More Praise _____ ty

"Readers craving full-on immersion in the ethos of Silicon Valley will love every page of *Escape Velocity*. Susan Wolfe's cast of colorful villains, con artists, and just plain folks caught up in high-stakes industry games is painstakingly drawn and always unpredictable. Good, clever fun with a thriller of an ending."

—Laura Benedict, author of *The Abandoned Heart*

"Susan Wolfe has achieved something extraordinary with this book: a financial and legal thriller with rich character development that creates an absolutely compelling stay-up-all-night read."

—Alice LaPlante, Award-winning author of *Turn of Mind*

"Instantly addictive and disconcertingly credible, *Escape Velocity* will send the unwary reader pell-mell through the mazy proceedings and gamesmanship of corporate Silicon Valley. If the adrenaline rush isn't enough, then the endearing vigilantism will close the deal. I never knew how much I wanted to know about the legal and economic ins-and-outs of the tech industry until Susan Wolfe, uniquely positioned to illuminate both, decided to write this exhilarating novel."

—Lynn Stegner, award-winning author of *For All the Obvious Reasons* & nominee for the National Book Award & the Pulitzer Prize

"Was there ever a more appealing character than this clever, hard-working Georgia Griffin of Piney, Arkansas, who has inherited her father's genius for the con? Not only highly entertaining, but also insightful and informative about Silicon Valley's high tech industry, whose principals are not always what they claim."

—Barbara Babcock, Professor Emerita of Stanford Law School, and author of *Fish Raincoats: A Woman Lawyer's Life*

"Wolfe made her debut in 1989 with *The Last Billable Hour*, which won an Edgar Award for Best First Novel. Her accomplished, amusing follow-up, a thriller set in California's Silicon Valley, stars paralegal Georgia Griffin. ... Wolfe, a lawyer who knows the high-tech world, makes a very welcome return."

—*Publishers Weekly*, starred review

Praise for *The Last Billable Hour*
Edgar Award Winner

"A funny, chilling view of big-time law."

—The New York Times Book Review

"Absolutely first class. Susan Wolfe has succeeded in bringing the reader into the profit-obsessed world of big-time corporate law without once talking down. *The Last Billable Hour* is a brilliant debut by a first-class writer."

—Collin Wilcox, author of *The Pariah* and *Night Games*

"The ultimate insider's look at the intrigues and infighting by which California's most hyperkinetic lawyers stay sharp in between multimillion-dollar deals."

—*Mystery News*

"A swift, complex plot, an unlikely romance and an intriguing glimpse at power politics among yuppie attorneys."

—*St. Louis Post-Dispatch*

"Fast-paced . . . humorous. These twists of plot and details of practice are drawn with accuracy and wit. *The Last Billable Hour* is also a moral tale, a thoughtful and colorful commentary on the legal profession."

—*California Lawyer*

"The writing is sharp, and the dialogue leaps from the page."

—Robert Barnard, author of *Death in a Cold Climate* and *Death on the High C's*

"An absolutely authentic view of law firm politics, written by someone who's obviously been there. If Samuel Butler had been a corporate lawyer, this is the kind of satire he'd have written. It will make readers laugh—and it will make lawyers blush."

—Lia Matera, author of *Where Lawyers Fear to Tread*

ESCAPE VELOCITY

A Novel by
Susan Wolfe

ESCAPE VELOCITY

A Novel by

Susan Wolfe

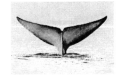

Steelkilt Press
Palo Alto, California

Hardcover: 978-0-9972117-0-2
Softcover: 978-0-9972117-1-9
Ebook: 978-0-9972117-2-6

Interior Design: Vicky Vaughn Shea, Ponderosa Pine Design
Editorial: Mark Woodworth
Publishing Strategist: Holly Brady
Logo: David Ivester

For more information, contact:
Steelkilt Press
P.O. Box 1344
Palo Alto, CA 94302
info@SteelkiltPress.com

To the rare and valuable Ken Madigans
of this world.

Acknowledgments

I thank fellow members of The Finishing School (Margit Look-Henry and Leslie Ingham) for their excellent editing and advice throughout; Susan Termohlen and Trish Kubal for their generous encouragement and expertise; Susan Maunders for her valuable editing of my first draft; and Brian Stine, for patiently reading more drafts of this book than it ever should have taken.

I thank Peter Lee for believing in this project and kindly insisting that I carry it to completion.

And most of all I thank my husband, Ralph DeVoe, and my daughter, Catherine Wolfe DeVoe, whose love and encouragement make everything possible.

PROLOGUE

"Now, as I see it, Gaddy," Drummer explained, setting his drink on the high gloss table and leaning his forearms onto his thighs, "we were partners in this deal, and then one of us kept quiet and went to jail so *you* could get away."

The other man sipped his drink, watching Drummer over the rim of his glass.

"I did the right thing, Gaddy," Drummer asserted. "Jail would've been tough on a punk like you. But it's been hard to get back on my feet after time in the pen. People look at you different. You can't get a good job."

"I suppose not," Gaddy said, raising his eyebrows. "You tried?"

Drummer stiffened and sat straight up. "Yeah I tried. And looked around for you. I thought sure we'd team up again. Figured you'd be in touch."

"How could I have gotten in touch?" Gaddy asked reasonably, lifting his palms for emphasis. "I was a fugitive."

"Yeah. Still are, I guess. Anyway, I see now you had bigger plans. These years have been good to my rookie partner, you could almost seem legit." Drummer shook his head in wonder and swept his arm in an expansive arc, taking in the rich wood paneling and the marble bar. "I bet your main house is in some fancy neighborhood full of movie stars and big-time athletes. Isn't it? I'm happy for you, kid."

Gaddy smiled slightly. "I appreciate that. But you didn't come all this way to congratulate me."

"No," Drummer acknowledged. He tried to conceal a sly smile

that deepened the cracks in his weathered face by tilting his head back to drain his glass. "It's a little more complicated. After all, we're still partners, and partners share."

"Of course. And we will. Let's start with sharing a little more of this fine scotch." Gaddy held the half empty bottle aloft. "More ice? Okay, tell me about the sharing. What do you have in mind?"

The drone of a motor through the open window was hypnotic. Drummer shook his head slightly to clear it. "So. You've got this whole enterprise because of me keeping my mouth shut."

Gaddy considered a moment and nodded. "Okay, let's say that's true. And now you want to be part of it. You want a job?"

Drummer's eyes darkened. "Working for you, you mean? That wouldn't seem right, now, would it? No, Gaddy, we'll settle this thing with cash. That way I get out of your hair, nobody the wiser. You go right on doing whatever you're doing so . . . prosprossy." He frowned and repeated carefully, "Prosper-ous-ly." He closed his eyes and dragged the back of his hand slowly across his forehead. "Seems a little close in here, even with that window open."

"Could be that flannel shirt you're wearing. And maybe go easy on the liquor," Gaddy advised. "It's pretty strong stuff."

"You didn't put something special in it, did you?" Drummer winked and set the drink down hard, splashing a little onto the table-top. "Oh, sorry . . . "

"No worries. Here, let me wipe it up so you won't get it on your sleeve. By the way," he mentioned, lifting Drummer's glass and using a white towel to carefully dry the rosewood underneath, "nobody's called me Gaddy for many years now."

Drummer slowly stood up. "That right? Whatever you say, Gaddy. I just need . . . move a little." He walked carefully over to the stairs. On the first step he wobbled and grabbed the banister.

"Hey there, take it easy," Gaddy warned, gripping Drummer's arm. "Maybe you better rest a minute, get your bearings." He guided the man to a sofa in the far corner. "We've got all evening if we need it."

"Well, I don't . . ."

"Here you go."

Drummer reacted to the shove by sitting down hard on the sofa.

"Tell you what," Gaddy continued conversationally, "you stay right here and let that scotch settle. I've got some stuff to do upstairs, and then I'll be back."

No response. Gaddy pushed Drummer so that he slumped over on the sofa. He closed the window and crossed over to the stairs. He paused on the bottom step, his hand on the light switch, and turned to look back at the man lying inert on the sofa. "Dammit Drummer," he muttered, "couldn't you have been just a little bit smarter? You've turned me into a killer." He shook his head ruefully, flicked off the light and ascended the stairs.

CHAPTER 1

Georgia followed the bouncing ponytail into a silent conference room with an immense black table. She perched on the edge of a fancy leather chair, quietly sniffed the air, and followed the scent to a tray of food on a side table: rows of colorful ripe fruit, cheerful little pots of yogurt, a tray of meat and cheese alongside glistening rolls. They hadn't mentioned it would be a lunch interview. She'd have to pace herself and not look greedy. Her empty stomach contracted in anticipation as she politely declined the offer of coffee.

"He'll be with you in a moment," the woman said. "Oh, sorry, let me get this out of here." She scooped up the food and carried it from the room, leaving only a scent of pineapple hovering in the air.

Well. Good riddance. The last thing Georgia needed was to get all gorged and sleepy right before an interview.

And this could be *the* interview. This could be the interview that landed the job that allowed her to bring Katie-Ann to California until her father got out of prison. Too bad her resume was sort of bare, but the economy was finally picking up and she only needed one solid foothold. It didn't matter how many jobs she hadn't gotten. What mattered was the one she did get, and this could be that one. So what if it had been more than three weeks since her last interview? That just meant she should make this one count.

As she moved her forearm slowly across the mahogany, she could see her pale skin reflected off the glistening finish. Sure was quiet in here. You couldn't hear anything of the big company that was supposedly operating at breakneck speed just outside the walls. Fast-paced was what they called themselves. Self-starter is what she was supposed to be. Well, she was a self-starter. How else had she gotten here? All the way from Piney, Arkansas, to Silicon Valley on bald tires, a million miles from the sound of Mama's sniffling, the acrid smell of her bright pink nail polish.

Georgia wasn't wearing any makeup at all. The woman with the bobbing ponytail had on perfect makeup that made her skin look like a baby's butt. Which was great if you also knew how to avoid making yourself a magnet for perverts, but Georgia hoped she could hold her own around here without makeup. Tall and lanky and fast-moving, like a colt, her father said. (He should know, he'd boarded enough of them.) She wasn't an athlete, exactly, but definitely a runner. Dark pin-stripe pantsuit from the Now and Again shop up in Palo Alto, scratchy at the back of her neck. Blueberry-colored eyes against pale, freckled skin, shiny black hair in a blunt bob as even as her dull scissors could chew through it. A smile so wide it sometimes startled people, seemed to give the fleeting impression she was unhinged. Careful with the smile. Enthusiastic, but not alarming.

The guy coming to interview her was late. She could have peed after all. This big San Jose industrial park was confusing, with boxy cement buildings that all looked exactly alike. Set back from the street behind gigantic parking lots full of glinting cars so it was impossible to see any street numbers, making it clear they couldn't care less whether a newcomer found her way. She'd ended up having to run in her heels just to get to the lobby on time.

Could she get to the john now? She squeezed her shoulder blades tightly and stretched the back of her neck away from the scratchy suit coat. The silence was making her jumpy. She left her resume on the polished table and opened the door just enough to look out.

The woman with the ponytail was nowhere to be seen. In fact, Georgia couldn't see a living soul. She took a couple of tentative steps into the hall. What if the interviewer showed up before she got back? Screw it. With a last look around the vacant executive area, she darted down the hallway.

The hall opened abruptly into an area crammed with battle-gray, fabric cubicles that created a maze the size of a football field. Had she wandered into a different company? The only thing the two areas had in common was that here, too, it was quiet. People must really be concentrating. Either that, or they'd had a bomb scare and nobody had bothered to tell her.

She was relieved to see a bald head appear above the fabric wall a few cubes down like a Jurassic Park dinosaur. (Now, that was quite an image. Did she feel *that* out of place around here?) She heard a printer spitting out copies somewhere in the distance as she headed toward the dinosaur, rounded a corner and stopped cold.

An unattended donut was resting on the work surface just inside one of the cubes. Barely even inside the cube, less than a foot away, almost as if it had been set down and forgotten by some passerby. The plate slapped down in a hurry, its edge sticking out precariously beyond the edge of the work surface. Yesterday's donut, perhaps, abandoned, stale.

But no, the donut was still puffy and golden, with minuscule cracks in that shiny sugar glaze. A donut still wafting the faintest scent of the fat it had been fried in. She could almost feel her lips touching the tender surface as her teeth ...

Had she whimpered out loud? She glanced both ways along the still-deserted hall and then returned her gaze to the donut resting on its lightly grease-stained white paper plate. Pretending to wonder if the cube was occupied, she leaned her head in and called a faint "hello?" resting her hand lightly on the work surface, a finger touching the paper plate. Staring straight ahead, she floated her fingers across the surface and up, until her palm was hovering just above the donut's sticky surface. One quick grab ...

"May I help you?" intoned a male voice.

Georgia snatched her hand back like the donut was a rattlesnake.

She turned and found herself face to face with the Jurassic Park dinosaur, who was looking distinctly human and downright suspicious. He looked past her and surveyed the vacant cube before resting his skeptical gaze on her most winsome smile.

"Oh, hi!" she said brightly. "I'm here for an interview, and I was hoping you could point me toward the restroom?"

"And you thought it might be in here?"

"Well no, but I thought a *person* ..."

"Follow me, please."

She heard her Arkansas twang vibrating the air between them as he led her down the hall a few yards, pointed a stern finger and said, "In there." He crossed his arms, and she felt the heat of his disapproving gaze on her back as she pushed through the heavy door into the privacy on the other side.

Now, that was just downright mortifying. Caught in the act of stealing a donut? A donut?? If he told somebody ... She cupped her palm over her closed eyes and dragged it slowly down until it covered her mouth.

Of course, she hadn't actually taken the donut, so what precisely had the guy seen? A woman standing at the edge of an empty cube, leaning her head in politely to look for someone. He probably hadn't noticed the donut, and even if he had he'd never imagine how desperately she wanted it. He'd probably had steak and gravy for breakfast, and thought a hungry person in Silicon Valley was as rare as a Jurassic Park dinosaur. If anything, he probably thought she was casing the empty cube for something valuable. Which was ridiculous, because what could a cube contain that was as valuable as a job?

But if he thought it was true, he might be waiting for her just outside the door with a security guard, planning to march her out of the building and away from this rare and essential person who could actually give her a job. Busted because of a donut.

The face that looked back from the mirror above the sink was staring at a firing squad as Georgia held her icy hands under the hot water.

But then the stare turned defiant.

4

She hadn't driven all the way from Arkansas to live in her car and get this job interview just to become distracted at the critical moment by some prissy, no-account donut police. Who did he think he was? It wasn't even his donut, and anyway, he wasn't doing the hiring. Her only task at this moment was to deliver the interview of a lifetime and get this job.

She squared her shoulders, practiced her smile in the mirror two or three times and strode with her head erect back along the deserted corridor to the interview room.

The man who entered the conference room five minutes later had the stiff-backed posture and shorn hair of a military man. He was well over six feet tall, lean, in his late forties, wearing neatly rolled blue chambray shirtsleeves and a bright yellow bow tie. As he shook her hand and sat opposite her, she saw that his stubble of hair was red and his eyes were a muted green. Fellow Irishman, maybe. Could she forge some connection from that?

"I'm Ken Madigan, the General Counsel here. Are you Georgia Griffin?"

"Yes, sir, I am." She offered her carefully calibrated, not-alarming smile.

"Appreciate you coming in today. Sorry to keep you waiting." He tapped a green folder with her name on the tab. "I've read your resume, so I won't ask you to repeat it. As you know, we have a key job to fill after quite a hiring freeze. Let's start with what's important to you in your next job."

"Well, sir, I just got my paralegal certificate, and I'm looking for the opportunity to put my learning and judgment to use. I intend to prove that I can make a real difference to my company, and then I'd like to advance."

His smile was encouraging. "Advance to what?"

This was a variant of the 'five years' question, and she answered confidently. "In five years I'd still like to be in the legal department, but I want to have learned everything there is to know about the other parts of the company, too. My goal is to become, well, indispensable."

"Is anything else important?" Those gray-green eyes were watching her with mild interest. She decided to take a chance and expose a tiny bit of her peculiar background to personalize this interview.

"Well, sir, I'm eager to get started, because I need to make enough money to get my baby sister here just as soon as I can make a place for her."

His raised his eyebrows slightly. "And how old is she?"

"Fifteen, sir, and needing a better future than the one she's got. I need to move pretty fast on that one."

"I see. Now tell me about your work experience." Which was where these interviews generally died. She shoved her cold hands between her thighs and the chair.

"I don't have a lot of glamorous experience, sir. I cleaned houses and worked as a waitress at the WhistleStop to get myself through school. And the whole time I was growing up I helped my father look after the horses he was boarding. In fact, he got so busy with his second job for a while that I just took over the horses myself. Horses are expensive, delicate animals, and things can go wrong in a heartbeat. With me in charge, our horses did fine."

"Okay, great." He ran his palm over his stubble of hair, considering. "Now tell me what kind of people you like to work with." Not one follow-up question about her experience. Did he think there was nothing worth talking about? *Just focus on the question.*

"The main thing is I want to work with smart people who like to do things right the first time. And people who just, you know, have common sense."

"I see. And what kind of people bug you?" This interviewer wasn't talking much, which made it hard to tell what impression she was making. A bead of sweat trickled between her shoulder blades.

"Well, I don't much like hypocrites." Which unfortunately eliminated about half the human race, but she wouldn't mention that. He waited. "And I don't like people who can't or won't do their jobs." She stopped there, in spite of his continued silence. No need to mention pedophiles, or that nasty prison guard who'd backed her against the wall on the catwalk. That probably wasn't what Ken Madigan had in mind.

"Thank you." He tapped his pen on her resume. "Now I'd like you to describe yourself with three adjectives."

Was this guy jerking her chain? He didn't much look like he'd jerk anybody's chain, but what did adjectives have to do with job qualifications? Maybe he was politely passing the time because he'd already decided not to hire her.

"Well," she said, glancing into the corner, "I guess I would say I'm effective. Quick at sizing up a situation." She paused. "And then I'm trying to decide between 'inventive' and 'tough.'"

"Okay, I'll give you both. Inventive and tough. Tell me about a time you were quick at sizing up a situation." This didn't feel like the other interviews she'd done. Not only were the questions weird, but he seemed to be listening to her so closely. She couldn't recall ever being listened to quite like this.

To her astonishment she said exactly what came into her head. "Well, like this one. I can already tell that you're a kind person who cares about the people who work for you. I think you're pretty smart, and you listen with a capital L. You might have a problem standing up to people who aren't as smart or above board as you are, though. That could be holding you back some."

Ken Madigan's eyebrows were suddenly up near his hairline. Why on earth was she spilling her insights about him to him? Too many weeks of isolation? Was it hunger? She should have taken that coffee after all, if only to dump plenty of sugar in it. Or was it something about him, that earnest-looking bow tie maybe, that made her idiotically want to be understood? Whatever it was, she'd blown the interview. Good thing she wasn't the sort of weakling who cried.

So move it along and get out of there. She dropped her forehead into her hand. "God, I can't believe I just said all that. You probably don't have any flaws at all, sir, and if you do it isn't my place to notice them. I guess I need another adjective."

"Which would be ...?"

"Blunt."

He lowered one eyebrow slightly. "Let's say 'forthright.' And I won't need an example."

"You know what, though?" There was nothing left to lose, really, and she was curious. "I'm not this 'forthright' with everybody. A lot of people must just talk to you."

"They do," he acknowledged with a single nod, his eyebrows resuming their natural location. "It's an accident of birth. But they usually don't say anything this interesting." He sounded amused. Could she salvage this?

"Well, I'm completely embarrassed I got so personal."

"You shouldn't be. I'm impressed with your insight."

"Really? Then maybe you see what I mean about being quick."

He laughed. "I believe I do."

"I mean, I can be quick about other things, too. Quick to see a problem starting up. Sometimes quick to see what'll solve it. Like when my father had to go away and I saw we'd have to sell the stable to pay the taxes..." Blah blah blah, there she went again. She resisted clapping her hand over her mouth. Was she trying to lose this job?

The woman with the bouncy ponytail stuck her head in. "I'm so sorry, but Roy would like to see you in his office right away. And your next appointment is already downstairs." She handed him another green folder. The tab said 'Sarah Millchamp.' "I'm going to lunch, but I'll have Maggie go down for her in ten minutes. She'll be in here whenever you're ready."

"Thanks, Nikki," he said, turning back to Georgia. "Unfortunately, it looks like our time's about up. Do you have a question for me before we stop?"

Sixty seconds left to make an impression. "I saw your stock's been going up. Do you think it's going up for the right reasons?"

There went his eyebrows again, and this time his mouth seemed to be restraining a smile. "Not entirely, no, as a matter of fact."

"I'm sorry to hear that. Do you have an opinion about improvements that would make your growth more sustainable?"

He allowed his smile to expand. "I have many opinions, and a small amount of real insight. Might be difficult to discuss right now…"

She held a hand up. "Oh, I understand. But do you think a paralegal could help make a difference?"

"A solid paralegal could make a big difference."

"I'd like to know more about the issues, sir, but they're probably confidential, and anyway, I know you have to leave." She leaned forward, preparing to stand up.

"You're a surprising person, Ms. Griffin, and an interesting one. I've enjoyed our conversation."

Like he enjoyed a circus freak, probably. She made her smile humble. "Thank you."

"If it's all right with you, I'd like to have somebody from Human Resources give you a call in the next day or two."

Was he serious? "That would be fine."

"If we decide to work together, could you start pretty quickly?"

The goal now was to leave without saying anything else stupid. "I'm sure I can meet your requirements."

As he walked her out to the elevator he lowered his voice. "You know, Ms. Griffin, you're an intuitive person, and you might have some insights about the Human Resources people you're about to meet…"

She held up her palm. "Don't worry, sir. If I do, I'll keep my mouth shut."

"Excellent. Great talking to you. Drive safely, now," he called as the elevator door closed between them.

Thank God that interview was finished. In another five minutes she'd have told him anything, she'd have told him about Robbie. Drive safely? What a cornball. But she must have said something right. He gave her that tip about getting past the Human Resources people, which meant he must like her. Landing a first job with her resume was like trying to freeze fire, but this time at least she had a chance.

Her stomach cramped with hunger as she emerged into the lobby and saw a woman in her mid-thirties glancing through a magazine. Tailored suit, precision-cut blond hair, leather case laid neatly across her lap. Completely professional, and she had ten years' experience on Georgia at least. No. No way. Georgia walked briskly over to the woman and stood between her and the receptionist.

"Ms. Millchamp?" she said quietly, extending her hand.

The woman stood up and smiled. "Sarah Millchamp. Nice to meet you. I know I'm early."

"I'm Misty. So sorry to tell you this, but Mr. Madigan's been called out of town unexpectedly. He's headed for the airport now."

"Oh!" The poised Ms. Millchamp quickly regained her composure. "That's too bad. But of course I understand."

"Thank you for being so understanding. This literally happened ten minutes ago, and I'm completely flustered. I know he wants to meet you. Are you parked out here? At least let me walk you to your car."

She put a sisterly hand against Ms. Millchamp's elbow and began steering her toward the exit. "Tell you what, can I call you to reschedule as soon as Mr. Madigan gets back? Maybe you two can have lunch. Just don't take that job at Google in the meantime."

"Google?"

"Now, don't pretend you haven't heard about the job at Google. In Brad Dormond's department? They're our worst nightmare when it comes to competing for good people." The air in the parking lot mingled the spicy scent of eucalyptus with the smell of rancid engine grease, and her stomach lurched. "So, see over there? That's the entrance to the freeway. Bye now. I'll call you soon."

Georgia waved as Sarah Millchamp backed her car out. Then she hurried back inside to the receptionist.

"Hi," she said. "That lady, Ms. Millchamp? She just let me know she has a migraine and will call to reschedule. Will you let Maggie know?"

The receptionist nodded and picked up her phone. "That's too bad."

"Isn't it, though?"

Done and dusted, as Gramma Griffin would say.

She still might not get the job, of course, she reminded herself as she pulled onto the freeway, nibbling a half-eaten dinner roll she'd squirreled away in the crack between her passenger seat cushions the night before. She'd gotten this far once before. And she didn't have to get it. She had another dozen resumes out, and one of those might still lead to something. Her cousin at Apple had turned out to be more useless than a well dug in a river, but that didn't mean she was desperate. If she continued sleeping in her car most nights her money could last for another five weeks. And Lumina Software might not be a great job, anyway. Ken Madigan probably just interviewed well. That's probably all it was.

CHAPTER 2

Georgia spent her first hour of employment at Lumina Software consuming donuts at what she hoped was a dignified pace and listening carefully in orientation. She spent the second hour sort of listening in orientation, and keeping her spirits up by reminding herself what a privilege it was to be paid $23.91 an hour to sit anywhere. She spent the third hour envisioning black smoke and a clanging fire alarm that would get her out of orientation, which was proving to be about as useful as pajamas on a pig.

Sally Kurtz, the senior vice president of Human Resources, was leading the dozen or so new employees through a discussion of company core values. The group had been herded together on metal folding chairs around one end of a wood-laminated table in a meeting room that had obviously been designed for larger crowds. Every nervous cough and every chair scrape on the speckled linoleum echoed faintly off the farthest white wall.

Senior Vice President was a fancy title, and Ms. Kurtz was not what Georgia expected. Ms. Kurtz smiled shyly and introduced herself in a voice so soft that the new employees had to tilt forward to hear her. She was in her mid-forties, with shoulder-length mousy brown hair that looked like she'd slept on it funny, and a kind of boney, angular body that put Georgia in mind of a Methodist missionary. She wore a cream-colored sweater with see-through material bunched at the neck, evidently intended to be feminine but modest. Could that be store bought? Well, dowdy was one way to show you were all business, and it must be working for this big shot.

"Let's start with Integrity," Sally said. The word Integrity faded in at the top of a PowerPoint slide that was projected onto a pull-down screen. "What do you think the company means by that?"

"We tell the truth?" said a slightly built man in a short-sleeved brown shirt.

"Absolutely." Sally wrote 'Tell the truth' with a purple marker on a flip chart. "That's an important element. What else?"

"We obey the law and do the right thing," said a woman with bright lipstick and orange hair. Uh-oh. If people really participated in this sorry nonsense they were going to prolong it.

"Good," Sally nodded, and wrote it down. "We rely on our legal team for that first part, and then we rely on our own moral compass for the second, don't we?"

Shouldn't the company orient them to something useful, like the technical terms on all the billboards around here? Terms like 'cloud computing' or 'SaaS'? Except maybe everybody else understood them already. Georgia had been memorizing one technical term from each trip down the freeway, and then looking it up on the Internet in the library. She knew she was coming from behind.

The door opened and a short, very fit woman sporting jeans and boyish blond hair entered. Close to forty, maybe. Without looking at anyone she sat next to Sally, pushed up the sleeves of her black turtle-neck, and opened her laptop. Runner or swimmer, Georgia thought. Hard to tell which.

Sally glanced in the direction of the newcomer and then continued. "That's great. What else?"

"We treat our customers fairly," someone said.

"Yes," Sally agreed. "Thank you. Just our customers?"

"And our partners."

"Good. And what about each other?" She added 'partners' and 'each other' to the flip chart. "Anything else? Okay, now let's see what our leadership team said about Integrity." She hit the button on her computer, and phrases came floating in one after the other:

We are truthful and candid.
We do what is right and ethical.
We treat each other, our customers and shareholders with fairness,
*   dignity and respect.*

"It's a pretty close match, isn't it? This group has good instincts." She rewarded them with a soft smile. "The leadership team added a couple of things. 'Dignity and respect.' Very important. And 'share- holders.' We don't want to forget about them. Good. That's the first core value. We'll look at these periodically throughout the day. At the moment, let me introduce Andrea Hancock, who's in charge of Research and Development ..."

A man in his fifties swung the door wide and entered the room. He was about 5'9", Georgia guessed, square and solid like a fireplug, wear- ing an expensive-looking black suit and red tie. He had the jowly, florid face of a middle-aged man who makes a half-hearted effort to control his weight. His forehead was elevated in a look of chronic skepticism, like he knew whoever he was talking to was full of shit and he intended to catch them at it as efficiently as possible.

He surveyed them briefly without enthusiasm, and signaled to Sally with a curt nod of his head.

"Class," Sally beamed with excitement, "we are very honored to have our CEO, Roy Zisko, take time from his terribly busy schedule to speak to us this morning. Roy?" He remained standing, feet planted apart, and consulted his watch, while Georgia and everyone else leaned forward in anticipation.

"Good morning," he said briskly, his small dark eyes glowering at them over the rims of his oval glasses. "As you may have been told, you're the first new hires since I joined Lumina just over a year ago. On the day I arrived, I initiated a hiring freeze as one of many strict cost- cutting measures, which also included eliminating the lowest ranked 20 percent of our workforce. You're here today because those cost-cut- ting measures have been effective, and because your departments have now convinced themselves they cannot function without you." He shrugged. "We'll see. I consider each of you an experiment in productivity, and, of course, inevitably, some experiments fail." Wait, was he glaring at her? Did she look unproductive? She squared her shoulders and gazed straight back at him, her mouth arranged in a pleasant, attentive smile. After a moment, his glare moved on to the woman with orange hair.

"If you glance around, you'll notice that this training room has the capacity for a much larger crowd than the one here today." He began to walk slowly up and back in the front of the room. "This is not an accident. This room will never again be filled during my tenure. It won't need to be, as long as each person we do hire contributes fully to this company's profitability. Some of you will find your workload too heavy, and I encourage you to seek a lighter one somewhere else." Andrea, the head of R&D, had closed her laptop and was staring into the distance, juggling her pen in an elaborate figure eight motion around the knuckles of her left hand.

"If you do remain at Lumina, as I expect some of you will, then you will quickly find that doing more with less is a habit we all subscribe to, one that will serve our shareholders well and secure your continued employment.

"Now, do any of you have questions for me?" he asked as he simultaneously shook his head from side to side. "No? Then good luck." He turned to Sally and muttered in what he apparently thought was an inaudible voice, "That guy in the back a stutterer?" They all glanced in the direction of the slight man in the short-sleeved shirt, who blinked rapidly and stared straight ahead. What made him even think of that, when the guy hadn't said one word?

Sally smiled confidently without turning to look. "Certainly not."

"Good. Talk to them about grooming, for God's sake." He turned abruptly and left the room.

Well. Wasn't he cuddly.

The temperature in the room seemed to have dropped several

degrees, and a couple of the new employees had slunk down in their seats. Trying to hide their bad grooming?

"Isn't he impressive?" Sally beamed. "Just so ... down-to-earth and ... straight-talking, isn't he?" Bully was more like it, Georgia thought, but Sally Kurtz could hardly say that. Andrea Hancock seemed decidedly less than dazzled. She drummed lightly with two fingers on a faint smile while she waited for the murmurs of timid agreement to subside, then launched into a twenty-minute presentation of Lumina's software product and left.

As the morning wore on, Georgia learned what it meant to be a company that sells stock to the public. Their next core value was "Passion."

Passion seemed a peculiar value for a software company, but she supposed they meant something other than *Fifty Shades of Grey*. Georgia personally had a passion for hanging onto her job, but that wouldn't be what they had in mind, either. After all, how could they know this job was her one big chance to cheat her fate?

She'd been thinking about cheating her fate quite a lot since her father got hauled off to prison for running his con artist business, exposing the rest of the family to ostracism (by a bunch of sorry rednecks, no less, like being ostracized by a chain gang) and to financial ruin. She'd had her doubts even before he got hauled off. How many times had she told him that she wasn't ready to enter the so-called family business, that she might want to do something other than what he had carefully trained her for? Of course she could never mention her real reason for wanting out: Making your living by tricking people out of their money, even if you loved it (which her father surely did), even if you were an outright genius at it (which her father surely was), was really just sort of no-account. She wanted to use her talents for something consequential.

But she and her father had both believed she would eventually give in. Her father probably knew as well as she did that it was nearly impossible to achieve escape velocity from the life you were born to, from a father you loved who was counting on you. Her father had just been biding his time, waiting patiently for her to grow up and quit stalling. He probably still was.

But the disaster with that no-account Robbie had changed everything. Her eyes narrowed. She'd never had to summon the fortitude to get in her car and drive away from her father, because he'd left her by going to prison. Suddenly all their lives were shifting, and she'd just decided to shift hers in the right direction. And it was the right direction, even if food was occasionally scarce, even if she was temporarily surrounded by acres of strangers who never spoke to her and wouldn't notice if she keeled over on a sidewalk and expired. Because now things had shifted again. She ducked her head to conceal a joyful little smile. Now she was seated in this room, experiencing her first day of a bona fide job that gave her a genuine presence in Silicon Valley and a real home for her and Katie-Ann. Her chance for the life she wanted was now.

Hanging on to this job and getting Katie-Ann through high school would be plenty consequential for now. She shifted on her folding chair and ran her thumb down through the condensation on the side of her coffee cup. Continuing to listen with one ear in case her name was called, she considered her finances.

It was important to get Katie-Ann out here by September so she could be in the same place for her last two years. If Georgia continued to live in her car entirely for another six weeks, she could scrape up the first and last month's rent on a one-bedroom apartment before school started. That wouldn't be so bad now that she could shower in the company gym, instead of waiting in line for that germy shower at the homeless center.

She'd found a second outfit at Goodwill, and another shirt for her pantsuit, so she would never have to wear anything more than twice a week. Hard to keep her clothes decent with her car for a closet, and the CEO evidently had a bee up his butt about grooming. Did they have an iron at the homeless center? Lousy having no refrigerator, but she was pretty sure they had one here in the kitchen she could use, and four nights a week they served a hot dinner at the church on First Street if she could get there on time. Once she started working late she could do frozen dinners in the microwave on the third floor.

Katie-Ann was working at the WhistleStop to save her bus money. She had $92 already, and was saving $20 a week. The bus fare was $209. Together, they could make this work.

∞

After the break they divided into small groups and competed to prepare the best "elevator pitch" for the company's software, which meant describing the software in the time it took to ride up in an elevator with a sales prospect. That actually seemed useful, and soon Georgia's team had the following pitch: *Our mission-critical, data mining software retrieves information from a company's database—or the Web!—according to search queries; analyzes the data for trends; organizes the results into presentation-ready reports; and distributes those reports throughout the enterprise.* They were debating whether to keep the semicolons when Sally called out, "Georgia Griffin? I need to speak to you, please."

About what?? Had they found out from the background check that her father was a con artist? Had the cops followed her here to harass her for sleeping in her car? Or had she just flunked grooming? She avoided the glances of her teammates and headed over to Sally, who absent-mindedly touched a scar just above her eyebrow as she introduced Georgia to Ken Madigan's secretary, Maggie.

Maggie looked friendly enough. She was wearing swingy white plastic earrings and a bright print dress. "I'm really embarrassed, but one of our lawyers flew to Boston today, and he needs somebody to witness an interview over the phone right now. We're so short-handed from this hiring freeze that you're the only person I can find."

This had nothing to do with her. Her shoulders dropped about three inches with relief.

"Do you mind terribly if we head upstairs for a few minutes?" Maggie continued. "I'll get you back down here just as soon as possible."

"No problem," Georgia responded, trotting happily down the corridor beside her. "I'll just remain disoriented for now."

Maggie showed Georgia into a little, windowless room with dirty maroon walls. "Zack's here on the speakerphone. Zack? I have Georgia Griffin."

"Hi, Georgia," came a rich, deep voice through the speakerphone. "Thanks for agreeing to help out." Get a load of that voice. She imagined a tall man, thirties maybe, curly black hair, lean shoulders inside a well-fitted suit. Not that she was remotely interested after that low-down skunk Deke. "I'm in the Boston office today to interview one of our sales reps regarding a sexual harassment case. The employee says the manager of the office, Buck Gibbons, is making homophobic remarks. If that's true, then it violates Massachusetts law and our Code of Ethics."

"And our company values," Georgia added.

"I'm sorry, what was that?" Zack called through the phone.

"You know. 'We treat each other with fairness, dignity and respect?'" There was a short silence.

"Georgia's in orientation today," Maggie explained brightly.

"Oh, right," Zack said. "So, the first step is to interview the person who complained and get his story, but he's afraid the manager will retaliate against him for complaining. He also thinks the Human Resources person is biased because she's scared to death of the manager. Which frankly she might be. So, will you be our witness? The guy's standing outside in the corridor right now."

"Love to," Georgia said, grinning as she accepted a pen from Maggie. Her fire alarm fantasy had come true. Out of that sorry orientation, smack into her real job.

∞

Three hours later Georgia was still next to the speakerphone in the little, windowless room, waiting to hear Zack's fifth and last face-to-face interview. Maggie had brought her a ham and cheese sandwich twice as thick as the ones they offered at the homeless center, and a few tiny crumbs dotted the pitted surface of the laminated conference table between the empty plate and her mouth. She'd drunk so much coffee her kidneys ached.

The sales rep who had complained was Andrew. He said his regional manager, Buck, consistently called people "faggots" and "queers" and "girly-men" when they didn't sell enough software. Two weeks ago Andrew had failed to close a deal by quarter-end, and Buck yelled that he was "a fucking homo" right out in the open office. Andrew was gay, but hadn't disclosed that to people at work. He wasn't sure who had overheard Buck that day, but he gave the names of four other sales reps who had either been the butt of similar remarks or had witnessed them.

Zack interviewed those four next. The first was named Jack. No, Buck had never called Jack a faggot, and Jack had no reason to think Buck was homophobic. Buck definitely got a little excited at times, but he was a good manager and the team performed well. Jack really had no complaints.

The second witness, Bill, might have heard Buck call somebody a "girly-man," but that was no big deal. He didn't think there was a homophobic atmosphere in the office, although maybe it was a little bit macho. If they were finished he'd like to get back to a deal he was trying to close.

The third witness, the only female sales rep, explained with irritation that the office atmosphere was just fine, and anyway who cared? What sales reps cared about was whether they were selling software and meeting quota. Anybody who had time to complain about office atmosphere probably wasn't doing their job.

The only interesting thing about these three interviews was that they utterly contradicted everything Andrew had told them. Why would Andrew make that stuff up and give specific names if there was nothing to it? Georgia wanted to ask Zack what he thought, but she could never be sure he was alone in the room there in Boston. Now they were waiting for Ben, the final sales rep.

She heard a muffled voice and then a door closed. She picked up her pen as Zack explained the purpose of the meeting and offered the standard assurance: "I will keep anything you tell me confidential to the extent I can, but it's possible that in order to complete the investigation I'll need to reveal what you've told me. If that happens, the company will protect you from retaliation. Okay?"

"Yeah."

"Okay, great. In the year and a half you've been working out of this office, have you noticed anything about the atmosphere that makes you uncomfortable?"

"No. Like what?" More of the same, evidently. Georgia sighed. This little, windowless room was getting stuffy.

"Do people talk to each other in a way that seems disrespectful or inappropriate?"

"No, not really."

"Have you ever heard anyone making homophobic remarks in the office?"

"I don't think so. Like what?"

"Have you ever heard anybody call someone a 'faggot' or a 'queer'?"

"No, I haven't heard that."

"How about 'girly-man'?"

"Is this about Buck Gibbons?"

"Why do you ask? Have you heard Buck Gibbons call somebody a 'girly-man'?"

"Not sure if I have or not. It's definitely the kind of thing he would say, though."

"I see. And do you think the way Buck talks to people makes them uncomfortable?"

"Can't really say if it does or not. Tell you what he does that makes me uncomfortable."

"What's that?"

"He flips me." Georgia frowned at the phone. 'Flips.' What did that mean?

"I'm sorry?" Zack said.

"He flips me. You know, like this." He apparently was demonstrating.

"Ben, could you be more specific? Are you saying that Buck Gibbons touches you in some way that makes you uncomfortable?"

"Yeah, he flips my nuts, man. I don't like it at all."

Georgia's hand flew to her mouth. Had she gasped out loud? Very unprofessional. She heard nothing on the phone for several seconds.

"Okay, Ben, from what you just told me, Buck Gibbons has put his hand under your ... genitals, and flipped them up. Is that right?"

"That's right."

"Has he done this more than once?"

Ben paused. "Five times." She remembered she should be taking notes and resumed scribbling.

"Five times in the office? Were there witnesses?"

"Four times in the office, once in a restaurant. And yeah, there were witnesses."

"Did you ever ask him to stop?"

"Yeah, I told him. Not the first time, because I was like, you know, a little bit not believing it had really happened. But the second time was in front of a couple of other guys, and I followed him back to his office and asked him not to do it anymore."

"And what did he say?"

"He just laughed and tried to flip me again. Then he did it to me again the very next night, only that time was in a restaurant in front of my girlfriend. I felt like he was getting even because I asked him to stop. So now I just try to keep away from him."

"Have you ever seen him do this to anyone else?"

"No."

"And you never went to Human Resources about it?"

"It's really kind of embarrassing, you know, and I thought I could just keep away from him. But he did it to me again last night, and now you're here today and it seems kind of relevant to what you're talking about..."

"Absolutely. I'm glad you told me. Now if you don't mind, I'd like to talk through the different times this has happened, and see who else was there who could corroborate it."

Ben gave Zack three names of people to talk to, including the Bill who'd just finished assuring them the office atmosphere was fine.

"Okay, Ben, is there anything else that Buck or anybody else does around here that you think I should know about?"

"No. That's it."

"Fine. Now, I'm going to investigate this, and if I confirm it we have to get him to stop."

"I want him to stop. I just don't want to lose my job."

"You won't lose your job. You have the right not to be retaliated against, and I'm going to make sure we enforce that right."

There was a brief silence. "Okay."

"You know, I've never heard anything quite like this."

"Pretty weird, isn't it?"

"Very weird. Thank you, Ben. We'll be in ... I'll get back to you."

Georgia heard footsteps and then the door closed again. "Georgia?" Zack called quietly into the phone. "You still there?"

"Right here," she assured him, leaning toward the speakerphone. "I fainted a while, but now I'm getting my color back."

"Can you believe this? Listen, I need to talk to Ken right away. Can you let Maggie know? Then you should probably go back to your orientation. We'll have plenty of time to talk about this later, especially if it turns out to be true."

"Well, if it's not true," Georgia said slowly, "how interesting does that make Ben?"

"Point taken. Hang onto your notes, okay? And welcome to Lumina Software."

Genital grabbing. Dignity and respect. Hard to reconcile those, really, Georgia thought as she followed Maggie back downstairs. Be fun to see how it played out. Look at that, 4:30. Less than an hour of orientation to go.

Sally was just finishing a discussion of the core value "Leadership." She'd recorded their thoughts on the flip chart.

"Fantastic," she said with her soft smile. "I can see that this group is already on the path to understanding and living the values. Now let's see how your answers compare to the Leadership Team's." She punched the key and the new employees watched the list appear:

Every one of us is a leader.
We set the right example.
We expect and help each person to make a difference.

Georgia read the last sentence twice. Why should something so obvious even need to be said? That ornery CEO could rest assured, Georgia Griffin fully intended to make a difference.

CHAPTER 3

On Wednesday she stopped by Mail Boxes Etc. and found her first letter from her father. So the mail drop to his lawyer was working. She had to rush to make it to the Lutheran church while they were still serving dinner, and then she needed a place she could park her car for the night. She finally settled on a shabby little two-block residential street called Little Portman Road near the Trimble Road entrance to the freeway. She climbed into the back seat, hung her two shirts on hangers over the rear side windows as curtains, and tore open the typed envelope to find the familiar, handwritten script:

Dearest Georgia,

Congratulations on your new job. Your talent for gaining the confidence of complete strangers has served you well again. It shows you were quite right to strike out on your own for the time being, instead of filling the vacancy created by Robbie's departure. And you managed to find work in this sorry economy without the assistance of that useless cousin of yours at Apple. I hope you feel proud of what you have accomplished.

She loved that stilted, formal tone of her father's letters. The proud autodidact, demonstrating facility with diction and grammar far beyond his eighth grade education. She and Katie-Ann both used a similar style for letter writing, because, well, that was just how letters should be.

Now you can provide for Katie-Ann while I am temporarily sidelined, which is a great relief. And you'll have useful experience when you're ready to join me in the business. Georgia sighed. Which would be never, right, Daddy? After all, why did he think she was out here? But her father was no fool. Many rockets never achieve escape velocity.

She noticed some cramped handwriting in the margin:

Horrible racket today, replacing the rail around the catwalk where that guard fell during your visit. Still don't know how he fell. Must mean they still couldn't ask him. Either that or he was too embarrassed to tell them he'd been shoved while he was busy unbuckling his belt. She shrugged slightly and continued reading.

As for your wish to make yourself indispensable to your new employer, there are bound to be a hundred opportunities if you expand your focus beyond the confines of your current job description. According to the literature, bad product seems like the number one killer of Silicon Valley companies. Bad go-to-market plans are a close second, and then you have lawsuits that just bleed the company dry. There's also bad sales training, which is either not knowing how to find a mark, or not being able to close with one after you do find him. (Dreadful waste! Heartbreaking, really.) And lurking behind every one of these problems could be a greedy employee, a stupid employee, or a complacent employee who consumes a salary but contributes nothing. Your first challenge is to figure out which of these problems are weighing down Lumina Software.

Well no, Daddy, strictly speaking that was about her third challenge. Number one was to avoid having the cops notice she was sleeping in her rusty Subaru again tonight. In a few minutes she'd be scrunched up inside her hot sleeping bag here in the back seat, trying to conceal her Itty Bitty Book Lite from nosey passersby. Assuming she could even stay here. This street had a good amount of through traffic for safety, but the neighbors might be noticers. Already in fifteen minutes she'd had some driver of a pickup with a missing headlight slow down like a real snoop before turning into the driveway a couple of doors down.

The number two challenge was to remain employed. Some of the legal issues she was hearing about at Lumina Software sounded a little more complicated than they let on at Heber Springs Correspondence School. She'd had to locate and then practically memorize about twenty different articles just in case she needed to help with Due Diligence one of these days. And there were several other subjects lined up right behind that one.

She appreciated her father's vote of confidence, especially when her finances were so precarious, and he was undoubtedly right about understanding the bigger issues of the business. With a little time she probably could figure out a thing or two that needed fixing, but what made him think a paralegal could just waltz in and fix them? She wasn't selling herself short, exactly, but before aiming at the stars around here she was going to aim for a tolerable document tracking system and a good night's sleep.

∞

She arrived early for the legal team meeting in Ken Madigan's conference room the next morning, and sat right across from the door where she could get a good look at every person who walked in. She was going to meet Zack in person, lay eyes on the rest of the legal team, and see Ken for the second time ever. Too bad she'd cut it so close getting to the Lutheran church last night. By the time she got there, there'd been nothing left but stale rolls and soggy salad. Now she was feeling lightheaded right when she needed to be alert. She blinked and sat up straight to clear her head. With luck, they'd have those big, sugary maple bars, and she could snag one before somebody else beat her to it.

Maggie finished snapping on lights in the yellow-walled, windowless room, and then opened a big pink pastry box in the center of the table in front of Georgia. "Go ahead and help yourself," she invited, holding out a flimsy white paper plate as she set the rest of the stack on the table. Hopefully Maggie was too busy with the coffee over at the credenza to hear Georgia's stomach gurgle its loud, descending scale as she triumphantly seized the only maple bar in the box.

Maggie was wearing a bright turquoise cotton blouse and big orange double-hoop earrings. Georgia's black pantsuit suddenly seemed too formal. She hooked a hand inside each lapel and started to slide the coat back off her shoulders, and then remembered her dark blue shirt had a soup stain on the sleeve. She shrugged the coat back up onto her shoulders and tapped her pen on her yellow pad.

Maggie dialed in the conference phone as people began filing into the room. Georgia stood and shook the hand of a slight Asian man with very thick black hair, who nodded and blinked at her from behind rimless glasses. This guy had to be older than he looked, because he looked like a Cub Scout. She wrote "Quan—lawyer" on her legal pad. Quan sat at the end of the table and busied himself with plugging in his laptop. She felt a surge of energy as donut sugar hit her bloodstream.

Five or six others filed into the room, greeting each other, waving at Georgia or shaking hands as Maggie introduced them. Georgia carefully wrote each name on her legal pad and continued watching the door.

She'd thought about Ken every day since her interview (he was the closest human contact she'd had since she left Piney), and actually seeing him appear in the doorway was startling. He was taller than she remembered, 6'5" at least, and leaner than a greyhound after a hard race. His bow tie was so red it almost glowed. She took in that military posture, thumbs hooked behind each hip and fingers fanned out along the front, and that close-cropped red hair.

"Hey, everybody," he said, holding up his long, thin fingers in greeting. "Severine, how's Paris?" he called into the phone. "Ang, you there? Thanks, no, Beatrice, I don't think I will have a donut, but they do look great." Georgia was pretty sure Ken Madigan hadn't eaten a donut in twenty years. "Tell you who isn't with us today, and that's Jennifer, because she had her baby about five hours ago." Exclamations and murmurs. "Yep, his name is Jacob Aaron, six and a half pounds, blue eyes ... what else, Maggie? Oh yes, he's bald." Laughter. "Good to be reminded of what really matters once in a while, isn't it?

"And I have one other important piece of news before we start. Did you all get a chance to meet Georgia?" He gestured with a sweep of his hand. "She joins us this morning as a much-needed addition to our team."

"Yay!" called Severine with her French accent through the speaker-phone. "We have a fresh troop!" More laughter.

"Georgia spent yesterday in orientation," Ken continued, "so maybe she can finally orient the rest of us."

"Actually, Ken," called Zack's voice through the phone. So he hadn't made his 6 o'clock plane after all. "Georgia didn't get to spend her entire day in orientation, because she was on the phone with me on the sexual harassment matter ..."

"... that of course we can't really talk about right now," Ken reminded him.

"No-o," Zack reined himself in with obvious reluctance, "but I bet Georgia wonders what she's gotten herself into."

"I consider it my true orientation," she assured him, and Zack's snicker sounded appreciative.

"Okay, our big item today is the SAP litigation, after my update. Anything else?"

Maggie raised her hand. "If there's time I'd like to bitch about the AP department."

Surprising somebody said 'bitch' around Ken. She made a note: AP?

"Therapeutic complaining," Ken rephrased with no evident disapproval, "onto the list. Anybody else? Okay, let's start with the news."

Georgia wrote one thing about every subject Ken mentioned. Software licensing. Must be what they called selling software. Somebody needed a nondisclosure agreement. Somebody had an ethics issue in China, and nobody seemed surprised.

"And then my last thing," Ken continued, "isn't quite news yet, but it's gonna be. As you know, our Business Development team scouts around for smaller companies to buy that have already created their own software. They've identified a little software company in the finance space, and we need somebody to take the lead on it. Could mean spending some time up in Seattle. Any takers?"

"I'll do it." Quan looked up from his computer and raised his hand.

"Perfect," Ken said. "And Georgia, how about if you help us with the NDA and due diligence process. Okay? That's great."

Georgia nodded confidently and wrote: "NDA?? Due diligence!"

"And that's the news. Okay, Zack. Give us an update on the SAP litigation. Maybe we can start with 60 seconds of background for Georgia." Georgia wrote: SAP?

"Sure," Zack said. "We bought a company three years ago when it was being sued for patent infringement by a little German company called Eichel. Then SAP bought Eichel, and our little patent lawsuit became a gigantic patent lawsuit with SAP." Snickers and groans.

"You know who SAP is?" Ken asked Georgia. "They're basically the German Microsoft. This lawsuit is now probably the single biggest threat our company faces." He was talking to her as if she mattered. Which was the oldest trick in the book, she reminded herself. Like vodka to an alcoholic.

"We're in the fight of our life with these guys," Zack continued. "As of last week they've accused us of violating thirteen of their patents, and we've asserted ten against them. We have to find some way to get leverage in this case before SAP drives us under with legal fees and pointless BS."

At least she knew what BS stood for.

"Our one real chance for leverage," Zack continued, "is our killer patent application that's been making its way through the Patent and Trademark Office now for almost three years. Called the '401, Georgia, because the PTO assigned that number to it. That one patent could change the case completely, because we could force SAP to stop manufacturing its own software." He paused. "That's the background."

Georgia wrote "401. Patent and Trademark Office = PTO."

"So what's going on now?" Ken asked.

"Well, that's the problem," Zack declared. "Absolutely nothing. This patent application is just stuck somewhere in the bowels of the PTO, and I'm going crazy trying to dislodge it and get the patent issued. On Friday, the judge set discovery cut-off for August 31st. If we don't get the patent before then, we can forget about using it in the lawsuit."

Georgia flipped back to "SAP" and wrote "Swiftly Acquire Patent" as a memory device. She needed some way to keep these acronyms straight.

"You don't think it's too late already?" Quan asked.

"Hard to say. Judge's discretion, so we won't know unless we try. And we can't try, because we don't have the damn patent."

"What does Archie say?"

Georgia wrote "Archie?"

"He says what Archie always says. 'Any day now. You can't speed it up. If you try to speed it up you might slow it down, blah blah blah.' At this point I just want to get an outside Washington lawyer who specializes in the PTO who can at least give me confidence we're giving this our best shot." PTO, thought Georgia, PTO. Patent's Terrible Obstacle. She flipped back to "Patent and Trademark Office = PTO" and added "Patent's Terrible Obstacle."

"Good idea," Ken was saying. "We just have to let Archie know. Other comments? Okay, Maggie, tell us about Accounts Payable."

"What's going on," Maggie sighed, "is that three different companies that work for us are threatening to cut us off because they haven't been paid. I've been calling AP for weeks to find out why they haven't gotten their money."

Georgia wrote "Accounts Payable = AP."

"First AP wouldn't call me back. Then they told me the invoices had been paid. Then this morning they found a whole box of our unpaid invoices that go all the way back to last year. The miracle is that only three vendors are threatening us."

"So they're paying them now?" Ken asked.

Maggie arched her back. "No!! They say they're backed up on current invoices already, and rather than frustrate a new batch of vendors they'll just have to pay these as their schedules permit. Meaning never. So I went to Holly Foxx with it, and she threatened to throw the invoices out and make me start over, because these invoices are 'stale.'" She made air quotes with her fingers. "I'm sorry to take the team's time with something so trivial..."

"It isn't trivial," Zack contradicted, as Georgia wrote 'Always Pigheaded' next to 'AP.' "I'm pretty sure one of the vendors is the firm defending our patent litigation. That must be why the senior partner tried to reach me yesterday."

"God bless Holly," Ken said with a game smile, "and all who are privileged to work with her. Let me talk to her. If I can't get her cooperation, I'll go to Cliff." Georgia wrote, 'Holly. Cliff.' "Sorry, Maggie. I don't know where accounts payable got the idea their job was to not pay bills.

"Okay, that's it? Well, gang, another fine day to be alive and working in the Lumina legal department. Thanks for your time, feel free to take an extra donut." He stood up.

Georgia dropped a glazed donut onto a clean plate as she filed out of the room with the others, who were joking and laughing. If that Swiftly Acquire Patent case was the company's biggest threat, then that's what she wanted to work on. Make herself indispensable before Mr. Slash-and-Burn CEO decided to fire another 20 percent of Lumina employees. But hey, she already had a company to buy, and a sexual harassment case to think about. That Due Diligence study was about to be put to good use.

∞

On her lunch hour she ducked into the little maroon-walled conference room, closed the door and dialed the phone. "Katie-Ann, can you talk?

Is Mama there?"

"I think she's at work, Georgia. Well, unless she's sleeping off her Jim Beam in the bedroom. Hold on." While she waited, Georgia shooed a fly that was sauntering along the laminated tabletop, and it began zigzagging around the room.

"Nope," Katie-Ann reported after a minute. "She's gone."

"So how are you and Mama doing?"

"We're all right, I guess. Mama's been very busy being comforted in her time of sorrow by that Reverend Johnny Awknell."

"Great. Do she and Awknell drink together?"

"Nah, it seems like Johnny wants her to cut back on her drinking. He wants her to go to AA. She doesn't drink when she's around him, and just makes up for it later. They do seem to spend a lot of time in the TV room with the door closed, though."

"The Lord must love hypocrites, to employ them so frequently. Is he leaving you alone?"

"Yeah, more or less."

Georgia narrowed her eyes. "What's the less?"

"Well, you know how the top of my baton-twirling uniform has buttons down the front? After the 4th of July parade on Saturday he got awfully interested in how smooth those buttons felt."

"Katie-Ann, I want you to start locking your door before you go to bed."

"He won't come in my room. Mama wouldn't let him."

"Mama would convince herself he's coming in to cleanse your soul. That's what she thinks he's doing to her in that TV room. Lock your door."

Katie-Ann expelled a deep sigh. "Fine. I'll lock it."

"If Johnny knows what's good for him he'll make sure the neighbors don't have a lot to tell Daddy when he gets home." The fly was back on the tabletop, and she shooed it off again. How had a fly gotten into this airless inner vault, anyway?

"They're being careful. I think he mostly just comes when I'm here with Mama. He told Miz Gaskell he's been helping me out with my Bible studies."

Georgia barked a laugh. "What if Daddy ever tests that by asking you to name an apostle?"

"I know, but can you imagine Daddy if I ever did start naming apostles? Then he'd really take out after Reverend Awknell."

"Probably true. So, how's business down at the WhistleStop?"

"Good. Your former suitor stopped by the other day. And guess who he had with him?"

"Don't want to hear about him, Katie-Ann," Georgia warned, fighting off a nasty stab of jealousy.

"You sure? Deke's come way down in the world since he decided he was too refined for a jailbird's daughter."

"Whoever she is, she's too good for him. Let's talk about something else." That cheeky fly was back, crawling on the phone this time. Georgia slapped it silly with her notepad and flicked its carcass onto the linoleum floor.

"Up to you," Katie-Ann said, "but just so you know, this new one looks like she's been rode hard and put away wet." Georgia snickered in spite of herself, but said nothing. After a moment Katie-Ann gave up. "You know what, Georgia? Those government guys were sniffing around here looking for Robbie again."

Robbie. She made her response sound nonchalant. "Persistent, aren't they?"

"It's driving Mama crazy. She keeps saying, 'What will the neighbors think?' I know it's mean to laugh, but what does she suppose they think now? What do they want with Robbie, anyway? Was he in on that pigeon-drop they got Daddy for?"

"Hard to say. What'd you tell 'em?"

"The truth again. He disappeared all of a sudden, and we haven't seen him in a long while. The trick is going to be if he does show up again one of these days. What'll we tell the government people then?"

"I wouldn't worry about it."

"Why not?" Katie-Ann's curiosity put Georgia on the alert.

"Oh, I just think you'll be out here with me by the time Robbie shows up. Mama can handle it fine when the time comes. I should probably get back to work now. Look out for Mama, okay? Make sure she gets up in the morning. She really needs to hang onto her job."

"I know. I'm helping her. I just worry how she's going to manage once I'm in California. Anyway, bye now."

Georgia set the receiver back in its cradle and stared at the phone. Katie-Ann had a very good question. Why *was* the government so interested in Robbie all of a sudden? Were they still after him on the pigeon-drop? Lot of effort for some dumb-ass grifter that her father never should've hired in the first place. Had another one of Robbie's reloaded marks gone to the police? She pushed back from the table and stood up. That was probably the worst it could be. If they'd actually found Robbie they wouldn't be asking for him.

Would they?

∞

After her second uneventful night on Little Portman Road, she decided to make it her permanent (temporary) sleeping place. Nobody had called the cops on her, and there was just the right amount of coming and going to keep her from feeling completely isolated and vulnerable. Wednesday night was peaceful like the rest, but hot, which thickened that sweet alfalfa smell from her days of hauling feed in her trunk. Amazing how she longed for the luxury of just stretching out to stop the sweat from pooling behind her bent knees. It wasn't safe to leave the windows down, so she stuck with the quarter-inch crack she always used for oxygen, and tried to sleep under the sleeping bag instead of in it. The slippery nylon bag slid off every time she managed to turn over, and beads of sweat broke free periodically to trickle sideways across her back. Her eyes were probably going to be Early Girl tomato red in the morning when she headed into her meeting with Ken.

∞

"Georgia, come on in." Ken was alert and cheerful at 7:30 a.m., and his clothes looked like they'd been pressed on the way up in the elevator. Today his bow tie was kelly green. "How you doin'? Your neck okay?"

"Yeah. Thanks." She stopped rubbing it. "I just slept funny." Ugh, was that a whiff of alfalfa coming from her shirt?

"Sometimes it takes a while to get used to sleeping in a new place."

"Yeah, that must be it."

He punched a final key on his computer and joined her at the table. "Appreciate you helping out while Nikki's sick. Let's start with the purpose of the board meeting. The board meets once a quarter to talk about how the company is performing and set the strategic ..."

Maggie knocked on the door and opened it. "It's the court reporter for the deposition tomorrow. She has a quick question."

"Excuse me, Georgia," Ken said. "This'll only take a minute. Hi, this is Ken Madigan. Yes, Ms. Krinker, nice to meet you. I know you've been doing some depositions with Zack Stern, and we appreciate your help. Haven't been paid for any of them? I'm very sorry, I'll look into it today. Why don't we meet at 9:45 tomorrow in the lobby and I can go over some of the names with you? Great, you can't miss me, I'm the one with the bow tie and the big nose. Bye, now."

"Sorry, Georgia. Now, the logistics for the meeting. I'd like you to help me keep track of everything that happens. Attendance, all official votes ..."

Maggie knocked on the door again. Georgia contemplated his profile as he picked up the phone.

"Yes," he said. "Ms. Weatherford, I understand you'll be defending our expert tomorrow. Great, I'd be happy to. How about 9 there in the lobby for a cup of coffee? You'll have no trouble recognizing me, I'm the one with the bow tie and the big nose. Bye, now."

Her curiosity got the better of her. "Ken?" she said as he hung up. "Yes."

"You don't have a big nose."

He turned to look at her. "Well, I know. But if you saw the trouble I've gotten into because of my appearance…"

She tilted her head, considering. "So saying you have a big nose is camouflage, so people won't notice you're really good-looking."

Red-haired people sure knew how to blush. Maybe she'd been too candid again. "Well, now that you put it that way, Georgia, it does sound a little ridiculous. Maybe I'm just incredibly vain."

She squinted, then shook her head. "Don't think you're vain. Does it work?"

"Does what work?"

"The nose thing."

"Would you mind if we talk about the board book now?"

So *that* was what the bow tie was for. She continued to study his profile surreptitiously while they finished up. Strong chin, slightly thin lips, and a straight, very medium-sized nose. He actually was good-looking, now that she thought about it. (She'd make darn sure he never knew she thought about it.) He seemed like such an unguarded person, a crab without a shell who didn't miss it. How had he lasted for forty-odd years without getting squashed?

∞

"Excuse me," she called quietly to the woman facing away from her in the cube. "Are you Holly Foxx?" Queen of AP? Ms. Always Pigheaded?

As the woman rotated her chair around, her wavy auburn hair cascaded over her shoulder in slow motion, exactly like in some vintage shampoo commercial. Long, black eyelashes framed her big hazel eyes. She was wearing a thin cotton top so tight it outlined the grommets in her bra straps. "Yes?"

"My name is Georgia Griffin, and I just started about a week ago with the legal team."

"And?"

"Ken Madigan has asked me to arrange for a simultaneous transcript of a deposition tomorrow for our huge patent litigation. It turns out the court reporter still hasn't been paid for the depositions she did last month, so I need to hand carry the check ..."

"Whoa!" Holly interrupted, and held up the palm of her hand. "I don't know what it is with you people. If you submitted the paperwork properly, then she'll be paid in due course. I'm way too busy for special requests. I've told you guys a thousand times."

"If we don't do the simultaneous transcript it might damage the litigation."

"Wouldn't it be great for you if that was my problem? See ya." She turned her back to Georgia and resumed shuffling through a pile of well-thumbed invoices.

Ah. Evidently a graduate of the Roy Zisko School of Courtly Manners.

"Oh, that's okay," Georgia said to her back. "Thanks for listening. Nice shirt, by the way. You have a great sense of style." Holly snickered into her stack of invoices. "Anyway, bye."

Okay, so Holly Foxx had no intention whatever of doing her job, Georgia thought as she ran lightly up the stairs to her floor. One of those destructive employees her father had just written about. So Holly's boss, Cliff, just needed to recognize the obvious, and then he'd step in to fix the problem. Well, unless he got distracted by that bright, shiny hair of hers. If for some reason Cliff didn't fix the problem, was there a way she could help? Definitely something to think about tonight while she dined on slightly gray broccoli at Grace Lutheran.

CHAPTER 4

In addition to the savings, the other big advantage of sleeping in her car was that it motivated her to work late in the office. The long, uninterrupted evening hours helped a lot with her burgeoning workload.

Well, mostly uninterrupted.

"Georgia, here again tonight? They don't believe in breaking you in easy, do they?"

Cliff Tanco again, the Chief Financial Officer and so-called manager of Holly Foxx and her Always Pigheaded gang. He leaned his fifty-year-old body companionably against the panel edge that formed the entrance to her cubicle, his pager and iPhone suspended from his belt in leather holsters like six-shooters. "Don't you have a boyfriend who wants you home?"

She didn't look up. "Just moved here about a month ago, Cliff. Too busy for a boyfriend." Not to mention Deke had turned out to be about as steadfast as a wig in a hurricane. A new boyfriend would be more trouble than he was worth. Second prize: two boyfriends.

"Well, that's too bad. Must be lonely for you, but maybe I can help. Come on down to my office for a nightcap. I have some single malt whiskey, and we can get to know each other better."

Great. Was there something she needed less than getting to know Cliff Tanco better? He evidently thought that battleship gray hair of his was quite the aphrodisiac with people who were still getting carded in bars. She studied her nondisclosure agreement, calibrating her response. Then she looked up at him with a polite smile. "You know, Cliff, that's sweet of you, it really is. Can't do it, though, 'cause I have to finish this for tomorrow."

"Well, but everybody needs a ..."

"You know what else, Cliff? I think we know each other the right amount already." Oops, take it easy. This wasn't the prison guard. She beamed a disarming smile. "I mean, I already know that I enjoy working with you, and I value that a lot. I just have to get back to my work. Talk to you later, okay?" She offered a little compensatory wave as he backed out of her cubicle and headed down the hall.

"Nicely done," whispered a voice behind her. Georgia jumped.

"Oh! Nikki!" Roy's secretary had her hair in the ponytail again, revealing her little square earrings. "I didn't know anybody else was here." She lowered her voice. "That must've sounded awfully rude..."

"Exactly the right amount of rude to get the job done," Nikki said, grinning. "I'm impressed."

"Does he, you know, flirt with a lot of women?"

"Only the ones who breathe." They giggled. "And I hear the third Mrs. Tanco has no sense of humor whatsoever. Anyway, he's easily deflected. There isn't a person alive who hates conflict more than Cliff Tanco. Gonna be here much longer? If you leave after me, could you switch off the coffee?"

So Cliff Tanco craved female attention, which would explain why the ordinary corrective channels didn't seem to be functioning with Holly Foxx. Holly probably figured (correctly) that her great big hazel eyes would keep her fully employed even if she folded all those invoices into paper airplanes and sailed them out the window.

At that instant a solution popped into Georgia's head.

Unfortunately, it was a lot like one her father would think up, and that stuff was off limits forever. She stretched her arms above her head and returned to marking up the Non-Disclosure Agreement.

Too bad, though. It was sort of clever, really, and it might even work. She finished marking up the Non-Disclosure Agreement, put down her pen and tapped the pages against the desktop to straighten them.

A hundred percent off limits, she admonished herself, narrowing her eyes. Forget about it.

She entered the final changes, shut down her computer, switched off the coffee machine and headed to her car.

Well, but hold on. She paused on the dimly lit sidewalk. What if it wasn't her father's special talents that caused so much misery, but the ill-advised use he made of them? What if those skills he'd taught her could be redirected to make the company more productive, and even prevent layoffs? Those very skills might make her a more effective employee and help her keep a roof over Katie-Ann's head. She resumed walking.

Not that solving this one tiny problem could accomplish all that, she thought as she turned on her headlights and backed her car out, but wasn't it always better to solve a problem than not to solve it? Maybe it was better to at least try to make a difference. She'd think about that more after tomorrow's board meeting.

It was after eleven by the time she pulled her car into her sleeping spot on Little Portman Road. She settled in on the passenger side of her Subaru with her Itty Bitty Book Light to read the front-page of Ken's discarded *Wall Street Journal*. He always left it on Maggie's chair at the end of the day, and ten minutes of cruising through the front page had become part of Georgia's daily ritual.

She'd decided to resist the urge to cover her car windows at night, because she wanted to avoid broadcasting her homelessness. Which meant she should turn her light off, but tonight she was restless. She needed to make a good impression with the big shots at tomorrow's board meeting. If they noticed her in a good way, if they thought she was useful, it could help her survive the next round of layoffs. One screw-up and she'd be out on the street.

No way those wrinkles were going to just fall out of her pantsuit, even though she'd stretched the pants as carefully as possible over the back of the driver's seat. And what if she smelled like alfalfa in the morning?

She had to get to sleep. She was thirsty, but if she drank too much she'd have to pee into the mason jar during the night. This Subaru living was becoming more vexatious by the day. Still keyed up, she ventured inside the paper and found an article on page 6 with patent news. Perfect. This would put her to sleep in no time. Cranking her passenger seat back as far as possible, she began to read.

Some guy in St. Louis had just gotten a patent on a new computer switch. A little company in Illinois had used a patent dispute to get the International Trade Commission to block the import of some French computer chip into the U.S. The patent office was now taking an average of 30 months to process a patent application, up from 28 months only a year ago. She suppressed a small yawn.

Sure enough, after ten minutes she jerked awake as the paper dropped onto her lap. She snapped off the light, slid the *Journal* over to the driver's seat, and crawled between the seats into the back. New moon tonight, she thought as she punched her pillow and settled in. What *was* the International Trade Commission? Cliff should flirt less and manage that shiftless Holly Foxx more. Katie-Ann better not be squandering her tip money...

∞

Since it was her first board meeting, she was in the room a good fifteen minutes before the start time. This was the fancy room she'd interviewed in, and look! Those fat, fragrant little sandwiches were there on the side table again. She sniffed the air. And something chocolate. She dropped her bag and notepad on the dark, shiny table, and followed the scent to a tray of frosted brownies with a walnut half in the center of each one. Probably ill-bred to pick through the lunch before the board got a chance, and anyway, she had to get the room ready. She'd bide her time.

She dialed in the conference number and muted it, exactly as Nikki had showed her. She tested the console to be sure she could switch between the three screens, and took out her copy of the agenda. She set her new smart phone on the table in case she needed to text Nikki for emergency advice.

The first to arrive was a man in his seventies, whose sweater and slacks draped elegantly from his tall, lean frame, and whose manner reminded her of Cary Grant. "Jared Winters," he said, gripping her telltale icy hand. "Where's Nikki today? Are you her able assistant?" This was the investment banker. One down, six to go.

Next to enter was Jean-Claude Hauwel, who was chairman of the board and head of the audit committee. He was small and wiry with stiff gray hair, wearing a green and black plaid shirt tucked into his jeans. Jared immediately began teasing him, and Jean-Claude smiled as he defended himself and finally laughed as he tossed his green parka onto a chair by the wall. That was quite a French accent he had. She hoped she'd be able to follow him.

Four more directors pushed into the room simultaneously, and she didn't have time to sort them out. Then Cliff Tanco (Don Juan of Finance) and Ken. Oh, and Sally Kurtz, that dowdy Human Resources person from orientation. Today's outfit didn't look homemade, but where did you go exactly to buy a mustard yellow suit? Georgia glanced at her list. Ken must have forgotten to mention Sally Kurtz.

When Roy Zisko pushed open the side door and entered the boardroom a few moments later, the cheerful noise abruptly subsided into stiff greetings and polite handshakes. Then Roy removed his suit coat, kept everyone waiting while he carefully squared its shoulders on the back of his chair, brushed away a piece of lint, held his maroon tie against his chest and finally sat down.

Ken began with an update on the patent litigation, then turned the meeting over to Roy for a twenty-minute corporate overview. After only two minutes a board member with raven black hair and a very square, determined jaw interrupted Roy in mid-sentence.

"You know, Roy, I wonder if you could talk to us about why the sales numbers for the new release are so abysmal, and what it means about our ability to make our numbers for the quarter?" His smile was polite unless you actually looked at it, but his black eyes looked like they could bore through rock. Georgia glanced at her list. Must be Larry Stockton, the one who was CEO of his own software company. Were the sales numbers a real problem?

Roy shrugged. "I intended to get to this in a couple of minutes, but I guess we can go there now. I know we all have different attention spans. The P&L, please?" Whoa! Hostile. Would his bold grin let him get away with it? The board members' expressions betrayed nothing, but Ken dropped one eyelid in a sly wink. He knew what she was thinking. Georgia ducked her chin to conceal a little smile, and punched a button on the console. Mercifully, the correct columns of numbers appeared, and Roy explained that weak software sales were being offset by better-than-expected maintenance revenue.

"That's fine," Larry countered, "but it's no plan for the long-term. Selling software is our core business, so why aren't we selling more of it? Is the market down generally?"

"No," Roy admitted, "this is specific to us. We're hearing that customers have lost confidence because of perceived defects in our 6.0 release."

"Perceived?" echoed a very tall board member with a shiny bald head. Must be Paul Holder, the tech guru. "So it's a marketing problem? Or are there actually fundamental problems with the 6.0?"

"I think it's a combination of things. Software is always buggy. This particular version has a few more problems than most. And then we have a pretty green sales force. And then ..."

She scribbled furiously, trying to catch all of Roy's reasons.

"You're right," Jared said. "Software is always buggy. So the question is, why are we getting hit harder for buggy software than our competitors are? And why does this version have more problems?"

Great question.

"I don't know if it really has more problems. Might just be that these are more noticeable to the customer."

Now, what on earth did that mean? Did the company have product problems, or didn't it? This whole conversation felt like trying to grab a bar of wet soap.

"We're getting hit pretty hard by the technical press," Paul Holder said, "and that might be scaring off some customers. This product is Andrea's baby. Shouldn't we get her in here to get her thoughts about it?"

Andrea, the swimmer from orientation. Ken looked up from his notes.

"Only if you want to hear some elegantly crafted excuses," Roy replied, his small dark eyes watching them over the rims of his narrow glasses. "I'm afraid Andrea is an executive who really struggles with the concept of cost control. I'd hate to see her use an invitation from the board to make another run at getting her budget restored."

He wanted to keep Andrea away from the board.

"Well, but she signed off on this release just like she has all the others, didn't she?" Paul persisted.

"Eventually, yes. Unfortunately, when it became necessary to reduce Andrea's budget, she spent her time lobbying me to get her surplus engineers back instead of finding ways to improve productivity. Then as the target release date for the 6.0 approached, she wanted to delay the release until she felt satisfied with it."

"But of course, Ship When Ready," Jean-Claude said with his elegant accent. "It's what we always have done, because our software is mission critical for our customers and must be reliable."

"I know it's what you've always done. This time I decided to call Andrea's bluff and insist that we support the sales team by delivering the product on time."

Roy was in a power struggle with the head of R&D.

"This has apparently resulted in a few more issues than we anticipated," Roy continued, "but it's nothing more than a blip on the radar screen. For one thing, we've just gotten B of A's permission to use their name as a reference. We don't have any worries here."

Board members exchanged silent glances.

"You know, in future, Roy," Jean-Claude said, "if we're going to change something as basic as Ship When Ready, the board would like to know about that in advance."

Roy gave a stiff nod that meant 'fuck you.' This guy was a real sniper, striking fast to keep his targets off balance. Her father would have enjoyed the marksmanship.

"And you also said the sales force is green," Jean-Claude continued, consulting his notes. "Why are they suddenly so green? Are we not able to compete for seasoned people?"

Which led to a presentation by Sally on employee satisfaction. As Georgia switched over to the third screen her stomach gave an angry growl, and she put a hand over her abdomen as Jared caught her eye with mock dismay. She should have seized that brownie when she had the chance.

To better understand the employees' state of mind, Sally was explaining, the company had once again used the Voice of the Team survey. Uh-oh. Was the board going to get a dose of that saccharine junk from orientation?

Sally clearly hoped so. She stood at the front of the room in her mustard yellow suit jacket and beamed with pride as she turned to her first slide. "Okay, the things the employees scored us very high on were …"

"Take us through the lowest scores," Larry directed.

"Certainly," she said with a soft smile, switching to a different slide. "The lowest scores were:

a) *I have the tools I need to do my job.*
b) *I believe compensation is generally fair and equitable.*
And finally:
c) *Management listens to its employees.*"

"Okay," Jared said, "and those actual scores were…"

"Let's see. 1 out of 10."

Brief silence. "Did they have the option of saying zero?" Jared asked mildly, and somebody snickered.

"No," she responded innocently. "One was the lowest."

Jean-Claude was flipping noisily through his board book. "I see this is a summary, but where are the actual scores for each question?"

"I'm afraid they aren't there, Jean-Claude. We thought the summary would be more helpful this year. Was there something in particular?"

"Yes, I remember a question about how many would leave for another job if they could?"

Sally glanced at Roy, who gave a barely perceptible shrug. "Yes," she acknowledged. "Do you mean 'I would leave Lumina if I received an equivalent job offer at another company?'"

"That's it. What were those scores, please?"

"Twenty percent agreed strongly, and another 38 percent agreed somewhat."

Jean-Claude sat up straighter and opened his eyes wide. "Have I misunderstood you? Over half of our employees would leave if they could? Is that possible?"

"It is troubling," Sally sighed softly. "It's really one of our biggest problems."

"Sally, speak up, please" Larry commanded. Sally responded with a slightly pained, ladylike smile. That smile was about right for *Gone With the Wind*, maybe, but a Silicon Valley boardroom? Sally was a puzzlement.

"We want to be careful here," Roy cautioned. "All we're really measuring is how much our employees like to complain. In spite of these scores, the actual voluntary attrition for the last twelve months was only 8 percent."

"Well, but galley slaves wouldn't have quit in last year's economy," Jared objected with a dismissive wave of his hand, "because there was nowhere to go. The question is, what's going to happen now that the economy's picking up? Will we have anyone left to turn out the lights?"

"Sally," Larry called, "can you tell us what the numbers were for that same question two years ago?"

Sally flipped quickly through a binder. "Two years ago the combined total for 'agreed' and 'agreed strongly' was, let's see, 12.5 percent."

"From 12.5 percent to 58 percent in two years." Larry adjusted his French cuff as he flashed a triumphant smirk around the room and then settled it on Roy. "So the change during your tenure is impressive." Did these two really dislike each other, or was this just executive testosterone gone wild?

Several board members began to speak at once, and Roy held up his hand. "Look, cost-cutting, and particularly downsizing, are never going to be popular with the rank and file. Morale is bound to be low when you first eliminate entitlements, like profit-sharing, that never should have been given in the first place. We just should have waited another six months to do the survey."

"Why not a year, when there'd be nobody left to respond?" Jared asked mildly.

His remark hung in the air until Sally finally offered, "We're finalizing plans now to focus on those bottom three scores, which we think will have the biggest impact."

"Great," Jean-Claude responded promptly. "How quickly do you expect to reduce this enthusiasm for escaping Lumina, and by how much?"

"We're confident we can reduce it to 40 percent in the next twelve months."

A couple of board members barked out laughs while Jean-Claude threw his hands high in the air. "I'm sorry, we cannot accept this at all. I ask you to return to the board in two weeks with a detailed plan for getting this 'defection' number down to 18 percent within one year, including quarterly milestones. Do the minutes reflect that requirement?"

"They do," Ken confirmed, nodding to Georgia.

"Fine," Jean-Claude said, consulting his watch. "Let's take a

10-minute break." Several people stood at once. Larry Stockton and Roy reached the exit simultaneously, where they flailed like overturned beetles with their shoulders wedged in the doorway. Then Larry broke free and exited first. Georgia and the others hurried out behind them.

Who knew that sorry-sounding survey might actually be good for something? Did most corporate boards have this much antagonism? And how bad were the product problems? She was pretty sure her father had warned her that bad product was the number one killer of Silicon Valley companies.

Whatever. Nothing she could do about product quality. Just so Lumina Software lasted long enough to get Katie-Ann through high school. The blueberry-colored eyes staring back from the bathroom mirror looked anxious as she reparted her black bob and used her comb to tuck the ends under.

This meeting was certainly thought-provoking, and for all her jitters she was performing her duties just fine. Too bad she was only wallpaper. She sighed as she tossed her paper towel into the wastebasket. Well, she'd just have to make herself indispensable somewhere else.

When she reentered the boardroom, three board members had already returned to their seats and were smiling politely as they listened to Roy.

"...and the wind was really kicking up the waves and my wife was starting to get seasick, when all of a sudden we were being pelted by hailstones the size of golf balls. They hurt like hell."

"Wow," a board member exclaimed dutifully, "that must have been something." So they were committed to being civil after all. Jared picked up his paper copy of the next PowerPoint presentation, keeping his smile focused on Roy.

"It was something," Roy continued. "But you know what? It turned out it wasn't hail. We were actually sailing under a huge flock of geese, and what we were being pelted by was huge bird droppings that must have been freezing on the way down. A literal shit storm." Roy grinned, and the board members seemed at a slight loss for how to respond.

Other board members were filing back in.

"Well," Jared remarked, "there's no telling with Mother Nature, is there? Jean-Claude, shouldn't we get started?" No need to get carried away with civility.

"And I ended up with bruises on my shoulders and even on my head from all that lousy bird shit. And then, when it started to melt …!"

"Cliff!" Jean-Claude almost shouted. "Start the presentation!"

The meeting ended at 12:30. Sally pushed through the door and disappeared. Now the board members would have lunch together and begin their confidential strategy session. Was Georgia going to miss out on those sandwiches again? No way. She headed for the door, darting her hand out to snag a ham on rye as she passed the side table. Too bad she couldn't get a brownie, too.

"Whose computer is this?" Jean-Claude asked, pointing to the space Sally had just vacated.

"Sally's," Roy responded. "I think she stepped out to the bathroom."

"Well, let's remove it now, so she doesn't interrupt the lunch or the strategy session. Georgia, can you take it to her, please?" So at least the Board Chairman knew her name.

"Wait," Roy instructed, and then he seemed to hesitate. "I'll do it." He scooped up Sally's computer and followed Georgia out into the hallway. "Nikki," he said, dumping the computer and papers onto her desk. "The Board has asked that the lunch and strategy session be confidential. Would you stop Sally before she comes back in? Thank her for me and let her know I'll call her if we need her." He disappeared back into the boardroom.

"Oh, this'll be fun," Nikki muttered. "You need something, Georgia?"

"Sorry to bother you, but can we just confirm which board member is which? I got some of them, but …"

"Hey, Sally," Nikki called cheerfully into the hallway, "I have your stuff over here."

Sally paused with her hand against the boardroom door, and then slowly turned a bright smile toward Nikki.

"What on earth would you be doing with it out here?"

"Roy gave it to me and told me to thank you. He'll call you if they need anything."

Sally kept her hand poised on the door for five full seconds. Then she lowered it and kept smiling as she sauntered to Nikki's desk.

"Oh, I'm sure there's a misunderstanding," she said sweetly. "Roy wants me to attend the strategy session."

Nikki shrugged. "He was pretty explicit, so something must've changed. I wouldn't go in there, if I were you. Here you go. I think it's all there."

Sally's smile vanished and her voice descended to a snarl. "This is so unacceptable." She snatched her computer from Nikki. "I need a meeting with Roy tomorrow, for an hour, to discuss this."

"Great," Nikki said. "I'll look at his calendar and see what I can manage."

"Manage an hour. Tomorrow." She marched out of Nikki's office.

Bingo. From Scarlett O'Hara to Clint Eastwood in under five seconds. Will the real Sally please stand up?

"Wow," Georgia offered after Sally was out of earshot. "That was a little intense."

"Everything about that woman is intense." Nikki rubbed wearily on the side of her forehead where the migraine was evidently still lodged. "All right, let's go over the board members. The French guy, Jean-Claude, is the chairman . . ."

∞

"So she still won't pay them?" Zack's disbelieving voice carried easily to Georgia's cubicle, and she glanced up from her computer screen.

"She isn't refusing to pay them anymore," Maggie clarified. "Cliff must've talked to her. Now she says she'll pay them as soon as she gets Roy's counter-signature on every one, because she wants him to authorize her in writing to process them ahead of other people's bills. And Roy just left for customer visits in Asia."

"This is preposterous. I'll take the bills to Cliff myself. If he signs them she'll have to pay."

"Be careful. If you make her mad, she'll think up a reason to delay even longer."

"I guess I'm confused," Zack said. "Wasn't she hired to pay bills? How much energy are we supposed to waste on this jerk?"

Sitting in her cube, tapping her pen on her patent notes, Georgia decided they had probably wasted enough.

CHAPTER 5

"Georgia!" Ken called, leaning out from behind his computer console. "Come on in. Good to see you." He seemed delighted to see her every time she crossed the threshold of this frenetic office, which of course couldn't always be true. He probably made everyone feel that way. Just like everybody telling him their inner thoughts, really. Another accident of birth.

"Have a seat," he said, joining her at the conference table. "Zack'll be here in a minute, and we'll head over to see Archie Moss about getting our patent issued." So he'd decided to let her help with Swiftly Acquire Patent, the biggest challenge facing the company, and she'd finally meet the elusive owner of that wonderful, deep voice. Fine start to the morning.

Ken's paisley bow tie was hornet yellow with dark blue kidneys, and his blue chambray sleeves were rolled neatly to his elbows, his bare forearm resting on the dark wood. Beyond his window the bright sun bounced joyfully off windshields in the parking lot, and heated the tops of the fragrant eucalyptus trees beyond. "So," he asked, "how'd you like the board meeting?"

"I would say interesting, and confusing."

"What's the confusing part?"

"Well, remember how Roy said this version of our product had more bugs than usual, and then he said maybe they were just more noticeable bugs?"

He suppressed a smile. "I guess he did say those things."

"So, does that mean we do have a product problem, or we don't?"

"Hard to say what it means, isn't it, Georgia?" he said, relaxing into a grin. Ah, so it really was bullshit. His smile faded. "I can tell you, though, we certainly do have a product problem, and I just hope Andrea's team gets us out of it quickly."

"Ah. Is it serious?" *Another reason for layoffs.* Suddenly that bright sun was glaring right in her eyes.

"Want to push the door closed? Thanks." He lifted his forearm off the table and waited until she resumed her seat. "You know how a software company constantly updates its software to add new features? Well, our software sits at the core of our customers' whole computer system. Like all good companies that make mission-critical software, we make very certain our product is fully functional before it goes out, even if it means missing our target release date. It's what we've always done.

"Until last time. Roy was under a lot of pressure to get his sales numbers up, and he decided to ship the product before Andrea signed off on it. Word got out that customers were having serious problems with the software, and now even our longtime customers are refusing to buy the new version."

"Andrea knows how to fix it?"

"Absolutely. We're very fortunate. A lot of people think Andrea's the best R&D person here in the Valley."

"So then it's temporary."

He tilted his head to one side, considering. "Well, the only reason it might not be temporary is that once you spook your customers with unreliable product, I'm not too sure how soon they trust you again. Just hope we don't compound the problem by making the same mistake twice."

"The board knows this?"

"Not sure they do. You heard what Roy told them."

"So, is the board's not knowing stuff one of the big problems we have around here?"

He brushed his hand over the top of his inch-high red hair. "It probably is, though I don't know how different that is from most companies. Boards are in a strange position. They pretty much only know what the people who run the company choose to tell them."

Georgia tucked her hair behind one ear and tried to make her next question sound casual. "And what about the rest of us? If we know how to fix some little thing, should we just go ahead and fix it?"

"Absolutely. If each of us took that initiative, we'd be a very successful company. Why? You have something in mind?"

She shook her head. "No. Just curious. This helps a lot." It really did.

"You're curious about a lot of things, Georgia, and that's good for the company. Next time we're in a meeting and you have a question, feel free to shoot me a text message. Maybe I can help."

"But won't that distract you?"

He shook his head. "I won't let it. I might not always see your message right away, but there's some real dead space in those meetings, and I'd prefer to use it for something worthwhile."

"Great, I'll try it. Thanks." She pointed at the photos on his desk. "Are those all your children?" One photo seemed to be of Ken's family: a dark-haired wife with a son and daughter who looked about nine and eleven. The second photo was of Ken and two girls, slightly older.

"All mine," he confirmed, glancing at the photos, "but my two older girls have grown up. Kristy's twenty-four, and Jenny's twenty-five."

"Wow. You must have been young when you had them."

"Nineteen with Jenny, and Kristy when I was twenty. Miracle they turned out okay. They stayed with their mother when we split up, and I ended up having to call them every night to make sure they were doing their homework and brushing their teeth."

"You called them every night?"

He nodded. "Every Sunday through Thursday evening, if I possibly could. Occasionally I'd be on a plane or something, and then I'd ask my older girl to make sure the younger one did her homework. For a while I had to call in the morning, too, just to get 'em out of bed."

"Sounds pretty hard."

"Not as hard as it was for them, and I owed them all the help I could give. Tiffany wasn't very organized, and I still feel guilty about leaving her and the girls. Catholic upbringing stays with you, even when you don't believe the religion anymore."

"If you're so Catholic, I'm surprised you could leave at all."

"I really couldn't stay. We were both eighteen when she got pregnant with Jenny, so of course we got married. I was working two jobs, one in construction, and I also had to finish college. I wasn't around much, and she got involved with someone else. You know, Tiffany's a good person, but she really isn't very practical. I'm not proud of this, but after all these years she still sort of irritates me."

Georgia's laugh seemed to surprise him. "You think that's not very surprising," he interpreted.

"I think there might be divorces where feelings run even stronger."

"Well, but she's the girls' mother, and I always wanted to like her for their sake." They heard a knock. "Here's Zack now."

Zack Sern didn't look one bit like she'd imagined him on the phone, which shouldn't have been a surprise but somehow always was. He had a blond buzz cut that made his head look triangular and exposed the jowls on either side of his big, disarming smile. He wore chinos and a shirt with narrow green stripes. Relaxed, friendly, approachable, ten years younger than Ken, but with a few more donuts and a lot less exercise.

Well. So much for lean shoulders. Good. Who needed the distraction?

"Hey, Georgia," Zack said as they stood in the hall, waiting for Ken to speak to Maggie. "Welcome to Mission Impossible."

"Why do you say that?"

"Our mission, should we choose to accept it, is to get Archibald Moss to say something sensible about getting our patent issued."

"Ah." Interesting. Sarcasm seemed slightly at odds with that friendly, open smile. Ken rejoined them and they set off for the other building. "So what is Mr. Moss's job exactly?"

"He's the lawyer in charge of developing our patent portfolio," Zack's rich voice ricocheted in the narrow stairwell as she followed him down the cement steps. "He talks to our software engineers about the ideas they're developing, and then gets their help on the patent applications."

"So, he's in our department?"

"No," Ken replied from behind her. "He's the only lawyer in the company who's not in the legal department. Technically he reports to Andrea, but it was Paul Holder—you met him, Georgia, that tall, thin board member who got Archie hired—so Archie thinks he reports to the board. He therefore deems his cooperation with us completely voluntary, and I guess in a way it is." The thick carpet of grass glistened in the sun as they crossed the patio, and the fountain gave off a cooling mist. "He's a good person, but he occasionally has some challenges with the practical side of things."

As he held the door for her to enter the engineering building, he lowered his voice. "I'm sure you know there's a law against smoking in public buildings here in California, but Archie is considered uniquely valuable because of his ability to get along with our engineers. So he gets certain privileges, and one of those, I'm afraid, is that he routinely smokes cigars."

"Cigars," Georgia repeated. Cigars made her throat close.

"Just in his own office, of course. But just a warning, it can get a little close in there. Here he is now. Hi, Archie."

Archibald Moss was short and squat, not fat exactly, but with a round belly sticking out in front of him, across which he had fastened a big, shiny buckle to hold up his pants. His corn-colored hair looked like a broom he had lopped off across the top so that short bristles stuck straight up above a cheerful face with thick red lips and a wide nose. One pointy felt hat, thought Georgia, and presto! Instant Gnome.

He closed his door after they entered, revealing a folded rollaway bed with My Little Pony sheets.

"Nice rollaway, Arch," Ken said companionably. "Comfortable?"

"Very comfortable. One of the engineer's wives lent it to me until I could get my own bed, and I haven't gotten it back to her yet."

"So you still cling to your bachelor ways."

"Just haven't met the woman who could make me want to give them up. Have a seat."

No cigar in sight, but an acrid smell burned her nasal passages.

"What can I do for you gentlemen?"

"Archibald, this is Georgia Griffin, who joined the company a couple of weeks ago."

"Right. So what can I do for you gentlemen?" Gentlemen. Nice to know she was invisible, introduction notwithstanding.

"We've come to see you about the '401 application," Ken explained.

"I'm very familiar with it. What would you like to know?"

"We'd like to know how we can speed things up so we have it in time for the SAP case."

Archie shrugged cheerfully. "You can't. This seems to be a common misperception, and I'm very happy to explain it yet again. When we file a patent application, what we control is how quickly we respond to inquiries. They control everything else. Simple as that."

"Is there any way to track the progress through the different stages?"

"Sure, for all the good it'll do you. Let me show you their website." They joined him behind his desk, where he clicked the mouse a few times. "Here, this is us."

Georgia studied the computer screen. "So our patent's been on that desk for 104 days?"

"Correct."

"Is that typical? None of the other applications seem to have been there for more than 60."

"So ours will probably get done first," he said breezily.

"For something this important," Zack said, "do you ever call up a human being at the PTO to find out what the hang-up is?"

"Completely pointless. The whole purpose of this database is to stop people from bugging them with useless questions. We're all grown men here." Except for little invisible me, Georgia thought sourly. "For months now I've assured Paul almost every day that this is a routine process with everything on track. I feel like I've become the patent shrink around here, but hey, whatever helps."

"What I'd like to do," Ken said, "is call one of the D.C. patent firms who deal with the PTO day in and day out, just to see if they have any suggestions for us."

"Be my guest. Never hurts to hear the same answer twice. Just don't use my name to pester the patent office."

"No, of course not. And once we get someone, Arch, would you take a few minutes to give them the background?"

"Always happy to share my expertise with anyone. Feel free to call on me any time. Coming to the picnic this afternoon?"

"That's right, it's today, isn't it?" Ken caught Zack's eye and made a tiny head gesture toward the door. "I'll definitely be there, 'cause I'm on hamburger duty with Laura and the kids." Laura must be his second wife.

Archie smiled as he stood to say good-bye, exposing teeth the color of Vaseline. "Fulfilling your civic duty. Shows everyone your fun side. Speaking of which, I'm still waiting to see you down at the Saloon after work for a beer."

"Guess you should both put in an appearance at that picnic, too," Ken advised as they headed back across the patio, with Georgia sucking in healing gulps of fountain-cooled air. "What do you think about what Archie said?"

"Predictably useless," Zack replied. "I think one of us should call the patent office today and talk to a human being about what's happening to our application."

"Should we have our outside lawyer do that?"

Could she make herself useful already? "What if I call them up as just a little green pea," she offered, "and find some friendly underling who'll explain a few things? If I step on any toes, you can apologize later and say I had no business calling in the first place."

Zack looked at Ken and nodded. "Great idea. She might learn something before we can even get our outside lawyer set up."

∞

By 4:30 the picnic on the patio was downright lively. There were a hundred people milling about, trying the face paint, the cotton candy, the ball toss. A line had already formed in front of the grill where Ken was flipping burgers, with the help of his willowy brunette wife who was wearing a yellow sundress and opening buns on paper plates. And that would be their 11-year-old dark-haired daughter, solemnly planting a pickle spear beside each bun before holding the plate up for her father to drop the burger in place.

"Great-looking family, aren't they?" said a voice at her elbow, and Georgia turned to see Nikki, ponytail cascading out her Giants cap, gesture with her head toward the hamburger station. Was she that obvious about staring at Ken? Stupid to be standing around gawking like this when she had a job to do. Georgia murmured her embarrassed agreement and hurried on.

A few daredevil employees had donned red velcro suits and were jumping on a trampoline to stick as high as possible on a big velcro wall. How exactly did the company have money for this, when it couldn't afford to hire Andrea's software engineers? Georgia read a sign that said the guy who stuck highest on the velcro wall won a dinner for two at some fancy restaurant. The very thought of dinner in a clean, well-lit restaurant almost made her knees buckle. Stand back, boys. She'd jump like a bullfrog just the minute she completed her final task for the day.

She stretched to see if she could find Cliff Tanco, Don Juan of Finance, anywhere in the crowd. He was over by the tricycle race, leading the finance team in its last-minute decorations. Sure enough, Holly, Queen of Always Pigheaded, was right there with him, her magnificent auburn hair cascading down her back and almost touching the tiny white shorts that showed off her long, tan legs.

Georgia hurried past Sally, who was leaning over a delivery man and hissing "...assure you I don't care what you...!" She waved at Cliff, and called, "Hi there, too bad you guys are wasting so much effort on a trike that has no chance of winning."

"Booo!" cried the finance team.

"Are your kids here?" she asked Cliff.

"Just the youngest one. She's the eight-year-old blond over there with my wife." He pointed toward the soft drink line.

Bingo. She hurried over while she could get right behind them at the back of the line. Mrs. Tanco was blond, attractive and no-nonsense, with deep crow's-feet etched in delicate skin.

"My," Georgia sighed after a moment, fanning herself with her hand. "Warm today, isn't it? I wish we could get this line moving a little bit faster. I'm just about parched."

"You don't mind the heat, do you, Sarah?" Mrs. Tanco said to her daughter. She clarified to Georgia, "Anything that gets Sarah out of piano practice into the sunshine is just fine with her."

"Oh," Georgia said to the girl, "Are you Sarah Tanco?" The girl nodded warily. "Nice to meet you. I'm Georgia. Your dad talks a lot about how good you are on the piano."

The woman held out her hand. "I'm Katherine. Nice to meet you. Are you part of Cliff's group?"

"No, I just work a lot with finance. Cliff's put together quite a team there. They're so loyal to him."

"Are they really?"

"Absolutely. From the controller right down to the lowliest clerk, they'd just do anything for him. I mean, Holly Foxx, our accounts payable clerk? She's so devoted she's there working all hours with him, night after night. Now, you know that isn't because of any huge salary they pay her. She's just so committed to getting all those payments out." God, this was rude, but you never knew how quick people were on the uptake, and she'd only get one shot. Just so the daughter didn't catch on.

"That is impressive," Katherine acknowledged, a faint flush darkening her pale skin. "Which one is Holly?"

"I don't know if she's here... Oh, there she is, getting ready to start the trike race." Holly's bare legs were protruding out the sides of the tricycle like wings as Cliff leaned over her, adjusting her handle bars.

"That's great," Katherine said evenly. "I must remember to thank Holly for her steadfast devotion to my husband."

"Oh, she might prefer if you didn't, actually. She's kind of a shy person, to tell the truth." At that instant Holly shrieked with excitement as the gun went off, and pedaled furiously, hair flying, toward the finish line.

"Is that so?" Katherine said lightly, watching Holly.

"Mom," Sarah called. "Mom! The man's trying to give you your soda."

Do your job, and then step back, her father always said. Georgia downed her Odwalla and headed for the trampoline.

CHAPTER 6

Nikki's migraines (unfortunately for Nikki) were proving Georgia's greatest ally in her quest to increase her value to company big shots. This morning she was keeping minutes for the executive team, those very top employees the board relied on to run the company day to day. When she snapped on the lights of the executive team meeting room, she saw a room just similar enough to the boardroom across the hall to emphasize the lower status. Was that deliberate? Same frosted-glass swinging entry door, but into a more cramped space with no windows. Generous white paper napkins, to be sure, but no linen. Tragically, even the food was scaled back: Instead of those fragrant, glistening strawberries, the cafeteria had delivered rubbery, fork-resistant melon cubes that gave off no scent whatever.

She dropped the least dry-looking sweet roll onto her styrofoam plate and noted with satisfaction that she already recognized several of the executives who were entering the room. Andrea Hancock, with her black turtleneck and swimmer's blond hair. Cliff Tanco, finance Don Juan, his pager and iPhone in their six-shooter holsters, to whom Georgia offered a smile and a little wave. Ken, of course, with military posture and bow tie firmly in place, who politely introduced her to Glen Terkes, head of worldwide sales.

Glen shook her hand firmly, cufflinks glinting, his gray-eyed gaze traveling frankly down and up her body before focusing slightly over her right shoulder to see who else was coming through the door. Tall and tan, slouching easily in his perfectly fitted European suit, Terkes reminded her of the guy from the Tanqueray ad, the one who believes drinking expensive gin really does demonstrate depth of character. When Terkes sipped gin, he probably felt more urbane than Hugh and Cary Grant combined.

Ken also introduced her to Mark Balog, who was in charge of maintenance and support. "Hi, Georgia! Welcome!" he called across the table with a bright, tense smile. As she watched him pull his laptop from its case she suspected it wasn't easy to be Mark Balog. He looked like a man who'd decided many years ago to look alert and positive, and who executed perfectly on this and every other intention. He was the right weight (165 lbs.) in the right tie (gold and blue paisley today) to match the right shirt (sky blue, starched, to match his eyes). Those wide eyes and very white teeth completed a careful, unassailable package that somehow exuded terror, as if he were determined to stave off for one more day the disaster and humiliation that threatened to crush him.

At 8:01 Roy and Sally swept into the room.

"Good morning." Roy walked briskly to the far end of the conference table, where he pulled out a chair and stood in front of it with legs planted in a wide boxer's stance. Sally sat down in the adjacent chair and tilted her face up to him with beaming admiration. Whoa, little early in the morning for the Big Beam. Georgia averted her eyes and sipped her steaming coffee, wrapping her hands around her cup. Cold in this room. Was it her job to manage the heat?

"This morning," Roy began, staring down at them over the tops of his narrow oval glasses, "I want to congratulate Charlie Reebuck, who just closed a deal with Harmer Industrial for $1.2 million. Glen, please give Charlie our congratulations." Glen nodded once, urbanely.

"To summarize yesterday's board meeting, I think they're pretty well satisfied with my leadership of the business." Startled, Georgia glanced at Ken, who closed one eyelid in a subtle wink. Good, she wasn't crazy. "They do want us to focus on our license revenue as a means of getting our stock price up, and they're concerned about technical issues with the 6.0. They'd like us to increase employee satisfaction, which we'll talk about in a few minutes.

"I tell you the board's view to keep you informed, but I don't mean to let it distract us. Like any board, this one thinks it knows more than it really does. It's my job to set the direction of the company, and that's what I'll continue to do. Okay, Nikki—No." He glanced around, located Georgia and nodded to her, apparently unable to recall her name. "What's on the agenda, please?"

Georgia consulted her list. "The agenda is business development by Burt Plowfield. Update on the 6.1 release by Andrea. Open plan building renovation by you and the architect, and then improving employee satisfaction by Sally."

"We'll get started. Burt?" Roy sat down.

"Oh, hi everybody." A person in his fifties raised his hand. That was weird. How had she completely overlooked this guy? Very sloppy. Even if his beige shirt did blend into the wall behind him, even if his round face was strangely blank under that thinning yellow hair. She'd better pay more attention.

She corrected her attendance record as Burt said, "Oh, Roy thought you might want to know about a deal we're putting together to buy a company up in Oregon called Futuresoft." This must be the company she was going to help buy. Perfect. She'd get the background.

"Their product is a finance application that sits on top of our software and is sold ..." Was he mumbling? She leaned forward to hear better. His words almost seemed to be muffled and absorbed by the air around him. Bad acoustics, maybe.

He continued for several minutes. "... $26 million in revenue last year with a cost of $24 million." She noticed that Mark Balog's hair had tracks where the teeth of his comb had passed through. Must use 'product' to hold it in place ...

She jerked herself back to attention. "... almost 200 employees, 80 of them ..." Boy, Andrea had sure nailed that trick of juggling her pen around her knuckles in a figure eight. Could Georgia do that? Her pen dropped noisily onto the table, and several heads turned toward the sound as she snatched it up.

Hopeless, and it definitely wasn't the acoustics. Listening to this guy's monotone was like listening to a refrigerator hum. She forgot everything he said before he even finished saying it. Impossible to take notes.

"… investors involved who are running the negotiation from …" Where had Sally found that zigzag print blouse with ruffles at the shoulders? So gaudy. Now 'gaudy' was a word you didn't …

"Can I just ask, Burt?" Mark's staccato voice snapped her back to the discussion. "How much do the two founders stand to make on the deal at closing?"

"About $15 million apiece." Georgia wrote down his answer.

Andrea looked up from her monitor. "And we currently have zero ability to develop the product ourselves. If we lose them before they train us to edit the product, the product will be worthless."

"Sounds risky," Ken commented. "Have we thought about putting part of their cash in escrow for a year or two? Maybe with payout milestones tied to knowledge transfer. That would keep them on the hook to help Andrea."

"Oh, they don't want an escrow," Burt stated. "They want their money free and clear."

Ken shifted in his seat. "Everybody always wants their money free and clear," he said mildly, "but they're usually willing to compromise to get their deal done."

Burt shook his head. "They don't have to compromise. There are other buyers who'll give them all unencumbered cash."

"How do we know that?" Ken sounded puzzled.

"Oh, they said so."

Honestly. If her father ever met this Burt guy he would chortle with anticipation. She sent her first text message to Ken: *Burt =gullible?*

She continued her notes. A text message appeared: *Definitely. u done deals B4?*

She snorted softly. No, she just knew how to recognize a pigeon when it had beady red eyes and sat in a pigeon coop. She thought a minute and messaged back: *Poker with my dad.* She glanced up to see

Ken looking at his iPhone, his hand covering a faint smile that played at the corners of his mouth.

"Okay, thanks, Burt," Roy said. "Andrea, status of version 6.1."

She noted Andrea's response: 35 of 71 major bugs in version 6.0 corrected so far.

"Oracle compatibility is one of those bugs?" Roy asked.

Andrea tilted her head to one side. "Well, I guess you could think of it as our biggest bug, sort of a giant, prehistoric cockroach." She seemed oblivious to his glare. "We think we've identified the problem for many of the configurations, but it's going to involve significant new programming. After being starved for programmers, I suddenly have so many people working on it that they're tripping over each other. We have to schedule the staff carefully to maximize the chance it'll be ready in five weeks."

"It *will* be ready," Roy pronounced, his close-set eyes boring into Andrea's forehead. "Failure is not an option. We're getting the crap knocked out of us in the marketplace because of these compatibility problems."

"I know the importance of Oracle compatibility," she said evenly, returning his gaze. "That's why I didn't want to release the 6.0 without it." The air in this room was suddenly so cold it made Georgia's skin hurt. She rubbed her forearms briskly through the fabric of her summer suit jacket.

"Hey, guys?" Mark Balog waved his hand like a student seeking permission. "I'd like to comment. I think we should take the time we need to make sure we Ship. When. Ready."

Terkes was slouched in his chair, a forefinger resting in the indentation between his closed lips. Now he lifted the finger away from his face long enough to say, "We don't release 6.1 on schedule, we miss the quarter. Simple as that," and let the finger drop back into place.

Mark persisted. "But isn't is better to take a revenue hit this quarter than to take yet another blow to our credibility that we'll be living with for years to come?"

"We aren't going to have a 'hit' either to our credibility or to the revenue," Roy declared, "because 6.1 is going to be released on time, and will be fully compatible with an Oracle environment. Andrea, I hold you accountable. Do I make myself clear?"

"Very clear. I hope I've been clear as well."

"Your clarity is not valuable. Your only value is execution. Enough on that subject. Let's talk about the open plan renovation."

As the architect led them through the plans, Georgia realized that "open plan" meant all the offices were disappearing. After he finished, Roy shook his head from side to side as he said, "Comments? Questions? I'm really very pleased with these designs."

"Oh, congratulations," Burt offered. "Very innovative."

"It really looks state of the art," Sally said with her soft smile. "The employees are very fortunate that you care about giving them such a good environment, Roy."

"I'm sure that's all true," Ken said, "but I'm worried about where my lawyers are going to work. The work they do is often highly confidential or fairly detailed, and a lot of times it's both. I don't see how they can work sitting out in the open."

Roy's smile was patronizing. "This is quite predictable. People always have status issues at first, and my job is to help them see past their own egos to the real benefits of the open floor plan." Hmph. That thick neck of his was downright unattractive.

"I'm not talking about status, Roy." Ken's direct gaze remained pleasant. "I'm talking about people losing their ability to do confidential work in the office. I just don't think the benefits outweigh the drawbacks for my team."

"Your team?" Cliff directed his protest at Ken. "What about *my* team? They're going to have exactly the same problem. I can't sell it to them if legal is going to get something special. I think we all just have to live with it."

"Why should anybody live with something that doesn't make sense?" Andrea inquired, looking up from her monitor and closing her palm to capture her pen in mid-juggle. "If open plan is bad for legal and finance, then we just shouldn't put them there."

"Maybe," Mark suggested brightly, "instead of spending $3 million to remove our offices, we could spend $300,000 to get fresh paint and lower cube walls, and then spend the rest replenishing Andrea's team? Hiring more quota-carrying salespeople? Filing more patent applications?"

Had Mark just said three million dollars to wreck people's work space? Surely he was misinformed.

"What a bunch of negative complainers," Sally chided with a sweet smile. "I think the plans are great. Every new CEO has the right, almost an obligation, to make his own mark on the company he leads. This new design for open communication really speaks very well to your personality, Roy. An important part of your legacy."

Roy didn't look at Sally, but held up his hands like a celebrity trying to suppress a wildly enthusiastic audience. "Okay, thanks to all of you for your candid comments." Georgia sighed. Did he say 'candid'? Or 'candied'? Probably shouldn't put that in a message to Ken. "Okay, and finally we have the employee satisfaction matter. Sally?"

"Thanks, Roy." Sally led them through the presentation she had given to the board the day before. "So I need help with a plan for these lowest three scores. How about this feeling that management doesn't listen to employees?"

Georgia shot a message to Ken: *Discussion groups on open plan?*

"One thought," Ken suggested, looking up from his iPhone, "is that we could hold a couple of focus groups on the open floor plan we were just talking about." This secret text thing was sort of fun, once you got the hang of it.

"I don't think we need to let the employees run the company," Sally snapped. She caught herself mid-snarl and smiled softly. "Or do we?"

"I don't see the point of it, either," Roy agreed. "We know what they think already. We just don't happen to agree with it."

"Oh, I have an idea." Burt held up his hand. "Why don't we ask the marketing team to do some posters about how management is listening? We just aren't getting credit for the listening we already do."

Andrea widened her eyes at her screen and shook her head rapidly, like she was trying to dislodge something.

Roy stroked his lips with his thumb and forefinger a couple of times, considering. "Might work. Sally, have the marketing people start work on an internal campaign."

"Got it," Sally said, tapping happily on her keyboard. "This is a great idea."

Message from Ken: *Jesus, Mary & Joseph!* Georgia coughed.

"Now, what about the company vision?" Roy continued. "I have to explain this damn vision every time I turn around." The conversation continued for another 10 minutes, and then Roy ended the meeting and disappeared through the swinging door. The executives began quietly packing up their laptops.

"Sally," Andrea said as she unplugged her power cord. "If you're going to keep sucking up like that, you need to issue barf bags to the rest of us."

"I beg your pardon?" Sally sounded ominously prim, as if she was stepping in high heels around a dog turd.

Ken caught Georgia's eye and tilted his head toward the exit. Everyone was suddenly packing more quickly.

"Barf bags," Andrea enunciated carefully, looking directly at Sally. "Like on airplanes. After all, you're the Queen of HR, aren't you supposed to anticipate our human needs?"

Ken and Georgia escaped into the hall.

"Yikes!" Georgia muttered, as executives streamed around them and scurried away.

"Yikes is right," he muttered back. "I hope Andrea isn't losing her ability to suffer fools gladly. That could be a real handicap around here."

∞

The second best thing about that remark was that it was clever, she decided later as she bent over the gutter next to her car, brushing her teeth in the dark. The best thing was that he trusted her enough to share it with her.

It had been a pretty solitary few months, she reflected as she climbed into her driver's seat and reached across to the side pocket of the passenger door to stash her toothbrush and cup. Maybe she was just grasping at straws, but it seemed like this uptight Catholic could actually make her feel as if she belonged in Silicon Valley. Colleagues could also be friends, couldn't they? Not that she was really a colleague of some big executive, but he made her feel as if she was. Exchanging text messages right there in the meeting today. His perceptive green eyes resting on her across his conference table, encouraging her to speak up. Being looked at by Ken felt like early morning sun on her face when she stepped...

Whoa! Important not to get confused by those eyes of his, as some other women apparently had (hence the bow tie to keep them at bay). She needed to keep that good-looking wife of his in mind. Not to mention his daughter, her thin arms confidently holding that plate aloft to let Ken slide the burger onto it.

She climbed between the front seats into the back and adjusted her pillow against the armrest, noticing that the usually bright stars were obscured by thin clouds tonight. What could it possibly feel like to be a young girl with a stable, sensible father like Ken Madigan? Of course, no amount of imagination was going to allow the daughter of George Griffin to imagine that. Might as well ask a frog to imagine yodeling.

Whatever. She gave her pillow an extra punch and lay down with her legs extended and her feet planted high up on the side window. If she was lucky enough to have Ken Madigan as a mentor, she surely had the brains to keep from squandering it with some half-baked fantasy about a guy (however appealing) twenty years older than she was. Wouldn't hurt to find a man her own age, though, just for inoculation. Lumina Software was so far proving an unfortunate paradox in that regard. Stuffed with male employees, and yet just sort of a man desert.

∞

She picked up her phone on the first ring the next morning, and recognized the voice of Angela Trapp, PTO Specialist One, Georgia's new ally in overcoming Patent's Terrible Obstacles and getting the patent issued in time for the SAP lawsuit. After performing her most soul-stirring rendition of how issuance of the '401 could save Lumina Software, Georgia had only half expected ever to hear from her again.

"Ms. Griffin, your patent file isn't here."

"Oh, please call me Georgia." She cradled the phone between her ear and shoulder as she pushed a button to activate her screensaver. "Isn't where, in your department?"

"Isn't anywhere that I can tell."

She sat up straighter and frowned. "But your database says it's in your department."

"I know it does, but I really took the place apart and we just don't have it."

"So it's still back in the other department?"

"That's possible, but I called a friend of mine over there, and it's not on the shelf where it should be."

"Ms. Trapp, thank you so much for discovering this. Can I just ask, how do I find our patent file?"

"I'll put a tracer on it today. They start with the last department that had it, but I have to tell you, this isn't something that's pursued very actively here. I think you should assume it's been lost."

Georgia was now clutching the receiver with both hands. "Lost?? Vanished out of the whole Patent and Trademark Office? How could that happen?"

Ms. Trapp sighed. "Lotta ways, I'm afraid. I personally found a file one time soaking in a mud puddle in the middle of W Street. I guess it had fallen from the truck on its way from one building to another, and if I hadn't just happened to see it … Or if it's been misfiled, it might as well have bounced off the truck, because we have tens of thousands of files here, and they all look pretty much alike. We won't find it again until somebody grabs it by mistake, which could take years."

"This is horrible. What should I do?"

"I suggest you reassemble the paperwork and submit a new file. Call your patent lawyer right away."

"Thank you thank you thank you," Georgia said, and hurried over to see Maggie. Ken and Zack were both in meetings. She left an urgent message with Maggie, considered a moment and decided to contact Archibald directly. He answered his phone on the first ring.

"Griffin," he repeated vaguely. "Don't think we've had the pleasure."

"Actually, we have. I came to see you with Ken Madigan about the '401 patent?"

"Yes, well, I'm about to begin an important patent review meeting. Please call me another time."

"Wait! I just got off the phone with a patent specialist at the PTO. She says our patent application has been missing for several months. It never made it to the illustrations department after second review."

"Well, that's their fault, then. Their database was wrong."

Her shoulders twitched. "Well, it might be their fault, but how does that help Lumina? The PTO person said we should assume it's lost and start over, Archibald." Her voice was rising to a wail. "She said we'd be lucky to get it now by Thanksgiving."

"Well, that's better than Christmas." He didn't sound like he was joking.

"But this means we won't have it for the patent litigation. Our last chance disappears in less than two weeks." He didn't respond. She heard papers shuffling. "Okay. Well. I just thought you'd want to know."

"Absolutely. I should be apprised of all matters related to our patent portfolio. Now, if you'll excuse me, our engineers can't start anything without me."

She hung up, and was staring at the phone when an unfamiliar voice drifted over the tops of the cubicles. "Are you Maggie Wallace?

I'm Robert Pinske, the new manager of accounts payable." Georgia's ears pricked up. Something new in Always Pigheaded?

Maggie obviously didn't think so, since her voice was polite but noncommittal. "Nice to meet you, Robert. So, you work with Holly?"

"Actually, I'm replacing Holly, who is no longer with the company."

Immediate, ear-splitting silence in the cubicles.

"I wanted to introduce myself," he went on, "and talk to you about how we're going to get your bills caught up. May we go to a conference room?"

"Oh, we certainly may," Maggie said with enthusiasm. "Let's find one now." The cubicles remained silent as Maggie's animated voice and Robert's deeper one grew fainter and then died out as they rounded a corner down the hall.

"Did that guy say 'no longer with the company'?" Beatrice called hesitantly from her cube.

"That's what he said," a male voice confirmed. "Shouldn't we tell Ken?"

A minute later Ken's door flew open and he led the department in a round of applause. Seated in her cubicle where nobody could see her, Georgia acknowledged their gratitude with a solemn bow, even though they would never realize they were clapping for her.

CHAPTER 7

Ken's jaw had just fallen open at Georgia's news of the lost patent application when Maggie knocked and ushered in Glen Terkes. Ken stared blankly at Lumina's head of worldwide sales for a moment, then stood, shook hands and invited him to be seated.

Did Glen always dress like a guy out of *GQ*, or had he dropped by on his way to some big customer meeting? His lightweight gray summer suit and pink dress shirt made Ken look downright drab in his neatly rolled white shirtsleeves, like a sparrow sitting on a lawn next to a peacock. Georgia was suddenly conscious of the smear on her shirt where she'd carefully rubbed away salad dressing in order to delay a trip to the laundromat.

"Okay," Glen said with an impudent smile. "To what do I owe the pleasure?"

He was worried about something.

"We'd like to talk to you about an employment matter in the Boston office."

Glen's shoulders relaxed. *So Glen's problem was somewhere else.* "What about it? They're my best sales office."

"I know, they're very good. We had a complaint about a sexual harassment issue there, no big deal. But in the course of investigating that, something potentially more serious came up."

Glen raised his eyebrows. "Which would be . . .?"

"We've had a complaint that Buck Gibbons has been 'flipping' the genitals of one of the male sales reps who reports to him. By that I mean putting his hand underneath the person's genitals and trying to flip them up. I'm sure you understand, we need to investigate."

"Don't bother to investigate," Glen replied, adjusting a French cuff. "I know it's true."

"I'm sorry?"

He looked slightly bored as he adjusted the other cuff. "I said it's true. I was there."

Ken squinted at Glen for several seconds, moving his head in little jerks. The sparrow was trying to bring the peacock into focus.

"You were present when Buck Gibbons touched the genitals of another male in the office?"

"Yeah. Ben Larkin."

Ken stared at Glen, who was sporting a slight smirk, until Georgia coughed to fill the silence. Then he leaned forward, frowning with concentration, and said: "Glen, if you were there... did you say anything?"

"No."

"Did you think Buck's behavior was appropriate?"

Glen shrugged. "He's just immature."

Ken leaned even farther forward as if he doubted his hearing. "Really. You think we all did that when we were younger?"

"Ha ha. Look, he was just team-building. Not the best way to go about it. I'll talk to him."

Ken's eyes grew wide as tennis balls as he sat back up, apparently convinced he'd heard correctly. "I don't know if it was team-building, Glen. To a D.A. it might look more like sexual assault. I do know we have a complaint of offensive bodily contact here, corroborated by an executive who witnessed the behavior and did nothing. The company has to take this seriously and investigate. If he does it again ...'"

"He won't do it again. I'll tell him to stop."

Ken's elbow was now on the table, his chin resting on his thumb, his cheek against his extended forefinger as he scrutinized Glen. "If it's that simple, Glen, why haven't you have told him to stop already?"

"Look!" Glen stabbed the air toward Ken. When Ken didn't blink or move, Glen let his hand drop back onto the table. "Hey, I told you

I'll deal with it. We're heading into the last month of the quarter, and I can't have the General Counsel screwing with Buck's head, all right?"

"I don't think it is all right, unfortunately. I have an immediate obligation to our other Boston employees."

Glen looked mildly alarmed for the first time. "You cannot go to Buck about this before he closes the deal with Sinclair Electronics. Should be tomorrow. Are we agreed on that?"

Ken stood up. "I agree to wait until tomorrow. Check back with me toward the end of the day." He escorted Glen from the office and leaned his back against the closed door.

"Georgia, are we or are we not losing our minds?"

Georgia clapped her palm against her mouth, and for an instant she managed to swallow a burgeoning laugh. But then in spite of herself, her smile widened into her slightly loony grin, and she began to laugh hard. "Sorry," she wheezed. "I know it's serious. You should've seen the look on your face ..." She circled her fingers around her eyes and mimed them getting wider. "... the look when he ..." She could feel tears welling up and she couldn't get her sentence out. "... Team-building! ..." she gasped.

Ken's glare melted into amusement. "Exactly. What kind of a team ...?" And then he began to laugh, too, until they both had tears in their eyes. "Oh, God, Georgia," he said after a moment, plunking a box of Kleenex onto the table between them. "Can you believe this? I'm in no shape to deal with this now. We'll have to figure it out tomorrow. Right now we need to deal with our patent disaster." With a final hiccup, he opened the door and asked Maggie to find Zack.

Within an hour they had retained Jim Prizine of the Banyon firm to re-create the patent file, physically escort the file through the PTO, and get the patent issued, all in twelve days. Was that even possible? She hoped they hadn't embraced delusion as their chosen strategy.

And what was that other, unspoken thing that was worrying Glen, she wondered as she headed along the corridor back to her cube. (Remembering Ken's astounded face, she let out a little laugh.) Glen didn't seem like the worrying kind, exactly, so if something was bothering him, it was bound to be downright ugly. Just so it wasn't ugly enough to threaten the whole company.

Problems seemed to sprout like dandelions in this company, didn't they? But she had now managed to light one little candle in the darkness. Holly Foxx, deposed queen of Always Pigheaded, was off to paralyze somebody else's company. Now the legal team could spend its time on more important things. Which wasn't enough to prevent layoffs and guarantee her job, of course, but hey, it was a start.

∞

That night she hunched under her scratchy wool blanket to conceal her Itty Bitty Book Light and tore open her latest letter from her father.

Dear Georgia,

Thank you for the heads up on Robbie. Someone was here last week asking about him as well. I hope you won't let these harmless inquiries distract you from more important matters. I attended to all aspects of Robbie personally, and can assure you he won't be making an appearance anytime soon.

Her blanket sure stank of alfalfa. And something else, something acrid that burned her nostrils. Good thing she had her sleeping bag. If she or Katie-Ann ever wanted to sleep under this thing, they'd have to get it dry cleaned to keep from smelling like hayseeds.

What I cannot forgive myself for is missing important clues to Robbie's real character before things reached the point where drastic remedy was necessary. And I ended up here anyway, with our little enterprise scattered to the four winds. This wound to my professional pride will not heal easily. Perhaps it never should.

Poor Daddy. Being cooped up in that jail was bound to make him restless, but now he was starting to doubt himself.

With several months still to go before his first parole hearing.

And so I repent at leisure. My brother thinks he's so educated with his Bachelor of Superstition from Searcy Bible College, but he's the only one in the whole family who might actually benefit from this sorry little prison library. I'm running a Spanish Prisoner scam to keep my spirits up, but there isn't much challenge in it, and to tell you the truth I'm bored. I haven't gone this long without a good challenge since Gramma Griffin and I sold the old dry goods store to Mr. Haney. I'll just have to get my satisfaction vicariously by watching you rise through the ranks of Lumina Software.
Take care of yourself, Georgia. I'm proud that you are my daughter.
Your Daddy

He was being too hard on himself. How could he have predicted that Robbie would be fool enough to sneak back and try to reload their marks on his own? After all, who could possibly be *more* primed to run straight to the cops than a guy who'd already been scammed once? On the other hand, in her father's line of business you didn't always get the pick of the litter. So who knew, maybe he should have known Robbie was dumb enough to piss in his own boot.

Whatever. She snapped off her book light, threw off the smelly blanket and adjusted her pillow to protect her head from the armrest as she settled deeper into the back seat. If she could manage to get Katie-Ann through high school, her father could surely take care of himself. She'd do what she could, of course. Seek his advice, keep him informed of her progress. Send him a real book or two, maybe entertain him with the whole Holly Foxx escapade. Of course, the only thing that would really cheer her father up was a juicy new scam of his own.

∞

With Jim Prizine, the new outside patent lawyer, on his single-minded mission to overcome Patent's Terrible Obstacle, the legal team could turn its attention to the acquisition of the Seattle company called Futuresoft. The acquisition team (Ken, Quan and Georgia) held their initial meeting in Ken's office.

"Okay, Georgia," Ken began, "you know what due diligence is?"

She certainly hoped so. She knew exactly what her class notes and ten hours of Internet research could tell her. "I think it's where you find the dirt and catch the crooks," she stated with more conviction than she felt.

Quan and Ken barked a laugh. "Perfect," Ken agreed, "though we wouldn't want to say that to everybody."

"It's a real battle of wits," Quan confirmed. "They desperately want to hide the dirt and the crooks, and we desperately need to find them." Good. She was apparently both right and slightly clever.

With a quiet sigh of relief she asked, "And we start with a list of documents we want from them?"

"Here's the list," Ken confirmed, handing her a multipage document. "Your job is to keep ironclad track of every document Futuresoft provides, which you will do by taking ownership of our new basement diligence room." He held up a key. "You'll log the documents, and then be in the room whenever one of our employees is in there reviewing them."

In the next several days, as Quan began negotiating the deal agreement and Ken conducted diligence interviews (two of which he invited her to attend!), Georgia dutifully spent her days down in the basement, cataloguing and labeling the documents contained in 37 white bankers' boxes, and then hoisting the boxes into neat stacks along the wall. She spent her evenings and the wee hours of the morning reading the documents, and noting her questions and observations. After all, this could be her chance to make herself indispensable. She wanted to dazzle Ken by finding her very own Crook or Dirt.

They held their second meeting four days after the first, the three of them again huddled around Ken's conference table, their three sets of hands absorbing heat from three Peet's coffee cups. Georgia saw over

Quan's right shoulder that dawn had just finished bleaching the stars from the night sky and was staining the undersides of fat clouds with brilliant pink. Steam from the coffee released its rich fragrance into the air above their notepads and binders.

Quan led off with concern that the deal negotiations being led by Burt Plowfield were spiraling out of control. It seemed Blank Burt, the executive with the soporific voice, was caving immediately on every single concession requested by the other side.

"I was so horrified that I asked our outside lawyer, Jill, to attend the second meeting," he said.

"And how did that work?" Ken asked.

Quan laughed. "He gave things away twice as fast."

"Well, Burt's a good person, but he isn't very forceful, is he? He also gets a bonus whenever he closes a deal, so maybe he doesn't care how much he gives away to get there. What's he giving up?" While Ken and Quan discussed four or five things that Georgia didn't fully follow, the clouds over the parking lot transformed from resplendent rose into plush, majestic white. As she watched the topmost sliver of sun appeared over the eucalyptus trees, something occurred to her.

"Are there any women on the other side?" she asked, turning her gaze away from the clouds toward Quan.

"Their outside lawyer is a woman, but I haven't met her yet. Why?"

"Burt might refuse to give things away to a woman."

"What makes you say that, Georgia?" Ken asked, looking up from his notes.

"The fact that he gave even more away with our outside lawyer there. Burt seems deferential, so you'd expect him to defer to our own expert. But weak people sometimes need to lord it over somebody weaker. And why would he think Jill was weaker, except that she's a woman?" She shrugged. "Just a thought."

"That might be quite insightful," Quan responded, turning to Ken. "It isn't just Jill he undermines. I've never seen him agree with Andrea about anything."

"Gosh, I hate to think that could be a factor, but if we can get their lawyer in the room, why not? As for the diligence reviews, I'd say I'm pretty much done. The only thing …" He tapped his notes with his pen. "Their CEO sure seems proud of the way he stole business from their European distributor. He bragged to me that Futuresoft ended up with all the salespeople and customers, and the distributor ended up with all the obligations."

"How did they manage that?" Quan laughed. "Sounds too good to be true."

"Was the distributor named Norditch?" Georgia asked.

Ken stopped tapping and looked up from his notes. "Yes. Why? You've heard of them?"

"I found the distribution agreement between Norditch and Futuresoft in the diligence materials. I also found an agreement for Norditch to sell their whole company to Futuresoft, but it wasn't signed."

He raised his eyebrows and smiled at her. "Really!" *Her document reading was paying off.* "So Futuresoft did their own diligence review of Norditch's confidential information as if they were going to buy them, and then never completed the sale." He considered a moment. "Do you suppose they misused Norditch's confidential information to steal their customers? It's just suspicious that the CEO is so proud of screwing them over." One decisive thump of his pen. "In fact, I'm going to fly up to meet him. Unless his answers put my mind at ease, we might have to focus on Crooks and Dirt related to Norditch."

∞

Stark, Georgia decided. The word for Sally's office was 'stark.' While Zack talked about copies of the Board's annual self-evaluations, she allowed her eye to wander from a sickly rubber plant in the corner, to the top of a credenza packed with leaded glass and acrylic business mementos, to a single, colorful, framed photo of Sally standing in front of a thatched hut with black children wearing bright African fabrics. Mounted on the wall next to the photo were what appeared to be two shrunken heads. Which couldn't be right, of course. Probably some HR joke, or else she'd been sleeping worse than she'd realized. She rubbed her eye and looked again, but the heads were still there.

"So," Zack was saying to Sally, who remained seated behind her expansive mahogany desk. "Your admin was just over asking Georgia for copies of board evaluations."

Sally lifted her eyes wearily to look at him, her pen still poised above the notepad. "And that required interrupting me because...?"

"Well, first because there's nothing to copy. I thought maybe if you explained what you wanted them for, I could help."

Sally rolled her eyes and made a notation. "Roy has asked me to prepare for the next board evaluation, and I wanted to see what's been done in the past. Obviously, nothing very sophisticated."

Zack cocked his head to one side. "I guess I'm a little confused. The legal department manages the board evaluations. Maybe Roy doesn't know that."

"I think, Zack, you do well to assume the confusion is yours." A yellow-brown leaf separated from the rubber plant and dropped limply onto the carpet. Maybe those really were shrunken heads. "If you'll excuse me..."

"Impressive," Zack muttered as they headed back down the hall. "Sally has managed to know less than nothing. I'm afraid we have to ask Ken to intervene."

"Too bad. Zack, did you see those ..." but then they found Ken at his oval table, making his way gamely through a tall stack of documents. He invited them to sit, and rubbed his hand over his stubble of hair while he listened.

"Did you explain to Sally that she can't be involved, because she'll destroy the confidentiality of the process?"

"No point, Ken. She was deeply committed to our department's being stupid."

"She and Roy are probably thinking up ways to give Sally more interaction with the board after the board members barred her from the strategy session. They'll just have to think up something else, though. I'll deal with it." Why exactly did Roy care whether Sally had more interaction with the board? She thought about asking, but Ken said, "While I have you both here, can we talk about the Ben Larkin complaint?"

"Our team-building nut-flipper?" Zack said, grinning.

Ken flushed as his eyes flicked to Georgia and away again. "Buck Gibbons, yes. What should we do about him? Zack, let's start with you."

"Well, there doesn't seem to be any question that Buck flipped Ben's nuts, since Glen saw it happen. In spite of Glen's ridiculous statement about team building, I think it pretty much amounted to a sexual assault. Can you imagine if Buck did that to a woman?"

Ken held up a cautionary palm. "Well, but he didn't do it to a woman. He did it to a man. Any chance that would fall outside the definition of sexual harassment?"

"You mean, no sexual intent? I doubt it." Zack was hunched forward, resting his forearms comfortably on his loose-fitting khakis. "Why would a guy do that except with sexual intent?"

Ken shrugged. "Just trying to humiliate him? No better, of course, just different. Anyway, please continue."

"In any case, we're still on notice of a harmful or offensive touching. Can you imagine our liability if he ever does this again? Can you imagine the publicity in the *Wall Street Journal*? I say we fire him, unless he has some compelling explanation."

Georgia snorted. "And what would that be? A signed invitation from Ben?"

Ken turned to her. "So I take it you agree with Zack?"

Did everybody like being asked their opinion this much? She sat up a little straighter. "Well, I agree we *ought* to fire Buck, but Glen loves the guy."

"Loves the revenue he brings in," Ken clarified.

"But if we don't fire him," Georgia continued, "will Ben sue us?"

Zack shook his head confidently. "Don't think so, as long as we protect his job. Doesn't seem much like a troublemaker to me."

"That's my biggest concern," Ken said, "both from a human and a legal standpoint. If we don't fire Buck, how do we protect Ben Larkin's job?"

"My concern is that he'll keep doing it," Georgia said, "because he won't be able to stop. I mean, would you do that even once if you could stop yourself?"

Ken's green eyes flashed with suppressed laughter. "Sorry, Georgia, that's one I'm really not equipped to answer." She wished those eyes of his were slightly less attractive. The bow ties truthfully didn't counteract them much.

"Who cares what Glen's opinion is?" Zack threw his hands wide above the table. "He doesn't run the company. Surely Roy's gonna see we have to fire him."

Ken allowed one vertebra to sag slightly. "Don't think so, Zack. His gut reaction will be to protect the revenue, same as Glen. But I agree, it's too risky to keep Buck around after this." He snapped the vertebra back into correct military formation. "Thanks, guys. I'll take it from here."

∞

Now that Georgia had organized the Futuresoft diligence documents, she was spending time with the employees who came down to the basement room to review them. This afternoon she was reading employment agreements with a young woman from Human Resources, whom Georgia had silently nicknamed Prim Lucy. Every hair Prim Lucy owned had been sprayed into rigid submission. Thick, coke-bottle lenses dragged her pink plastic frames down her nose, so that she constantly scooted them up again.

"Oh!" Prim Lucy said, looking at her watch. "Almost six already. I have to go." She jumped up, smoothing the skirt of a shapeless, tan dress with a priestly collar. "I'm due at my mom's to make dinner."

"That's nice of you."

She pushed her glasses up her nose." Well, she's in a wheelchair, so it's not easy for her to get out any more. My sister goes over there on Sundays, and I do dinner every Wednesday."

"You should get going, then. I'll put this stuff away."

A few minutes later Georgia glanced up through the strip of window into the parking lot and was surprised to see Prim Lucy climb into a bright red Mini Cooper with black racing stripes and zoom out the back exit. How exactly did that car fit with coke bottle glasses?

She snapped the agreements back into their binder, then climbed to the second floor conference room and called Katie-Ann.

"Katie-Ann, it's me. Can you talk?"

"No problem. Mama's got the TV on and she's, you know."

"Johnny's not there?"

"Nope. Haven't seen him all day."

"Okay. Well, I signed the lease yesterday."

"We have an apartment?"

"Yep."

"Oh my God, that's fabulous!"

"I know. I was so excited I went straight to Salvation Army and bought two pots with lids and some serving spoons."

"Please tell me our life isn't going to be that boring when I get there."

"When you get here we will party big time, I promise. I pick the key up on the 30th. Gonna be a little under-furnished for a while."

"Who cares? I love camping. You have my sleeping bag, right?"

"Right there in my trunk with the new pots. Now I can go next week and get you registered for school. I checked the Greyhound schedule. You can walk into Searcy and catch the 3 p.m. bus on the Friday before Labor Day. Then you change to the bus for San Jose in Little

Rock, and you'll be here by Sunday noon."

"Hope I can sleep on the bus."

"You sleep anywhere, Katie-Ann. Just pretend you're in geometry."

"Cut it out. I got a B."

"Nice. How's your money?"

"I'll have enough for the bus fare by the end of this week, so I should have some extra by the time of the trip."

"Just don't spend it on cigarettes, okay?" Stubborn silence. "How are your clothes?"

"Getting there. I sneak out one backpackful a day to my school locker. Doing pajamas and stuff next." She lowered her voice and almost whispered into the phone, "Can't believe it's only two weeks now."

"Just two more weeks to avoid Johnny's laying on of hands."

"I can do it."

"I know you can. You're locking your bedroom door?"

"Yeah, but he and Mama are gonna be madder'n yellow jackets if they figure that out."

"If they figure it out, that means you needed your door locked, Katie-Ann. We have to make sure he doesn't get a whiff of this trip you're taking. He's the one that would be upset."

Katie-Ann was silent a moment, and Georgia pictured her winding a strand of blond hair around her finger. "I just hope he doesn't drop Mama like a hot potato when he finds out I'm gone."

"She'll be better off if he does. Maybe she'll wake up and realize what a hypocrite he is. Mama's a great big grown-up, you know. She needs to save herself." Now Katie-Ann's silence sounded sad. "Listen, we'll call her as soon as you're out here. We'll tell her it's temporary, just until she gets back on her feet. She'll be okay."

"I got an extra shift at the WhistleStop, Georgia."

"Way to hustle. Heard any more about Robbie?"

"No. Deke hasn't paraded any more ugly girlfriends through, either."

"Good on both counts. Well, I guess we'd better hang up now. I'll try to call you again before the big day. You have my number at work in case you need anything?"

"I have it. Bye, Georgia. I'm thrilled about the apartment."

∞

She sat in the passenger seat of her car that night, teeth brushed, doors locked, gazing up through the windshield at Orion glittering in the night sky. They had the apartment. Katie-Ann had her ticket money. They were ready for the school year. Grit and determination had caused these wonderful circumstances to converge. This wasn't yet escape velocity, but with Georgia's able assistance Katie-Ann Griffin was about to launch.

CHAPTER 8

Georgia and Zack were the first to arrive for their Crooks and Dirt document review. (She'd been warned never to call it that around Bland Burt.) Burt arrived late, while Zack was under the table plugging in his laptop, and he shoved Zack's laptop aside and supplanted him at the head of the table. "Before we start," Burt announced, "I want to point out that I have a mandate from Roy to get this deal done and signed in the next five days."

Zack hoisted himself up from the floor and agreeably moved to a side seat. "Great. Hope we can do it. Let's start with Lucy regarding HR." Ah yes. Prim Lucy, who made dinner for her mom on Wednesday nights. Andrea began juggling her pen in its customary figure eight around the knuckles of her right hand.

"This little company has been sued five times by its own employees in three years," Lucy warned as she pushed her heavy glasses up her nose. "That just sets off alarm bells for a company this size. We need to follow up with interviews, make sure the employees are committed to the company."

"That won't be necessary," Burt stated firmly. "The investment bankers and CEO assure me that the employees are very happy. They don't want us in there disrupting people while they're trying to run the business."

Honestly. What else would the bankers say, when they were the ones trying to sell the company? Georgia sighed. It was just sad her father was stuck in jail with this fat, luscious Burt pigeon strutting up and back under everyone's nose. It would be heaven to watch his feathers shoot forty feet in the air.

"Well, this is my recommendation to Sally," Lucy reiterated. "I'm sure she'd be happy to hear your perspective, Burt."

Interesting. Lucy had that schoolmarmish way of dressing, with her body-concealing dresses and those pink, coke-bottle glasses, but she confidently stood her ground with the likes of Burt Plowfield. And she had those racing stripes on her car.

"Thanks, Lucy," Zack said. "Let's move to Georgia and Jill on key contracts."

Jill Chamberlain, their outside lawyer from Woodrow, Mantella, had a bad haircut and rumpled suit that made her look like an unmade bed. After working with her for several days, Georgia admired her as a bottomless well of patience and expertise.

"Most of the contracts we reviewed are in decent shape," Jill told the group. "However ..." The word 'however' caused Andrea to stop juggling her pen. "... they do seem to have dangerous agreements with two of our major competitors. They sold unlimited product to Cordova and Oracle for a flat fee, including rights to all future related products."

"That's no problem," Burt explained. "Once we acquire them, there won't *be* any future related products."

"I'm afraid it's the opposite," Jill corrected him. "If you ever integrate one piece of Futuresoft code into your Lumina code—which of course you will—your two chief competitors can claim that every one of your products is a 'related product' and try to get them for free."

"Oh no," Quan said quietly, touching the wire temples of his glasses. "And could they modify and sell them?"

"Yes," Jill confirmed. "That's exactly what they could do."

"You gotta be kiddin' me," Zack said, dropping his forearms heavily onto the table.

"Deal-killer," Andrea pronounced.

"So how do we fix it?" Burt asked. "Remember, Roy wants this deal done in the next five days."

"I think," Jill said, wincing slightly in anticipation of Burt's response, "Futuresoft has to go back and renegotiate those contracts."

"That's ridiculous," Burt snapped. "The minute they try it, Oracle will know something's up and jack the price sky high." His tone suddenly turned patient. "Okay, Jill and Georgia, you girls have done a good job of bringing this to my attention, but now I think it's time to turn it over to my team to take it from here." Take it and bury it somewhere, no doubt.

"Well," Jill replied evenly, "we'll report our findings to Ken, and he'll guide us on next steps."

"Don't bother with that," Burt said generously. "You girls just leave it with me, and I'll work it out with Ken."

"You keep saying 'girls,'" Andrea noted, glancing around with mock curiosity. "Are there children in this room?"

"Oh, pardon me. Lay-dees. I know some lay-dees who prefer to be called girls."

Andrea laughed cheerfully. "Is there a special school to learn 'patronizing,' Burt, or is it all natural talent?"

So Bland Burt had a nasty little tiger in his tank. They should definitely get Futuresoft's woman lawyer into that negotiating room. She glanced at Quan, who caught her eye and nodded to acknowledge he was thinking the same thing.

"Let's move on," Zack said briskly, "to Quan and Andrea on intellectual property."

Quan held up some papers. "We've learned that Futuresoft freely uses open source in their product, including GPL licensed code. You all know what GPL is?" Georgia knew open source was free software you could download from the Internet, but she wrote "GPL?" on her notepad.

"GPL is a special subset of open source, isn't it?" Zack offered. "It turns all your code into open source."

"Exactly. If you integrate free GPL source code into your own private source code, then you have to make your entire product available for free as well. It completely destroys the commercial value of your software."

Was she hearing this correctly? Next to 'GPL' she wrote 'Greatly Poisons Lucre?'

"Well, that can't be right," Burt protested. "How has Futuresoft gotten around it?"

"It appears Futuresoft is so small that nobody ever noticed, and demanded free software," Quan replied.

"Well, they've been around for almost ten years," Burt said. "If nobody's noticed it by now, it's nothing to worry about."

"We need to worry about it a lot, I'm afraid," Andrea said. "We could gut the value of our intellectual property. For this very reason, by the way, we warrant to Microsoft that our code contains no GPL of any kind."

"Good point," Quan confirmed. "If we acquire their software the way it is now, we'll be in immediate breach of our warranties to Microsoft."

Okay, so she was hearing it right. She crossed out the question mark after Greatly Poisons Lucre. This whole Futuresoft deal was starting to smell like a hog pen at high noon.

"Well, so what's the solution?" Burt demanded. His round, white face had turned a mottled red.

"They have to get the GPL code out of their product before we buy it," Andrea stated.

"They'll *never* agree to that," Burt growled with disgust. "This is ridiculous. I'm going to take it to the investment bankers."

"You should," Andrea agreed, "and I'll talk to the two founders in charge of the code. It's not a deal breaker, just some work. But they've got to understand this isn't negotiable."

"Everything's negotiable," Burt snapped. "If you could just find a way to talk to the other side so they don't feel like their manhood is at risk."

All action in the room ceased. For an instant Andrea looked genuinely puzzled. "Manhood?" she repeated. "Oh, I get it. Your imitation of a fifties moron." She nodded appreciatively, eyebrows elevated.

"Convincing. But shouldn't we focus on our deal? Two problems if we let them think it's negotiable. First, it'll slow things down while they fight about it, and second, they'll eventually feel like we've pulled the rug out from under them when they have to do it anyway."

Burt's face was now an alarming, dark red. "I abso...!"

"It sounds like Andrea and Burt will talk to their respective counterparts," Quan summarized helpfully.

"Great." Zack stood up, practically shooing them from the room. "I'd say we're done. Ten minutes early, too. Thanks everybody. See you Thursday."

Georgia watched quietly while everyone but Zack grabbed their laptops and hurried from the room. "Wow," she said as the door to the stairwell banged shut, "does this dry business stuff always get people so riled up?"

"More than you'd expect," he acknowledged. "Business is done by people, and people can be pretty emotional."

"Do Burt and Andrea hate each other?"

He grinned. "They don't seem to like each other much, do they? But they do make a fine vaudeville team."

"That's a positive take on it."

"Yeah, I get accused of being positive sometimes. Even by my wife. I remember when she was pregnant, she had a lot of freaky, vivid dreams. One morning she clutched my arm and said, 'Zack! I dreamed our baby was born without a head!' So I said 'Oh, Cindy, don't worry. If the baby's born without a head, we'll give it the best life it can possibly have.'"

Georgia snorted. "Okay, but are you feeling positive about this Futuresoft deal? The problems seem insurmountable."

"They do, don't they?" He tucked his laptop under his arm and headed for the door. "I think it'll probably work out, but now you know my outlook."

∞

"How cool is this!" Nikki exclaimed quietly over her shoulder as they followed the elegant young hostess to their table at Evvia restaurant. Seen from behind, Nikki's tight jeans and high boots accentuated the grace of her healthy body. Georgia's jeans were squeaky clean, and her second-hand black Ralph Lauren shirt fit well enough. After three sweaty nights sleeping in her car, she'd stood for twenty minutes in the hot shower at the office gym just to steam the grit out of her pores and feel she belonged in this fancy Palo Alto restaurant. Which had sort of worked. She was probably still the only person in the room trying not to smell like alfalfa.

Over the tops of their menus, they took in the noisy atmosphere of the deep, cool room. Light from the open rotisserie fire danced on the high oak beam ceilings and flickered on the gleaming, hammered copper pots hanging above the open kitchen. Bottles of different shapes and sizes had been filled with brightly colored liquid, arranged on shelves, and then backlit on the rear wall. Nikki accepted the wine list, and said, "Don't you just love this place? I still can't believe you jumped higher than all those guys on the trampoline. You won the big prize, and now I get to share it with you."

"Well, it's only fair." Georgia shook open her linen napkin. "After all the work you did to put that party together, the least you deserve is a good meal." Not to mention that if Nikki had turned her down, there wouldn't have been one other person within a thousand miles she wanted to ask.

She'd never eaten Greek food, but the smells of garlic and lemon were certainly promising. Lots of lamb on the menu, and she hadn't had a real hunk of meat in a while. She just had to remember not to eat enough to make herself sick.

"Did you know anybody when you moved here, Georgia?" Nikki asked as they waited to order.

"Cousin at Apple, but mostly just wanted to be in California. My sister, Katie-Ann, is going to join me when school starts. Can't wait to see her."

"That's great. Older or younger?"

"Fifteen. She'll be a junior. I just hope she'll be able to make friends."

Nikki raised her eyebrows. "Oh wow, a little sister. Big responsibility. So where are your mom and dad?"

Uh-oh.

"Look, here's our waiter!" Georgia beamed at him a little too enthusiastically and pointed to her menu. "I'd like to start with this salad, please."

"The Horiatiki?" The waiter smiled back and held her eyes for an instant. She noticed he had curly dark hair and those excellent lank shoulders.

"Oh wow," Nikki commented as soon as he left, "that waiter thinks you're hot. He's cute, isn't he?"

At least they were off the parents thing. Georgia shrugged. "Whatever. I probably just look like a big spender. So how about you, Nikki? You have a boyfriend?" Nikki recounted how she had almost gotten married a couple of years earlier, until her fiancé decided she was already married to her job. Now she was dating one of the software developers, which led to a mutual lament that there were so few plausible guys in a fairly big company. The salads arrived, and the cubes of cheese with the salty olives were delicious. As they sipped the red wine Nikki had chosen, the conversation turned to work.

"Are the executives at least nice to you?" Georgia asked.

Nikki's grin was wolfish. "The smart ones are."

The waiter appeared to replace the empty salad plates with plump, glistening lamb chops and roasted potatoes. Georgia closed her eyes as she bit down on her first bite of lamb and felt the juices spurt onto her tongue. She chewed slowly, and when she opened her eyes again Nikki was beaming at Georgia's evident pleasure. The wine was so good with the lamb that for several minutes they spoke only of food.

"Hey, let's do a toast." Nikki's brown eyes sparkled as she lifted her glass. Then she snatched the glass back, sloshing the wine a little. "No, make that two toasts. First: To the highest trampoline jumper on the Peninsula, and, for all we know, the world!" They drank, and her grin became conspiratorial. "Second, and also miraculous in its way: To the memory of Holly Foxx, bill-paying obstructionist, who has obstructed her last bill for Lumina Software!" They clinked glasses and drank again.

"So why'd they fire her?" Georgia asked. "Something worse than never paying bills?"

"Had to be!" Nikki laughed, throwing her hands in the air. "... Since she hadn't paid a bill in years. I heard Cliff's wife, Kathleen, forced the issue, but I really don't believe it." A boisterous multigeneration Greek family at the next table erupted in laughter, forcing them to lean forward to hear each other.

"Why? Were Holly and Cliff..."

"That's just it. I don't think they were. Holly has a boyfriend she's crazy about." Nikki shrugged. "Who knows what happened? All I know is the company's going to work a whole lot better without her."

"I keep hearing that. You know what, though, Nikki? Does it seem to you like there are some other people at Lumina who don't do their jobs very well?"

Nikki rolled her eyes. "Oh-h-h, yeah! And some of them have a much bigger impact than Holly. This company is such a sinkhole of mediocrity, I sometimes wonder how we keep our doors open."

"Like who? I mean, is, um, Burt Plowfield good at his job?"

"Who?" Nikki leaned closer, since somebody at the family table had apparently told another fine joke. Georgia cupped her hands around her mouth and leaned across the table as she repeated the name.

Nikki's cheerful face turned downcast. "Poor Burt. He's kind of a sad case. You know, he used to have Andrea's job at another company."

"Really! How'd he end up here?"

"As I understand it, he couldn't get along with their new CEO. Evidently the two of them were just at constant loggerheads, and after a while she canned him. Funny, he's so mild-mannered you'd think he could get along with everybody." Mild-mannered with sneaky punches to the diaphragm. Evidently he'd been smart enough never to throw a punch at Nikki.

"But otherwise, he was good at his job?" Georgia persisted.

"Well, I assume so." Nikki shrugged. "He has a Master's from Caltech, so he must have something on the ball. I know he looked for another R&D job, but if that CEO wouldn't give him a recommendation ... Anyway, Roy hired him to find software companies to buy. The other side always seems to think he's great, but I've heard he doesn't hold his own too well in negotiations." She tilted her head back and drained her wine glass.

"Isn't that just two ways of saying the same thing?"

Nikki laughed. "Good point. So maybe he doesn't get all the fine points of negotiation." Her attention was drifting, and they watched the hostess brush past them with a woman whose glittering necklace would have funded Georgia's lifestyle for about five years. Then Nikki glowered. "You know who I think's an even bigger problem? Sally Kurtz."

"Sally? How come? I mean, I notice she's a little Jekyll and Hyde, but she certainly seems quite devoted to Roy."

Nikki rolled her eyes. "Yeah. Devoted. That woman sidled in here on her very first day, determined to make him her own entirely. She sneaks in without an appointment when my back is turned. She writes him little emails saying how exhausted he must be after his big long trip with those nasty old analysts. She just kind of oozes all over him in every meeting with empathy and understanding until you want to puke."

"Yeah, I might've seen some of that."

"It's actually sort of sci-fi. She's the alien who creeps into the captain's office disguised as a human, stings him to paralyze him and then plays with his insides for a while."

"Blech!" They both laughed.

"And for the rest of the movie everybody keeps saying"—Nikki deepened her voice and scrunched her eyebrows—'Is something wrong with the captain? He doesn't seem quite like himself.'"

Georgia shuddered. "Gross! You think she really influences him, though? In a funny way, he doesn't even seem to acknowledge her much." Partyers at a big table in the center of the room erupted in an enthusiastic rendition of Happy Birthday, to a smattering of applause.

"Oh, she influences him all right. If nothing else, she reinforces every completely lame idea he comes up with by telling him it's genius. If he had even a little bit of people smarts he'd see right through her. But Roy has the emotional IQ of a fire plug."

"So, why's she doing that? Just insecure? Or does she have something bigger in mind?"

"Good question." Nikki scrunched her mouth to one side, considering. "You know, I saw some form she filled out a few months ago, and for where she wanted to be in five years, she put 'CAO.'"

Acronyms at dinner. Georgia sighed. "Sorry, what does that mean?"

"Chief Administrative Officer. Some companies put everything that isn't sales or finance under a CAO. And then the CAO and the CEO and the CFO make a little triumvirate that runs the company."

"Does CAO include the legal department?"

"Yep."

"Sally wants to be in charge of our legal department?" Those cozy rotisserie flames dancing at the edge of her vision suddenly seemed devilish.

Nikki grinned. "She wants to be in charge of the solar system, Georgia, but for now she'll settle for legal." Noticing Georgia's face, she stopped smiling and held up her palm. "Hey, bad joke. Just some stupid form, and she had to put something in the blank to look ambitious. Anyway, don't let Sally ruin your great mood. You still have important choices to make, like baklava with Greek coffee, or chocolate with espresso? This is your night, Georgia."

Nikki was absolutely right, of course. No reason whatever to let some hypothetical future trouble interfere with this rare and sumptuous dinner. She'd think about Sally later. And that good-looking waiter did sort of think she was hot. She flashed Nikki a reassuring smile as she settled back in her chair and speared a wedge of perfectly roasted potato.

∞

Georgia was blessed with an innate talent for deep and restful sleep, even with the Futuresoft deal in deep trouble, even with Jim Prizine's heroic efforts to Swiftly Acquire Patent hanging by a single thread. Even when she was wedged into the back seat of her Subaru. She almost never woke up before sunlight slanted onto her face through the windshield, so maybe it was that late night espresso with Nikki that caused her eyes to blink wide open in the middle of the night. The first thing she saw was a bright moon shining in through the slanted back window. The second thing she saw was a man's face pressed against the window six inches from her own.

She started violently and scrambled upright against the back of the driver's seat as far from him as possible. Had she screamed? His tangled hair obscured the faint outline of his face, but she could make out sloping shoulders and a wide, saggy body. He cupped a hand around his mouth and said slowly, "I live there." He pointed to the house behind him and said something else. When she didn't respond, he moved around the car to where she had left the passenger window open a crack.

"I said, you should start sleeping in my driveway." Only his thick lips were visible in the crack in the window. "I see you out here every night, and you'll be safer in the driveway. The police won't hassle you there."

Georgia was suddenly furious. "You needed to tell me that at, what, four in the morning? You scared the living shit out of me!"

"I didn't mean to scare you," he said defensively. "I wasn't even going to wake you up. I just wanted to see if you were all right, like I do every night. But then your eyes opened."

She watched in fascination as the lips in the crack above the window said, "You're pretty when you sleep, you know?"

Her heavy wrench was under the front of the driver's seat where she couldn't reach it. Had she locked her doors? Her pulse was thundering as she forced a smile and said calmly, "Thanks. Appreciate the invitation, but I wouldn't want to be a nuisance. You sure it would really be all right?"

He pulled his ear away from the crack in the window and his lips reappeared. "It's definitely all right. You could come in sometimes and watch TV."

"Wow, that would be great. Now, where should I park?"

He pointed. "Over on that side, away from the streetlight."

"On the far side of your pickup? Great. Would you mind standing exactly where you'd like me to stop my front wheels? I don't want to be in the way. I'm going to get in the front seat and start the car, okay? This'll be great." She snaked a leg between the front seats and hoisted herself into the driver's side.

She caught a glimpse of his bare legs as he disappeared into the dark driveway on the far side of his pickup. "Over here," she heard him call.

Starting her engine, she popped off the brake and accelerated so fast that the car fish-tailed. She turned the corner and kept speeding, checking her rearview mirror every five seconds. The street behind her remained dark.

Crazy fucker! Looking in at her every night? She shuddered. No more uncovered windows, even if the coverings did attract attention. No more staying in one place for more than a night. Should she check into the Castlekeep to calm down? It was already 4:30, big waste of money. She was done sleeping for this night.

Stupid creep. What if this made her scared to sleep in her car for the next two weeks? One thing for sure, she'd spring for a can of Mace tomorrow, and sleep with it right next to her head. What if he had her license plate number? Would that let him find their new apartment? She confirmed that her doors were locked, and headed to the all-night Happy Donuts in Palo Alto.

CHAPTER 9

By the time Georgia and Quan entered Ken's office at 9 a.m. that morning, she had jogged, showered and consumed an impressive quantity of donut holes. Now she welcomed any distraction that would dislodge last night's drama from her mind.

"So," Ken began, "I went over this Norditch relationship with the CEO of Futuresoft yesterday. I'd say my suspicions grew instead of diminishing."

"Oh no," Quan said, raking his fingers through his thick black hair. "You think there really might be Crooks and Dirt?"

"I'm afraid I do, but it's still only speculation, and we can't let suspicions slow us down. We have to go all out to get answers and then fix any problems if we possibly can."

"Did you find out how Norditch managed to stay in business with no customers or salespeople?" Quan asked

Ken shrugged. "They didn't. After Futuresoft stripped out the bulk of their business, Norditch sold the little sliver that remained to Cordova."

"Cordova," Georgia repeated. "Our big rivals again? So, if we buy Futuresoft, and Futuresoft cheated Norditch, and Norditch is now Cordova, is it really the same as us having cheated Cordova?"

"You got it." Ken nodded decisively.

Quan laughed. "Oh, no! Exact repeat of the SAP disaster, where we buy our way into horrible legal problems with our worst enemies."

"Yes, but only if Futuresoft really did cheat Nordich," Ken said, "which is what we have to find out. I've asked Futuresoft to produce every piece of paper that relates to Norditch employees and customers becoming employees and customers of Futuresoft. Georgia, you okay?"

"Fine." Georgia jerked herself out of the image of those thick red lips moving in the crack above her car window. God, had she shuddered or something? "Sorry. Weird dream last night. So we need a new document request." She picked up her pen.

"Unfortunately, Futuresoft has refused any new document request," Ken replied. "They said if we slow the deal down that much, they'll just walk away. What they *will* do is put a lot of documents they've supposedly never reviewed into a room up in Seattle. We can go in the room and look through them, as long as we don't take notes or make copies."

Georgia's eyes narrowed. "So there must be something nasty. "

Quan laughed. " I wish Burt had your insight. So the battle of wits continues. They want to increase the odds that we'll overlook something horrible in their documents, and then they'll be off the hook because technically they allowed us to see them."

How gratifying that a smart person like Quan thought she had insight. "So now what?"

"Now we go up to Seattle and look at all that paper," Ken stated. "Quan, can you make it up there for a day this week?"

"I'll go tomorrow, but can we get this done in a day?"

"We have to try. Let's make a list of what we're looking for." Twenty minutes later Georgia and Quan stood to go, and Ken said, "Before you leave, Georgia, update on the '401 patent application?"

She turned back as Quan continued down the hall. "Our new patent lawyer, Jim Prizine, is sitting on a wooden bench outside the office of the Director of Drawing and Diagram Review somewhere in the bowels of the Patent and Trademark Office. Jim delivered the file into the Director's hands yesterday, jumps to attention every time she goes in or out, and will hand carry the file to the next guy. Two more departments and two days to go."

Ken pressed his lips into a tight line. "Boy, this really is a cliffhanger, isn't it? Exactly what you don't want with something this important. Does Archie have any ideas?"

"Archie? Haven't spoken to him since we hired Prizine. Hasn't he called you?"

"No."

"Wouldn't you think he'd be curious?" Probably reckless to criticize a big shot, but also irresistible. "For months he pretended to be Paul Holder's patent psychiatrist instead of actually tracking the patent, which is why we have this disaster on our hands. Now he acts like it has nothing to do with him."

Ken stood up, brushing his palm across the stubble of his military-style haircut. "To be honest, Georgia, you're much more capable of managing this kind of thing than Archie is. He's a good person, but he doesn't seem to be very practical."

"He's about as practical as wings on a cucumber. I'm happy to track the patent, but shouldn't he feel slightly responsible for jeopardizing our whole patent case?"

Ken's green eyes searched her face for a moment. "Maybe you should talk that through with him. He's a person we have to work with, and it's better not to have the whole relationship poisoned if you can avoid it."

"Really?" Her dread must have been obvious, because Ken's smile was sympathetic.

"Do what you think best. I just think one way or another it might help if you get to know him a little better."

∞

After lunch she dutifully crossed the fountain-cooled patio to Archibald's office unannounced.

"Archibald?" she called, rapping against the half-open door. Somebody was seated across from him, a man in his thirties with stringy dishwater-colored hair that matched his dishwater-colored T-shirt. One of their software engineers, probably.

Archie set a smoldering cigar in his ashtray as he looked up. "Don't believe I've had the honor."

Maybe she could make a career out of introducing herself to this guy. "I'm Georgia Griffin, about the '401 patent. You have a minute?"

"That again?" he said. "I'm afraid I'm in a ..."

"No problem," the man said hastily, standing up. "I was done for now, anyway." He motioned her into his vacated chair with an exaggerated sweep of his arm, his eyes locked onto hers just a moment too long before he turned and left.

"Fine," Archie said cheerfully, waving her in. "Hope you don't mind the smoke." Were those flakes of tobacco that were stuck on his yellow teeth?

"Mind if I close the door?" The rollaway bed was still there, being gassed within an inch of its life. "I wanted to talk to you about the stuff Ken and I have been doing with the '401. We're desperate to get that patent issued in time for our SAP case, and it sort of seems like you don't even think it's a problem."

"I'm glad you came to discuss this with me," he said, gesturing for her to sit as smoke spiraled slowly into the air above his desk. "See, when you've had my education and experience, you realize it isn't any big deal. The patent office loses applications all the time."

Georgia paused, considering. His red lips were curved in a patient smile, waiting for her slower mental faculties to catch up. "Isn't a big deal to whom? I mean, it might not be a big deal from the perspective of the patent office, but shouldn't we take Lumina's perspective? Ken and Paul Holder think it's a big deal."

"I know, and I'm very disappointed in them. I thought they were grown men."

Had this imbecile ever gotten a point in his life? "Maybe they're afraid we'll lose the patent case." She paused again, while he continued to smile patiently. The guy's confidence was as unassailable as Napoleon's. "Actually, I find it frustrating to be the one trying to get the patent on time, when it's your area of expertise."

"Really," he said, tapping the ash from his cigar. "I just assumed you loved the work. I hear you spend almost all your time on it."

She searched in vain for some appropriate response, and then gave up. "Right," she said, standing to go. "Well, I just thought I should mention it, because I didn't want resentment to build between us."

He waved his hand dismissively. "No worries. I'm not the resentful type. Glad you stopped by. Feel free to take advantage of my expertise any time."

A few minutes later she was bent over the bathroom sink, coughing and splashing cold water into her smoke-stung eyes. Well, that was a failure. She now found him even more irritating, and she'd bet her gas money he still wouldn't remember who she was. Next time she'd introduce herself as Meryl Streep.

So Archie was prized because he related well to software engineers. A vital skill, no doubt. But it seemed safer to drive a hog across a field of land mines than let him be in charge of anything. She just hoped she and Ken had taken control before it was too late.

∞

"Now, why are we here at the Saloon?" Nikki wrinkled her nose as they pushed through the padded, red leather doors into the long, dim room. A back-lit bar spanned the far wall, beyond a bunch of sticky-looking varnished tables, beneath electrical fixtures that gave off flickering yellow light. "Isn't this the place where Mandy gets drunk sometimes, and dusts it up with her boyfriend?"

"Who?"

"Mandy. That curly-haired brunette who works in payroll and kinda looks like Salma Hayak?" Georgia shrugged and shook her head. "Latina accent?"

"Sorry. Haven't met her."

"Doesn't matter. I'm just saying our last destination had more class."

"True. But Ken thinks I should get to know Archibald better, since we're working together so much." She was scanning the tables, trying to find him in the deep gloom. The place felt like it was just heating up.

"Yeah, I heard Archie's here a lot. There he is. At the end of the bar." Nikki waved. "I think he's cute."

"So was Nero," Georgia muttered.

"Sorry?"

"I said it's a good thing we came. He's all by himself."

Archibald was stirring his drink slowly and talking to the bartender. "Nikki," he nodded, smiling. "Here's a pleasant surprise. Have I met your friend? What'll you ladies have?"

"Wow, so who else comes here?" Nikki asked after they settled on their bar stools.

"It varies a lot," Archibald said. "I usually count on Charlie and David, but then a lot of other people show up sometimes. Like the two of you, for example."

"Do a lot of women come here?"

"Enough to keep hope alive."

"Oh, Archie, don't pretend," Nikki chided him with her thousand-watt grin, sipping her wine. "I bet you can get a date whenever you want one. Women just want to take care of you." Surely that was a joke, so why was nobody laughing?

"To some extent you're right," Archibald acknowledged. "Women are such nice people that they're drawn to hopeless cases. Not exactly the same as romantic interest, though, and I sometimes seem to have trouble telling the difference."

"Really." Georgia's polite tone belied her flash of curiosity. "How so?" They'd gotten their stools just in time. The area around the bar was getting crowded, and the guy behind her kept brushing against her shoulder blades. She wished he'd back up a little.

"Well," Archibald said, "when I used to work at the law firm, there was this gorgeous secretary named Linda. Linda and I had lunch a few times, and sometimes I went out with her and her friends. Then she started dating some associate, and when I told her friends I missed her, they said it served me right. Said she decided she'd been pining for me long enough. I almost fainted. Pining?? For me?? I had absolutely no idea."

"Shame," Georgia commiserated with a slow shake of her head. Somebody jostled against her back again, and smiled apologetically when she turned to glare at him. "Did she end up with the other guy?"

"Married him. I presume they're living happily ever after. But then another time I had this very sexy woman really coming on to me in a bar, not this bar, one in New York. The place was jammed, and she was right behind my stool. She kept putting her hand on my back, and then on my shoulder, and every time I turned around she'd give me this big, sexy smile. Pretty soon she was practically squirming against me, and when I finally suggested we go back to her place, she threw her drink at me!"

"Ouch!"

"Yeah, it was awful. Tell you the truth, I was so embarrassed I had to find another bar for a while. So I've been very careful not to make that mistake again. Here comes David now. Let's get a table. David! Look! Female companionship!"

"Georgia?" Nikki was waving a hand in front of her face. "Georgia! You with us? We're moving to a table."

"Oh. Sure," she murmured, reluctantly emerging from her mesmerizing vision of Archie undone. She lifted her beer glass, dropped from her stool onto the floor and smiled dreamily as she threaded her way through the bodies, following Nikki deeper into the atmospheric gloom.

∞

After her scare with the creep on Little Portman Road, Georgia decided to treat herself to the profound luxury of a real bed (and locked door!) at Castlekeep Inn for the night. Thankfully they had a room, and at 7:30 she raced upstairs to soak in her tub, periodically adding hot water until her toes looked like ten happy raisins. She dried her hair slowly, and then danced all around her big, private room in the hotel's frayed terrycloth robe until she flopped into the overstuffed chair from exhaustion. By 8:30 she was bouncing on the queen-sized bed, sniffing appreciatively the faint scent of bleach from the blindingly white sheets. She wasn't quite ready for sleep. This would be a great time to use her free wi-fi to get some answers about her idea (well, notion really) for the patent case. She got online and went at it.

At 10:00 she set her computer down on the bed and pressed her fingers against her closed eyes. This was about as far as she could go on her own. Her idea actually looked workable to her, but of course she was probably blind to the obvious, insurmountable barrier that was blocking her way. After all, if Lumina could do this for the patent case, wouldn't their famous patent firm be doing it already?

Well. There were worse things than making a fool of yourself, and one of them was being too chicken to live. If you thought you could make a difference you just went for it, and then learned something if they bothered to explain how stupid it was. In the meantime, what could be better than a glorious night's sleep, spread out wide in the center of a real bed? She double-checked her alarm, burrowed blissfully into the cool sheets and snapped off the light.

∞

Around 9 a.m. Ken forwarded Quan's first report that he was in the Seattle conference room with thousands of documents piled on the long table and thousands more stacked in drifts on along the walls. A pleasant young attendant had assured him regretfully that there was no index and was now watching him like a hawk. Must be quite a needle to warrant that much haystack, Georgia thought.

Ken asked her to join him for Quan's 3:30 phone call. When Quan came on the line he was breathing hard.

"Quan, what's goin' on there, buddy?" Ken called into the phone. "You sound like you've been running."

"I literally just ran away from Burt. He seemed quite angry that I wouldn't stop and talk to him."

"Burt Plowfield? What's he doin' up there?"

"I'd say several important things. Fraternizing with the enemy. Asking what's taking so long. And letting me know ahead of time that anything I find is either misunderstood or irrelevant."

"Sorry, Quan, you had more than enough to deal with today without that guy. Tell us what you've found."

"Well, keep in mind I couldn't take notes or make copies, but I did jot down a list right before this call." He described his findings for twenty minutes.

"Okay," Ken said when he had finished, "first of all, you've done an amazing job of organizing your search and your findings. You're like the guy from *The Thirty-nine Steps*. Here's what I think you found:

"First, looks like the way they got the Norditch customers was legal.

"Second, they put two Norditch employees on the Futuresoft payroll while they were still employees of Norditch. Probably illegal, definitely sleazy, but not in itself the crime of the century.

"But third, the information the Norditch employees brought with them to Futuresoft is clearly illegal. They brought a prototype of a Cordova product that hadn't been released yet. And confidential pricing information about deals where Cordova was competing with Futuresoft.

"And what's really bad is that the Futuresoft CEO himself was personally right in the thick of it. He—personally!—set up secret email accounts for the Norditch employees. The obvious reason to do that is to help them funnel stolen information to him without getting caught. Also, he counseled his Singapore employees to clean their drives of any Norditch information 'just in case.' We can only presume the 'just in case' was to prevent us from finding out what they had."

He paused a moment, considering. "That's what I recall. Is it accurate?"

"Yes," Quan confirmed, "but keep in mind I looked at less than 1 percent of the documents in the room. There may be innocent explanations of some stuff I saw that we don't know about, and it's also possible that I misread something in my haste."

"True. But you didn't misread everything, and there's enough in what you found to fuel a great lawsuit if Cordova cares to bring one. The fact is, we're on notice that Futuresoft has stolen Cordova's intellectual property."

"I think that's right." Quan's breath had returned to normal. "And even if the CEO isn't outright crooked, he doesn't seem very ethical. How can he explain setting up those top secret email accounts for somebody else's employees?"

"He was team building," Georgia offered.

Ken snorted. "He certainly wasn't doing anything sensible."

"So, he's either a crook or as dumb as a sack of hammers," Georgia summarized. "Is that a person we want on our management team?"

"Sadly, Georgia, that depends on who 'we' is. Speaking of which, Quan, have you briefed Burt?"

"No," Quan said, "I refused to speak to him. I just didn't have time. I'm sure that's part of what he's angry about."

"Also scared you found something. Tell you what, just head directly for the airport, and I'll deal with Burt. You've done a great job for the company, Mr. Memory. Terrific work."

"You don't want me to stay here and continue for at least another day? There are still thousands of unread documents."

"Unfortunately for the deal, I think we have enough already. Let's meet tomorrow morning. Safe trip back."

So was the whole Futuresoft deal dead, she wondered as she headed back to her cube. God, that bed last night had been glorious. She was well rested. The thought of folding herself up into her back seat again tonight seemed a little like being buried alive.

Suck it up. Two more weeks and Katie-Ann would be here, and they'd stretch out in their sleeping bags on a big, wide carpeted floor night after heated night. Hot food whenever they wanted it, without having to worry about whether there would be any mystery meat left by the time she got to the front of the homeless line. No more trying to sit upwind of redolent dinner companions, or avoiding people who chewed with their mouths open. A person could surely manage for two short weeks, with the promise of such luxury so close behind.

CHAPTER 10

Quan and Georgia were helping Ken finalize his Futuresoft presentation to Roy when Zack stuck his head in Ken's office.

"Ken, did you tell Archibald Moss to get involved with the Western Analytics lawsuit?" Western Analytics was a patent case Georgia had nothing to do with. Zack's buzz cut looked the same, but something about him was different.

"No," Ken replied. "Does he think I did?"

"Western Analytics missed a discovery deadline last week. I just called their lawyer because I hadn't heard from them, and they said they'd already agreed with our general counsel to stop all discovery."

"That's ridiculous. I haven't even talked to them."

"I know you haven't. They worked it out with our 'general counsel,' Archibald Moss." Zack used his middle finger to push his glasses up his nose, and she realized that was the difference. His contacts must be hurting him, because he was wearing thick black-rimmed glasses.

"You gotta be kiddin' me. How did they even find Archie?" Ken trapped a sigh in his puffed-out cheeks. "Would you ask Maggie to see if she can get him on the speakerphone? Excuse me a minute, guys." He set down his pen and rubbed his fingers across his closed eyes.

It was so quiet while they waited that they could hear employees cut their engines as they arrived in the parking lot. Morning sun had reached the edge of Ken's conference table, and was spreading its slow stain across Quan's notepad and up the side of his paper coffee cup.

Maggie put Archibald through. "Hey, Arch. I'm here with Zack Stern. He just got off the phone with … who was it, their general counsel? Zack just got off the phone with the general counsel of Western Analytics. Did you tell him we agreed to stop all discovery in our patent litigation?"

"No. I did say that it made sense to stop fighting, because we were all grown men."

Ken exchanged a pointed glance with Zack as he said to the phone, "Did you put anything in writing?"

"Not unless it's on a bar napkin somewhere."

"You met him in a bar?"

"Yeah, down at the Saloon."

He touched his canary yellow bow tie as he leaned closer to the speakerphone. "Did you tell him you were Lumina's general counsel?"

"Certainly not."

"Why do they think you're the general counsel?"

"How should I know? Must be my regal bearing."

He glanced quickly at each of them in the room. "Archibald, you shouldn't even be talking to the lawyers at Western Analytics about the patent case."

"I disagree. I have a broad mandate to manage our intellectual property here at Lumina, and this lawsuit is impeding the free and unfettered development of our software."

"But it's not your mandate to decide or communicate litigation strategy."

"Never said it was."

"Okay. If you run into those guys at the Saloon again, could you please not talk about the patent litigation?"

"Too restrictive."

"If anybody from Western Analytics tries to reach any agreement with you, will you refer them to Zack?"

"More than happy to."

"Thanks, Arch. See you later." He punched the off button. "Zack, you know how to deal with this, but let me know if I can help."

"Thanks." Zack put his hand on the door handle, but then turned back. "Ken, do we need man-on-man defense for this guy?" Well, exactly. Archie's behavior was about as predictable as a grapefruit squirt.

Ken smiled ruefully. "He does seem to get around, doesn't he?"

"Wouldn't our jobs be a lot easier if we got him under control?"

Georgia leaned forward to hear the answer.

"They probably would, Zack, if we could do it. But how? Archibald's a good person, but he's also an out-and-out anarchist. I think he's just our cross to bear."

Zack used his middle finger to push his glasses up his nose again. "He's going to make a mess we can't fix one of these days. I think maybe he already did with the '401 patent."

"He's pretty destructive, I'll grant you that. Wish I knew a better answer."

Georgia leaned back. She wished he did, too. Ken's passive acceptance was sort of embarrassing.

"By the way, Georgia," Ken said as Zack left, "did you ever talk to Archie about the lost patent?"

"I did," she nodded. "Helped a lot. In fact, we've had drinks twice now down at the Saloon." Which she considered literally true and compassionately misleading.

"No kidding. Fantastic. Maybe you can run interference between him and the Western Analytics lawyer. Thanks for the outline, guys. I think I'm ready."

"You have a minute on another subject?" she asked.

"I do. Thanks, Quan. See you later." Quan closed the door behind him, and Ken's eyes rested on her with friendly concern. "What's up? You look tired. Your workload too much?"

She probably did look tired from being folded up like an accordion again all night. "I'm fine, Ken. Thanks. I had two quick things I wanted to talk to you about. The first is Glen Terkes. Did you notice how he relaxed that day when you told him your issue was in the Boston office?"

"No. Did he really?"

"I think he did. If I'm right, that means there's something worse outside of Boston that we don't know about yet. We just might keep our eyes open."

His eyes dutifully opened wider. "No kidding. I hope to God you're wrong, Georgia, but thanks for the heads up."

"The second thing is an idea I had for the patent case." Her voice suddenly sounded like it had caught down in her throat somewhere.

"Let's hear it," he invited, fully attentive. Okay, she thought. Here goes.

"Well, I think there's a huge chance we won't get the '401 patent in time to use it in the lawsuit."

"Completely agree. Probably too late already, though we have to keep trying."

"Well, I saw an article in the *Wall Street Journal* about the International Trade Commission. I just wondered if we could bring a separate lawsuit there."

"International Trade Commission. The people who do import regulations?"

"Absolutely. But they also have their own judges, and a U.S. company can start a whole separate lawsuit with them if a foreign company is stealing their intellectual property. You can stop the foreign company from selling its software here in the U.S." She knew she was talking too fast. "Does SAP create its software in Germany?"

He raised his eyebrows, considering. "I presume so, at least part of it."

"Well, if SAP's product violates our new patent, maybe we could stop them from selling it here."

"I think I've heard of these lawsuits, but they're pretty rare, aren't they? Can they be based on patents?"

"I think they can. I printed these pages from the ITC web site, and each lawsuit lists either 'no patent' or else a patent number. See?" Ken took the papers from her, and looked where she was pointing, while she rushed ahead. "The good thing is that the cases move really fast, and the preliminary injunction can be done in a couple of weeks. Maybe we could leapfrog the whole patent case." There it was, she thought. ITC: Ingenious Tricky Countersuit?

Ken brushed a hand across his military-cut red hair as he looked through the pages.

"Georgia, I have no idea if this will work. I do think it's the first new idea we've had in a while, and I'll call the Banyon lawyers today. Any news on the patent?"

"Jim Prizine is sitting on a wooden bench outside the office of the person with the official seal, but he hasn't been allowed to speak to her. He says from a distance she looks dumb, bureaucratic and arrogant."

"Great. Let's just hope he can charm her into giving us that seal. One day left before discovery cutoff. Thanks, Georgia."

At least he hadn't said it was ridiculous, Georgia thought as she headed back to her cube. He had listened respectfully, exactly the way he always did, and he was going to ask the Banyon lawyers. The way he listened made all those hours seem worth it, whether her idea panned out or not.

He wasn't going to deal with Archibald, though, and Zack was right. The guy was a whole new Marx Brother, and they were only funny in movies.

Of course, it was hard to deal with problem employees, especially if you were a nice person like Ken. Even her father had waited too long with no-good Robbie, which accounted for his current misfortune.

Was that why she saw this more clearly than Ken did? It seemed obvious that letting an overconfident person do stupid stuff day after endless day would eventually bring the whole company down around their heads. This doofus was Robbie all over again, and somebody needed to stop him before it was too late.

As she rounded the corner and glanced into the empty break room, her vision from the night down at the Saloon resurfaced in breathtaking clarity. Archie Undone. Could she pull it off? Maybe, if she was willing to use her special talents again. Probably, if she could get Archie to trust her enough.

The cleanest approach, she knew from her father, was to complete your scam and get out before the mark ever got his bearings. Which of course wasn't always possible. So he also taught that when you need time to prepare your gambit, you should give the mark preliminary opportunities to confirm your reliability, so that he has confidence in you when you spring your trap.

But wait. She paused on the carpet a few cubes down from her own. This was exactly what she'd turned her back on forever. Wasn't it? She'd gone to years of trouble to get her paralegal degree and extract herself from a life of conning people. Of course, that was conning people for profit. Was this different? She resumed walking.

Her con artist training had been put to excellent use once already, getting that no-account Holly Foxx off the payroll. And so efficiently, compared to more traditional methods of dealing with a problem employee. Archibald Moss posed a way bigger threat to the company than Holly Foxx had, so the benefit would be a lot greater. Unfortunately, so was the risk. She turned into her cube.

Not a great time to be taking risks of any kind with Katie-Ann coming, but of course there was also risk in doing nothing. Or was there? Maybe she was overreacting. Maybe somebody else would step up and solve the problem. She sighed. Probably wouldn't hurt to prepare, just in case. Suddenly she missed her father terribly.

∞

On Wednesday afternoon she watched her time carefully, and at 5:45 she was in her Subaru, waiting just outside the back exit. Sure enough, at five before six Prim Lucy's bright red Mini Cooper with black racing stripes pulled out onto the street. Georgia followed it for fifteen minutes, watched it turn into the underground lot of an apartment building. The building had external stairs, and she ducked down below the window in her driver's seat to watch without being noticed.

A few moments later Lucy appeared on the stairs and climbed to the third floor, where she used a key to let herself in. Georgia waited five long minutes, then jumped from her car and walked briskly up the same stairs until she could read the number on the door through which Lucy had disappeared. She hurried to her car and sped back to the office.

∞

She didn't get to the Saloon until 10:30 that night, and at first she thought Archibald had gone home. When she scanned the room more slowly, she spotted him at a table at the far end. No wonder she'd missed him. A curly-haired woman in her thirties had her arm around Archie's nonexistent neck. Really? How could any sentient being voluntarily touch this guy? Well, Gramma Griffin always said that every pot has its lid. In any case, Georgia obviously wasn't going to be building any rapport with Archie tonight. The woman was even sort of good looking. In fact, she looked a little bit like that actress, what was her name? Salma Hayak.

Salma Hayak. Wait, was this that woman Nikki had talked about? The one who liked to 'dust it up' with her boyfriend? Maybe that explained it. Maybe she'd pretend to like anybody to get her boyfriend jealous. Whatever the explanation, this could be a great way to build trust with Archie. She hurried over behind the woman so that Archibald was facing her, and waved to get his attention. He ignored her completely.

"Excuse me, Archie, could I talk to you for a minute?"

Archie's face was spread in a wide, dreamy grin as his eyes stared into Salma's. "Not a good time, Georgia. Maybe you could, you know, take a number?"

"I'm afraid it's kind of urgent."

"Can you believe it?" he said to the woman, holding her gaze as he disentangled himself reluctantly from her arm. "I'm in such demand all of a sudden. Don't go anywhere, now." He slid off his stool and followed Georgia into the thick part of the crowd. "What're you, jealous? This better be good."

"It is good, in a bad sort of way. That woman you're with? I think she's trouble."

"What're you talking about? She totally hot, and she thinks I'm fascinating."

"Yeah. She's also got a mean husband."

"What husband? She sure doesn't act like she has a husband."

"Maybe he isn't here. Could be a boyfriend. But anyway, I've heard about her, and she definitely has one. Sort of a physical type who shows up and shoves people."

"No way. You sure it's the same woman?"

"No," she admitted. "It looks like her, though. Does she have a Latina accent?"

"Oh, yeah. Very sexy."

"I'm sure it is. Her boyfriend thinks so, too."

"Nah, you've got ..." and at that instant the red leather doors swung inward to reveal a stocky man with tattoos on his muscled forearms, who surveyed the room, marched over to the curly-haired woman and said something in a low, growly voice. She turned away dismissively as he pointed to Archie's drink and asked a question. He scanned the crowded, dimly lit room and asked the question louder. Archie ducked behind Georgia, his back to the table. Georgia saw the guy lift the woman onto her feet by her arm and move her toward the door, his hand so high up inside her armpit that her shoulder was squeezed against her ear. They disappeared through the swinging doors.

"Holy shit!" Archibald muttered. "Guess she does have a boyfriend. Has he seen me?"

Could something this wonderful possibly happen? "No. They're gone."

"You sure?"

"Yep."

He peeked fearfully at the now-vacant table and then stood up.

"You were right."

"Yeah. I thought I might be." She coughed to keep from laughing at his terrified expression.

"Thanks for getting me outta that. I had no idea."

"Glad I could help. But now you lost your female companionship."

"True, but I kept my teeth. And my dignity. Let's sit somewhere far from that dangerous table to celebrate."

Manna from heaven, Daddy, she thought as she followed Archibald to his customary seat at the bar. She really had saved Archie's bacon, and he knew it. Ha! In fact, ha-ha! She still hoped she'd never need to use her special talents to curb Archie the Anarchist, but it was satisfying to have a plan shaping up, just in case.

∞

Burt Plowfield's admin was away from her desk, and his office was empty. At least it seemed empty. As she turned to go, she heard a cough. Turning back, she saw that Burt was actually behind his monitor with the lights off, his beige shirt blending perfectly with the wall behind him. Weird. When this guy didn't have a woman to fight with, he was a regular polar bear in a snowstorm.

"Oh, hi," she called, waving from the doorway. "You have a minute to sign some things?"

"Happy to. Come in."

"Your office is so big I didn't see you at first. Are those your boxing gloves?" Simpering for a purpose wasn't actually simpering, she reassured herself.

"Absolutely. I was the first-ranked boxer on the Caltech team for two years."

"Wow. I didn't know you had a degree from Caltech." She explained the documents, then looked around as he began signing. The only photo on his desk was a snapshot of a stout, middle-aged woman glaring sternly at the camera with her arms akimbo across the front of her battle-gray suit. Wife? Mother? Whoever it was, why exactly would that be a favorite photo?

She pointed to two large wall photos of sand formations in beige frames. "Fabulous photographs. You been there?"

He kept signing. "I took those photographs." He didn't seem to notice she was laying it on a little thick.

"They're beautiful. I have a cousin back home who loves to take nature photographs. There's a lot of art to it, isn't there?"

There was silence for a moment except for the scratching of the pen.

"I've enjoyed learning a little bit about acquiring companies," Georgia ventured. "It's an important part of the business, isn't it? Must be hard to identify the right companies to acquire. Is that what you do?"

He didn't look up. "Part of what I do. You have to be an expert in the technology, and a jack of all trades in everything else. No point in acquiring a company with great technology if you're stuck with a business model that won't let you make money with it."

"I'm sure that's right. I'll bet there's a lot of different things you have to look out for. All signed? Now, I have you as 'Executive Vice President' here on the signature line. That's right, isn't it? Really? You know, I just assumed that with your importance to the company … That's okay, just cross out the 'Executive' and initial it. Anyway, I'm so interested in your part of the business and all, if you ever need help with something, just let me know."

"I'm afraid what we do is a little bit sophisticated for you."

"Oh, of course, and I'd never want to be in the way. Just keep me in mind in case, okay?"

She escaped into the hallway and pumped her forefinger toward her open mouth a couple of times in a gagging gesture.

∞

The Crooks and Dirt Team (Ken, Quan, Andrea, Burt and Georgia) were waiting in the boardroom for Roy, who had allotted 30 minutes to hear about the issues with Futuresoft. Roy was already ten minutes late, and Ken was reviewing the agenda with the group. "Okay, and then Andrea will handle the open source, and then..."

"Andrea," Burt interrupted, "when you present that, if you could just try not to be irrational..."

Andrea laughed merrily. "Oh, well, I could try not to be irrational, Burt, but you know how women are."

Roy descended on them through the connecting door to his office, and assumed his boxer's stance at the head of the table. "Okay. Let's do this efficiently. Who's in charge here?"

"There are three issues we want to brief you on, Roy," Ken said. "I'd like to start with the most difficult one, something Quan found on Friday up in Seattle."

Roy managed to further elevate his chronically skeptical eyebrows. "And?"

Ken took 10 minutes to describe what they had found, during which Roy relinquished his boxer's stance and sat down. "From a legal perspective," Ken concluded, "this is a very serious problem that would have to be cleaned up before we could acquire the company."

"Why's that?" Roy asked, waving a hand in the air. "Everybody does this stuff."

Ken kept his expression pleasantly neutral. "Well, I'm not sure I want to comment on that, except to tell you it isn't much of a defense if you end up in court. If we buy the company knowing about its theft of Cordova intellectual property, it's like buying a TV off the back of a truck in an alley. That isn't just a civil issue, it's a crime."

"What does their CEO say?"

"Oh, they haven't asked him," Burt explained. "These guys saw this stuff—or think they saw it—and decided they'd be judge and jury." Aggressive, in his passive way, thought Georgia. Must be confident of where Roy was going to come out on this.

"Well," Ken said, "That's not really the point. No matter what the CEO says, those documents exist and they aren't going to disappear.

You have to think about how this would play out in a trial, even a civil trial. First of all, let's assume Cordova is unhappy about our acquisition of Futuresoft."

"They're going to be miserable." Roy's wolfish grin was actually more frightening than his scowl. "We're going to annihilate them in the financial reporting space."

"Great. But then they find out about their prototype being in our hands, and see the chance to give us a real black eye. I think they'll just flat-out sue us. Wouldn't you?"

Roy shrugged. "How would they ever find out about it?"

"The same way everybody always finds this stuff out. A disgruntled Futuresoft employee goes and tells them about it, either trying to make trouble or trying to get a job after we lay him off in the acquisition. Of course, there's another way the U.S. Attorney would have to find out about this, that you and I can discuss privately."

The U.S. attorney? What was that about? Roy didn't respond, but his grin wavered.

"Now," Ken continued, leaning forward and focusing intently on Roy. "Imagine Cordova's lawsuit. These documents are all they need to get a huge civil action going and get the attention of the U.S. Attorney. How would the Futuresoft CEO go about offering his innocent explanation, assuming he has one?" Ken lifted his hands and opened them wide above the table. "Answer: We'd spend two years waiting for him to get the chance to present it in court, while our reputation gets dragged through the mud in the marketplace." He dropped his hands back onto the table. "So I didn't ask the CEO, Roy, because there isn't anything he can say that solves the problem."

Roy waved his hand dismissively. "So tell them to clean it up."

"The only way they can clean it up is to go to Cordova, disclose what they did and get a release."

"They're obviously not going to do that," Roy snapped, glaring at Ken over the rims of his narrow oval glasses. "They'd be putting their heads in a noose."

"They might do it if they know it's the only way to do the acquisition."

"We're doing the acquisition," Roy declared. "We need this company to hit our growth plan."

"Oh, that's what I told them," Burt spoke up helpfully. "Instead of thinking up reasons not to do the deal, it would be refreshing if they'd actually help us get it done."

"Evidently I need to get it done," Roy said with a burdened sigh. "Get their CEO in here tomorrow. I want the investment bankers, too, in person. Then I'll decide what to do." He disappeared through the door to his office.

"This is bad, isn't it?" Georgia asked in a low voice as she and Quan and Ken headed down the corridor.

"It has the potential to be very bad," Ken agreed. He paused outside his office and looked at them. "Should I be in those meetings tomorrow?"

"Won't that make it seem like what they have to say is relevant?" Quan asked. "'Not relevant' is a cleaner message."

"I think so, too. I must not be expressing it very well."

"It would be great for the company if that were the problem," Quan remarked mildly.

Ken looked at Quan's calm, impassive face for an instant and then snorted. "Okay, guys, another fine day to be alive and working in the Lumina Software legal department. Let's go wrestle our alligators."

∞

Thursday was the last day before discovery cutoff in the SAP patent case, and at 10 a.m. Georgia ducked into a conference room to call Jim Prizine on his cell. "Jim, it's Georgia. Today's the big day, so I'm just checking in. Have you seen Mrs. Important-slash-Busy?"

"I won't see her today, Georgia. I'm here in Boston for my cousin's wedding."

"You're where?"

"Boston. Just landed. Didn't Archibald Moss tell you?"

Surely impossible. "Tell me what, Jim? Why are you talking to Archibald Moss?"

"He called me. Said Paul Holder, one of your board members, wanted to know how the patent was coming. Explained that he's in charge of intellectual property for the company, and that it was too late to get the patent into the lawsuit. So I talked to him about coming to Boston for my cousin's wedding, and he told me to go for it."

Georgia had to loosen her grip on the receiver to stop her hand from hurting. "Okay, first of all, Archibald Moss has nothing to do with this lawsuit. That's why Ken never told you about him. Second of all, he's the person who didn't keep track of the patent and let it be lost for a hundred years. Third of all, if you're in Boston for your cousin's wedding, then who's sitting outside Important-slash-Busy's door waiting to leap up and get her to give you the seal?"

"Actually ... nobody." He sounded sheepish. "Sounds like maybe you guys have your wires crossed. Archibald Moss said it was too late to get the patent into the lawsuit, and he didn't like to see work interfere with family obligations. That's why I'm here."

When she got this angry her muscles locked, and the air sort of rippled.

"Jim, nothing about the status of this patent has changed. Every day has been precious to us, and this is the most precious day of all. We're desperate. I know this probably seems horrible, but if you aren't actually in your cousin's wedding, would you please, please get back on a plane and head to the PTO as fast as you can? I'm holding out hope we might still get the patent issued today."

"Can I just ask? Why do you and Moss have such different ideas about the urgency of this?"

"Because only one of us inhabits Planet Earth. Time is evidently more plentiful wherever Archibald lives. Can I get Ken to call you back in the next ninety seconds? No reason you should do this on my say-so."

"No need, Georgia. I'm still in the airport, and I'm walking to a ticket counter now." She heard a gasp through the phone, followed by a woman's urgent question. "I really screwed this up by not confirming with you about Moss," Jim continued. "I hope we haven't lost a day because of it."

"Not *a* day, Jim, *the* day. The only one left. And we haven't lost it yet. Text me the minute you get to the PTO, okay?" She hung up.

"Georgia," Maggie said, sticking her head in a few minutes later. "Are you okay in here? If you keep glaring at that phone you're gonna melt it."

Georgia lifted her eyes without moving her head, and made herself inhale. "Momentary loss of perspective, Maggie," she managed to declare through her tightly constricted throat. "You know what? I think I'll stay in here a bit and do my mountain meditation. Would you mind closing the door?" In Arkansas her father kept their meditation private, but here it was practically a badge of honor.

Sure enough, twenty minutes later she felt refreshed and clear. Two truths were now evident: First, Archibald Moss's vigorous incompetence had defeated their monumental efforts to Swiftly Acquire Patent. Second, Lumina Software was about to receive a clean-up service she was peculiarly qualified to provide.

CHAPTER 11

She was marching with conviction to Archibald's office the next morning when Ken called out to her from his office. "Georgia! Come on in. Maggie's looking for you." It wasn't like Ken to call out like that. He thought it was impolite. Couldn't be the old news that they had failed in their efforts to Swiftly Acquire Patent in time for the patent case. She hurried in to see what had happened.

Must not be anything bad. Ken and Zack were tilted back in their chairs like a couple of satisfied gluttons after a big meal. Ken sat up when she entered and announced, "Big news, Georgia. Zack and I just got off the phone with our outside lawyers defending the SAP case. They've looked at your International Trade Commission idea, and they want to file the new lawsuit."

So Ingenious Tricky Countersuit was going to happen.

Zack was grinning, his hands resting comfortably on top of his head. "In fact, they've decided they're real geniuses for thinking it up."

Ken laughed. "Some things never change, do they? Anyway, they're pulling together the complaint and the injunction papers now, and need some help checking on facts. Are you available?"

Now Georgia was grinning, too. "Of course I'm available. This is fabulous." And it was. Archie had slammed one door, but they'd managed to pry open another one.

"Good. I said you and Zack would call them back in ten minutes. The idea is to deliver the papers to Jim Prizine in forty-eight hours. The minute the PTO issues our patent, he takes a taxi across town and files with the ITC."

"How do you know they're going to issue it?" Zack asked pleasantly, pushing his glasses up his nose with his middle finger. "Is somebody spread-eagled on top of Archie Moss?"

Ken's look turned sober. "God, Zack, I know how frustrated you must be. It's frustrating to me, too, but we have to move past it. Jim's onto him now, he'll never listen to another word Archie says." He ducked his head and half-swallowed a laugh. "You know, though, let's not tell Archie about the ITC action till after it's filed." Zack didn't join in the laugh, and why should he, Georgia thought. It tarnished her satisfaction to see Ken looking weak again.

"I want Jim to call us from the ITC steps just as soon as the action is filed," Ken continued. "Zack, can you take the lead on the press release?" He turned to Georgia. "If this succeeds, you'll deserve the gratitude of this entire company. Now that we finally have something worthwhile to do, let's get going."

Her idea had worked, she exulted as she hurried down the hallway behind Zack. Ha! They could use the new patent after all, despite the antics of Archie Moss. What a gratifying way of helping the company, right out in the open where Ken could know about it. Maybe this really could make her seem indispensable, and not a moment too soon. Katie-Ann was heading to California in three days, and Georgia's financial responsibilities would really kick in.

Did this mean she could forget about trying to rein in Archie for now? No, she decided, exactly the opposite. Now that she had the Ingenious Tricky Countersuit to protect, the visit to Archie was more urgent than ever. She'd head over there right after this call to the patent lawyers.

∞

She knocked politely against the frame of his open door. "Archie?"

He was seated behind his desk, cigar smoke curling around his wide nostrils and up over his corn-colored hair. "Georgia! Savior! My knight-ess in shining armor!" As he spread his arms wide in greeting, a few flakes of cigar ash fell onto his carpet. "Come right in and have a seat."

"Okay if I close the door?"

He arms dropped heavily onto his desk and his smile faded. "Uh-oh. You mad about the '401 again?"

"The patent?" She waved a hand dismissively as she closed the door. The My Little Ponies dotting the rollaway looked limp and defeated. "Nah, I've let it go. I mean, what's the point? The judge was never going to let a whole new patent in on the last day of discovery, anyway."

"Happy to see my superior perspective is finally rubbing off. You might share it with your buddy, Zack, by the way. He seems a little put out by the whole thing."

"Does he?"

"Very disappointing. I thought we were all grown men here."

"I know you did. He'll get over it. Anyway, I'm here on a whole different subject. Something social," she confided, tugging his visitor chair a little closer to his desk as she sat down.

"Social?"

She pressed the heels of her hands against her eyes, which were already burning from the smoke. "Yeah. Remember that first night we met at the Saloon? You were saying how hard it can be to know if somebody's interested in you romantically."

"Yeah. Don't remind me. Just look what happened the other night."

"Well, that was different. That lady seemed very interested, she was just unavailable. But after what happened, it occurred to me you might be happier if you had a steady girlfriend."

"No kidding. Safer, too. Why? You have someone in mind?" He bared his yellow teeth in a rakish grin and tapped his cigar against the rim of the ash tray.

"I might," she said with a slight shrug. "If you're interested. You know who Lucy Feiffer is?"

"Lucy. Certainly. Lucy in HR."

"Well, I happen to know she thinks you're hot."

"Really? I had no idea. She's very pretty."

"I thought you might have missed the signals, and you wouldn't want to waste another opportunity. The thing is, she's on the shy side and a little uptight, so it takes a fairly assertive person to get her to respond. She really needs someone to push through her shyness and sweep her off her feet. She's drawn to nice men, but then she complains they have trouble being as, you know, assertive as she wants. Oh, this is a little embarrassing."

"She would be foolish to think that about me. I'm a grown man. I can be very assertive if I know it's what the lady wants."

"Really?"

"Absolutely." He leaned back and blew a smoke ring.

"Well, and do you like Lucy?"

He spread his arms expansively. "I like all pretty women. She'd be fine."

"Well, if that's the case . . ."

"By the way, assertive in what way, exactly?"

"Well . . ." Georgia hesitated. "I don't mean hurting her, of course, or anything physical. All I really mean is she, um, sort of likes dirty talk. You know Henry Miller?"

"Yeah. Saw his play once. Very depressing."

"Actually, that might be Arthur. Henry's a different guy. Henry Miller lived in Paris for a while, and he wrote the book called *Tropic of Cancer*. You heard of it?"

"No."

"Well, anyway, Lucy loves Paris, and she really loves the language of that book."

He shrugged. "Okay. Anything in particular?"

"Well, if you want you can google 'Henry Miller' and just say 'six inches' and 'bone'. You'll see the kind of thing Lucy goes for."

"You don't just wanna tell me?"

Georgia held up a flat palm, and gave her lowered head an embarrassed little shake.

"Hold on," he said, setting his cigar in the ashtray and turning to his keyboard. He studied his screen, punched his keyboard a few times and then studied some more. While she waited, smoke spiraled lazily into the air and then bent into an unmistakable beeline for her face.

"You kidding me? She wants me to say that? Not very romantic." Suddenly she felt mortified by how ridiculous it all sounded. Come on, even a numb-nut like Archie was too smart for this crap. What on earth had she been thinking? She almost groaned with humiliation.

Maybe she could still back-peddle. "I mean, I just thought it could be an example..."

"Wow," he said appreciatively, turning to grin at her. "Who knew?" He shrugged. "If it works for the lady it works for me."

"Really? She'd like that." She coughed as the smoke touched the tip of her nose and began to fan sideways across her cheeks.

"I'll have to sort of build up to it over time, though, won't I?"

"No, no," she said, coughing and fanning the air. "Not sure that would even work. The thing that excites her is knowing she's driving a man wild. So just put it right out there, and I'm pretty sure she'll take it from there."

"I'd be happy to take her out this weekend."

"Perfect. Or, you know what?"

"What?"

"Tomorrow's her birthday. Her sister was coming to see her, but then the sister's baby got sick. So I was going to cook dinner at her place, but wouldn't it be a nice surprise if you showed up instead of me?"

He shook his head. "Don't know how to cook." Georgia smiled gently. "Oh, I get it, maybe if it's me we won't have to cook. I can take her somewhere after. Shall I tell her you sent me?"

"Oh, don't give me the credit. Just let it be that you've been thinking about her, and could no longer stay away. It would be so great if the two of you got started on the right foot. Just say it like you mean it, okay?"

"Don't worry. I can be very dramatic." He took a giant drag on his cigar and then exhaled through a smirk.

"I'm sure you can, Archie. Maybe have a couple of other, you know, similar remarks in reserve, just in case. Let your words work their magic, and then just follow her lead. I know that's important to her. I was supposed to get there about 6:30. 1201 White Oak Avenue here in San Jose. She's in number 14." She peered through the smoke to make sure he wrote it down correctly, and then stood up.

He turned back to his computer screen and tapped the ash from his cigar. "You're sure about this. Sounds kind of, I don't know, aggressive."

She held both palms up vertically, fingers spread in a gesture of full disclosure. "Let's just say I'm as sure as I was about the boyfriend."

"Good enough for me. Thanks, Georgia. If this pans out I'll owe you a whole barrel of scotch."

Did scotch even come in barrels, she wondered as she headed back to her building. She wished he'd been slightly less grateful. Too bad he wasn't an out-and-out crook instead of just a relentless, serial fuck-up.

But he really was relentless. And serial. He'd wrecked their patent case as surely as if he'd been trying, and would wreck the Ingenious Tricky Countersuit with equal oblivion if she didn't stop him. Do your work and step back. Time to turn her attention to those facts for the new lawsuit.

∞

The next morning she strung a homemade "Do not disturb" sign over the corner of her cube while she chased down a few final facts for the ITC complaint. She still needed to confirm the approximate value of all software sold by SAP into the U.S. in the last five calendar years, and so far all she could find was fiscal year ... She ignored the phone for the first three rings, then changed her mind and snatched it up just before it went into voicemail.

"Will you accept a collect call from Katie-Ann Griffin?"

Georgia went on hyper-alert. "I will, operator. Thank you. Katie-Ann, is that you?"

Katie-Ann was crying. "Georgia, the money's gone."

"The money for your ticket?"

"Yes, and the extra."

"Are you sure? Where was it?"

"Really sure. I had it in the back of our closet, in the jewelry box Daddy gave me. The jewelry box is right where I left it, but the money's gone. Over three hundred dollars, and nothing left but the pennies. I think Mama found my hiding place and just drank it."

Georgia was mindful that Beatrice's cube had gone very quiet. She lowered her voice. "When was the last time you saw it?"

"Two days ago. I put my tip money in there every day as soon as Mama leaves for work, but she didn't go yesterday."

"Did you count it two days ago?"

"No, I haven't counted it since last week. Oh, Georgia, what's the difference? I have no way to get there now. What'll we do?"

Georgia considered. If Mama had 'borrowed' the money for whiskey, she probably would have done it little by little to keep from being noticed. If she took the whole thing at once, maybe she'd gone to Johnny with it to get his advice about what Katie-Ann was up to. Damn those AA people. "Was Johnny there last night when you got home?"

"They were talking in the TV room with the door closed."

Why hadn't they mentioned the money to Katie-Ann? She felt a chill across the back of her neck.

"Katie-Ann, how much money do you have now?"

"About twenty-two dollars in cash, and my paycheck for forty-seven."

"Good. Here's what I want you to do. Put on your uniform like you're going to work, but then call and tell them you're sick. You need to get out of there today. Take some food that will keep for a day or two, but don't clean the place out so it gives you away. Cash your check at the bank, and then try to be on the 5:30 bus to Little Rock. Can you collect your clothes and get there in time?"

"Yes, if I hurry."

"Take your jacket. The bus might get cold. Try to change out of your uniform so you won't be conspicuous. The minute you get to Little Rock, call me collect again. I'll figure something out in the meantime."

"I'm scared, Georgia. What'll I do in Little Rock with no money?"

"I'll figure something out, Katie-Ann. Whose daughter are you?"

"George Griffin's daughter. Same as you."

"Then we know you can do it. Keep your head clear, you're going to need it today. I think you should meditate on the bus."

"Okay, I will." She had stopped crying. "I should go. Call you this afternoon."

Georgia looked at her watch. Four and a half hours to come up with $250 and get it to Katie-Ann in Little Rock. Would their snooty cousin at Apple help, or would he just rat her out to her mother? Probably neither. Just politely ignore her, the way he'd ignore a fart at a fancy dinner party. Useless. Could she reach her father's lawyer? She rushed into a conference room to make some calls.

∞

"Georgia," Maggie said, opening the conference room door a couple of hours later. She wore swingy hoop earrings and a salmon-colored bandana in her hair. "Ken would like to see you in his office."

That's right, the ITC complaint. Georgia put the phone down and pressed the heels of her hands against her closed eyelids. She still didn't have the money, and she surely didn't have those facts. She didn't even have time to talk to him, but of course that wasn't optional. She made herself breathe deeply as she walked to his office.

"Georgia," Ken said, "have a seat." He came and sat across from her at his conference table. His shirt was yellow, his bow tie was kelly green, and his open face immediately registered that she didn't look so good. "I'm concerned that something is worrying you."

"I know you need those last facts for the ITC complaint..."

He waved a hand in dismissal. "I'll have somebody at the firm do it. But Beatrice thought you sounded worried on a phone call earlier. Something about your sister?"

News travelled fast. Telephone. Telegraph. Tell a Beatrice. She knew she looked like a rabbit caught in the headlights, but she couldn't think of a single response.

"The reason I'm asking, Georgia, is I'm wondering if I can help you. You're a very important member of our team, and you won't be able to focus if you're upset about something personal. Looking out for our team members is looking out for the company."

Georgia's skin was flushed with danger. She searched frantically for a way to avoid exposing her private life.

"Ken, you so don't have time to be thinking about my personal stuff."

He shrugged. "Looks like I am thinking about it."

If you can't say nothing, her father said, try to tell a limited truth. Truth is easier to remember. "My sister's coming to live with me to go to school."

"Yes. You told me you have a sister you've been worried about. How's she doing?" Oh right, she thought, staring back into those attentive, green eyes. This was the guy who made you want to tell everything.

"Well, ever since I got here, I've been saving up to get us an apartment before school starts. It took every penny I could save for first and last months' rent, so Katie-Ann was waitressing to get the money for her bus ticket. She called me a little while ago, and her money's disappeared. School starts next Wednesday, and well ..." She shrugged, hoping to offset her faltering voice. "I don't know how to get her here."

"I see. That really is a problem. Would you mind if I get my wife, Laura, on the line? I don't mean to broadcast your personal life, but she's my primary confidante and I'd like to get her help on this. Okay with you?"

He got Laura on the speakerphone, and introduced them. Georgia repeated her story.

"Georgia," Laura asked, "does Katie-Ann's mother agree with her plan to come to California?"

Why was she asking that? Were they going to try to stop her? Too late.

"She doesn't know about it, ma'am. We're going to call and let her know as soon as my sister gets here. My father's the one who wants her to be here, but he's not in a position to help out with the money right now."

"Does he have custody?"

Did parents in prison have custody? "I'm pretty sure they have joint custody."

"Can you enroll her in school?"

"I've already done that. I just needed the lease and her birth certificate."

"Georgia, Ken and I would like to contribute the money for your sister's bus ticket. It sounds like you and your dad have a very good plan to help her, and I don't see how there's time to get the money from anywhere else. It isn't often that a reasonable amount of money can make a difference, but this sounds to me like one of those times. How much is it?"

Dangerous. These people had no idea who they were dealing with, and she wasn't about to let them find out.

"I appreciate that, I really do," she said, "but I don't think it's good to complicate our professional relationship. I need this job to support Katie-Ann."

"Good instincts, Georgia," Ken agreed. "We definitely won't make a habit of it. But I believe in this particular instance, it's in the company's best interest."

"And in your sister's best interest," Laura added. "I know you'll take that into account."

Georgia looked at her watch. Katie-Ann would be calling again in an hour. This was probably her one chance to get the money. She watched the second hand tick for a full ten seconds. "Mrs. Madigan?"

Her voice actually sounded sort of timid. "Would you loan me the money, and let me sign a promissory note?"

"Absolutely. I'll have Ken review it for me to make sure it's legally binding."

Well. No going back, even if she did feel slightly dizzy and her hands were cold. "I certainly do appreciate it. My sister's already on the bus to Little Rock with the money she had in her wallet, and I could sure use a plan for when she calls me in an hour."

"I see," Ken said, glancing at his watch. "Then we should probably get started."

"You need me for this part, Ken?" Laura asked.

"We'll take care of it from here, Laura. Love you. Bye now.

"Georgia," he continued, "why don't we put in a call to Greyhound? Let's see if we can get this resolved before your sister calls. What's her name?"

"Katie-Ann." Saying the name suddenly brought tears to her eyes. Ken seemed not to notice.

"Katie-Ann's probably a very competent 15-year-old, but let's try to put her mind at rest as soon as possible."

An hour later Katie-Ann had boarded her bus for San Francisco, and Georgia was in hot pursuit of that five-year revenue number for the ITC complaint.

∞

Dear Daddy, she wrote that evening, huddled under her sleeping bag with her Itty Bitty Book Light. *I have had an unusual day. I hit a fairly serious glitch in our plans to get Katie-Ann out here. I am happy to report that things are all right again, and she is on the bus as I write this letter.*

Of course, that is not the unusual part. The unusual part is that a man in my office gave me the money and some other help to solve the problem, and honestly Daddy, I believe he just wanted to help. He involved his wife and had the money come from her, I think just so I wouldn't worry that he was looking for sexual favors. He already thinks I'm doing a good job, so I don't think he's trying to get me to work harder. He has a big job that pays him plenty of money, and anyway, how much could he hope to scam out of somebody who needs to borrow bus fare for her little sister?

Have you ever encountered a similar situation? Do you think I'm being naive? I work with this person on a daily basis, and would benefit from your insight soonest. In any case, the apartment is ready and waiting, and we will inform you promptly when Katie-Ann has safely arrived.
Your loving daughter,
Georgia

She lay holding the sealed envelope, gazing up through her back window. Honestly, it was a relief that Ken was married, which made him even more off-limits than he was already. Well, sort of a relief. Funny, the thing that made Mr. Straight-Edge Upright totally unavailable also made him even more appealing. Thank God he was a million years older than she was. The Anti-Deke. Good to know there was one.

The stars were sure sparkly tonight, like every speck of cosmic dust had been washed out of the sky. There was Orion, for example, with his shiny belt and sword, exactly where he belonged, just like he'd always been for at least a billion years.

Up until tonight it would never have occurred to Georgia Griffin, not in those billion years since Orion first appeared, that somebody else might watch her back once her father was in jail. And Katie-Ann's back, too, just because she was important to Georgia. She closed her eyes and let the unfamiliar sensation of gratitude spread slowly through her whole body.

CHAPTER 12

"Excuse me, are you Georgia?"

Georgia looked up to see a stranger in the entrance to her cube. "Sally would like to see you rather urgently." Must be Sally's new admin. Georgia set down her document index and glanced at her watch. Barely 7:15 a.m. Then she remembered: the "dinner" with Archibald and Lucy had been scheduled for the night before. In all the excitement about Katie-Ann, she'd sort of forgotten about Archie. Her word against his, she reminded herself, no matter what he'd told Sally. And his word was—by design—preposterous.

"Lucky I was here this early," she commented as she followed the woman down the still-empty hallway. "You know what it's about?"

"Not really. Paul Holder's in there."

"The board member? Hope I didn't mess up the board compensation." Had Archie gone to the board with this? Holder was Archie's champion, so she could be in for a difficult discussion. She was pretty sure she was ready.

But when she heard Sally's office door click shut behind her, she felt a hint of panic. Better not look at those shrunken heads just now.

Paul and Sally were seated at her conference table, and Paul stood to greet her, revealing sage-colored jeans on his stork-like legs. They both looked grim.

"You remember Mr. Holder?" Sally began.

"Absolutely." Georgia shook his hand, hoping her clammy skin didn't give her away. "How are you, Mr. Holder?"

"Well, I'm not great at the moment, as a matter of fact. Have a seat. Are you aware of an incident involving Archibald Moss and somebody named Lucy Feiffer?"

Incident. So he'd gone through with it.

"No." She made her eyes widen with curiosity as her pulse began to thud rhythmically in her ears.

"Well, it's rather unfortunate," Paul continued. "Lucy claims Archibald showed up at her mother's apartment last night, began shouting sexual obscenities, and then tried to kiss her."

She frowned with feigned confusion. "Archibald tried to kiss Lucy's mother?"

"No, Lucy. Lucy was there."

"Oh." Pause. Still confused. "He shouted sexual obscenities at Lucy in front of her mother?" *Kissing wasn't part of the plan. Had he attacked her?* Her pulse began thudding faster.

"It seems surprising for a number of reasons, doesn't it? But the mother confirms that she heard Lucy shouting, and rushed into the living room in her wheelchair just as Lucy threw her drink at a man who turned out to be Archibald."

"Wow. And what did he do?"

"Well, he apparently just stood in the doorway looking shocked, Campari running down his face. But then he said ... well, he said something horribly vulgar that I'm not going to repeat, and then he said, 'Can I kiss you now?'"

She reared back slightly to register surprise. "So he was asking permission?" *Didn't sound like assault. Good.*

Paul spread his hands above the table. "I ... guess. And then Lucy was so freaked out she started screaming that he was a pervert, and to get out of her mother's house or they'd call the cops. And he said 'Mother?,' apparently noticed her mother for the first time, and then said, 'Oh God, not again!'"

Score!

"'Oh God, not again,'" she echoed, musing. "So this had happened before. And then what?"

Paul shrugged. "Then he left. That was it."

"He just walked away?" *So mere lunatic ranting.* She exhaled with quiet relief.

"Well, ran actually. I guess the neighbors had opened their door to see what the noise was, and he just … ran away."

"Wow. This is bizarre. And of course you want to find Ken." She consulted her watch and stood up. "Let me see if he's here now. My guess is he'll want to talk to Archie."

"I already did that. Archie called me this morning."

"Really. And what does he say?"

"Well, in some ways that's the most surprising of all. He admits—sheepishly—that he said those repulsive things, and that he was hoping to have sex with Lucy. But he claims he was invited."

Georgia shrugged. "Well, she might have invited him to dinner, but not to hear that kind of stuff."

"Actually, Georgia, he claims to have been invited by you." *He'd told them everything.* She could hear her pulse picking up speed again.

She sat back down. "Archie says I invited him to dinner with Lucy?"

Paul nodded. "Says you gave him the address and everything."

"But I didn't know anything about it. I wasn't invited to dinner." She considered a moment, and pointed a forefinger at her own face. "You sure it's me he's talking about?"

"Quite sure. He claims you invited him to show up at Lucy's, gave him her mother's address, and put him up to the whole thing."

She folded her right hand over her left fist on top of the table and leaned forward, frowning. "He says I told him to shout obscenities at Lucy? And knew her mother's address?" Then she shook her head like she was trying to clear it. "Sorry, I don't mean to sound like a parrot, but I'm a little confused. I don't even know Lucy Feiffer. I wonder why he wants to involve me in this."

"Paul, may I ask a couple of questions?" Sally asked. "Georgia, you had a conversation with Archibald about Lucy being interested in him, didn't you?" *Leading question. Classic cross-examination technique.*

"No," she answered promptly, shaking her head. "I didn't know she was interested."

"Didn't you tell Archibald that Lucy was very interested in him, and liked her men to talk dirty?"

"Ugh!" She stiffened with surprise and aversion. "How would I know that?"

"Didn't you give him a line from Henry Miller to recite to her?"

"Who's Henry Miller? The playwright?"

"Thanks, Georgia," Paul interrupted, with a meaningful glance at Sally. "We won't trouble you with this any further. I'm not surprised you're confused, since the whole thing makes absolutely no sense. But we needed to ask, it was just such a strange story..." He frowned at the wall behind her. "Shame, really. Our engineers just love the guy." Sally was studying her through narrowed eyes.

"Well, let me find Ken for you. He's the one who can sort it all out." She stood up again.

"I can probably decide who to involve in the investigation," Sally said coolly. "In the meantime, you can appreciate this is completely confidential, even from Ken. Close the door on your way out."

Well, *that* surely got the old heart pumping, she thought as she briskly retraced her steps along the still-empty, carpeted corridor. Halfway back to her cube, she changed course and sought the privacy of a toilet stall, where she leaned her head against the closed door and took several deep breaths. Was it over? Probably. Better not mention Henry Miller for a while. Sally looked entirely too curious, but what could she or anyone do with such a ridiculous story and no evidence? Talk to Ken about it, maybe. She really would prefer not to repeat this charade with Ken.

She splashed water on her face at the sink, then headed back to her cube. Poor Archie. Even if somebody believed his silly story, did he think for one second it would excuse his behavior? His capacity for terrible judgment was impeccable, right up to the end.

∞

She and Ken were going over the latest diligence results, when Ken's door flew open and Roy declared, "Need to talk to you."

Archie. Well, she could do it again, even with Ken.

"Sure. Georgia, would you…?"

"Don't bother," Roy said, raising a palm. He closed the door and assumed his wide boxer's stance, his neck stuffed into a tight collar. "Just finished my meeting with the Futuresoft bankers and the CEO. Problem solved." *This had nothing to do with Archie. Get a grip.*

"Really," Ken said. "How so? Have a seat."

"Stupid misunderstanding," he said, ignoring the invitation to sit. "They did get the prototype, but they knew it was inappropriate and gave it right back again. And the CEO agrees it wasn't the brightest to set up that alternate email account, but he assures me he never received anything confidential on it. Doesn't think they even hired the guy."

Guy? Singular? There had been at least four secret accounts.

"And the document destruction was a misunderstanding, too. Bottom line, they explained very convincingly that they never did anything wrong. And anyway, nobody's going to find this stuff. We're boxing with our own shadows here." Interesting, how Roy's brain train kept jumping from the 'did no wrong' track onto the 'won't get caught' track. Somebody had laid those tracks awfully close together.

"But …" Ken said.

Roy held his hand up. "We're going ahead with the deal."

"You think the board will agree?"

"I'm sure they will, since we won't alarm them with this crap."

"I'll have to notify the U.S. Attorney."

"Why is that?"

Ken flicked a glance in Georgia's direction. "I have the ongoing obligation to tell them about any suspected wrongdoing, my investigation, and the outcome."

"But this isn't our wrongdoing in any case. It's theirs."

143

"Ours will be knowing about it, Roy, and buying the company anyway."

"We don't know anything, Ken. We know our good friends and business partners say they've done nothing." His mouth was puckered just like he'd sucked a lemon, as he stood over Ken and glared at him. "Don't make this more complicated than it needs to be. Wrap it up. Now I have to make a call on another matter."

Silence filled the office after the door closed behind him. Georgia noted with alarm that Ken's mouth had become a straight, thin line in a very white face.

"Ken?"

"Will you excuse me for a moment?" he said stiffly. Georgia sat staring at the door after it closed behind him. Did he want her to wait?

When he returned a few minutes later, his mouth had resumed its normal shape, but his face was still white between his red hair and vermillion bow tie. "Forgive me, Georgia. I showed poor leadership just now."

"By getting mad? Everybody gets mad."

He sat on his conference table with a palm on either side. "By getting so mad I had to interrupt our conversation and walk around to control myself. I have a real Irish temper, and you'd have seen plenty of evidence of it if you'd been around when I was growing up. My brothers and I got into more fist fights than you can imagine. My mother was convinced she'd produced a bunch of hooligans."

"Hey," she grinned, "I'm a proud Irish Griffin myself, so I've seen temper. You still get in fights as an adult?"

"Once, with my older brother. My mother wouldn't let either of us back in the house after that for six months. And I came close another time, in a deposition. The lawyer on the other side was irritating me, and I decided I was going to lunge across the table and take him out. I knew I'd be fired, and I was going to do it anyway."

"But you didn't?"

"The court reporter saw what was happening, and she just stood up and stopped the deposition. Then she sat on the table to block my view of the guy, and told me to leave the room. Gutsy lady. Saved my butt, and possibly my career. And ever since then, whenever I get really angry, I get up and walk away, and then keep walking until I'm over it. But I'm sorry to keep you waiting."

"No problem. Honestly." She suppressed the urge to touch his arm.

He brushed his palm over the top of his short hair. "I tell you, this Futuresoft problem is a nasty one." He walked over and opened his door. "Maggie, would you see if you can get Andrea and Quan in here right away?" He closed the door again. "And while she's doing that, Georgia, I need to explain something you just heard.

"Our company got in some trouble a couple of years ago. Several of our employees were playing fast and loose with a competitor's intellectual property, and we very nearly got ourselves indicted. We persuaded the U.S. Attorney to give us something called a Letter of Non-Prosecution, which requires me to report any suspected wrongdoing related to intellectual property for a period of three years.

"Our criminal defense lawyer agrees I'd have to report this Futuresoft deal. Roy's living in a dream world if he thinks it wouldn't blow up in our faces. Here are Andrea and Quan."

Twenty minutes later the group looked glumly at one another around the table.

"Don't you know Plowfield's as happy as a pig in mud?" Andrea muttered, raking her short blond hair back from her face.

"Burt and Roy do seem to amplify each other's folly," Quan agreed rather primly.

"Mark Twain would call them the two finest quarter-wits who ever combined to make a half-wit," Georgia contributed.

"Georgia?" Ken asked in surprise. "What did you say?"

Andrea was choking back a laugh.

"Sorry. I was just quoting Mark Twain. Probably inappropriate."

"Definitely inappropriate. I can't have anybody speak so disrespectfully about the leadership of this company, including Mark Twain."

She felt her face redden. "I'm very sorry." Now she'd distracted them, embarrassed herself, and disappointed Ken, just because she was trying to be clever.

Quan came to her rescue. "Perhaps we can quote Upton Sinclair instead. 'It's difficult to get a man to understand something, when his salary depends upon his not understanding it.'"

Ken laughed. "Now *that* I can agree with. Roy wants to buy this company so much that he's refusing to think through the consequences." He spread his palms on the table. "But I don't have that luxury. I'd be committing an ethical violation to let this deal go through while I'm the general counsel. I'd have to resign."

"If you explain that to the board, they'll stop the deal," Andrea said.

Ken nodded slowly, his mouth bunched to one side. "Probably. But how would that affect my relationship with Roy? And maybe the board as well? An executive who threatens to resign over an ethical matter shouldn't plan to keep his job for long."

Outside Ken's window, they could hear car doors slamming and engines revving in the parking lot. After 6 already. She'd have to start managing her schedule once Katie-Ann got here.

"Isn't this a terrible deal even without the criminal stuff?" she asked.

"It is, but the board won't know that." Ken sagged slightly into his chair. "Roy will just package it up with a bow, and they'll defer to him without ever hearing the issues."

"We can't let that happen," Andrea pronounced, lifting her chin out of her palm. They all looked at her. "Georgia's onto something. You have to carry the burden on this criminal stuff, but I can slow them down on the intellectual property before we ever get there. We've got that horrible Oracle contract, the source code problem, the ridiculous plan to pay the founders all cash. Maybe we never even get to the ethical stuff."

Ken shook his head. "Roy won't let you criticize this deal to the board."

"Not up to him. The board will insist on talking to me, and once

I'm in there I'll let it rip. He can't fire me for being candid with the board."

Ken shook his head again. "He can do other stuff. Too risky for you."

"It's risky for both of us, but what's the alternative? Not right for you to shoulder this alone."

Ken considered. "Well, I don't need to contact the U.S. Attorney unless the board actually approves the deal …" He brushed his hand over his stubble of red hair. "Okay. Let's try it. Boy, Andrea, appreciate the support."

"Happy to help. You know what, though, I wish we could make Burt take the heat for this Frankenstein deal he created. Why are we the ones putting our jobs on the line to kill it?"

Andrea was right, Georgia reflected as she headed back to her cube. Why should either of them be jeopardized for Burt's stupidity? He should clean up his own mess, but there was no way to make that happen. Was there?

Most people are surprisingly inclined to believe what they want to believe, her father had taught her. Identify what the mark wants to believe.

She was pretty sure she knew what Burt wanted to believe. He wanted to believe he was a forceful, effective leader instead of some wobbly-kneed wimp who bullied women. There might be a way to work with that, and have some fun in the bargain. In fact … She slowed her walk, a little smile on her face.

Then she caught herself, and the smile evaporated. What was she thinking? She had to lie lower than a snake's belly until this Archie thing got resolved. Just when Katie-Ann was coming, the last thing she needed was to generate another distraction and even more risk.

Too bad, though. Could really have taken the heat off Ken and Andrea, if she'd managed to pull it off. Another time, maybe. She hoped being responsible for Katie-Ann wasn't going to make her jump at her own shadow.

∞

"You hear about Archie?" Nikki whispered when Georgia picked up her phone.

Georgia whispered back. "No. What about him?"

"He's leaving the company. Today."

"He quit?"

"Ssh. Don't know if he quit. He might've gotten fired. Paul Holder and Sally came to see Roy a while ago, looking really upset. And then Roy called your boss in."

"Wow."

"You could tell they were trying to talk Ken into something, but he was pretty emphatic. The meeting just ended, and now Sally told me to go to Archie's office and pack up his personal stuff. You think he's done something horrible with our intellectual property?"

"Sure hope not. If I hear anything, I'll let you know."

"Ditto on this end. Bye."

Well, she thought, plunking her receiver back into its cradle. Done and dusted, as Gramma Griffin used to say. Now the Ingenious Tricky Countersuit could proceed with nary a Marx Brother in sight. And guys like Archie always had nine lives for some reason, maybe because they were all grown men. He'd get a recommendation from Paul and be wrecking somebody else's company in no time. If Lumina was really lucky, his new company would be SAP.

∞

She'd been anticipating Katie-Ann's arrival for so long that when she actually appeared in the narrow bus doorway, Georgia thought for an instant she wasn't real. Then Katie-Ann leaned forward into the bright California sun, grabbed the handrails and swung herself down onto the pavement in that loose-jointed way of hers, and Georgia knew she was one hundred percent Katie-Ann Griffin. They hugged while the driver extracted Katie-Ann's duffels from the luggage compartment, and then lugged the duffels across the parking lot to the newly scrubbed and downright cavernous Subaru.

Katie-Ann exclaimed at least fifteen times on their way to the apartment:

"These houses are all bubblegum colors. That one's bright pink! What's the stuff they're made of?"

"Stucco."

"Where are the yards, Georgia? Everybody has these tiny little manicured lawns."

"Oh my God! Are those palm trees?? They're so ... primeval."

"Why's everything so clean here? Where's all the crap on the ground?"

Georgia stole glances at her as they drove. Her blond hair was wound into a samurai knot high on the back of her head, and her gray sweatpants were bagged out at the knees. She was tall and lanky like Georgia, and her dark blue eyes were red from exhaustion and wide with excitement.

"People on that last bus were pretty weird," she reported enthusiastically. "This one old guy kept talking to himself, and then getting all pissed off about what he said. Nutty as a pet coon."

Georgia winced. "Katie-Ann, there are some expressions you don't really want to use out here."

"Like what?"

"Well, a good example is 'nutty as a pet coon.' People might wonder what a 'coon' is, and not like it much."

"Wow. So I'm an immigrant here, trying to blend in the way Gramma Griffin did."

"Not sure it's that dramatic."

"Yeah, it is. Look at that billboard." She read slowly, "Visualization alone does not an effective cloud environment make.' Must mean they still need water." Georgia laughed. "Hey, if Grandma Griffin could make it in the New World, so can I. You can coach me, and I'll listen to that national news guy at night, the way you did. Assimilation is hunky-dory with me."

'Hunky-dory.' Georgia sighed. "You'll have it in no time. Here we are." She pulled up to the curb to let Katie-Ann get a good view of the shabby, two-story, stucco building with chipped Spanish tiles accenting the outside stairwells. Katie-Ann actually squealed with excitement, and Georgia was grinning as they each hauled a duffel up to the second floor and she unlocked the door.

"Like I said, it's pretty empty." Her voice echoed as Katie-Ann surveyed the room. "Just moved in yesterday."

"You kidding?" Katie-Ann raced into the bedroom and flipped on the light in the bathroom. "We have this whole huge place to ourselves? It has great carpet, and look at all the windows." She ran over and looked out eight feet across the alley to a filthy stucco wall. "Plenty of light. We'll do stuff to make it homey."

"You want a shower? I gave you the blue towels, and I'll take the green ones."

"Great. Then what?" Katie-Ann was using her foot to scoot a heavy duffel toward the bedroom.

"Then we head to a grocery store, and think about your school supplies. If there's time, we can always drive to the beach."

"I totally want to go to the beach. Ready in fifteen."

Totally? Georgia laughed. "Katie-Ann, you're totally assimilating already."

Fifteen minutes later Georgia heard the shower stop. Five minutes after that she found Katie-Ann face down on her sleeping bag, blowing small snores into the pillow, the water from her hair spreading a slow stain across her new pillowcase. Unbelievable, how many things had finally come together to allow this vulnerable girl to fall asleep in this clean, secure apartment. Georgia covered her with the green blanket and settled herself at the card table in the otherwise empty living room to send her father the good news.

CHAPTER 13

"Congratulations," Georgia said, opening a blue vinyl document binder to the correct page and handing it to Burt in the basement diligence room. "I hear Roy decided to go ahead with the deal." Galling, really, to be stuck down here, helping this guy make trouble for Ken and Andrea. Springing her little trap on him would be so much more satisfying. Well, she'd happily settle for the satisfaction of knowing this was Katie-Ann's very first day at Liberty High.

"Finally," Burt responded as he ran his finger down the margin of the document. "We sure wasted enough time on that Norditch sideshow. Yeah, I'll take this one." *So integrity was a sideshow.* She took the binder he held out to her, stuck a Post-It on the open page, and handed him the next open binder.

"Yeah," she responded, and then heard herself add, "If we'd listened to you from the beginning we'd have saved a lot of time, wouldn't we?" *Why was she provoking his obnoxious comments? Like pushing your tongue against a sore tooth.*

He paused with his finger halfway down the page and looked up at her. "Well, exactly. I wish your boss could figure that out. We're just lucky the investment bankers didn't scuttle the whole deal." *Oh, so Ken lacked Burt's excellent judgment. Strutty little pigeon!*

She forced herself not to glare. "Be a relief to get it through the board next week. Are these documents for your presentation?"

He resumed reading. "Roy's presentation. I'm getting it ready for him." *Perfect opening. She could maybe take one little jab.*

"Really." She arched her eyebrows. "Is that how he does it? I just assumed that since you did all the work..."

"Yeah, that would be nice. But Roy does all the presentations to the board." *So tantalizing.* She decided to allow herself one more jab.

"Along with Andrea, you mean," she clarified, with only the faintest emphasis on the name. "You prepare her presentation, too?"

His fleshy shoulders jerked in a little twitch of annoyance. "Andrea isn't doing a presentation. She has nothing to do with this." He closed a binder with a snap and handed it back to her.

Georgia shrugged. "I must be wrong, then. I thought I heard something..."

"Andrea doesn't begin to understand this deal well enough to do a presentation. She can't even manage the job she does have." *The hell with it. For the sake of women everywhere, this pigeon was going down!*

"Well, then he's probably..."

"If anybody were presenting with him, it would be me."

"Seems only fair, doesn't it? Maybe you could mention that to him. Have you presented to the board in the past?"

"Never been invited. Hand me that brown binder, will you?"

"Here you go. Does Andrea get invited?"

"Yeah, she does sometimes, but only about R&D. She doesn't talk about deals."

"I must've misunderstood then, or else this is a special case and Roy has his reasons. Maybe because she's, you know, an *executive* vice president, which is such a silly distinction. Anyway, you probably don't care who gets the credit, so long as the deal gets done."

"Yeah, that's right. Make me a copy of this one, will you? I might look into it, though. Maybe he wants me to present with him."

She marked the document with a Post-It. "Would Andrea like that? Should you maybe talk to her about it first?" *How was that for ham-fisted?*

His fatty shoulders twitched again, and he slammed the binder shut. "I probably don't need Andrea's permission to do my job."

"Of course you don't," she reassured him with a little smile.

"Anyway, I'm sure the board would like to hear from you directly. Here, let me get that out of your way."

∞

She was in her cube later, sighing with boredom and tapping her pen on the Futuresoft log, when Maggie's telephone voice drifted over the tops of the cubes. "Hi, Mary. Find anybody to go to the airport? What about Sally's admin? Another one??" She lowered her voice to a jokey, conspiratorial whisper. "She isn't having much luck with admins, is she?" She resumed speaking normally. "Okay, let me ask around."

Georgia stood up, stretched her arms in a luxurious Y, and wandered over to Maggie's cube. "Somebody need to go to the airport?"

Maggie was holding the receiver against her chest, and her double hoop earrings gyrated as she turned to Georgia. "Glen Terkes left for the European customer conference without his meds. Sally could take them in her carry-on, but Mary can't find anybody to get them to her."

Georgia rubbed her eye and shrugged. "Why don't I take them? I could use an excuse to get out of my cube for a while."

The big manila envelope that Glen's admin rushed into her hands ten minutes later had only been closed with the clasp. What was she hauling, anyway? She got into her car, unbent the clasp and glanced inside. Afrin nose spray, big deal. But there was also a bulky little manila envelope with Terkes' name handwritten across the seal, and that little envelope had been sealed so very carefully.

Made a person curious, really.

She pulled into the Starbucks just before the freeway entrance, and carried the smaller manila envelope inside. "Could I ask just a great big favor?" She smiled wistfully at the barista, a thin young man with the posture of a comma.

"Wudjya need?" he asked warily.

"I'm taking this medicine to my grandfather at the nursing home, and I forgot to put in one of the bottles." She flashed her Motrin bottle. "I only have this one envelope. Do you think you could hold the flap over the steam for about 15 seconds so that I can reuse it?"

He glanced up at the blinking computer screen of pending drink orders. "I guess so. Yeah." He reached for the envelope.

"Just count slow to fifteen. Wrap your hand in a towel, now, so you don't get burned."

He glanced at her curiously as he took the envelope. A minute later he handed it back. "That do it?"

"Oh, I'm sure it does. Did you count slow? Grandpa and I sure do appreciate it."

Back in her car she laid the envelope flat on her copy of *Crazy in Alabama*, took the knife from her Salvation Army box and slid the blade gently under the flap. She used a Kleenex to lift out the bottle. Cordarone. What was that for? Maybe if she was still bored when she got back, she'd look it up. She wrote the name, dosage, and prescription number of the bottle in her spiral-bound pad. Then she pulled a glue stick from her purse, dabbed very lightly along the gummed edge of the envelope, and realigned the signature precisely along the former glue line. The whole procedure had taken less than five minutes, and her boredom was pretty much cured. She felt almost perky as she pulled onto the freeway and headed for the airport.

∞

"Done and dusted, as Gramma Griffin would say," she reported to Maggie later. Ken wanted to see her.

"Hey, Georgia, come on in. Zack and I need your help with a new problem." Ken was wearing a long, red tie today, and she didn't like it at all. She didn't like having a new drain on her time with Katie-Ann starting school, either. But the new problem might not be urgent. Zack was leaning back comfortably in his spring-back conference chair, his fingers intertwined with palms down on top of his head, and his elbows spread wide to either side.

"But first," Ken said, "I want to let you know there's going to be a personnel announcement in a few hours. Archibald Moss is leaving the company."

Archie undone.

"He is??" Zack dropped his hands and leaned forward. "Wow. So maybe there is a God."

"Zack, you're all sentiment," Ken snorted.

"Because of the patent?" Georgia inquired. *So this really was wrapped up.* She pursed her mouth to prevent her smile from expanding into a slightly loony grin.

"The announcement is going to say he has health problems that need to be addressed immediately."

"'The announcement is going to say ...'" Zack repeated. "So does that mean we never find out the real reason?"

"Actually, it is a kind of health problem. Nothing life-threatening, fortunately."

"That is fortunate." Zack's laughing eyes contradicted his solemn tone. "So, is he just on sick leave then, or is he really gone? I need to manage my optimism."

"He's definitely gone for good. His replacement will report to me, so I'll lead the search."

Zack grinned. "So, at the risk of sounding heartless, don't we need champagne?"

"This is certainly going to make it easier for us to do our jobs," Ken agreed, "but Archie was a good person, and this isn't very good for him. He was popular with the programmers and oddly enough with a lot of nice women in this company who seemed to enjoy taking care of him. We might want to keep our enthusiasm to ourselves."

"Will do," Georgia responded, dutifully wiping the smile from her face.

"Point taken," Zack agreed.

"Okay, now the new problem. Georgia, you know what a side deal is?"

"No." She picked up her plastic pen and wrote 'side deal.'

"As a publicly traded company, we file quarterly public reports called the 10-Q, so that investors can decide whether to buy our stock."

"Catchy name." She wrote it down.

"A more descriptive name would be 'Let's Reveal Our Crooks and Dirt,'" Zack offered, returning his hands to the top of his head.

"Really?" Georgia asked.

"Well," Ken said, "let's just say that we report our sales numbers in these 10-Qs, and they have to be 100 percent accurate. If they're wrong, we have to file a public correction, which invites a shareholder lawsuit, and then all hell breaks loose.

"Which is why there are strict rules. One rule is that you can only count revenue for a software sale if you've delivered every single thing the contract says you'll deliver. If you promise software and a stick of gum, then you'd better deliver the gum before you count the revenue for the software. You follow me?"

"Yep."

"And the only way our controller knows what's been promised is for every single promise to be right there in the contract. If you're the sales guy, you can't write a separate letter promising a stick of gum, and you can't promise even one lousy stick of gum in a phone call, either. In other words, no side deals. Every single salesperson acknowledges in writing that if they do a side deal they'll be fired."

"Okay."

"And we really do fire them. Every single time. Consequently, side deals are rare. To give you some perspective, in the five years I've been here, there've been exactly two. So imagine Zack's surprise . . . Zack?"

"Three days ago I got a call from the controller in the San Francisco office about a possible side deal. A customer called up and said he'd like to return the software he'd purchased. The contract explicitly said he couldn't return the software, so of course the controller said no.

"But the customer insisted he'd been promised the right of return over the phone, by a sales guy who left our company about a month ago. We're investigating it now.

"So far, so bad," he continued cheerfully. "The total value of the contract is under $200,000, which isn't enough to require a public correction even if we do have to reverse the revenue. But then this morning I got another call from the controller. In the last 24 hours, she found three more side deals."

"Ouch." Georgia winced.

"Now, in all likelihood," Zack reassured them, "the controller just got spooked by the first side deal, and is being overly cautious. But we need to do some digging to make sure of that."

"No kidding," Ken agreed. "If all four of these deals turn out to be bad, how likely is it that we happen to have found the only four? We have to move quickly on this one."

Georgia had planned to spend this evening getting Katie-Ann settled into her new homework routine. Of course, Katie-Ann was only here at all because of Ken Madigan.

"Just tell me how I can help," she said.

∞

She was still preparing binders for the side deal investigation in her cube that night at 9:30, working just by the light of her computer screen and trying to ignore voices down the hall near Roy's office. She hated to leave Katie-Ann eating a sandwich by herself for dinner. She hoped she wasn't going to start feeling pulled between work and home like this all the time.

Somebody knocked on the metal rim of her cube. She swung around to see a man in his thirties with dishwater-colored hair that touched the collar of a polo shirt stretched tightly across his belly. She'd seen him somewhere before.

"Oh hi," he said. "I'm Joshua, and I met you in Archie's office a few days ago?"

"Oh, right. Now I remember, though I could hardly see you through the cigar smoke."

"Really? I could see you just fine, so maybe my vision is slightly better than yours. Although I'm sure your vision is good, also."

"Right. So what's up?"

He scratched his forearm and gazed at her right shoulder. "Well, I was just wondering if you'd like to get a beer together sometime down at the Saloon."

No, she would not. Good grief.

"That's very kind, Joshua, and I appreciate it. You know what, though, my little sister just moved here to live with me, so I can't really do stuff outside of work right now." Nice to have a completely genuine excuse.

"Oh." He paused a moment and scratched his forearm again. "Then we can have lunch instead."

She shook her head with regret. "Wish I could, but I pretty much have to work through lunch so I can get home to my sister for dinner. You can see even that didn't work today, since I'm still here. Thanks, though. I'm sure I'll see you around." She gave a friendly wave to signal the conversation was over, and turned back to her binders. Poor guy. Poor herself. Stupid fucking Deke.

Those voices down the hall were still at it. One of them was Roy, but she couldn't place a second male voice that sounded ... terrorized, really. She set her computer on sleep mode and crept silently down the hall to listen.

"You're asking me to get on board with no longer reporting to you, and you don't want to tell me who I will be reporting to?" Ah. Mark Balog, that fanatically groomed customer service guy with the hyper-alert blue eyes. She ducked into a dark cube a few feet from Mark's office.

"Can't say who you'll report to, because I haven't decided."

"If it isn't decided, why tell me anything?"

"You're leaving on vacation tomorrow, and I want to announce it before you get back."

Mark squeaked with horror. "You're going to announce my demotion to the whole world while I'm in Hawaii, and you won't tell me who I'm reporting to? How can I agree to this?"

"You don't need to agree to it, Mark. My mind's made up. But I do expect you to be cooperative. I expect you to position it well with your team."

"If I'm not here, how can I position it with my team at all? Can you at least tell me why this is happening? Aren't I one of the best performers in the company?"

There was a brief silence. "What do you want me to say, Mark? It's happening because I've decided it's in the best interests of the company. That's why reorgs always happen."

There was a long silence, and then Mark seemed to acknowledge defeat. "You know I'm a team player, Roy. I'll be as enthusiastic about this with my team as I possibly can be."

"Then I won't keep you any longer. Have a good vacation."

Mr. Cuddly the CEO had struck again.

∞

She stopped by the Mail Boxes Etc. on her way home, and found she already had a response from her father. She sat in her car and tore it open.

Dearest Georgia,

It puts my mind at rest to know that Katie-Ann is there with you, and out of the clutches of our Most Reverend. Encourage her to lose a bit of her southern accent if you can. For reasons of out-and-out prejudice, I find a southern accent sometimes creates an impression of stupidity that can be inconvenient in many circumstances, (though of course a decided advantage in others).

As to your confrere at work (does this paragon have a name?) I *have met genuinely good-hearted people twice in my life, and find they make excellent marks. There was a third person, who over a period of several months convinced me she was good-hearted, and then cleverly conned me out of $10,000. Sexual attraction was a factor there, so I encourage you to be self-aware.*

As for me, I am keeping my spirits up by writing a little fiction. Of course this isn't where my primary talents lie, but I'm striving for an air of authenticity, and believe I am making headway. I may have something to show you soon.

Take care, Georgia. I am so proud of you.
Love,
Daddy

Georgia smiled and shook her head. Like she would ever give him Ken's name. Daddy was losing his subtlety there in that prison with his talents going to waste. At least he had his new fiction project to keep him out of trouble.

She read through the letter again. Her father would be even prouder if he could see how his teachings were being put to use. Holly Foxx had just been a nuisance, but Archibald Moss really mattered, and she'd pulled it off without a hitch. Now that Archibald was gone, the new Ingenious Tricky Countersuit had a chance. 'I did it, Daddy,' she thought, gazing up through her windshield at a tree whose lightly swaying branches etched a black lace pattern across the moon. 'First I observed him with my open mind, and then closed my eyes and visualized his fault lines, like I was looking at a map, exactly the way you taught me.' Pride is a dangerous emotion, she knew, but after months of feeling overwhelmed every single day, surely she could luxuriate in this moment of out-and-out competence.

CHAPTER 14

Georgia was dashing from one perimeter shelf to the next in the diligence room, snapping documents into binders at lightning speed. She filed the last document in her hand, turned back for more, and almost shrieked with fright. Bland Burt was standing in the basement gloom less than two feet away from her.

"Oh God, Burt! Didn't hear you come in." *Fucking jerk!* She moved her palm from her mouth to her collarbone. "Here, can I get you some coffee? How's the board presentation coming?"

"Almost done, but I need a few more documents."

"Great. Have a seat, let me move those for you." She was determined not to let her thudding pulse cause her to miss an opportunity. "So, are you going to present to the board?"

"No." He seated himself under the hanging light and reached both hands up to take the steaming cup from her. "I talked to Roy about it, but he wants to do it himself. I really had to push just to get myself invited into the meeting. You were right about Andrea, by the way. The Board wants to hear from her on the intellectual property."

She could feel her heart rate slowing to normal, and her gasping was already just little puffs of exhalation. "Well, but isn't this a big success? Now that you're in the meeting, you can step in to make sure the board gets an accurate picture. I'm sure that's what Roy expects."

Burt frowned, then nodded. "Yeah, I can't just sit there and let Andrea confuse people. I'll have to jump in if they need me."

"It's your duty as an officer of the company, isn't it? I know Ken always feels that way. Once the board sees how much you know, they'll probably ask for you explicitly from now on. You'll be an executive vice president in no time." Was it possible to go too far with this guy?

"I should've been one a long time ago. Put some milk in this coffee, will you? Not too much." Georgia smiled sweetly and stirred it for him.

∞

She rapped her knuckles on the frame of Ken's open door. He wheeled back from his computer and stretched his arms above his head. His butter yellow shirt was crisp as always, but he looked a little groggy this morning. "Hey, Georgia, what's up?"

Something she hoped would seem like her business.

"I saw Mark Balog in the hall this morning. Isn't he supposed to be on vacation?"

"Yeah, I think he is." He rubbed his hand across his eyes and blinked. "Something must be going on in his part of the company."

"I might know what it is."

"Really?" He yawned, and stretched his eyes open. "What's that?"

"I overheard Roy the other night, telling Mark he's going to start reporting to somebody else."

He stopped yawning and sat up straight. "No kidding. Who's he reporting to now?"

"Roy wouldn't tell him."

"Pardon?"

"Roy's going to announce the change while Mark's on vacation, but hasn't decided who his new boss is."

"That's ridiculous. No wonder Mark's upset."

"Now I think he might be too freaked out to take his vacation. Is there any chance you could talk to him?"

He cocked his head, his green eyes studying her face. "You're afraid he'll quit."

"Well, and wouldn't that be bad? He seems like one of the

people around here who does his job." She felt herself flush under his friendly gaze.

"He is. Absolutely. I could try, Georgia, but Mark and I don't really talk about personal matters. He might be upset that I know anything about it."

"I bet he won't be. Everyone likes to talk to you, remember? It's an accident of birth."

He snorted softly and drummed his fingers on the desk, considering. "Okay, I'll try it. Don't know what good it'll ..."

"Ken?" Mark poked his head in the door as if on cue. "Can I come in and hide?" His smile was so tight it looked like his skin would split.

"That bad, huh? Come on in. Should I ask Georgia to step out?"

"Hi, Georgia. Don't leave. Nikki told me you overheard the bomb being dropped. You told Ken?" He sat stiffly on the edge of his chair. "This morning I talked to him again, and it got worse. He's decided I'm reporting to Glen Terkes. Can you believe that? I told him it won't work, because Glen doesn't respect customer service and he doesn't respect me. He never returns my calls, and my attempts to collaborate are always rejected." Painful, really, to hear those sounds of anguish issue through those tight, smiling lips. Made her jumpy just to watch.

"Roy says I'm making too big a deal about it," Mark continued. "He says there are lots of job opportunities, and in six months if I'm not happy, I can just move into another job."

"Interesting," Ken said. "Like what?"

"So I said exactly that, 'Like what, Roy? Tech support and maintenance is what I do.' And Roy said, 'Don't worry. Maybe you can have Andrea's job.'"

Ken stiffened. "He said what?"

Mark leaned toward Ken, his blue eyes glittering ominously, and repeated more slowly, "He said, 'Maybe you can have Andrea's job.' Does that make any sense to you?"

"None whatever. Jesus, Mary and Joseph!!"

"So I said, 'Roy, how could that be? I don't even have an engineering degree.' And he just laughed. And Ken, I'm telling you, it was a pretty weird laugh. Either he's losing his marbles or I'm losing mine. Is he really thinking of replacing Andrea?" *Stop smiling, Mark.*

"Hard to tell what it means, 'cause it makes no sense."

"Maybe he needs a scapegoat for the problems with the 6.0, but he'd be crazy to replace Andrea. And anyway," Mark asked, his voice rising to a higher register, "why tell me? She's my peer, and it's just totally embarrassing."

"Boy, no kidding." Ken was frowning, searching for an answer in the air beyond Mark's right shoulder.

"Okay," Mark continued, "but even aside from Andrea, putting me under Glen makes no sense, either. Does it?"

Ken returned his gaze to Mark. "My guess is Glen wants to be more than just a sales guy, so Roy thought up this 'reorg' to give him a bigger title."

"Glen could never be more than a sales guy. He's completely incapable of thinking beyond his next deal." He slumped a little, his smile burning even brighter. "So Roy's just sacrificing me to Glen."

"He probably figures he can't afford to lose Glen, and he's counting on you not to quit. Thinks you'll keep doing your job no matter where you are, because that's the way you're built."

"Great," Mark said bitterly. "I thought consistent execution was a good thing." *Please stop smiling.*

"It is a good thing. You're the most reliable person on our team, and a critical person for this company. What you need to decide now is, should you stay here and fight this, or should you set it aside and go on vacation?"

"If I go, I'll feel like shit the whole time. Why did he tell me this now?"

"Because he was thinking about his own comfort instead of yours. Not good leadership. Think you can change his mind?"

Mark resisted a moment before admitting, "No."

"Then do you need to be here for your team, or should you head out of here now and spend some time with your family?"

He stared at Ken for a moment, then puffed out his cheeks and finally let his smile collapse. Georgia almost gasped with relief. "I should go with my family. They're sitting at home surrounded by suitcases, completely freaked out. And my team will probably go ballistic if they see me here. Listen, if I give you my cell phone number, will you call me about absolutely anything that involves my team and this reorg?"

Ken gave an emphatic nod. "You have my commitment. So if you don't hear from me, you know it's business as usual."

"Thanks, Ken. I can't tell you how much I appreciate the support. You, too, Georgia. Thanks."

Ken closed his door and turned to Georgia. "Boy, I tell you, Roy's taking quite a chance with Mark. And that Andrea comment, which was probably just made for Mark's benefit..." He exhaled slowly.

"You think Roy really is losing his marbles?"

He shook his head. "Nah. This isn't degenerative. He's pretty much always had intermittent marble loss." Georgia snorted. "The truth is that Wall Street loves Roy for slashing costs and getting our profits up, while the rest of us have to live with ever decreasing resources and his ham-fisted interpersonal skills. I have to say, Roy's a good person, but I'm beginning to have doubts. Would you follow that guy into battle?"

The notion almost made her laugh. She would never follow anybody into battle if she could possibly avoid it. Which of course wasn't Ken Madigan's point, or a position he would admire. So she solemnly replied, "I hope not. Sort of like following General Custer."

∞

She was perched on the edge of a deep brown leather armchair in Roy's lavishly decorated office, and taking notes while Roy briefed Ken on expected quarter-end deals. "By the way," Roy said, "I've decided not to fire Buck Gibbons over this Larkin thing."

"Even though he grabbed his subordinate's genitals? Why is that?" Ken's mouth was tightening into a straight line. Uh-oh, she'd seen that look before.

Roy's starched white sleeves were rolled up, and he waved a hand dismissively. "I asked Sally to look into it, and she doesn't think we have to."

Ken sat forward, his feel planted on the oriental carpet. "We probably don't have to, Roy, but that really isn't the question. The question is what's best for the company."

"I talked to Glen about it, too," Roy added, "and he's confident he can keep the situation under control. Seems this guy Larkin isn't much of a salesman anyway, so he might not be here long."

"Roy, he's gone to Quota Club three years in a row."

"That right? Well, Glen isn't very impressed with what he's done lately."

"This sounds exactly like retaliation, Roy, and it'll really set us up for a lawsuit. It will also have a terrible impact on employee morale, which won't do much for Sally's efforts to reduce attrition." Ken's tolerance for bullshit seemed a little diminished since his conversation with Mark Balog. Interesting, when he flushed like that, his hair looked more orange.

"Who said anything about retaliation?" Roy asked. "Talk to Sally about putting some kind of warning in Buck's file as soon as the quarter's over. Just go over the content with Glen beforehand, so we don't upset Buck. We're done here." And not a moment too soon. She hurried out after Ken, who marched right past his office and kept on going.

"This pisses me off," Zack pronounced a few minutes later after Ken described the conversation. "I gave Ben Larkin my word that he wouldn't lose his job."

Ken had regained his composure. "I feel angry about it, too, Zack. We'll just have to do our best to keep him from getting fired. I'll warn Buck not to retaliate. Glen, too."

"Which might work if they believed for one second they could get in trouble for retaliating. How successful can Ben possibly be with a manager who hates him now?"

"That's always a problem, Zack. If I were Ben, I'd start thinking about my alternatives in and outside the company. Keep in mind that the situation he was in was already pretty intolerable. I doubt he was going to put up with that indefinitely, in any case."

"Yeah. The situation was pretty intolerable, and now I've made it utterly intolerable. This place sucks sometimes."

"Every place sucks sometimes, because things aren't always fair. The company is very fortunate to have you here, committed to doing the right thing. That's about all we can ask of ourselves."

Was it? thought Georgia as she headed back to her cube. How did being committed to the right thing help Ben Larkin, if the right thing didn't get done?

∞

Katie-Ann stood holding the front door at 7:30 while Georgia climbed the stairs. "Hurry up. I'm starving."

"Me, too. Sorry I'm late, and it's my turn to cook. Should we just do macaroni and cheese?" She dropped her computer bag on the carpet.

"Dinner is served," Katie-Ann announced, opening the oven door with a flourish. "I got this whole turkey leg for only four dollars." She peered into the dark interior. "Just hope it's not all dry . . ."

"I'm sure it's wonderful," Georgia grinned as she handed her the potholder. "Serious protein. How 'bout I make salad, while you set the table and tell me about your, let's see, fourth day of school?"

Soon they were seated on folding chairs at the card table in the living room, paper towels across their laps. "Anyway," Katie-Ann was saying, "I kind of felt like a freak at lunch. This group of girls were all polite enough to my face, but something about the way they were watching each other the whole time gave me the willies. One of them said she liked my skirt, but she had this little smirk on her face, you know? Assimilation might be harder than I thought, Georgia. Every single thing is just so ... new every day. Kinda wears me out."

"Yeah, I know what you mean. It does get better, though. Pretty soon some of the new stuff will start to seem familiar."

Katie-Ann took a sip of milk. "I guess. Honestly, I wish Daddy was here. I could sure use one of his stories about now. Something to bring tears to a glass eye." Georgia snickered and then they were silent a long moment, their dull knives scraping the chipped, mismatched plates as they sawed on the (frankly dry) turkey leg. The air in the room suddenly threatened to turn stale.

"I know!" Katie-Ann said. "Why don't you tell one of his stories? You're a good story-teller."

Georgia snorted and held her hand up. "No, no. Only Daddy can tell a Daddy story. And anyway, we're leaving that stuff behind us, remember?"

"Well, but not the stories. The stories don't hurt anybody, and it'll seem more like he's here with us. Just for tonight. Come on, Georgia. Please?"

Georgia tapped two fingernails on the green vinyl surface of the card table. "Tell you what. If you want, we'll do one together. How 'bout the Scroggins boys?"

Katie-Ann squinted, appraising. "Fun, but not enough Daddy in it. I know. How 'bout Grandma Griffin and poor old Mr. Haney? You start."

Georgia relented with a smile, and set down her fork. "Okay. Well, when Daddy was little, he and Uncle Levi lived with Grandma and Grandpa Griffin over the old dry goods store. Grandpa Griffin was down there watching the store every day, doing the same exact thing, day in and day out, for less and less money. Daddy thought that was what he'd be doing when he grew up. I think Grandpa Griffin actually told him that sometimes, to help him imagine becoming a man, but Daddy couldn't stand the idea. Almost made him feel like not growing up at all."

Katie-Ann sighed luxuriously, her eyes already dreamy and unfocused. "Poor little Daddy. Can you imagine, with his creativity?"

"But then when Daddy was around nine, rumors got out that a Wal-Mart City Discount Store was coming, practically right next door in Searcy. Okay, your turn. Want more turkey?"

Katie-Ann handed over her plate, and held both hands up in front of her, like she was receiving a basketball. "Well, the instant Grandma Griffin heard the rumor, she knew they needed to sell their scrawny little dry goods store and get out while the gettin' was good. But everybody else had heard the rumor, too, so the trick was to find someone to sell it to." She paused and took her refilled plate from Georgia. "How'd she zero in on Mr. Haney, exactly?"

Georgia helped herself to a few more ropey strands of turkey. "He was that teacher who got his high school student pregnant over in the next county, remember? Had to find new work in a real big hurry. Don't remember how Grandma Griffin figured out he had the money, though."

"Okay, anyway," Katie-Ann continued, "she came and found little Daddy one afternoon, when he was skipping rocks across the pond out behind the store. Told him she was going to do some make-believe with Mr. Haney, and would he help? 'But it has to be our secret, okay, George? Just you and me. Your papa doesn't put as much store in make-believe as we do.'

"So, Daddy and Grandma Griffin did play-acting out by the pond every day for the better part of a week. When Grandma Griffin told him Mr. Haney would be coming the next day, Daddy got so excited he did somersaults all the way around the pond.

"And the next afternoon, little Daddy sat in the corner of the store with his fire truck and made noises for it, while Grandma Griffin showed Mr. Haney her tax returns and let him look over the inventory. When she told Mr. Haney her asking price, he practically laughed in her face. Truth be told, she knew her price was too high, even without the Wal-Mart. But it was what she needed to buy the stables over in

Piney, so otherwise what was the point?

"She and Mr. Haney commenced to arguin', and all the while Daddy's heart was beating faster and faster, and he was scared he'd have to go pee at the crucial moment, but he just kept making those engine noises for his truck. And when Grandma finally excused herself to go out back with a customer to look at a new blade for his bush hog, that's when Little Daddy went to work. Okay, now you tell what he did," she instructed, picking up her fork to spear a radish while Georgia took over the story.

"Well, he kept making his fire engine noises louder, until he was practically shouting 'Clang! Clang!' to get Mr. Haney's attention. Sure enough, Mr. Haney strolled over and smiled down at him, and asked whether he planned to be a fireman.

" 'Maybe,' little Daddy mumbled, looking shyly at the floor. Then he looked up. 'Are you from the tax office?'

" 'The tax office!' Mr. Haney laughed. 'Why, no, young feller! What makes you think that?'

"Little Daddy shrugged, like this, and answered slowly. 'Well, I just noticed she didn't show you her red book. And that brown book'—he nodded toward the one they'd been going through—'is the one she keeps for the tax office.'

"Mr. Haney was quiet a moment, while Daddy went back to rolling his fire engine, and then he said, 'You say she keeps a red book for somebody else?'

"Daddy shrugged again and stared at the floor, like this, pretending he was suddenly wary." Katie-Ann giggled at the pantomime.

" 'She does, doesn't she, young man?' " Georgia continued in a fake, deep voice. " 'She must have forgotten to show it to me, 'cause I'm definitely not the tax man. Why don't you help your mama out, and show me where she keeps that red book?'

"And that was when Daddy gave a long, scared look at the cupboard underneath the shelves of fabrics, and then looked up at Mr. Haney. 'Don't know where,' he said solemnly. 'And anyway, Mamma would hit me with the belt for sure.' And then he ran out, and they left Mr. Haney by himself in the store for a good fifteen minutes. Okay, Katie-Ann, now you finish up."

Katie-Ann had laid her knife and fork neatly across the center of her empty plate, and was tilted back in her chair, listening. She leaned forward and rested her forearms on the table, not really seeing Georgia or anything else in their living room. "Once they'd given Mr. Haney plenty of time to study the jacked-up sales numbers in the fake ledger, Grandma Griffin came back and they recommenced to arguin'. Before the bank closed that day, they had written up and signed a bill of sale for almost Grandma's original asking price. She took his money straight over to Piney the next morning and bought the stables."

"Yay!" Georgia said quietly.

"She and Grandpa Griffin were just hooking up the stove in the new home place a few days later, when Mr. Haney came calling. Little Daddy spotted him coming up the path, so he shouted to Grandma and then squished himself into the front corner of the room, where he could see Grandma, but Mr. Haney couldn't see him. Seems Mr. Haney'd finally figured out about the Wal-Mart, and was experiencing some buyer's remorse." Georgia guffawed. "Said he was gonna turn her in to the IRS if she didn't give his money back.

"And little Grandma stood her ground in the doorway, in her print dress and that apron, just looking sweet and confused with her big, round eyes. 'Lan' sake, Mr. Haney, now what would the IRS want with the likes of me? I pay my taxes. You saw the forms your own self … Now, Mr. Haney, you took all the time you wanted to study over my ledger. There some other book you might be calling a ledger? … Are you suggesting you did business in reliance on the word of a nine-year-old boy? Oh sorry, Mr. Haney, I know I oughtn't to laugh.' Until finally, Mr. Haney stopped yelling threats and turned away, saying he'd be back with the sheriff. Which of course he never was."

"Well, he couldn't," Georgia scoffed. "Lucky for Grandma Griffin, he wasn't exactly a pillar of the community, with that pregnant child bride of his. Needed to be a right good neighbor to keep from getting run out of the community altogether. So little Daddy not only escaped the dry goods business, but he got an actual taste of the most thrilling work he could possibly think of." She dropped her voice an octave and pumped her fist in the air. " 'The mastery, Georgia! The adrenaline pump!' He was hooked for life.

"And so very proud of his daredevil little mama. The fact that she got the money for the stables was secondary. What he really admired was her gumption. That was when he realized he was no shopkeeper like his father but was Grandma Griffin's son first and foremost. And he's never looked back."

Katie-Ann was staring into space over Georgia's shoulder. "Gumptious Grandma," she murmured. Then she snapped back into the present and looked ruefully at Georgia. "I sure miss her, Georgia, but aren't you glad she didn't live to see Daddy locked up in that jail? Might've killed 'em both." They were silent a moment. "She kind of retired after Mr. Haney, didn't she? Went back to taking care of the family and helping Grandpa Griffin with the stable."

"Well, sort of," Georgia clarified. "Credit where credit is due. She did get a good price for some sorry-looking swaybacks over the years."

Katie-Ann chortled. "That is so true. Remember that appaloosa yearling with the short leg?" She stood up with her empty plate and started lurching with one stiff leg into the kitchen, while they both laughed.

"I remember perfectly," Georgia said. "So anyway, that was that. Grandpa Griffin knew plenty about horses from back in Ireland. He rebuilt the stables, and Little Daddy loved those horses. He worked hard, learned everything he could, and did whatever Grandpa Griffin wanted him to. But his heart had been stolen by Grandma Griffin's special talents, and there it remains to this day."

"To this day," Katie-Ann reiterated. She set her plate in the sink and leaned against the counter, one bare foot on top of the other as she gazed through the kitchen window at the stucco building across the alley. "Not bad," she decided, turning to Georgia. "Not quite

Daddy-caliber, maybe, but I sure forgot about school for a while. You know what, can we have ice cream for dessert? I got that really dark chocolate stuff from Dove."

∞

"Hope you don't mind the road trip." Zack's ample body was cushioned by the white leather seat of his black Lexus convertible, and his wraparound sunglasses made him look like a bug in a tan suit.

"You kidding? It's gorgeous out here." Georgia was sunk deep in the passenger seat, and they were inching toward the 4th Street exit in San Francisco. The morning sun glinted off the little ripples in the Bay, and a line of pelicans wheeled in formation above the water. The breeze from the bay was blowing sharp and fresh over the snaking line of cars, holding its own admirably against the exhaust. Too bad they couldn't just hang out in Golden Gate Park all day.

"So, can I ask some stuff?" She rolled her head on its cushioned headrest away from the blue bay to look at him. "What's a distributor, and why do we care what they say about side deals?"

"Distributor's a middleman," The Bug explained, watching the traffic. "Sort of like Fry's, only without the storefront. The disti just gives us the name of his end customer, and then we sell him the software at a discount. That way we get a bigger sales force without having to cope with their ludicrous, vulgar shenanigans."

"And what are we hoping to get from these distributors—disti's—today?"

"We want them to admit they lied to us about having the right to return the software."

She frowned. "Is that likely?"

"Not very," he admitted cheerfully. "They'll probably say our sales guy promised them they could return the product if they couldn't find an end user. If they say that, then we're cynically hoping they have no proof. And if they do have proof, then at least we're hoping they'll tell us that these are the only three deals they've ever done with no end user and a side deal."

"I see. Our job is to contain the toxic spill before we clean it up."

"Exactly. With a whole set of progressively less optimistic containment rings."

Georgia made quick notes on the yellow notepad that was propped on her knees. "Okay. But why would we even care whether they have an end customer, if they don't have the right to return the software? Isn't that just their problem?"

"Sadly, it is not," he sighed. "It's also our nasty problem, called channel-stuffing," He nosed ahead of a Camry onto the exit, and the Camry honked. "If a distributor buys more software than he needs, and we won't let him sell it back to us, then he'll stop buying until he uses up what he has. So that inflates the sales number in one quarter, and tricks the public into thinking we're selling software at a faster rate than we really are. Channel stuffing. Which makes our public reports misleading, which can take our whole company down in flames. Can you see, is that a garage entrance on our right?"

"And why exactly would our sales guy stuff the channel by getting disti's to buy product they don't need?" she asked as Zack locked the car.

"Why do sales guys do everything? They're coin-operated. They get crazy at quarter-end if it looks like their commissions aren't gonna be big enough. And there might be pressure from the boss, who's also coin-operated. So occasionally, one of them does a side deal—knowing they'll get fired if we find it—just to pull future revenue into the present quarter. Here we are. I think they're on the fourteenth floor."

"So do all salespeople engage in ludicrous, vulgar shenanigans?" she asked as the elevator began to ascend.

"Certainly not. Our licensing lawyers work with a number of perfectly sensible professionals." He removed his bug glasses and slid them into his inner suit pocket.

"So, we have no reason to think these disti's are out of control."

"Well, that's not entirely true ..." He grinned slyly. "They wanted me to hold this meeting at the Wanton Wendy Club."

"At nine in the morning?"

"They asked me to wait until ten." *Was he teasing her?*

"So, why aren't we there?" she asked suspiciously.

"I said the tassels make me dizzy before I've had my coffee." He looked straight ahead as the elevator doors opened into the plush reception area of Chipotle Software Solutions.

The receptionist seated them in a conference room, and a moment later two virtually identical men with professionally mussed hair entered, their narrow-waisted, 'sharp' suits differentiated only by their red-and-yellow versus blue-and-maroon striped ties. Their cufflinks caught the light as they each firmly shook Zack's hand.

"Good, I see you found the coffee," Ron Davis said with a wink. "I heard it's your morning beverage of choice." *Reference to Wanton Wendy?* "So how can we help?"

"Well," Zack began, "I wanted to better understand your right to return software in those three deals you called us about. By the way, are those all the deals that you view as issues between us?"

"At the moment, yes," Mr. Davis said. "We ran a check, and the other deals like this have all sold through."

'The other deals . . .' So much for only three.

Zack's demeanor was deadpan. "When you say 'deals like this,' can you say what exactly you mean by that?"

"Sure. From time to time one of your sales guys asks us to 'pull forward' a deal that would logically occur later on. Either we don't have an end user, or the end user isn't ready for the software. We always go along if we can, because it helps Lumina and we know we won't be stuck with the product if we can't sell it." *Boom. Channel-stuffing.*

"I see. So you say 'we go along.' Have you been asked to go along very often?"

Ron Davis shrugged. "Dale, did you bring the chart? We thought you might be curious, so we did a little research."

Georgia glanced at the two-page chart. Eight customers were listed down the left-hand column.

"Thank you," Zack said. "Very helpful. So, on the three deals you called us about, I see that Bill Barrows is listed as the rep. He's the guy that just left the company.

"Right."

"And in the same column where Bill Barrow's name appears, I see other names. Are those the names of other Lumina salespeople?"

"Dora Hickox and Danny Villus, yeah. Those are the only three that ever approach us directly. And we know how it is. We have quotas too. So we help Charlie out if we can."

"Charlie?"

"Yeah. You know. Reebuck."

"Ah. Charlie Reebuck, the head of our western region," Zack said pleasantly.

Excellent poker face, thought Georgia. Must be from his days as a litigator. He often came across as good-natured and slightly obtuse. Looking at his cheerful smile, you'd never know bad news registered with him at all.

"But Charlie's name isn't on here," Zack continued. "Have you spoken to him about these deals?"

"Dale, have you?" Ron Davis asked. "No, we never spoke to Charlie directly about this, but your sales reps always emphasize that the request is from Charlie—you know, to help him get across the finish line for the quarter."

"I see. So with any of these deals, how would you document the agreement with Lumina?"

"Well, it looks like we haven't been too careful about that. We found one email on the Ramco deal." Burt handed Zack and Georgia a copy. "I think that lays it out pretty clearly." *So much for no proof. The disti's score!* "To tell you the truth we didn't feel we needed to document anything. Lumina always makes good on its promises."

"When you say 'we make good,' do you mean we've refunded money to you?"

"Well, it was never that direct. We understood the situation. We just quietly returned the product, and then we got a good discount on product in a subsequent deal. Charlie's very fair. It's just, you know, with Barrows gone all of a sudden, we got a little skittish about these three."

"I see. So this is a complete list of all the deals that were done in this way?" *The toxic spill was now leaking into the biggest containment facility.*

"We think so, yeah." He shrugged. "We don't like to do them too often, because it creates a few accounting issues of our own, if you know what I mean."

Zack leaned toward Ron Davis. "Mr. Davis, I plan to do everything in my power to make sure we don't ask Chipotle to do this for us again. Ever. If anybody does approach you with another request, we'd prefer that you stall him and call me. You've got my number on the card."

Mr. Davis picked up the card and glanced at it. "Sounds great." He tossed it back onto the table. "So I assume we're free to ship back the product? Glad we got that behind us by,"—he glanced at his watch— "9:35 in the morning. If only we had some entertainment to help us celebrate." He winked. "Next time let's find a better meeting place." The wink was her answer.

"Absolutely. Next time we will. Thanks, guys."

Zack said nothing on the way down in the elevator. As soon as they were safely enclosed in his Lexus, he dropped his head onto the steering wheel and bellowed, "Holy shit!" Georgia glanced quickly out the window to see who else had heard. "And those other two sales guys are probably still with the company, cranking out side deals faster than Krispy Kreme cranks out donuts." He sat up and smacked the steering wheel, hard, with his open hand.

Probably not a good time to ask how his optimism was holding up.

∞

"So that's what we know," Zack concluded a couple of hours later to Ken, Quan, Georgia, and Cliff Tanco, the Don Juan of finance. "Are you all suitably aghast?"

"I'm not sure 'aghast' really covers it," Ken said. "If this means we have to publicly restate our earnings for the past year, then we can practically guarantee a hit to our stock price."

"I know," Zack said, "when we've already got the patent lawsuit and that toxic Futuresoft deal. Sorry to drop this on you as well."

"Hardly your fault. That's why we have jobs. So let's list what needs to be done."

The group briskly agreed to restore eighteen months of email for the two still-employed sales reps, and hire eight outside lawyers to start reviewing the email for evidence of more side deals.

"Great." Zack actually sounded upbeat half an hour later, as he dropped his pen onto his yellow pad. "I think that covers it for now."

"I tell you," Ken said, touching his bow tie, "I'm scared to death we'll find out Reebuck was involved in this, because it could spread beyond the San Francisco office."

"But we have no evidence that he was involved," Zack reassured him. "Just speculation from a couple of ludicrous … sales guys." He shot a conspiratorial smile at Georgia.

"What happens if we miss the deadline for filing the 10-Q this quarter?" Quan asked.

"We can't let that happen," Ken stated flatly. "It's even worse than a restatement, because the investors know something is wrong, but they can't size the problem. Tell you what, let's get Reebuck's email restored now, just in case, and hope to hell we never need to read it."

"Boy," Quan remarked. "Six weeks to file the Q suddenly doesn't seem like much time."

Had it occurred to Ken that even Reebuck might not be the worst of it, Georgia wondered as she hurried back to her cube. What if *this* was what Terkes had been so worried about the day they told him about the Flipper? If Glen was involved, would they have to look at email for the whole world?

Those puny little half-empty side deal binders suddenly seemed ridiculous, like hummingbird wings on a moose.

∞

Although Georgia shared her father's love of the adrenalin pump, she had more patience for routine than he did. That was why she could get her college degree when her father never did. It was the reason she could manage a desk job (with maybe one or two little embellishments). But Georgia did have limits. After spending several hours meticulously arranging the tracking system for side deal evidence, she needed a break.

Why not go on the Internet and check out that prescription medication Glen Terkes used? Cordarone. Hm. Heart stuff. Interesting. Looked like it might be serious heart stuff. She was deciphering an article from the *Journal of American Medicine* when her phone rang.

"Georgia, it's Jim Prizine. I'm standing on the steps of the International Trade Commission."

"Oh my God! Hold on a minute, okay?"

A moment later she and Ken and Zack were standing expectantly around Ken's conference table, and Ken called into his speakerphone, "Jim? Tell us what's happening."

"Well, I'm standing on the steps of the International Trade Commission here in our capital, with a copy of your ITC lawsuit, which was file-stamped exactly seven minutes ago."

"I have goosebumps," Zack said. "Like I'm talking to Neil Armstrong on the moon." They all cheered with giddy delight.

Georgia cut out the headline from the *Wall Street Journal* the next morning and stuck it up in her cube: "Plucky Lumina Software Fires ITC Salvo at German Giant SAP." By the end of the day, Lumina stock was trading up five points.

CHAPTER 15

"I'm having a second thought or two about this, Nikki," Georgia warned as she followed Nikki's bobbing ponytail along the wooden dock. The bright sunshine was warm on Georgia's back as she tied her windbreaker around her waist. "I'm a little bit of a chicken in certain ways."

Nikki spoke over her shoulder without breaking her stride. "Legal people always are. Professional hazard. But there's no risk to this, as long as the two of us stick together. Just don't let the fat guy get you alone."

"That's not really the risk I'm worried about, Nikki, though now I know why you invited me."

Nikki flashed a grin over her shoulder. "Now, that's not fair. It was maybe one little reason. Roy has to sail the boat, which means he's up on deck the whole time, and I couldn't really take a chance on getting stuck alone in the cabin with Large Romeo. But I could have asked a dozen different people to join me, and I chose you because it'll be the most fun for me."

"What if I get seasick? What if the boat tips over?"

"Those would make it less fun," Nikki acknowledged, "but they're not gonna happen. Catered food, gorgeous weather, fine wine. And we'll get all your documents signed." She patted her messenger bag.

"Who is the fat guy, anyway, and why do you think he'd come on to you?

"Jonathan Bascom. Head of sales for a company called WizBiz. Larry Stockton, our board member, asked Roy to spend a little time with him. Not clear why. As to his manners, just a feeling from when I met him for thirty seconds. Could be totally wrong. Here we are."

Georgia paused to read the name on the back of the gently bobbing boat. "The *'Chaucer.'* Now, that's a surprise."

"Yeah, that's the new name. Look where it's painted over."

Georgia squinted. "Is that ... *'Salt'* ...?"

"Yeah. Used to be the *'Salty Fart,'* but Jean-Francois made him clean it up for customers. Watch your step. Hey, Roy!"

"Guy's not here," Roy grumbled, reaching a hand out to steady Nikki as she stepped onto the boat. He offered a steadying hand to Georgia without looking at her.

"Thanks," Georgia murmured to the side of his head.

"Should be here any minute," Nikki said. "I gave him directions myself." She put her cell phone to her ear and gestured for Georgia to carry the messenger bag down a short flight of steep steps into the cabin, a claustrophobic little room with cushioned bench seats, a fold-down table and a twin bed under a low ceiling. Narrow horizontal windows were cranked open to provide a cross breeze, but it was still stuffy. She dropped the bag on the table next to the food and went back up to look around, a light breeze blowing strands of her black hair across her face. Somehow "yacht" sounded a lot bigger than this ... boat, but what did she know? Beat hell out of a houseboat on Waxahachie Lake.

Roy's glare had slightly less malice in it here on the boat, and Nikki was still on her cell phone, so Georgia ventured, "Nice boat. You're a fan of Chaucer?"

"I was a big fan of Chaucer the dog. Named the boat after him."

"I see. What kind of dog was he?"

"Pit bull. Much better sailing companion than my wife. He sailed out to the Farallons with me every year for twelve years."

"You must really miss him. Aren't the Farallons ...?"

"Here he is. Johnny!" Nikki pocketed her cell phone and turned to greet the man who stepped heavily onto the bobbing deck. His broad chest sloped out and culminated in a distended belly that left his belt buckle peeking out underneath, exactly like Baby Huey's diaper pin. His big head was topped by a tiny baseball cap that accentuated his red, translucent ears. This was a sales guy? Must be big money in the sympathy appeal.

Georgia shook his hand as he said hello to her boobs. He pointed out how much he and Larry appreciated Roy taking the time. They chatted a moment while Nikki poured him some wine, and then Georgia followed her down into the cabin to set up lunch.

"I take your point," Georgia whispered when they got downstairs. "We can't let Large Romeo within a million miles of either of us."

"Absolutely not," Nikki agreed. "We stick together every minute." First there was Cliff, the Don Juan of Finance, and now Large Romeo. A regular Who's Who of sexual pests. Where were the decent guys looking for action in this company?

"Probably a nice enough person," Georgia conceded, "though he sure has a mouth on him. He says either 'fuck' or 'Larry' in every other sentence."

"Boy, I'll take 'fuck' any day. How insecure would you have to be to drop Larry's name every ten seconds? Let's get the food ready, then we'll go rescue Roy."

But Roy didn't need rescuing. Within ten minutes he and Large Romeo were howling with laughter about where Chaucer had pooped on the boat while they were sailing. Evidently a match made in the latrines of heaven.

∞

Zack knocked and stuck his head in Ken's office, where Georgia was helping to prepare for the board meeting. "Buck Gibbons called Human Resources today. He wants help putting Ben Larkin on a PIP."

"Jesus, Mary and Joseph!" When Ken pushed back from the table and turned to him, Georgia could see out over the parking lot that the gray-green eucalyptuses were deathly still. Today was going to be hot.

"PIP stands for ... ?'" she asked, turning away from the window and flipping to a clean page of her yellow pad.

"Persecute Innocent Person," Zack responded, pushing his glasses up his nose with his middle finger. Interesting, his eyes didn't look red any more. Was he keeping those glasses as a prop to express his views about Buck Gibbons?

"Close enough in this case, probably," Ken acknowledged. "It's actually 'Performance Improvement Plan,' often the first step toward firing someone."

"That didn't take long, did it?" she commented.

"No," Ken agreed, "I guess it didn't. What's the basis?"

"They say he hasn't sold enough in the first month of the quarter," Zack responded, "and doesn't have enough leads in the pipeline."

"Do we know how he compares with other guys' sales and pipeline?"

"No, and I'm sure Buck Gibbons doesn't know, either."

"So let's tell HR to find out before we take any action. In the mean-time, Zack, why don't you check in with Ben and see how he's doing?"

"Can you make the call with me, Georgia?" Zack asked. "I might not be Ben's favorite person at the moment."

"Ben, it's Zack Stern," he said into his speakerphone a moment later. "You remember Georgia Griffin?"

"Yeah. Hey, guys."

"It's been a few weeks since I talked to you, and we just wanted to check in and see how your quarter's going?"

"Exactly the way they knew it would go when they changed my territory."

Georgia and Zack exchanged glances. "They changed your territory?"

"Yeah. Cut my old territory in half, gave my biggest accounts to Linda, and gave me some new territory where I don't have a single contact."

"And your quota?" Zack asked.

"Same as it's always been."

"Can you meet it?"

A snort came through the speakerphone. "No way. I'm spending my time cold-calling in the new territory, just to find people who'll talk to me for ten minutes. That's the only reason you caught me here in the office."

"Did they change anybody else's territory?" Georgia asked.

"Nope. Just me and Linda."

"Ben, this is just wrong," Zack said. "We need to force them to give you your old territory back."

"So then they'll just raise my quota. Or say I have attitude problems. I think the handwriting's on the wall here. Not sure it's worth your time."

"But I feel responsible for this. At least let me give it a shot."

There was a short silence. "Up to you, but can you find me a bullet-proof vest? Your shots seem to end up lodged in me, somehow."

"Well," Zack said after they'd hung up, "I guess that's a kind of progress. Ben has developed sarcasm." His jokey tone was belied by the angry glitter in his eyes.

"Are Buck and Glen really going to get away with this?"

He lifted his hands in a gesture of helpless resignation. "Honestly, Georgia, I sorta think they are. I don't see any way to stop it at this point. Do you?"

Well, no she didn't, really. Not at the moment. And they were so overwhelmed by the side deal investigation that she couldn't even try to think of one.

∞

At 9:30 that night the self-denominated Hideous Facts Team was huddled around the cheap laminated table in the windowless red-walled conference room. Quan, Zack, Georgia, and a guy from Internal Audit were reviewing the "hot" email regarding side deals that had been culled by the now thirteen outside lawyers who were set up around a server over at the outside law firm, Woodrow, Mantella.

Although they were almost stacked on top of one another the airless little room was silent, with each reader taking notes and keeping his own counsel about what he was finding. From the email Georgia had read so far, both Dora Hickox and Danny Villus, the two sales executives from the San Francisco office, were up to their eyeballs in side deals, not all of them confined to Chipotle Software. She hoped she was misinterpreting something.

Then Quan said, "Uh-oh."

They all looked up. "Uh-oh what?" the Internal Audit guy said warily.

"Uh-oh I think I found a smoking gun. May I read it to you?" He blinked rapidly behind his rimless glasses. "This is Charlie Reebuck to Danny Villus on the Ramco deal: 'As for the buyback, don't use it unless you have to. You're a top salesman, out-negotiate him.'"

"Shit," Zack said decisively after a moment of silence. "We gotta do Reebuck." Georgia wished those walls had been painted something other than the color of dried blood.

∞

Georgia watched Ken read the 'smoking gun' email the next morning, his palm absent-mindedly brushing the top of his military haircut. Cliff Tanco was seated sideways at the table, his legs stretched out in front of him, and their outside lawyer, Jill, was on the speakerphone. Beyond the window, the utterly motionless trees seemed as lifeless as the parking lot itself, where the only movement was sun ricocheting off hot chrome.

Ken tossed the email onto his table and looked up. "This is quite unfortunate. We now have to review all of Charlie's email for the San Francisco office, and still find a way to file the Q on time. Has his email been restored?"

"It has." Georgia glanced at her notes. "And for three years it's another 54,000 emails." Somebody whistled. "And don't we have to look at his other direct reports in San Francisco, too?"

They had a plan in twenty minutes, which included Quan locating thirty new email readers by the end of the day. Was that even possible? Right now they had only thirteen.

"God bless Charlie Reebuck," Ken said. "Let's hope he hasn't cost the shareholders a billion dollars in market cap. I briefed Roy and the board, by the way. The board wonders if this whole investigation should be turned over to an outside firm so there's no claim of bias. Opinions?"

"My opinion," Zack replied promptly, "is that the minute you hand this over to an outside firm you can forget about filing on time."

"I agree with Zack," Jill said, "and I think it's unnecessary, unless we find evidence that an executive is involved. Meaning you, Cliff, or you, Ken, or Glen Terkes." Georgia felt Ken's eyes flick in her direction without making contact. *So he was worried about Glen, too.*

"If that happened," Quan said, "we might have to review the whole world."

"To be clear," Jill warned, "if this expands to *any* office beyond San Francisco for any reason, then we cannot expect to finish on time."

Ken looked askance at the phone. "Understand the issue, Jill, but we're here to get this done. Georgia, I'm afraid we need to ask IT to restore all email for all offices, starting with the rest of Charlie's Western Region offices. Unbelievable, that a high-tech company tries to save money by backing up their email on these Stone Age tapes. Okay, anything else? Thanks, everybody. Zack and Georgia, can I talk to you for one more minute?" They waited while the others filed from the room.

"Just got a call from the number two guy in SAP's legal department, Jochen Volkmann, the guy who's handling both the patent and now the ITC case. Evidently he called me as soon as he found out Archie Moss isn't here anymore."

"That's a joke, right?" Zack asked. "We could use a good joke about now. He wasn't really talking to Archie."

Ken shrugged with helpless bewilderment. "I think he must've been. How else would he even know Archie's name? Anyway, Volkmann asked me to meet him in New York this week to talk settlement. This would be a lot to dump on you, Zack, because we basically can't lose one second on the side deals. You good with it?"

"I'm fine with it. By all means, go settle SAP."

"Well, not in this first meeting, but it shows we've got their attention."

∞

Two mornings later, Maggie appeared in the entrance to Georgia's cube. "Ken's calling from New York. He'd like to speak to you and Zack on his speakerphone."

"Georgia, Zack, you there?" He was whispering. "Have to talk fast, they'll be back any minute now. This meeting with SAP is unbelievable. They just made a demand so low it's laughable. I'm supposedly talking to Roy about it now."

"What's the demand?" Zack asked.

"Sworn to secrecy, even from you, but it's down in the low triple-digits."

"NFW! After two and a half years?"

"And $24 million in legal fees. Wish you guys were here to see it, the fight's just drained out of 'em. I tell you, Georgia, your ITC idea was even better than we thought." *Wait, he was giving her credit?*

"And we buy peace?" Zack asked.

"You bet we buy peace. Up, gotta go!" The line went dead, and she continued to stare at the phone with a half-smile on her face, bobbing on a little sea of happiness.

∞

Charlie Reebuck probably weighed 130 pounds. Small, skinny, constantly in motion, dressed in a tailored and well-fitting suit that must have begun life in some boys' department. Georgia's hand throbbed after he shook it.

Zack directed him to a seat in the windowless conference room on the first floor. "Okay, Mr. Reebuck, I'd like to ask you some questions this afternoon, and Georgia will keep track of what we say. Thanks for coming in today."

Charlie's darting brown eyes settled earnestly on Zack. "Happy to help. Just need to get back into the field as quickly as possible."

"I'll try to move it along. You're in charge of sales for the Western Region, is that right?"

"Right. And then I moonlight as a boy prostitute."

"Great." Zack smiled appreciatively. "Just so you know, this might go a little faster if I don't have to figure out what's real and what's joking."

"No problem. That was real." Slight pause. "So, what am I in trouble for?" *He wanted to keep Zack off balance. Afraid, or just a control freak?*

"I don't know that you are in trouble," Zack clarified. "We're investigating a string of side deals that originated in your San Francisco office."

"You're kidding. Side deals? What deals were those?" Charlie looked very concerned.

"I'll go over them with you in a few minutes. First, I'd like to ask you whether you ever authorized any deals out of your San Francisco office, in which a distributor was given a right of return outside the signed contract."

Charlie's shoulders twitched. "Of course not. That's against company policy."

"Okay. I'd like to start with the Ramco deal. You're familiar with that?"

"Yeah, but that was a while ago. Wasn't it?" His torso was quivering from his leg jiggling under the table. *Was this normal for him? Could he be on drugs?*

"Closed in Q4 of last year," Zack continued. "Did you authorize Danny Villus to offer the distributor a full right of return if he took $200K of product in Q4?"

"Certainly not."

"Then can you tell me how you explain this email?"

Charlie tapped his middle finger rapidly on the table as he read. He must have been a fairly slow reader. Finally, he looked up. "Yeah?"

"Would you read the second paragraph, please?"

" 'I'm giving this my best, but I may need the ability to guarantee that he won't lose his money. Can you authorize me to offer a buyback for up to $200,000?' Unquote."

"Okay, great," Zack said. "And then would you please read your response? Second paragraph, first sentence I've highlighted for you?"

"Surprised you can't read it yourself. 'As for the buyback, don't use it unless you have to. You're a top salesman, out-negotiate him.' "

"Does that refresh your recollection about whether you authorized Danny Villus to offer the distributor a full right of return if he took $200K of product in Q4?"

"Not really, no."

"Do you recall that you sent this email?"

Charlie shrugged. "If you say it came from my computer, I must have sent it."

"And do you agree that it authorizes the offer of a $200K buyback?"

He considered a minute. "No."

"No?" Zack raised his eyebrows. "Can you explain what else it might mean?"

"Well, it just says don't use it unless you have to. That isn't the same as saying it's authorized."

Zack pushed his glasses up his nose with his middle finger. "Fine, Mr. Reebuck, I can take those from you. Now I'd like to move to the Lucas Solutions deal. That was a deal for $170K. You remember it?"

"Vaguely."

"Well, let's try to sharpen your memory. Take a look at this email exchange, please." He handed him two sheets of paper.

Again, Charlie looked at them for several minutes. Then he looked up.

"You see," Zack said, "paragraph two of Bill Litcomb's email to you says, 'I can close this by promising we'll work with him next quarter if he's stuck with the product. Please confirm you are okay with that.' You see that?"

"Yes."

"Can you tell me the meaning of 'we'll work with him next quarter?'"

He shrugged. "Bill wrote it. Have to ask him."

"Well, you agreed to 'work with him next quarter,' didn't you?"

"Don't know."

Zack raised his eyebrows. "You don't know? Mr. Reebuck, look at the language in your response email that I have highlighted for you. Do you see where you say, 'Of course we'll work with him. He's a preferred customer.' Do you see that?"

"Yes."

"Well, when you agreed to 'work with him' what did you think it meant?"

"Don't remember."

"Mr. Reebuck." Zack suddenly stood up and locked his elbows as he leaned forward across the table, looking down at Charlie's startled face. "I thought you were going to stop kidding around. I think you know exactly what it meant to 'work with him,' and I think you know very well that you agreed to the $200K buyback in the Ramco deal. You're lying to me, and I want you to start telling me the truth."

Whoa. What happened to Mr. Friendly?

Charlie held his palms up, and ducked his head. "Okay. Don't get excited. I'll tell you the truth." *When woodpeckers hummed Beethoven.*

Zack sat back down. "Great. You can start by telling me what you meant by 'work with him.'"

His shoulders twitched again. "Don't remember."

Zack expelled an exasperated sigh. Georgia passed him a note: "*Ask about his Mattel deal. Say it was fake.*"

"Okay, Mr. Reebuck ..."

"Call me Charlie," he offered expansively.

"Thank you, Mr. Reebuck, I don't think I will. I'd like to move to your Mattel deal."

Charlie stiffened. "Mattel! Now wait a minute. Nothing wrong with that deal. 100% legit."

Zack flashed Georgia a meaningful look. "As opposed to the Ramco and Lucas Solutions deals?"

"Whatever. If there's anything wrong with the Mattel deal, I had nothin' to do with it."

Zack's sigh was theatrical. "I'd like to believe you, Mr. Reebuck. But you lie so much, how can I believe anything you say?"

"I know. I know. I'm working on that." His staccato admission was tinged with regret, and he lifted his hands in a gesture of surrender.

Hide and Seek continued for another two hours.

∞

Zack and Georgia were sorting through their Reebuck notes and vying with each other for blackest humor at 6:30 that evening, when Ken called again. "Guys, we're done."

"For the day?" Zack asked, consulting his watch.

"Done entirely. We settled."

Georgia turned to stare at the speakerphone. "You settled the whole ITC lawsuit??"

"And the patent case. They're finalizing the agreement now."

"And the terms?" Zack asked.

"Verboten to say, but believe me, it's the deal of the millennium." He actually chortled. "I think they looked into the abyss of having their

U.S. sales blocked, and just capitulated. So Georgia, I just emailed you the language for the press release. Can you run it by Roy, and then get it out on the wire before the market opens tomorrow?"

"Absolutely."

"Woohoo!" Zack yelled, and they did a high five.

"This has certainly been quite a day for the company," Ken said. "How's the investigation coming?"

"We interviewed Charlie Reebuck." Zack caught Georgia's eye and she shook her head. "Tell you about him later. And then we found a way to squeeze three more email readers onto the system, so we're up to forty-eight. All a little precarious, but we're gettin' there."

"Good. Stay with it. I know you will. I'll see you in the morning as soon as my plane lands. In the meantime, savor the victory, guys. We don't get them often enough."

Zack ended the call, put his palms against the sides of his head and began alternating them. "We're up. We're down. We're up. We're down. Is the company better or worse off after today, Georgia? What do you think?"

"Better off, of course. One miserable little sales guy can't begin to cause the kind of damage the patent suit did."

Zack's silence was disconcerting.

∞

She wanted to forget about Charlie Reebuck during dinner, but Katie-Ann wasn't cooperating. She muttered grudging monosyllables until Georgia finally asked, "Hey. What's up? Spaghetti once too often?"

Katie-Ann paused, her noodles half wound around her fork, and looked up from her plate. "I got my first geometry quiz back today. I really don't know my butt from a dry well."

Poor time to criticize a metaphor. "Well, but you're great in English and history, they've put you in the AP classes. French is fine, art should be a snap. Maybe you just need a lower level of geometry."

"There *is* no lower level of geometry. Everybody else in my grade is doing trig." She abandoned all pretense of eating and rested her temples against her fists.

"You sure? I can talk to the teacher. Maybe you and I have to become really good math buddies for a while. Assuming I can figure it out. Otherwise, we'll get help from somebody who does."

"Might not be a quick fix."

"Doesn't need to be a quick fix. Remember how Grandma Griffin always wished she'd gone to high school? Well, you're in high school, and you have all the time you need to get it right."

"Whatever." Katie-Ann reorganized herself on her chair, and one knee appeared above the table top. "Tell you the truth, everything sucks. Everybody in the whole school has already known each other for two years. And I don't sound like anybody else. And my clothes are stupid. There's a girl named Ginger who's making fun of them."

"Go ahead, say you're ugly and I'll know you're delusional."

Katie-Ann didn't smile.

Georgia rested her fork on the chipped rim of her plate. "Look, I think you ought to join something. You get along fine with people, and I guarantee some of those students think your accent makes you interesting."

"Lepers are interesting."

Georgia inhaled sharply. "Okay, slightly soon for whining, Katie-Ann. Can you give me a couple of weeks to lose that vivid memory of sleeping in my small"—she jabbed her fork to punctuate each adjective—"uncomfortable, moderately unsafe, car for six weeks to get this apartment for us? Then you can start whining."

"You're right. Sorry." She picked up her fork and started pushing the spaghetti around, evidently trying not to cry.

Of course, it wasn't Katie-Ann's fault Charlie Reebuck was a low-down skunk. "In the meantime, let's go to Now & Again this weekend. You can get some new stuff that looks the way you want."

"Thanks," she said to her plate, "but Now & Again won't help. I need to look like an Aberzombie."

"A what?" Then Georgia pushed the heel of her hand against her eyebrow. She would not yell at her sister. She would not. "Fine. We'll go to Abercrombie."

Katie-Ann looked up. "We have the money?"

Georgia shrugged. "Emergency money. Evidently this is an emergency. But we're only getting two outfits, Katie-Ann, so plan carefully."

"That's so great. It really is." She was twirling her spaghetti faster. "And can we talk to Mr. Farber together? Whatever the math fix is, I need to start yesterday."

CHAPTER 16

Jean-Claude called the board meeting to order the instant Paul Holder's bald head appeared in the boardroom doorway. Georgia's head had been bent over her board book for a good fifteen minutes, watching Roy through her dark eyelashes, monitoring the manifestations of his increasing annoyance.

"If you don't mind, Paul, I think we should immediately begin," Jean-Claude called cheerfully in his heavy accent, inclining his head slightly in Roy's direction. Was he warning Paul, or sharing a joke at Roy's expense? Roy, so clearly the outsider in this room, with his hot-looking black suit and his neck stuffed into his tight collar, appeared oblivious to whatever the chairman was doing. He watched coldly while Paul bumped his computer and gym bags against his stork-like legs and squeezed into his seat.

Five board members were now seated around the glistening, dark table, including Jared Winters, the elegant 70-year-old investment banker who increasingly reminded Georgia of Cary Grant; and Larry Stockton, the software CEO with his determined square jaw and fierce black eyes. The remaining board members had begged off, probably because they expected this Futuresoft review to be nothing more than the customary rubber stamp ceremony. The only other people in the room were Ken and Georgia herself. Where were Andrea and Burt? She sipped her Starbucks coffee to offset the chronic chill of the boardroom.

"Okay," Jean-Claude began, "the biggest purpose of our meeting today is to discuss the Futuresoft acquisition. But we must begin with two other important subjects. First, even though we know it already, we must acknowledge the SAP nightmare is behind us."

"We can tell that by our stock price," Jared Winters called, against a background of heavy claps and cheers.

"That's true," Jean-Claude confirmed with a grin. "You remember our stock increased five points the day we announced our new lawsuit, and now since we settled it has gone up another ... Where is it today, Ken? So that's another seven. So a total of twelve points, or about $1.2 billion, that we really may say are due entirely to the excellent work of our General Counsel. I would like to speak for the company, and give our very big thanks to Ken for his great work on the shareholders' behalf."

"Absolutely," Larry Stockton said, his square jaw framing a deliberate, aggressive smile.

"Thank you," Ken nodded, smiling. "Appreciate the appreciation. Of course, you know that a success like this is always a collaborative effort. In this particular case, I would like the board to know where we got the idea for our ITC lawsuit." *Was this about her?*

"From you, of course," Jean-Claude pronounced confidently.

Ken shook his head ruefully. "Wish it had been me."

"The Banyon firm," Larry guessed.

Ken pointed to Georgia, who tried not to look like a deer caught in the headlights. "The idea came from our paralegal, Georgia Griffin. She read about an International Trade Commission lawsuit in the *Wall Street Journal*, and had the extraordinary creativity to suggest that we might bring one to preempt the patent litigation. Maybe the rest of us should have thought of it, but it was Georgia who actually did." He beamed at her frankly, inviting others to do the same.

She felt her skin heat up as the board members turned to stare at her. A lifetime of not sticking her head above the crowd, and now Ken had hoisted her onto his tall shoulders. Knowing about Katie-Ann, he also knew how desperately she needed layoff insurance. She made herself breathe, and smiled what she hoped was a pleasantly normal smile.

"Thanks, Georgia," Jared said lightly, with a nod of encouragement and a fleeting smile.

"Well done, Georgia," Paul agreed, and they all turned back to Ken.

And that was it. Not so dangerous, really. She felt her chest relax, and her deeper breathing resume. And very generous of Ken, really, who could easily have kept all the credit for himself. She stole a glance at him, and he dropped one eyelid in a wink.

"In any event," Jean-Claude concluded, "we are very happy to have this fine legal team working for us instead of SAP." After a slight pause he continued, "Okay, second subject, which is not such a happy one. Where are we with the side deal investigation?"

"In other words, Ken," Jared said, "what have you done for us lately?"

Laughter.

"I'm afraid it's very much a work in progress," Ken said. "We're making headway, but the size of the problem is still changing on a daily basis. Which is somewhat concerning, since the deadline remains the same." He described the findings to date, which elicited grunts of dismay and surprise around the table. "So far, no change for any quarter is big enough to require public restatement of our 10-Q, but a couple of quarters are getting close."

"Those are a lot of bad deals, Ken," Jared noted. "Do these guys not understand the rules, or is somebody encouraging them to violate rules they understand perfectly?"

"Really too soon to answer that. I have my suspicions, but I'd prefer to come back to you when the investigation is farther along."

"Fair enough," Jean-Claude said. "But if it becomes clear that we have a management problem, we really must deal with it firmly. With cancer, you must remove the entire tumor." Murmured agreement.

"Can we anticipate the cost of this massive effort?" Larry asked.

"I've told finance to budget $2 million." Whistles of surprise. "We'll do it for less if we can. We're asking our outside lawyers to get this done under extreme time pressure, and it isn't coming cheap."

"Okay, Ken," Jean-Claude said, "just keep the pressure on them to finish, so that we file the Q on time. It's the most important thing. Any other questions? Now we are ready for the Futuresoft deal. Roy?"

"Thanks, Jean-Claude." Roy said as he walked to the door and admitted Andrea and Burt. Andrea had honored the occasion by pairing her black turtleneck with slacks instead of her customary jeans. She and the board members exchanged hellos with muted nods and smiles.

Burt didn't make eye contact with anyone as he took a chair next to Andrea, his round, bland face even whiter than usual. That beige suit with a nondescript brown tie made him entirely too easy to ignore, in Georgia's opinion. After all, the whole point here was for Burt to get noticed. Was that at least a faint flicker of determination she saw in his eyes?

"Okay," Roy said, "you know Andrea, and some of you may have met Burt Plowfield, who's in charge of our Corporate Development team.

"This morning I want to present an opportunity in the financial planning space, which, as you know, is currently dominated by Cordova. I believe the acquisition of Futuresoft Corporation will allow us to leapfrog into first place in as little as twelve months, representing a revenue opportunity of $13 million in the first year. Andrea will tell you about the intellectual property benefits."

Andrea spoke about the key features of the technology and the opportunities for cross-selling the existing Lumina products. After ten minutes Paul asked, "Andrea, do you see any weaknesses or vulnerabilities in the intellectual property?"

"No worries there," Roy responded. "The ownership of the intellectual property is very sound."

"They've done a good job with that in many ways," Andrea agreed, shifting in her seat so that Roy was outside her line of vision. *Good, she saw her chance.* "There are a couple of areas of vulnerability, though..." Roy's expression remained fixed, but his posture stiffened.

"I don't agree," Burt Plowfield interjected firmly. "The intellectual property is in excellent shape."

Board members, including Roy, gave a startled glance at Burt, and then returned their attention to Andrea. "What are you seeing, Andrea?" Paul asked.

"Well, we know they have open source in their product, which could be a problem for us in terms of any GPL code. As you know, GPL makes all source code of any product completely free to the buyer as a matter of law. Also, if we acquire GPL, it could put us in breach of our warranties to Microsoft."

Georgia was probably the only one in the room who noticed the rose-colored stain spreading across Burt's cheeks. *Go for it!* she thought. *Now's your moment. Put that uppity Andrea Hancock in her place.*

"It might or might not be a big problem," Andrea went on, "but I'd be more comfortable if we could determine the extent of the GPL before signing."

"You'd be more comfortable," Burt interjected, "but we wouldn't get the deal done." Georgia tucked her chin, and pressed the back of her hand against her rogue smile.

Larry turned to Burt. "Why is that? Why not just run a diagnostic test to see the extent of it?"

"Oh, they won't allow it," Burt said. "They say if it's so important to us, we can do it on our own time after the software changes hands."

"But that's quite unreasonable," Jean-Claude objected. "If they don't want us to investigate it, they should agree to remove it all as a condition to closing."

"They won't do that, either" Burt said. "They say it makes the time of closing too uncertain."

"I see." Jean-Claude elevated his wiry, gray eyebrows. "They feel quite powerful about what they will and won't accept." He turned back to Andrea. "Is there anything else?"

"There's also the issue of the Oracle contract ..."

"The Oracle contract is not an issue," Burt contradicted.

"Burt," Roy barked. "You're not here to ...!"

"Hold on, Roy," Jared countered, his palm raised in Roy's direction and his eyes on Burt. "Burt, did you negotiate this deal?"

"From start to finish," Burt confirmed, sitting slightly straighter.

"Then I'd like to hear what you have to say. First, though, Andrea, what Oracle issue do you see?"

"Basically, Futuresoft wrote an all-you-can-eat contract with Oracle that includes 'all follow-on product' for another ten years. The way the contract's written, 'follow-on product' can mean not only all Futuresoft product, but all Lumina product as well."

"Okay, Burt," Jared said reasonably, "sounds like they get free access to all of our product. Tell us why that isn't a problem."

Roy opened his mouth, then silently closed it again, his jaw rippling.

"That was never the intent of the parties when the agreement was signed," Burt responded, "and Oracle has never interpreted it that way. Why would they suddenly interpret it that way now?"

"How about because a dangerous rival just made a strategic acquisition?" Larry responded. "Ken, do you agree with Andrea's interpretation of the contract?"

"I do. It might or might not have been intended to cover all product of an acquiring company, but it could be interpreted that way now. I'd say it's a small chance of complete catastrophe."

"How can you know it wasn't the intent of the parties?" Jean-Claude asked Burt.

"The bankers were involved in the negotiation, and that's what they tell me."

"Well, if the bankers are so confident it isn't a problem, are they prepared to indemnify us against it?" Larry asked.

"Didn't ask," Burt admitted. His face had resumed its normal color and his chin was higher. "They're pretty fed up with us already, because we delayed the deal with so many other irrelevant issues."

"What issues were those?" Jared asked pleasantly.

"Gentlemen," Roy cut in, "this isn't fair to Burt. I didn't ask him to present this morning, and it will be less confusing if we ask him to step out." *No! No! He wasn't finished yet.*

"Well, but it's his deal, evidently," Jared objected, gesturing toward Burt. "He probably knows it backward and forward without preparing, don't you, Burt?"

"I know the deal quite well ... yes," he hesitated, glancing fearfully at Roy for the first time. So now he suspected he was in trouble. He glanced at Georgia, who delivered a small, reassuring smile and beamed encouragement with her eyes. *Take her down, Burt! Take Andrea down!* Burt squared his shoulders.

"So tell us about these irrelevant issues we've been wasting time on," Jared invited. All the directors were leaning forward and listening intently to Burt Plowfield. Something he had dreamed of many times, no doubt. It should have been his shining moment.

"We basically insulted them by accusing them of stealing Cordova intellectual property, when they had an innocent explanation for everything. Perfect example of how an overzealous legal department prevents a deal from getting done."

"Well, thank God it turned out to be innocent," Jared said. "Ken, I assume you agree with Burt's conclusion?"

"Unfortunately, I don't agree at all."

"You don't agree?" Jean-Claude said in surprise. "Then we must explore it further. Just to finish with Andrea, though, have we understood all the intellectual property issues?"

Andrea kept her face angled away from Roy. "There's only one other issue. Their code has to be adapted for integration with larger, more complex systems, and for that we badly need the ongoing effort of the two founders."

"Well, surely we've got that sewn up," Paul stated with alarm.

"It's subject to debate. I ..."

"No it's not!" Burt hissed. "They are rock solid."

Roy expelled a furious sigh, and Georgia glanced over to see his face bent toward the clenched knot of his own two fists on the table. He was surely hating himself about now for letting Burt into the meeting.

Andrea continued. "We certainly hope they're going to stay, but with each of them getting $15 million when the deal closes, I perceive some vulnerability."

"I'd say that's a lot of vulnerability," Larry said. "Do we have retention agreements?"

"We don't need them," Burt stated.

"Tell us why we don't need them, Burt," Larry invited. "You agree the founders are vital?"

Burt seemed oblivious to the purring menace in Larry's voice. "Yes, but they've given me their personal assurances that they are very enthusiastic about staying on to help the merger succeed."

Paul's eyebrows shot up toward the ceiling. "You kidding? Everybody's enthusiastic, until they see how hard the integration's gonna be. Have they committed to a specific period of time in writing?"

"No."

"Have they agreed to put part of their money into escrow, and then earn it out over a period of time as milestones are met?"

"No."

While Burt was talking, Larry had begun watching Roy, a faint, acid smile curling the corners of his lips.

"Why not?" Paul persisted.

"Oh, they didn't want an escrow. They wanted their money free and clear." Jared and another board member snorted.

"I'm sure that's what they wanted, Burt," Larry said, his eyes still on Roy, his predatory smile stretching until his eyeteeth gleamed. "But why would we agree to it?"

"We had no choice," Burt responded hesitantly. "They had another suitor ready to pay all cash."

"And you know that because ...?"

"Oh, the bankers told me so," he almost whispered.

"The bankers are playing rope-a-dope with you, son," Jared said kindly. Fifty-year-old Burt Plowfield was a 'son.' Ken winced.

Jean-Claude turned to Roy. "I'm very sorry, Roy. Even with the substantial deference due to you as the CEO, we cannot accept this deal under the present terms." Paul had buried his face in his hands, and the overhead lights glinted on his shiny head.

"Perfectly understood, gentlemen," Roy said grimly. "I apologize for bringing it to you in the present condition."

Georgia could feel Burt's confounded gaze resting on her. She glanced up from her notes and gave a small, innocent shrug.

Larry asked, "Would it be helpful to the executive team, Roy, if we outline what we think would be acceptable?"

"I don't think we should bother with that now," Jared said. "I mean, Ken, what about this apparent theft of Cordova intellectual property? If that's a real problem, how can this company ever be safe for us to buy?"

"The way it could be safe, Jared, is for Futuresoft to go to Cordova, confess what they've done, and clean it up with them."

"It is perfect," Jean-Claude pronounced with a chuckle. "We must deliver this message. List every issue we have as a board, and then tell them we cannot agree to any further discussion until they have corrected the problem with Cordova. And if they do it," he said, grinning, "we may be certain there was no other buyer."

Laughter.

"So Roy," Larry said, "you'll see that the message gets delivered?"

"Certainly." Roy's stone cold eyes remained focused on the far wall.

Larry's smile was almost sadistic. "And I think you'd be wise to start thinking about Plan B."

"Okay, thank you everyone," Jean-Claude said. "I think we are finished with our meeting. Roy, could you remain for another minute? The board would like to speak to you alone."

Burt almost ran out through the swinging door of the boardroom. A moment later Georgia, Ken and Andrea were huddled outside in the hall.

"Jesus, Mary and Joseph!" Ken whispered.

"What do you know?" Andrea said softly, glancing both ways along the hall. "Justice sometimes prevails."

"Awfully nice of Burt to take the heat for us in there. That deal's as dead as a doornail."

"Might be the most useful thing he's ever done for this company," Georgia whispered.

"Even if not the most popular," Andrea agreed. "Did you see the look on Roy's face?" Their gleeful laughter was tinged with guilt.

"What I don't understand is how he got into that meeting in the first place," Ken said. "Roy makes blunders, but usually not the tactical kind. Painful to watch."

"It diminishes my pain," Andrea declared, "to remember that Burt's both incompetent *and* a Grade A asshole. Better him than us by a long shot."

"Put 'er there, pal," Ken said quietly, shaking Andrea's hand. "We're quite a team. Appreciate the support."

"Let's get out of here before the meeting breaks up," Andrea suggested, glancing back at the boardroom. "See you later. Thanks, Georgia."

Back in her cubicle, Georgia stared blankly at her whiteboard, trying not to let any hint of dissatisfaction dilute her feeling of triumph. Ken had praised her to the Board for the ITC lawsuit. It was perfectly appropriate for him to thank Andrea for killing the Futuresoft deal. After all, he had no way of knowing Georgia had anything to do with it.

At that instant she heard an engine roar to life in the parking lot. She ran to the hall window just in time to see Burt's red Ferrari zoom out the exit. She sighed. Well, as her father and Harry Truman liked to say, you can accomplish quite a lot in this world, as long as you don't care too much who gets the credit. It was going to be fun to tell this story to her father. Beyond that, she would emulate President Truman and savor her triumph herself.

CHAPTER 17

Georgia was so focused on her non-disclosure agreement that she jumped when she heard papers *whap!* like a beaver tail onto Beatrice's desk in the adjoining cubicle.

"You gave me a document to sign as the chairman of a committee I know nothing about." Sally's furious voice brought instant silence to the double row of cubicles.

"Ann," Beatrice said into her phone, "I'm sorry to interrupt, but somebody is ..."

"I don't sign things without explanation," Sally hissed, "and no one with an ounce of professional pride would ask me to. And evidently you don't proofread, either. The date on your mystery document doesn't even match the date of the minutes. Let's chat one day about what it is you *do* do." Georgia could hear Sally's footsteps receding down the hall.

The cubicles remained utterly silent, and Georgia felt heat rising in her face. Every person in every cube probably shared her dilemma right now: Should she race over and offer sympathy or pretend for Beatrice's sake she hadn't heard?

"Ann," she heard Beatrice say after a moment, "I will call you back." The phone went back into its base, and gradually the sounds from the cubicles resumed. She heard Beatrice pull a Kleenex from her box, and then Maggie said quietly, "Beatrice, you okay?"

"I did give her an explanation," Beatrice said softly, "but I guess she didn't read it." Georgia could hear her crying. "See, I put it here in this email. And the date in my document is correct. I don't know who prepared the minutes. Oh, Maggie, I feel ashamed. All these years I thought I was doing a good job here. Nobody ever made me feel stupid, until today. This is not the company I joined ten years ago."

"Forget about her!" Maggie whispered fiercely. "She's an unspeakable bitch, and you just happened to get in her line of fire. Come on, let's go for a walk around the building."

"I can't, Maggie. I need to sit here for now and calm down." Twenty minutes later Georgia saw Beatrice enter an empty office across the hall and close the door. She had stopped crying.

Georgia finished the non-disclosure agreement and headed over to Ken's office. She found him standing in his open doorway, shrugging his shoulders into his suit coat. He glanced at his watch, and then stood back to let her enter. "What's goin' on? I have a couple of minutes before I head out to Mass."

"You mean 'Mass' as in 'religious ceremony?' I thought you were a *lapsed* Catholic."

His smile was sheepish. "I am. Definitely haven't believed the stuff for quite a while. The funny thing is, though, that sometimes if I go to the service, I just feel better anyway. I know that's pretty irrational."

"So what, if it doesn't hurt anybody?" she said with a shrug. "Anyway, I wondered if you knew what happened to Beatrice a while ago."

"Maggie told me about her encounter with Sally. I went by to see her, but she'd gone home early."

"What if she quits?" Georgia asked. "Yonatan quit because of Sally, and so did that woman from payroll. When the board told Sally to deal with attrition, didn't they mean reduce it?"

"Well, hopefully Beatrice won't quit." Ken sounded alarmed. "She's a very important person to the department and to the company. I guess I didn't realize it was quite that bad."

"Sally's meaner than a snake on sandpaper," Georgia declared with narrowed eyes. "Severine doesn't even use her name any more. She just calls her 'the Nusty Beech.'" Severine was their poised and refined French lawyer.

"Didn't know our Severine was so poetic. I'll talk to Beatrice tomorrow, and then Sally."

Georgia shook her head. "Don't think talking's gonna help, Ken. The Nusty Beech needs a character transplant." Ken laughed. "Should she even work here? I think a Human Resources director who terrorizes people should go work for SAP."

"Appreciate your loyalty to Beatrice, Georgia, but Sally has complete job security here as long as Roy Zisko runs the company. He's tied to her with hoops of steel. I'm afraid she's just our cross to bear. I'll talk to her, though. She might be capable of feeling embarrassed."

"I'm sure Beatrice will appreciate it. Have fun at your Mass." She turned to go with a little wave and heard him pull his door closed.

That was the only thing about Ken, she sighed as she passed Beatrice's cube, pausing to confirm that Beatrice's computer was shut down and her purse nowhere in evidence. He would fearlessly tackle a problem the size of Mount Rushmore unless it involved weeding out a problem employee. Too bad so many managers didn't do that part of their jobs. It meant you lost the Beatrices and kept the Sallies, time and time again. Or worse, as her father well knew. Did Ken realize the Nusty Beech wanted control of the legal department?

Of course, you couldn't just 'weed out' a muckety-muck like Sally, even if you were Ken Madigan, especially as long as she and Roy were—what did Ken say?—bound together with hoops of steel.

Too bad there wasn't some way to loosen those rivets.

∞

Georgia couldn't have said why she preferred to sit in her car to read her father's letters. Maybe she felt proud to remember what she'd been through just to get to herself and Katie-Ann to their present circumstance. Maybe it was because her car was now the only place she had real privacy. In any case, she waited impatiently until after dinner and the geometry lesson to carry his letter down to her car:

Dearest Georgia,

Thank you so much for your kind words regarding my mentoring. You have rekindled vivid memories of our long afternoons together in the barn, with the late afternoon sun slanting in through the dust motes and releasing that clean smell of fresh hay. While we groomed the horses and mucked the stalls, I would illustrate some little aspect of our special talents by describing one or two of my adventures.

Georgia smiled out her side window, picturing five-year-old Katie-Ann solemnly grooming a horse's knees.

I say "our" because I knew even then that you shared my innate skills. I encouraged you to put them to good use, but never envisioned your creativity in adapting them to the corporate environment.

Isn't it amazing how certain methods that would seem laughably transparent to any objective observer can be so completely effective? When we align these simple methods with the mark's deepest desires, our preposterous assertions take root in his mind as unassailable truth. A mark's self-awareness is the only effective barrier to this process, and fortunately for hucksters everywhere, self-awareness is in short supply.

By my count, you have now rescued your company from no less than three destructive characters, and will probably identify others as you continue your worthy efforts to improve your company's performance. I'm honored to have contributed in some small way.

Will you allow me to remind you of a few things going forward? Well, but there was no "going forward," not in the way he meant. She'd maybe had one or two successes, but she wasn't going to keep tricking people for the sake of the company. Her open and above-board success with the International Trade Commission was a much better way to secure her job because Ken (and now even the Board!) knew and gave her credit. Another success or two like that and she could forget about unsavory cons forever. She read on.

For example, when you need to build confidence over time in order to execute a complex gambit, you must monitor your progress constantly. Although your mark seems to believe your disinformation, keep testing the strength and duration of that belief right up to the moment you spring your trap. After all, just as you perceive ways to entangle your mark, your mark might be able to perceive your intentions. This is a particular risk with the intelligent mark (which you seem not to have encountered so far at Lumina, but don't become complacent!).

Glancing out her side window again, she watched a raccoon pop up out of a storm drain and waddle off beyond the slanting illumination of a street light. As usual, her father had a point. Wouldn't hurt to cultivate a little rapport with Sally, just in case.

In the meantime, isn't it all just a hoot? I selfishly hope this experience of professional satisfaction will persuade you to cast off your colorless desk job and join me in the Business as soon as I can resume it. Combining your creativity with my experience would make us unstoppable, my dear.

As for me, I continue my literary efforts as best I can, and believe I am making progress. I have also begun to collect a bit of information about the probable composition of my parole board, even though the hearing is still months away. Too bad. She'd been hoping for a sample of his literary endeavor, but of course he had to take the time to get it right.

My only other entertainment is these ongoing efforts to locate Robbie. Earlier this week they actually had me observe a lineup. So I am practicing my thespian skills along with my literary ones, pausing just the right length of time before rejecting each 'suspect.' Poor old Robbie would no doubt feel he is finally getting the attention that is his due, though I continue to wonder why they want him so badly. You don't suppose he had hidden depths? Too bad he isn't here to enjoy it.

Give my love to Katie-Ann. Happy to hear she plans to write to me, but I wouldn't like her to be pressured. The two of you are managing exceptionally well under these difficult circumstances, and she needs to focus on her new life in California.
With love to both of you,
Daddy

Georgia smiled up through her windshield at the silver, silent man in the moon. The most cheerful letter she'd received from her father since the day he went into that awful place. But the man in the moon looked uneasy tonight, his ghostly mouth forming an alarmed 'o'. She wished she could share her father's optimism that he had nothing to fear from that ongoing search for Robbie. What if they decided Robbie was dead? If they developed the slightest suspicion her father was involved in murder, his hopes for early parole would vanish faster than a June bug on a duck. Well. He had a long, proud record of knowing exactly what he was doing, marred only by one unfortunate failure to assess a business colleague's stupidity. If she could manage to take care of herself and Katie-Ann, her father could surely manage to take care of one half-wit grifter.

But maybe the man in the moon was worried about Georgia, simply because he understood the power of gravitational pull. What did it say about her, that she kept thinking up solutions that required her special talents, when she knew she needed to retire those so-called talents forever? Here was an unanticipated drag against escape velocity: She'd had the grit to get herself and Katie-Ann to California, but George Griffin's daughter she would always remain. And yes Daddy, it really *was* a hoot.

∞

"Georgia, the company has awarded you this bonus of $5,000."

"It has?" she said stupidly, reaching across Ken's conference table to accept the check from his outstretched hand.

"Your work on the new lawsuit against SAP was really extraordinary. The company has also decided to grant you 5,000 stock options. Gives you a little piece of ownership in the company, so that if the company does well, you'll see some financial benefit there as well."

Georgia realized she was still staring at the check, and looked up. "I know you're not a practical joker, Ken, so what's the catch?"

"Why would there be a catch?" He sounded taken aback, and slightly offended.

"Sorry, that came out wrong. Stupid joke. I'm just surprised. You must have done a lot to make this happen."

"You're the one who made it happen, Georgia, and it's very well deserved. Now, I don't know what you'll want to do with the money…"

"I want to repay your wife, and the rest is going straight into the bank as a cushion for Katie-Ann and me. The truth is, we need this bonus right now. Turning her into an Aberzombie was expensive."

"A what?" Her dismissive head shake convinced him to let it go. "Saving's a great plan, only, I hope you won't mind me saying this…"

She raised her eyebrows and smiled slightly, waiting.

"I'm just wondering if you might want to use a few hundred dollars to put new tires on your car. I couldn't help noticing your tread's a little thin. I know it's none of my business…"

She carefully hid how flattered she was that he'd cared enough to notice. "Great idea. New tires all around! And that still leaves a cushion, because the bonus is huge. Thank you thank you thank you. This is so great."

He seemed slightly embarrassed. "Fine. Well, that's the first thing." He held up his keys. "The second thing is, I'm headed over to Woodrow, Mantella, and thought you might want to join me to look at the set-up for reviewing Charlie Reebuck's email."

Moments later they were in Ken's Camry, taking the twenty-minute trip to the law firm. "We're up to fifty-five email reviewers," he recounted as they turned onto El Camino Real. "Another five will be trained tomorrow. The hourly output of each reviewer is up to seventy-one, so that helps."

"You know what they've found so far?"

"As of this morning, we know Reebuck was on notice of the bad deal practice, although we still haven't found an email that shows he actively encouraged it. Two pieces of excellent news: So far, no office outside of San Francisco has been implicated. And there's nothing to suggest that Glen Terkes was informed." He pulled into the parking lot.

"So we can file the Q on time?"

"Looks like it, by the skin of our teeth. But I'd feel a whole lot safer if we could find some way to speed things up. Here we are. Let's see how the team is doing."

Jill's admin led them up coffee-colored, carpeted stairs and opened a door located in the interior of the second floor. Twenty-odd pairs of eyes flicked up as they entered, and then all but one pair flicked back to their computer screens. The remaining pair of eyes, pale gray in a prominently freckled face, lingered on her a moment before their owner looked back at his screen. These twenty-odd people were situated elbow to elbow around a group of mismatched tables dotted with half-empty water bottles and abandoned Starbucks cups. The floor beneath the tables was littered with wadded paper. The combination of heat and lack of oxygen in the room made Georgia immediately lightheaded.

A young woman rose from a desk in a far corner of the room and came to greet them.

"Mr. Madigan?" she asked, shaking his hand. "I'm Catherine DeVoe, I work with Jill." She looked younger than Georgia, but that couldn't be right. It must have been her china-blue eyes and the way her hair was swept into a ponytail. She was still wearing her tailored tan suit jacket in spite of the heat, and sported tiny beads of sweat across her nose.

"Here's the setup. We've got twenty-seven readers in this room, and then the others in the room next door. I don't know where the next five will go. Each of them is hooked to this very unimpressive server over here. We're calling it the Little Server That Could to keep its spirits up."

She pointed to a box about five feet square with yellow and green lights glowing in the far back corner of the room. It looked like something from a low-budget sci-fi movie.

"Our fate is in the hands of that?" Ken asked in disbelief.

"Careful," Catherine warned, "don't blow too hard on it. We had trouble finding anything that could work with those troglodyte tapes of yours, and had no idea it would turn into something this huge. We're afraid any tiny trauma will shut it down and bring all these lawyers to a halt."

"This looks like a huge effort, Catherine. I'd like to say hi to them if that's okay."

"I'm sure they welcome all evidence that somebody knows they exist," she said as one of the readers touched her arm and handed her a document.

"Hello?" Ken called. Twenty-seven pairs of eyes flicked up and fastened on him. Well, twenty-six. The man with gray eyes was watching Georgia again, his asymmetric smile a little wistful in an open, intelligent face. "I'm Ken Madigan, the General Counsel for Lumina Software. Gee, I've never been in a roomful of lawyers that was this quiet." Laughter. "I came here to see your operations, and I'm very impressed with your efforts, if not the equipment." The man who was watching her had brown hair that wouldn't lie flat, evidently, and the sky blue dress shirt that fitted loosely over his lean shoulders had sweat stains under the armpits. Late twenties, she guessed, that slightly asymmetric smile just shy of gorgeous, which made him even more engaging. She smiled faintly back.

"... really appreciate your dedication," Ken was saying. "You could probably all be doing something quite a bit more glamorous than this."

"Yeah, like brushing our teeth," one of the lawyers called out, and Ken laughed with them.

"Although," Ken pointed out, "it might be hard to find something more important to our company. We're grateful for your efforts, and just nobody sneeze in the direction of that unfortunate server." They laughed again as they turned back to their screens. He held the door for Georgia and Catherine as they exited the room. She didn't glance back to see if the man with gray eyes was following her departure.

"We're preparing another batch of hot email to send over to Zack and Jill," Catherine said, holding out the document she'd been given. "But you might want to look at this one now."

Georgia was trying to think of an excuse to ask Catherine the gray-eyed lawyer's name, when Ken handed her the document. "Well!" he said with gallows cheer, "looks like we have problems in Phoenix."

∞

"That's totally awesome about your bonus," Katie-Ann said. "If I'd known, I'd have made another turkey leg." She glanced with faint dismay at the plate of steaming tuna casserole that Georgia had just set in front of her on the folding table. The sun was slanting long rays in through the living room window and across the faded red beanbag chair they'd bought from Goodwill.

"Why don't we have turkey leg tomorrow night, if you have time to make it?" Georgia suggested. "Don't want to spend this bonus money on daily stuff, but we can forget about saving for a while. We can have meat and vegetables more often, instead of so much pasta."

"You know what else, Georgia? Could we use the money to bring Blizzard out here?"

"Blizzard!" Blizzard was their white tomcat. "You know we can't take the slightest chance of letting Johnny and Mama know where we are."

"I guess. Probably freak him out to be by himself in a crate, anyway. But I really miss him. He used to just hang out and lie on my books all the time. Now I'm stuck here doing way more homework than I used to, and he'd be such good company." She poked at her casserole without loading it onto her fork.

"Yeah, he'd be great company. Maybe when Daddy gets out, he'll bring him when he comes to visit."

"Daddy's who I miss the most. You think he'll really get out in six months?"

Georgia poured buttermilk for Katie-Ann and then herself. "No guarantees, but he's giving it his best shot. Worst case, he'll be out next September."

Katie-Ann set her fork down. "Why'd he get caught in the first place? I don't really get what Robbie did."

Georgia considered. Where was the harm, really? "Well. You know Robbie was Daddy's favorite shill for a long time."

"Yeah. Robbie knew how to pretend he was evaluating a situation ve-ry carefully." She mugged a thoughtful frown. "Gave the marks confidence."

"Exactly. So when Daddy decided to expand the business, he let Robbie start running his own scams, with his own shills and everything, just paying Daddy a small percentage."

"That's when Daddy started using Lena Mae for his shill."

"Right. Eat your casserole before it gets cold. Well, one day, Robbie said something that made Lena Mae suspect he was running extra scams on the sly. Turned out Robbie wasn't just holding out on Daddy's percentage. He actually had a list of his and Daddy's old marks, and he was going back and scamming them all over again. It's called 'reloading,' and Daddy was horrified that Robbie could be such a moron."

"Because the marks were onto them already?" Katie-Ann scooped up a forkful of casserole.

Georgia nodded grimly. "The marks were onto them, and of course they were pissed off. The risk was they'd pretend to be fooled and then run to the police. Which is exactly what happened. Daddy shut the reloading down immediately, but one of the recycled marks had already gone to the police about Robbie and Daddy both for some ancient melon drop."

Katie-Ann shook her head in disbelief. "All this trouble for a stupid melon drop! So why isn't Robbie in jail, too?"

"Evidently they couldn't find him. Daddy and I both thought

they'd forget about him fast enough. Not exactly the crime of the century we're dealing with here." She shrugged. "For some reason, they're still interested."

"Wow, do you think they want him for something worse than Daddy knows about?"

Georgia shrugged again, deeply. "We really just don't know. I do know Daddy will think twice before he lets some dumb shill go out on his own again."

"That's why he wants you to go in with him."

"Well, that, and he thinks it would just be fun."

"That's partly why I'm worried about him, Georgia. Daddy doesn't cope with boredom very well. I hope he doesn't get himself in trouble there in that prison."

"He won't," Georgia said with more conviction than she felt. "Daddy knows what's at stake. Anyway, his first parole hearing is coming up in a few months, and he can focus on that. The ultimate scam. He's already working up profiles on all the parole board members."

"Well, Daddy can con the stripes off a skunk, so I guess he's got as good a chance as anybody."

"Absolutely. Daddy's going to be out of jail and causing trouble again in no time." Katie-Ann was poking her food listlessly. "In the meantime, why don't I see if the landlord allows cats? Maybe Blizzard would like a nice buddy when he gets here."

∞

Zack called the meeting to order behind the firmly shut door of the windowless executive conference room early the next morning. Their outside lawyer Jill sat silently, looking rumpled and grim while Ken, Cliff and the rest of the team filed in around her.

"Okay, guys," Zack said in a slightly hushed voice, "I'm sure you all know the review of Reebuck's email has turned up two bad deals in Phoenix. Nothing anywhere else. Cliff, you've told the auditors?"

"We have. Now they insist we do a full-blown review of Phoenix. They're making noise about a full review of all the offices under Charlie Reebuck, but I think I've persuaded them to just do Phoenix, and then if a third office surfaces we'll have to do the whole region."

"Quan," Zack continued, "you've looked at the numbers?"

Quan nodded, raking his thick hair back from his eyes. "Their restored email for the three-year period amounts to another 120,000 emails." Muffled groans.

"So how many hours of reading will that take?" Ken asked. He was the only person in the room who looked fully alert at this hour, with hornet yellow kidney shapes marching in military precision across his red bow tie.

Jill said, "Ken, if I could interject here. I believe it is no longer possible for you to file your 10-Q on time."

The room went deadly quiet. Now they were all awake.

"We see how hard you're driving," she continued, "how committed you are, and we would do anything to help you reach your goals. At some point, though, we've got to confront the fact that it isn't going to happen." *That was why she was here in person. She'd come to take the heat for delivering bad news.*

Ken was sitting ramrod straight as usual, and he pulled his thin lips into a determined line. "Why can't it be done?"

"You heard Quan. You just added another 120,000 emails. Your readers are already going at maximum output, and they're exhausted. They cannot absorb the Phoenix emails."

"Then add more readers."

"Where would you get them?" she objected evenly. "Quan has moved heaven and earth to get the readers you do have. And if you did find more you'd still have to train them, and then it takes a couple of days before they achieve full productivity."

Ken turned to Quan. "How many more readers would we need to get through these additional 120,000 emails in the next eight days?"

Quan flicked his pen over his notepad. "Assuming full productivity for eight to ten hours a day starting in two days…fifteen more readers."

"We can't add fifteen more readers to this server," Jill protested. "It cannot handle the additional volume."

"So get another server," Ken said evenly.

"We have another server, and it's sitting in our delivery bay. The problem is that we have to shut down for at least two days to switch over. That blows your timing right there." *She was determined to persuade him to give up.*

"Ken," Zack added almost gently, "you know how you always accuse me of being an optimist? In this case even I don't see how we can finish in eight more days. The readers we have can't do this much longer."

"Why not?" Georgia objected. "Some people did the entire Civil War." *No reason to get into a whine fest here.*

Everybody glanced at Georgia and then back at Zack. A smile flickered at the corners of Ken's mouth.

"Sad to say, I agree with Zack," Cliff pressed ahead.

"Okay, guys," Ken said, leaning over the table and looking at each of them one by one. "I know you're tired. I also know you realize what's at stake here. Jill tells us we can expect to lose 25 percent of our market cap the day we announce that we're not going to file on time." He pointed a finger for emphasis. "That's 25 percent for being late, irrespective of whether we end up having to file a restatement. Do you recommend I tell Jean-Claude we're losing a quarter of the value of our company because we can't find a way to read some emails?"

Nobody was looking at Ken except Georgia, who struggled not to beam brighter than a lighthouse.

"Believe me," he continued, "I understand doubt. I understand and embrace despair, as long as we don't let it slow us down. I don't know whether we can do this. I know a lot of people are counting on us to do it, and if we don't do it, I want it to be because it was utterly, completely impossible. And how can we know that unless we give it our best shot?"

There was a long, uncomfortable silence, and then Jill said, "I hear you. We'll give it everything we've got."

"Thank you, Jill. That's all I can ask. Zack?"

"I'm in."

"Finance will go all out," Cliff confirmed.

"So, if we can't add more email readers to the server," Georgia asked, "can we add a midnight shift and run around the clock?"

Jill raised an eyebrow. "Good thought. Let me ask our IT guy."

"I will locate fifteen more readers ready to be trained at 10 a.m. tomorrow morning," Quan stated, touching the temples of his rimless glasses.

"I'd like to be one of them," Georgia offered. Who knew? Maybe that gray-eyed lawyer would show up. She could use another look at that asymmetric smile.

"Me, too." Zack stuck his hand in the air and grinned at Georgia. "Maybe we'll get that coveted midnight shift."

"Me, too," Ken said. "In fact, I need to let Roy know he really doesn't have a legal team until this audit is finished."

"I prefer to avoid having you read email if at all possible, Ken," Quan countered politely. "We need you to review whatever we find, and handle any crisis that comes up. If I can find twelve outside readers before the end of the day, then Zack, Georgia and I will round out the team."

"One more thing, Ken," Jill said. "I hope your board is prepared for the level of expense we'll incur when we really pull out the stops."

"They're fully prepared. Jean-Claude told me, 'Ken, you will never hear me say this again in my lifetime, but you have no budget constraints here. Your only constraint is to finish on time.'"

Jill's eyes grew round. "From a former Chief Financial Officer? I've heard enough. Let's go do it."

∞

"I guess I'm confused," Katie-Ann said later, as she proudly set a roast chicken surrounded by carrots and potatoes on the card table. "If you're going to be at a law office from midnight to five every night, when are you going to sleep?" Jill had confirmed the addition of a five-hour nightly graveyard shift, leaving three hours a day to maintain the rickety, retrograde server.

"Haven't figured that out yet," Georgia said, helping herself to the glistening, bright carrots. "God, look at this dinner! It'll be a night or two before I have to sleep, and by then I'll think of something."

"But you'll still be home for dinner?"

"And geometry. Absolutely. You gonna be all right by yourself here at night?"

"You kidding? Alone is way safer than having Reverend Johnny Awknell in the house."

"Good point. I'll have my iPhone in case you need me for something."

"What would I need you for?" Katie-Ann asked breezily with a wave of her hand. "And anyway, it's only a few days."

∞

At 3 o'clock in the morning on Day Four of her midnight-to-five shift, Georgia had read just over half of her nightly target of three hundred twenty emails. She rubbed her eye with the heel of her hand, and took a bitter sip of stone cold coffee. Couldn't conk out now. Just two more hours before the server went offline for its nightly maintenance. She slapped her cheek a few times as quietly as possible, trying not to distract the twenty-three other readers.

Both Zack and Quan were completely lost in concentration. Sartorial standards had sunk to a comfortable new low with this crowd. Zack was wearing cargo shorts and a faded red T-shirt. Even Eddie Fallon (the freckle-faced lawyer with gray eyes) had given up his suit in favor of jeans and an open-necked plaid shirt, which revealed a downright attractive collarbone. He was sitting right across from her now. Any chance she could glimpse those gray eyes through his black eyelashes . . . ?

"Georgia, you need something?" Catherine whispered behind her. Catherine's eyes were blood-shot, and her blond hair had taken on a flat look that meant it could use a washing.

Georgia waved her hand dismissively and covered her yawn. "I'm fine. My zombie just left me dead for a minute while it ran to the bathroom." She was rewarded with Eddie's appreciative snicker and his gray eyes resting on the side of her face. "Don't you have the 8 o'clock shift today?"

Catherine held up a small zippered bag. "My personal grooming kit. Deodorant. Dental floss. Isn't this fun? Backpacking without the view." Catherine was now pulling 36-hour shifts, sleeping in her jeans under her desk during the nightly maintenance.

Georgia acknowledged Eddie with a little smile and went back to reading. The room was completely silent except for the hum of the server and the muffled clicking of keyboards. She was all the way up to two hundred fifty when Quan broke the silence. "Uh-oh."

Zack rotated his bleary eyes sideways onto Georgia. "Did Quan just say 'uh-oh'?"

"I'm afraid he did," she confirmed with a heavy sigh. "Remember what happened the last time he said 'uh-oh'?"

"I sure do. But maybe this is a personal 'uh-oh.' Uh-oh, I'm out of chewing gum. Uh-oh, my fly is open."

Quan laughed. "Unfortunately, this is a sincere, professional uh-oh. But I might very well have misunderstood. I'm printing it for you now."

A moment later he handed an email to Zack and Georgia. It was from someone at Home Depot to Charlie Reebuck:

Charlie,
I have carried your latest proposal to our CEO, and we have a deal. Lumina is obviously very confident that Oracle compatibility will be achieved within the four months we have agreed upon, and

that is sufficient for us. I share your optimism that the promised
de-installation and refund will be unnecessary.
Best,
Rod

"So Charlie did his own side deal directly," Georgia concluded, her pulse starting to thud in her ears.

"It seems he did indeed," Quan confirmed. "And look who it's copied to."

The email was copied to Glen Terkes.

CHAPTER 18

"Terkes??" Ken exclaimed the next morning after a moment of shocked silence. "You gotta be kiddin' me. What are we, four days from filing the Q?" Interesting, Georgia thought, how quickly "Glen" had become "Terkes." Ken was distancing himself already, and the morning sun was just flashing its first glittery rays between the tops of the eucalyptus trees on the far side of the parking lot.

"Maybe it's not as bad as it looks," Zack offered. "Can we tell whether he opened it? Can we tell whether he responded?"

"But that's not up to us anymore, is it?" Ken asked, his green eyes pleading to be contradicted. "Jill said if it's somebody at the executive level, it has to go to the independent firm." He buried his face in his open palms for a long moment, before sliding them down to his chin and puffing his cheeks in a deep sigh. "I tell you, this really is taking on the quality of a nightmare. The ledge we're on gets narrower and narrower. Any minute now we're going to plunge forty stories."

"Can we carve this part out to give to the independent?" Quan suggested. "Maybe we can still complete the rest of the investigation ourselves."

"Has the independent lawyer been briefed?"

"Yes," Quan replied. "Horace. I brief him every morning."

By now Georgia knew Ken well enough to recognize his momentary inner struggle as he set aside panic and began to lead. "That's an excellent idea, Quan. Get Horace on the line, will you? Ask him to stand by for a call from Jean-Claude and me in half an hour."

When they reconvened an hour later, Ken's navy bow tie had been yanked sideways, but his gaze was steady and direct. "Okay, Horace and Jean-Claude agree that we'll split the investigation for now. Horace takes over every aspect of Terkes. He wants restoration of Terkes' email in the two weeks before and after the suspect email. Zack, can you make that happen today? He'll use his own readers to do the review, and then interview Terkes himself, together with a second lawyer from his firm. He intends to finish that and report back to Jean-Claude in three days."

"That's the day before the filing deadline," Quan observed.

"And that's the challenge. Here's where we are, guys. If Horace or the auditors decide to force a complete review of worldwide deals because of this, then it's out of our hands completely. We've done our absolute best, and we turn our attention to minimizing the inevitable delay in filing. However, *if* Horace concludes that Terkes' explanation obviates the need for a broader search, then this was just a momentary distraction that cannot be permitted to slow us down. My suggestion is that we avoid distracting the rest of the email team and say nothing whatever about Terkes until we know which way it's going. Thoughts?"

"Too late," Zack warned. "They were there when we found the email. If you want them to keep killing themselves, you have to tell them it's a false alarm."

"Lie to our team?" Ken said, slightly shocked.

"Not *lying*, Ken. Merely misdirecting with wild optimism. I'm perfect for that. If you want, I'll apologize the minute the Q is filed."

"Do it," Ken decided. "I'll apologize to them personally after the fact, and explain our reasoning. Okay, team, let's finish strong."

∞

It showed excellent foresight not to tell the email army that their heroic efforts could be scuttled in a heartbeat by the independent review of Glen Terkes. Georgia, who fully understood the importance of rushing flat out, still caught herself staring at her screen in the stuffy, windowless email room in the early morning hours, wondering if her time would be better spent at home in bed. Or at least flirting with gray-eyed Eddie.

Eddie sauntered over to where she was watching the printer spit out what looked to her like yet another side deal. "How's your zombie doing this evening?" he asked, gazing down at her with his slightly wistful smile. How did he manage to look that good in the middle of the night? She'd worn her dark blue silk blouse that matched her eyes, but what good was that if her eyes were puffy? Never mind. She felt the heavy silk slide along her arm as she tucked a strand of black hair behind her ear in what she hoped was a seductive gesture.

"My zombie is excellent, thank you, enjoying itself and growing more confident by the hour. It'll miss me terribly if I ever get a good night's sleep again."

"No worries about that anytime soon. But I was wondering, after we do get caught up on our sleep and buying groceries and stuff, would you maybe like to ..."

Her iPhone rang. Ten after three. "Sorry, probably a wrong number."

The screen said Katie-Ann. Georgia snatched it up.

"Somebody's trying to get in the front door!" Katie-Ann's whisper was constricted with fear.

Georgia was on instant hyper-alert. "Have you called 9-1-1?" Eddie's face registered alarm, and she shrugged an apology as she turned away.

"No! They'll start snooping! The door is locked."

"Jesus! You hear someone?"

"I heard something on our doorstep, and then ..."

"What?"

"I—I just saw the door knob move."

Georgia flashed on the creep who'd stared into her car. "Is the chain lock on?"

"No. I left it off for you. But I pushed in the button on the handle."

"Can you hear them now?"

"No."

Georgia race-walked toward the door, leaving Eddie stranded by the printer looking worried. "Okay, Katie-Ann, I'm headed home, walking out the door now. I want you to fake a really loud call to the cops." Zack was calling her name. She gestured impatiently and kept walking.

"You sure?"

"Now, Katie-Ann!"

"HELLO! POLICE? I NEED HELP RIGHT NOW AT 237 WILLOW DRIVE! NUMBER 3-B. THAT'S RIGHT! HURRY!"

"Good! Can you hear anything?"

"Someone's running down the steps!"

"You got 'em," Georgia's voice was confident, but her knees were suddenly weak. "Now go to the door and lock the chain."

"No way!! What if they come through the door?"

"Then go to the kitchen and get a knife." She slammed her car door and started the engine.

"No! I'm sitting here with my back to the wall."

Her tires squealed as she accelerated out of the lot. "Then hang onto the phone and scoot around with your back to the wall until you get to the kitchen. You can do it. I'm in my car, Katie-Ann. Ten minutes. I want you to sit with the knife in one hand and the phone in the other and watch the door. If you hear them come back you have to call 9-1-1. Hear me?"

Katie-Ann's voice was suddenly tiny. "I feel more afraid with this knife in my hand."

"You aren't going to need it. They're gone."

"Who is it, Georgia? Johnny Awknell? Or that weirdo who watched you in your car?"

"Weirdo wouldn't have waited this long. And Awknell would thump his Bible and march right in with a bunch of cops to save your soul," she asserted with more conviction than she felt. Could Awknell be a kidnapper? "Probably just some addict doing rounds for an

226

unlocked door. Long gone by now." Her car was now straddling several lanes as she hurtled down the center of the ghostly, deserted Central Expressway, streaking past multicolored street lights that stretched in a bright confetti parade into the distance.

"Do they know I'm alone?" Her voice was barely audible.

"Doubt it. Five more minutes, Katie-Ann. Stay on the phone with me."

"Shouldn't you put the phone down while you're driving?"

Georgia snorted softly. "Just keep talking to me, okay? Nobody out here for me to hit even if I wanted to." She hoped that was true.

"I don't want to be here alone at night anymore."

"Agree completely," Georgia said grimly. "I'm turning onto our street now. That'll be me at the door in one minute."

Her tires squealed as she braked hard at the curb, and jumped out to find two fat raccoons on the bottom steps leading to her apartment. They stared at her insolently for several seconds, revealing nothing, before waddling over to the storm drain and disappearing below the street.

∞

Two hours later she was still staring up at her dark bedroom ceiling and listening to Katie-Ann's deep breathing, when she suddenly remembered that Eddie Fallon had been abruptly cut off in mid-invitation. Probably the end of that. Not very romantic, really, shouting directives into her cell phone as she ran for the door. Just as well, maybe, since he'd have found out about Katie-Ann soon enough, and who wanted to wade into that kind of domestic hassle? He probably looked a lot better than he really was, anyway. Nobody could possibly be as good as Eddie Fallon looked. She sighed and turned over to face the window.

Could that really be dawn already beyond her blinds? Sure enough, the clock said almost 6. She groaned, threw off her sleeping bag and went to stand in a hot shower.

∽

For the next two nights, Ken took Georgia's shift on the email review. When she protested (weakly) he said it was simply the best allocation of resources to keep all critical functions moving ahead. Very objective, nodding soberly, his bow tie firmly in place. She smiled each time she remembered it, as she worked alone through the night in her living room, surrounded by stacks of documents, brewing coffee to keep herself awake while Katie-Ann slept peacefully in the next room. At one point she jerked awake from a deep sleep, her cheek pockmarked and tender from the coarse living-room carpet, bright sun backlighting the thin, yellow kitchen curtains. She realized how little it mattered that she'd fallen asleep and tried not to feel side-lined. She wondered if she'd ever lay eyes on Eddie Fallon again.

On the third morning she joined Ken, Zack and Quan in Jill's office. "Boy," Ken said appreciatively, "we all look like hell." Quan quickly calculated a collective sleep deficit of fifty-seven hours.

"Okay," Ken continued, "here's the result Horace just delivered to Jean-Claude. The independent email search shows no response to the Reebuck email and no other related correspondence. Horace interviewed Terkes, who has no recollection of seeing the email, and states if he had he would have stopped the deal."

"Wow," Quan said. "Perfect answer. Do you believe it?" Evidently not, thought Georgia, since Ken was still calling him 'Terkes.'

"Fortunately for Lumina Software, it doesn't matter what I believe," Ken responded with a muted smile. "What matters is what the independent investigator believes, and he believes the story is credible and that no further investigation of Glen Terkes is necessary."

"Perfect," Zack pronounced, "so we'll assume the teeth on this gift horse are pearly white. Have the auditors bought off on it?"

"Horace will report directly to the auditors today, with Jean-Claude present. Between the two of them, they think the auditors can be convinced."

"In that case," Quan declared, standing up, "all we have to do is read 30,000 emails in the next"—he consulted his watch—"forty-six hours."

∞

At dawn on the morning before the filing deadline, the Lumina side deal team (minus Ken) filed into the long-deserted basement Diligence room, and dropped themselves wearily onto metal folding chairs. After the hell-hot sensory deprivation of the email reading room at Woodrow, Mantella, the foot-high window overlooking a parking lot seemed like open air in a meadow.

"All right guys, let's get started," Zack said. "Big news from Quan."

"As of 5:25 this morning," Quan reported, "the email review is complete." The group whistled and applauded, which Zack immediately suppressed by pushing his flat palms firmly toward them. "Unfortunately, we're now three days behind schedule, so we don't know whether finance can finish its evaluation on time."

"We can do it," pronounced Terry of Internal Audit. Sotto voce cheers. "We will meet the goal of pencils down and handover to the auditors by midnight tonight.

"The crazy thing is," Terry continued, "we still don't know what the answer will be. Right now, the change in Q4 of last year is big enough to require a restatement." The crowd caught its collective breath. "Unless a deal gets re-bucketed into that quarter, we'll have to publicly restate our earnings for that quarter. And if another ten thousand falls out of Q2 of '09, we'll have to restate our earnings there as well."

"Guys, we don't control the outcome," Zack reminded them. "It would be terrible to lose market value, but we didn't make this mess. Ken told us our job was to get the answer in time, and it looks like we're gonna make it. I think we should be very proud of ourselves." Which was sort of like something Ken would say.

∞

At 7:05 the following morning Ken informed Jean-Claude and the Audit Committee that the results of the investigation had been handed over to the auditors, and (to everyone's astonishment) no restatement of earnings was required after all. Jean-Claude convened a board meeting one hour later.

"Okay," he pronounced to the only four members who were physically present, "we are here to review the 10-Q before we file it today. It seems we must owe another big congratulation to Ken and his team. This time we don't get a bump up in our stock, but we avoid a big bump down, which is slightly less thrilling but equally valuable." He grinned broadly. "Some of you may know that Ken and I spoke at least twice per week for the last six weeks, and it really was—how do you say—hair lifting? I must say I am extremely surprised and impressed by this outcome."

"Very impressive," Larry agreed with a patrician nod. Roy nodded stiffly and silently, his small black eyes watchful over the rims of his narrow oval glasses.

"And what have we done about the people responsible?" Jared called through the speakerphone.

"We haven't finalized that," Ken said. "I hope to resolve it by the end of next week."

"In any event," Jean-Claude said, "now that we have this dangerous episode behind us, we may expect an impressive quarter."

Later that day Lumina Software quietly filed its 10-Q on time. Shareholders learned that the company had achieved solid 7 percent revenue growth and that the SAP litigation was now behind them. Happily, they learned nothing of the near-death experience that had been averted by a matter of hours.

∞

"Georgia, could I speak to you a moment in the conference room?" Beatrice was standing in the door of her cube, looking delicate and demure with her dark skirt and white Peter Pan collar covering her compact forty-year-old frame. She'd been looking tired ever since the incident with Sally, but this morning she seemed calm and rested. "I wanted to let you know," she continued, closing the conference room door, "that I have decided to accept a position at Seagate Technology." *So that's why she looked better. She was escaping the Nusty Beech.*

"That's terrible," Georgia responded. "Does Ken know?"

"Oh, yes. And Sally. I spoke to her quite frankly when she came to me, right after Ken forced her to …" Beatrice smiled knowingly. "But she didn't apologize. She told me I misunderstood her, but, Georgia, I didn't misunderstand her tone of voice to me. She believes I am nothing. If I stayed here, I would have to work with her, so it's time for me to go. Even though I am so sorry to be leaving Ken."

"What a huge loss for all of us. I just hope this penetrates the dense skull of our HR queen, and she learns something from it."

"I do, too, Georgia, but I don't think you should expect it. She acts this way because it gratifies her. Thank you for taking this time with me. I think it's really good for the company that you're here."

Georgia wandered down to Ken's office, and found Maggie and Beatrice's assistant Suzanne already with him. "This a Beatrice meeting?" she asked. "Can I join?"

"Come on in, Georgia," Ken said. "We'll probably all be in here before the end of the day."

"Can you talk her out of it?" Georgia asked.

"No." Ken shook his head sadly. "If it was about more money, I could get her more money. But Beatrice didn't say a word to me until her mind was completely made up. We've lost her."

"What I don't understand," Suzanne said, "is how we're going to cope until we get her replacement. How are we going to finish the options memo?"

"What memo is that?" Georgia asked.

"Oh, you know, all this backdating stuff. The board asked us to research all the company's option practices going back three years. Beatrice is the one who knows everything."

"Sally said her team can pick up the slack," Ken said.

"No way!" Suzanne protested. "It's impossible to get the basic data out of her team as it is." She put her face in her hands. "I'm gonna be next. If Beatrice couldn't stand it, how will I?"

Georgia thought it was a very good question.

"Hi," Zack interrupted, knocking on Ken's door frame. "Is this the Sally Kurtz hanging posse? Can I join?" Clever, Georgia noted sourly, but a clever joke was still useless. If there was ever going to be a real hanging posse, it would consist entirely of one Georgia Griffin. Too late to help Beatrice, of course, but time for Georgia and the Nusty Beech to develop some rapport.

∞

Georgia was relieved that Nikki showed no interest in taking back management of the executive committee and board meetings as her migraines diminished. When Georgia arrived in the boardroom just before 9 a.m. for the next executive team meeting, Andrea was already in the room with her laptop open, her black turtleneck accentuating her blond, no-nonsense hair. Georgia was setting up the speakerphone when Sally entered, hugging her laptop and thereby obscuring one or two of the gigantic orange poppies on her salmon pink dress. That dress would make a strobe light squint.

"Sally," Andrea called, her eyes still on her computer screen.

"Yes?" Sally answered warily.

"I understand you told Lucy Feiffer you want to be in on the interviews for my new head of product."

"Yes. Just the finalists."

"No," Andrea said.

"No, what?"

"No, you cannot interview my new head of product. Lucy's great."

"I know she's great, but this is an important position."

"Precisely," Andrea agreed, and now she looked squarely at Sally. "A very important position, whose sole criterion needs to be talent and experience for doing the job. You'll just have to hire your political allies somewhere else."

Georgia tried to seem deaf and oblivious as she lowered the PowerPoint screen in the front of the room and adjusted the blinds.

Sally drew herself up until her spine threatened to fly into pieces. "Roy wants me involved in all key hires. Shall I talk to him?"

"Hmm." Andrea tapped her cheek with an index finger, feigning deliberation. "Wow. I don't seem to care who you talk to, as long as you don't talk to my candidates."

The skirmish ended abruptly as Glen Terkes slouched into the room in his finest silver Armani summer suit, carefully paired with a royal blue silk shirt. He smirked faintly in apparent recognition of the charged atmosphere, ran his eyes along Georgia's body, and then adjusted his cuffs as he seated himself loftily at the far end of the table. Well, she thought, his self-confidence certainly hadn't been diminished by his encounter with Horace regarding the side deal email. If anything, it had been enhanced.

She made sure the latest renovation drawings were up on easels and covered by flip chart paper. She began taking attendance as the rest of the executive team filed into the room.

"Good morning," Roy called as he entered, glancing around the room with free-floating contempt. "I have some preliminary announcements." He held his blue and gold striped tie against his chest as he seated himself at the head of the table.

"This is our first meeting since we put the SAP lawsuit behind us, and I want to start by acknowledging Ken for making that happen. It should have happened before we lined our lawyers' pockets to the tune of twenty-four million, but still, it is behind us." Sort of a grudging compliment. Georgia glanced at Ken, who without looking at her dropped his eyelid in a slow wink.

"Second, I wanted to let you know that our acquisition of Futuresoft has been delayed, perhaps indefinitely." She felt rather than saw Burt contract into himself, as if expecting a blow. "Some quite zealous investigation on the part of our legal department has revealed certain issues that Futuresoft will have to address before we proceed." The word 'zealous' apparently tasted like biting down on a lime. Was he planning to blame Ken instead of Burt, after all? "I'll let you know if and when we revive it, but this leaves a fairly big hole in our revenue planning for the rest of this year and next. We'll be talking later about how we're going to fill in that gap.

"Speaking of revenue gaps, we have learned that our Home Depot deal for $1.2 million won't be booked in this quarter after all. It seems Home Depot is insisting that we deliver Oracle-compatible updates within 160 days, so we can't book the revenue until we've done that. Glen will also need us to help him make up that revenue in the short amount of time remaining in the quarter."

"I need Oracle compatibility in the worst way," Glen stated.

"Of course you do. Andrea will report on that shortly, and I fully expect the news to be good.

"Finally, I have two important organizational announcements. First, I have decided to consolidate sales and technical support under a single leader, to facilitate better coordination between the two groups. Mark will therefore report to Glen, effective immediately."

The only reaction in the silent room was that Mark Balog's tight smile got slightly tighter. So everybody knew already.

Roy continued, "Mark will continue to attend our executive committee meetings, at least for the time being. I want to congratulate Glen on his new role, which I am confident he will fill most ably." Glen acknowledged his promotion with one regal, unsmiling nod.

"Second, I have decided to consolidate employee communication under Sally. Internal communication is a vital part of reducing attrition, and I want Sally to have all relevant resources at her disposal."

Georgia text message to Ken: *'queen xpands hr fiefdom. now she can lv us alone for a while?'*

Text message back: *'enjoy yr pleasant dream.'*

"And I'd also like to announce," Roy continued, "that employee communication itself has a new leader, reporting to Sally. That new leader, as of next week, is Burt Plowfield." Around the table the whole team seemed to jerk in unison. Burt's pale face turned pink, and his neck disappeared into his rounded shoulders. "Burt has already started work on the new 'management is listening' posters, and will have a proposal for us on that shortly. He will no longer remain on the executive committee, although he will join us from time to time at Sally's discretion. Congratulations, Sally and Burt, on your new roles."

Surely Burt had been told. Just as surely, nobody else had. The entire team was looking everywhere except at Burt. Andrea was suddenly extremely busy with her keyboard.

Text message from Ken: *'Jesus Mary & Joseph!'*

Georgia to Ken: *'kinder to just fire him?'*

"Thank you for this vote of confidence, Roy," Sally was saying with her fake shy smile. "I will certainly try to live up to it."

"Of course, you all realize this creates a vacancy at the head of corporate development. I expect to announce a new leader there in a few weeks.

"Okay, Andrea, the 6.1."

Andrea reported that the 6.1 would fix 52 of the 76 major bugs in the 6.0. "Of course the big issue is Oracle compatibility. We expect to have 10 of the 13 most likely configurations by the scheduled release date."

"I need every configuration," Glen asserted flatly. "What would it take to get that?"

Andrea scratched her eyebrow with a fingernail. "Supernatural intervention. You have a contact?"

"That's cleverly put, as usual, Andrea," Roy said, "but your results are inadequate and disappointing."

"I'm sure they are, Roy, but they have the advantage of being real. In the meantime, Mark has put together a plan to allow a surge in 6.1 sales with the degree of SAP compatibility we will have. Mark, can you describe it?"

"I will, Andrea, thank you," Mark said. "My team has developed a diagnostic to tell within twenty minutes whether a customer who needs Oracle compatibility will have it with the 6.1. Here's the matrix up on the screen now. Isn't this perfect? Great teamwork by Andrea's team and mine."

"Good work, Mark," Ken said. Other EC members murmured their agreement.

"Now there's just one thing," Mark continued. "Because of the increased business we anticipate from this, as well as the extensive workaround time to get existing customers updated to the new version, I need eight additional headcount approval immediately so that I can get them up to speed by day one. The total additional cost would be..."

"Glen," Roy interrupted, "your evaluation of this need?"

"Haven't studied it yet," Glen said, his voice deepening with importance. "With the loss of the $1.2 million and the other anticipated revenue shortfall, I'm inclined to think we need to just stretch the people Mark already has."

"I'm glad you suggested that, Glen," Mark beamed crazily, "because I can show everybody why it won't work. This chart I've put up shows the average number of hours my team has been putting in daily, beginning two weeks after we shipped the 6.0. You'll see that 70 percent of them have put in 15.2 hours per day seven days a week for..."

"Mark," interrupted Roy, holding up his hand, "you need to share this data with Glen rather than the rest of us. It's up to him to make the right recommendation."

"But we only have three..."

"Thanks, Mark," Glen said, holding up the palm of his hand. "We'll discuss this privately." He nodded to Roy.

"Good. Andrea, I'd like to see you in my office immediately

following this meeting. Okay, Georgia, will you ask our architect to join us regarding the renovation?"

"Let me get him for you," Mark said, his smile approaching rictus. "I need to step out anyway." He hurried out through the swinging door.

"Okay," the architect said a moment later, standing next to the flip chart, "here's the latest iteration of our plans for this floor. We've made a number of changes in response to your comments. For example, legal now has three designated meeting rooms instead of two."

"Take a good look at this version," Roy advised, "because I think we're getting close. We've addressed your concerns. Any major problems?" he asked, shaking his head from side to side.

"I'm afraid so, Roy," Ken said. "I appreciate the addition of one more meeting room, but it really doesn't solve my problem. I still have three work spaces for nine lawyers, and that just isn't going to work."

"We pay lawyers to argue, don't we?" Roy said to the group with a little smirk, "so I guess we can't criticize him for arguing with me. But you're just going to have to make do with what you've got, Ken. Anything else?"

"If we're worried about making our revenue numbers," Andrea said, "would this renovation be a good place to delay expense? That might allow us to give Mark the headcount he needs to respond quickly to our 6.1 customers."

Roy glared at her over his tented fingers. "If you focus on delivering what you've owed us for a very long time now, the necessary revenue will follow. Anything else?"

The team sat politely, their hands folded in their laps or their arms crossed.

"Looks like we have a go," Sally said, quivering with excitement. "How soon can we expect to be in our great new space?"

"We're going to start with this floor," the architect replied. "You should be in your new space by October."

"Thank you," Roy said with a nod of dismissal. "Sally, are you ready to talk about attrition?"

"I am, Roy," An image floated in on the PowerPoint screen with three big, purple arrows curving out of an oval marked 'stable employee base.' "Let's start with the 'management is listening' initiative, which as you know is being headed up by Burt. Burt, would you like to comment on that?"

"Oh, thanks, Sally. I'd prefer to address it in two weeks, when I'll have actual mock-ups of some of the posters we're planning to use."

Text to Ken: *'How did Burt get ths job? We all wnted it.'*

Ken to Georgia: *'Andrea and I almst got it.'*

Georgia considered as her fingers flew over the keyboard. Burt Plowfield thanking Sally Kurtz for the opportunity to speak to the executive team? That relationship was about as stable as ice cream in a hot skillet. Nikki had called Roy tone deaf, but how could anybody be this oblivious?

She hurried into Nikki's office as soon as the meeting ended, closed the door and pulled a chair close to Nikki's desk to report the highlights.

"Wow," Nikki said, her brown eyes wide with astonishment, "I guess that answers your question about Burt being good at his job. I must say, Roy was beside himself after that Futuresoft board meeting. He thinks Burt cost him the deal."

Georgia grimaced. "Yeah, the board didn't seem to like him much. What impresses me from this morning is the way Andrea took on the Nusty Beech."

Nikki laughed. "I'd have loved to see that. I think baiting Sally is blood sport for Andrea. Just wish I had her chutzpah. By the way, did you know Sally's newest admin quit?"

"Marta? She just got here."

Nikki nodded, her forefinger partly obscuring a knowing smile. "Under two weeks. Sally's record is actually deteriorating, and now Roy wants me to help her, since 'we're all on the same team.'" She used her fingers to make air quotes.

"Just be too busy."

Nikki smiled ruefully and shook her head. "Wouldn't be very professional. I'm sure she does need help. In fact, I need to go over there now to get her approval on this invoice before I pay it."

Perfect opportunity.

"Let me take it to her. I need to talk to her about something else, anyway."

"You sure? She bites."

Georgia held out her hand to take the invoice. "Since she poisoned Beatrice I carry anti-venom syrup at all times."

∞

Sally heaved an aggrieved sigh as she initialed the invoice, thrust it back at Georgia and resumed reading, leaving Georgia stranded on the carpet in front of her desk. The last leaf on the rubber plant was as limp as a handkerchief.

"I, um, was sorry to hear that Marta left." Sally slowly lifted her eyes, and pivoted her head to stare at Georgia with weary disbelief.

Georgia rushed ahead. "I know it can take time to find the right fit with an admin. I just wanted to let you know if you need a liaison with the legal department in the meantime, I'm happy to help. After all, we're all on the same team."

Sally resumed reading. "That'll be all. Thanks."

Georgia stood her ground, until Sally looked up with murder in her eyes.

"For example," Georgia continued, "I wanted to be sure you know there's a new ethics investigation." Painful to reveal this, but she had to get Sally's confidence somehow. What would Ken say? Out of the corner of her eye, she saw those two little heads on the wall stare at her in baleful warning.

"Really." Sally put her document down and touched the scar just above her eyebrow, granting Georgia her full attention. "Tell me about it."

"Well." Georgia lowered her voice and leaned closer. "This one is possible credit card fraud by one of our employees. He might have been double billing for his travel expenses."

Sally's face relaxed into a gracious smile. "And whose department is this?"

"I'm not supposed to tell anyone that." Georgia hesitated. "Well, but I'm sure they don't mean the head of Human Resources. Just don't tell anybody I told you, okay?"

"Of course not." Sally probably thought her smile was reassuring, but it reminded Georgia of that prison guard's wolfish grin, right before she shoved him.

"Okay, well, it was the procurement department. They're still collecting facts, so I don't know when they'll interview him. If you'd like, I can stop by now and then to keep you updated, you know, generally."

"Thank you, Georgia, I would appreciate that very much. After all, as you say, we're all on the same team. I wonder why some other people in this company don't have your common sense."

It wasn't really common sense, Georgia thought modestly as she carried the invoice back to Nikki. It was more the ability to look at somebody and see the actual person, instead of just your own ideas about the person. It was the ability to quiet your mind and contemplate someone, and then wait until the person's fault lines floated to the surface like a magic map to buried treasure. Even scarcer than common sense, she suspected, and sometimes a lot more useful.

∞

Dear Daddy,
I hope you are doing well under your difficult circumstances and keeping your spirits up. How is your novel coming along?
I myself am feeling discouraged. Although I have now eliminated three incompetents from our ranks, we are still beset by morons on every side. How did a whole company get to be so

dysfunctional, and why doesn't it just collapse under the weight of its own idiocy?

Your loving daughter,

Georgia

Dearest Georgia,

Idiocy doesn't weigh much.

I wish I could offer shock and surprise in response to your no-doubt accurate description of half-wits and lazy people infesting your company. Instead I can only offer empathy, along with profound respect for your zero tolerance approach. Sometimes it seems that all organizations are dysfunctional, and it's only a matter of degree and variety. I don't think you should accept that, ever. Only think of the competitive advantage if you ever create an environment in which every person pulls her own weight and cares about the outcome. Persist, my dear! (By the way, would you feel better if you relieved a few of these lesser employees of their spare cash? I'm sure Katie-Ann would enjoy some new clothes.)

As for me, in addition to my fiction project, I am keeping my skills and spirits up by evaluating every guard and inmate and then devising the perfect, customized scam for each of them. I can't actually do anything while I'm in here, of course, as it is fairly close quarters and you might say everyone knows my address. I do believe, however, that I have devised one or two promising schemes that will be great fun to implement as soon as I return to my rightful environment.

And of course I have the pleasure of the books you sent me. I finished Await Your Reply *in twenty-four hours. That main character was a man of true talent, and I was sorry to see his career cut short in such an unpleasant way.*

I am now enjoying Team of Rivals *a few chapters at a time. We are very fortunate that we love learning new things. Not like my pseudo-intellectual brother, who acts so high and mighty around us, as if one paltry degree from some middling religious school makes him the educated member of the family.*

Take care, Georgia, and don't let the chuckleheads get you down.

Love as always,
Your Daddy

CHAPTER 19

"These recommendations are devoid of all business sense," Roy stated flatly, his black eyes boring into Zack. Seven people, including Roy and Sally, were meeting to get sign-off to fire the ten wrongdoers in the side deal debacle. It was so cold in the boardroom that Georgia's skin was tender.

"I know from Glen that losing Charlie Reebuck would be a devastating blow, as would the loss of the San Francisco manager," Roy continued, tossing the list back across the table. "You need a different conclusion." So he intended to choose his desired outcome, and then marshal facts to support it. This could be a long meeting.

"We certainly want to go over the facts with you, Roy," Ken said quickly, drawing Roy's glare away from Zack and pointing to a stack of green vinyl binders. "We want you to see the evidence for yourself. Should we start with Charlie?"

For the next hour Quan, Zack and Terry from Internal Audit led a discussion in painstaking detail of each of the ten employees for whom termination was recommended. At the end of the discussion, there was consensus that the seven sales executives and the controller would be fired. The fates of Charlie Reebuck and the head of the San Francisco office remained undecided.

"In spite of your 'evidence'," Roy said, "I do not accept that it is in the shareholders' interest to terminate an extraordinary sales executive like Charlie Reebuck. We've let this investigation get out of hand."

Ken's eyes widened in surprise. "How so, Roy?"

Too many facts, thought Georgia sourly. Too risky to text message right under Roy's nose in such a little meeting, but how did people survive these meetings?

"Somehow we managed to spend over $4 million dollars to unearth less than $1 million in bad revenue. We had huge teams of lawyers reviewing a mountain of irrelevant email, and now you're suggesting we lose a substantial portion of our most productive sales team as well. I wouldn't permit our company to be dragged into something like this again."

"So unfortunate," Sally echoed, shaking her head soberly.

"I guess I'm a little confused." Ken's eyebrows were squeezed together, his head cocked to one side. "Are you saying we had a choice? This investigation was driven by the auditors and by SEC requirements. We consulted Jean-Claude every step of the way. We found bad deals that required moving several million dollars from one quarter to another, and we're extremely fortunate they didn't trigger a restatement." He ignored Roy's impatient hand signal that tried to cut him off. "As to the employees, Roy, I share your disappointment that we found so many who were willing to violate the rules. It's painful to fire them, but how else do we avoid the same problem all over again?"

"We're not going to have the same problem all over again," Roy responded. "I won't allow it. I shouldn't have allowed it this time."

Ken looked genuinely mystified. Not surprising, thought Georgia, since Roy was making no sense. Another case of intermittent marble loss? Or did Roy think he was so powerful he could rewrite history, and people would embrace it as truth? She glanced at Zack, whose face was carefully impassive. Her thumbs were just itching to text him about it.

"Well..." Ken began and then paused, reconsidering. "In any event, the immediate decision is whether to terminate Charlie Reebuck. Given the wealth of evidence, I just don't see how we justify terminating the individual players and not the manager who actively encouraged them. And by the way, he did acknowledge he's a compulsive liar."

"Sally?" Roy asked.

Sally heaved a sigh of deep regret. "Well, it's just so unfortunate

that it got this far. We really should have contained it better." *Uh-oh.*
Shared delusion? Or Sally just sucking up again? "Given where we are,
though, I don't really see how we can be harder on the sales executives
than we are on Charlie. Maybe we need to let them all off with a
warning."

"No!" the Internal Audit person shouted, apparently startling even
himself. "I mean, please," he continued more quietly, pressing his palm
to his tie, "I could never enforce our finance rules if word got out that
we let these guys off."

"He's right," Ken said. "How would we justify firing the next guy,
if we let all of these go free?"

"Well," Roy said, "then you're telling me we have no choice. I
don't accept that. Ken and Sally, I want you to come back to me in
twenty-four hours with a sound basis for keeping Charlie Reebuck. Tell
Nikki to schedule fifteen minutes." He rose from his chair. "I think
that's quite enough for today on this subject. I'll see the two of you
tomorrow." He disappeared through the door into his office.

Zack and Quan exchanged glances in the silence fostered by
Sally's continued presence. Ken began to speak to Sally about Charlie
Reebuck as Georgia and the others filed out of the room. Well, she
had no idea how Ken would manage his interaction with Sally, but she
knew how to manage hers. Time to feed Sally some more harmless,
rapport-building information.

She knocked on Sally's door an hour later and stuck her head in.
Sally was at her table with Lucy Feiffer. "Oh. Sorry," Georgia mumbled, and started to back out again.

"No, Georgia, it's fine," Sally called with a welcoming smile. "Lucy
and I were just finishing. Come in, have a seat. Would you like an
Odwalla?" Hostess with the mostest. Georgia ignored Lucy's curious
gaze as she disappeared behind the closing door.

"How go the admin interviews?" Georgia asked.

Sally waved her hand and sighed. "I've seen two resumes, and they
were both completely unqualified. But never mind that. What's new in

the legal department?" Her canine teeth sparkled.

"Well, not too much, I guess. The paper trail on that credit card fraud looks pretty damaging, but they still have to interview the guy. And then the only other thing is that situation in Italy."

"Italy," Sally repeated, interlacing her fingers into one big, braided fist on the table top. "Tell me about that."

"Well, they just hired a new head of sales for Italy, and now somebody told Ken in confidence that the guy was dismissed from his last job because of an ethics violation."

"That's ridiculous." Sally curled her lip with disgust. "Didn't they do a background check?"

"Well, they might have, but it didn't turn this up. In fact, the only reason Ken found out about it is that somebody who used to work at the guy's former company contacted Ken in complete confidence."

"I see," Sally said. "So what is Ken's plan?"

"I'm pretty sure he's going to ask for Roy's help with it. He mentioned they have a meeting tomorrow."

"Interesting. Thank you, Georgia. And what else?"

Georgia shrugged. "Nothing else, really. We're busy, but it's pretty routine stuff."

"Great. Thanks for stopping by. I really appreciate your efforts to keep our departments working well together."

"Oh, no problem. Good luck with your admin search. It's worth holding out for somebody terrific."

∞

"Thanks for making dinner tonight, Katie-Ann," Georgia said, resting a pot on a stained potholder on their rickety card table. "Big help." She began spooning black-eyed pea chili into Katie-Ann's bowl.

"No problem. I got my geometry test back today."

"And?" Georgia paused, the serving spoon suspended over her bowl. Katie-Ann shrugged. "C plus."

"C plus? That's a huge improvement over F. The tutoring must be paying off."

"I guess. That girl Ginger saw my paper, though, and she still made fun of me to those other girls who follow her around."

Georgia joined Katie-Ann at the table and spread her paper towel across her lap. "Ginger and her friends don't amount to a wart on the backside of a sorry hog, Katie-Ann. You're making real progress. I hope you feel proud of yourself."

"And I think I can do better for sure. Ginger Bitch is more important than you think, though. People really listen to her."

"Don't say 'bitch.' Yeah, those so-called popular girls can cause a lot of misery. Just don't let her see that she's getting to you." She held up her car keys. "Forget Ginger. After dinner, we'll head over to Happy Donuts and celebrate."

∞

"Guys, I just had an odd conversation with Roy." Ken had asked Zack and Georgia to join him in his office, and they were standing in the area between his desk and his oval conference table.

"Odder than usual?" Zack asked mildly.

"I take your point, but yes. I went to talk to him about the Italy matter, and he said Sally had already told him about it."

Zack frowned. "How did Sally know?"

"Exactly my point. Anton was absolutely clear that he couldn't go through Human Resources, because he didn't trust their discretion. So who told Sally?"

"Maybe the head of sales for Europe?"

"Don't think he knew about it, either. I hope we don't have a leak here in the department." Georgia began breathing deeply, careful not to look startled as her pulse began to sound in her ears.

"But the three of us are the only ones who know about it," Zack objected. *Argh! Really?*

247

Georgia tried to make her voice casual. "Anton must have told somebody else. Or maybe Sally overheard something through the walls?" *Fucking hell. Would Sally be smart enough to cover if Ken asked her about it?*

"Don't know," Ken said, "but we need to be careful. I'll mention it at our next team meeting. This one turned out okay, but next time it could cause real trouble."

Big trouble, Georgia concurred as she hurried out of his office, though not in the way Ken feared. She'd been so intent on choosing information that was harmless that she'd forgotten almost nobody knew about it. Didn't sound like Ken would pursue it, but you didn't get a lot of chances to be sloppy with this stuff. Imagining how disappointed her father would have been, Georgia winced.

∞

Georgia responded to Ken's summons and found him standing next to his oval conference table, his laptop under one arm and a notepad in his hand. His pale gray bow tie set off the green of his eyes as he looked at her in greeting. "Georgia, there you are. I'd like your help with something. Roy was just in here, and it looks like the company might be doing an earnings preannouncement. You know what that is?"

Georgia shook her head. "Sorry. Maybe you should start with what a plain old 'earnings announcement' is." That tie also brought out the red in his military-style hair. It was a good tie.

"Happy to," he agreed, "but can we start walking? Okay, so our 10-Q is the official public document that tells investors how we did for the quarter."

"Right."

"Frankly, it's a little dry."

Georgia's laugh caused two people to glance up from their desks.

"Fine. Make that very dry. So we also do a conference call at the end of every quarter for two reasons. First, we 'announce' in plain English how we did for the quarter, and answer questions about it. That's the 'announcement.' Second, we predict how we're going to do in the upcoming quarter. That's called 'guidance.' So it's an announcement about the past, and then guidance for the future. With me so far?"

Georgia nodded, hurrying to keep up. Good thing she was 'lanky' as her father called her.

"Great." He lowered his voice, and held his notepad at an angle near his mouth to muffle the sound. "Now, if we find out in the middle of a quarter that the guidance we've given is wrong, then we sometimes have a legal obligation to go out with a press release to correct the guidance. That's called a preannouncement, and it's both rare and very unfortunate. Our shareholders could easily lose several hundred million dollars when the stock drops. Evidently, Roy thinks we might have to do one for this quarter that's about to end."

He dropped the notepad away from his face and resumed his normal volume. "So. I'm headed into a meeting to discuss it, and we need your help with the press release. Here we are." He held the frosted swinging glass door so that she could enter the boardroom.

The room had been transformed by sheer body count and nervous energy into command central. Cliff was walking back and forth behind a tightly packed row of finance people, whose voices created a low, urgent hum as they reviewed and debated the data on each other's screens. Someone handed her a set of financial charts, and she squeezed herself in next to Ken at the far end of the table and opened her laptop. After a moment Roy entered through the side door from his office and the room fell silent.

"Okay, Cliff, tell us where we are."

Cliff stood behind his chair and rested his hands on the chair back. "We've just done a region-by-region summary for this quarter, and the news isn't good. The bottom line is we think we're going to be at least $8 million below street expectation on license revenue.

"We think it's big enough," he added, "that we should do a preannouncement in the next forty-eight hours."

"Wait a minute, though," Ken said as he studied his copy of the chart. "This is about license revenue? We don't give guidance on license revenue. We only give guidance on total revenue."

"True," Cliff said, "but that doesn't stop the analysts from making their own predictions. This is going to be such a big disappointment in the marketplace that we ought to get the word out early so that we don't look like we're trying to hide anything."

"I must be missing something," Ken responded, looking up from the charts. "We never have any obligation to comment on analysts' speculations about our company. That includes their speculations about license revenue. So how could we be accused of hiding anything? We don't want to hurt ourselves in the market if we don't have to."

"We're going to miss on total revenue and earnings as well," Cliff said. "And we did give guidance on those."

"By how much?"

"We don't know that yet. It looks like about $3 million to $5 million on revenue, and probably a point or two on earnings."

"When will you know?" Ken asked.

"To know exactly will take another two or three weeks, after the auditors sign off."

"Then I guess I have two issues," Ken said. "My first issue is that we have no obligation to say anything at all about license revenue. You seem to be saying you might want to do that for nonlegal reasons."

"Right," Cliff said.

"Setting that aside for a moment, my second issue is that we shouldn't 'correct' our guidance before we have accurate information to correct it with. I mean, isn't there a chance that we'll find more revenue and hit the low end of our guidance?"

"Nice wishing, Ken," Cliff said, "but we're not going to find another $5 million in revenue."

Ken ignored Cliff's patronizing smile. "Okay, but whenever you preannounce something, you call a lot more attention to how bad it is. And here's a basic truth: You go out into the market with a correction, the correction had better be right. Otherwise, you get clobbered once now, and then clobbered again when your correction is wrong." He sounded like he wouldn't mind doing some clobbering himself. She noticed with alarm that his face was taking on the dark red tinge that she associated with Irish temper.

"Nobody's going to get clobbered," Roy declared, holding up his hand. "My decision is made. We're going out with the preannouncement."

Ken was silent a moment, his lips in that alarming straight line. "Have we told the board?"

"Not yet," Roy replied. "I'll do that as soon as I have the draft press release," Roy replied. "We'll turn to that now."

Two days later the preannouncement regarding Lumina Software's anticipated disappointing quarterly results hit the wires. By the end of the day the stock price had dropped from 38 to 32. On day three it stabilized at 26. The company had lost $1.2 billion, roughly a third of its market value, in three days. Georgia found the plunge terrifying, but Roy appeared to take grim comfort in the fact that they had gotten the news out promptly, and thereby preserved their credibility with the street.

∾

Roy was sporting an uncharacteristic smile as he entered the Executive Committee meeting through the connecting door from his office. Georgia watched an elegantly dressed man in his late thirties follow Roy into the room, a tall man with curly black hair and the subtle swagger of a man who believes women find him attractive.

"Over here, Giuseppe," Sally called enthusiastically, pulling out the chair next to her. He dutifully joined her.

"We have an important agenda this morning," Roy said, holding his maroon and gold striped tie against his chest as he seated himself. "I'd like to begin by introducing our new head of business development,

Giuseppe Coppola."

From the looks of astonishment and intense interest around the table, Georgia guessed that most team members hadn't interviewed Mr. Coppola. Text message to Ken: *u know him?*

Response: *Didn't knw we wr interviewing.*

"I'm going to let Giuseppe introduce himself in a minute, but I'd like to begin by saying we are very fortunate to have found a person with such a strong background on such short notice. For that we must thank Sally, who worked with him at a previous company."

Text from Ken: *Jsus, Mary & Jseph!*

Georgia: *Certainly 1 way 2 get allies.*

Ken: *Mybe he's good. Dresses better thn Burt.*

Georgia glanced at Mr. Coppola's very tailored summer weight gray suit and crimson silk tie: *Dresses better thn Jacki O'.*

Ken: *LOL. Cld b why I'm suspicious.*

Indeed, by now the men on the executive team were so colorfully dressed that the women were starting to look like drab little peahens.

"… and after three years with Sangallo Software I felt is a good time for making a change," Mr. Coppola was saying. "So I am here, and I think I will be good for work with you. Thank you very much."

"Giuseppe," Mark called out as if he were thrilled, "can you say a bit about why you view this as a step up from your previous position?"

"Is chance to work in business development," Giuseppe replied. "And of course, is a much bigger company."

"So, if you're new to business development," Mark pursued brightly, "what was your focus at Sangallo?"

"R&D, the product development," Giuseppe explained, shrugging. "I think is similar, but I prefer now to do business development."

"Giuseppe's too modest to say this," Sally said with an admiring smile, "but he's fluent in five languages."

Text to Ken: *English 1 of them?* Ken frowned at his iPhone and set it down. Uh-oh, too snarky?

"I know you'll want to introduce yourselves to Giuseppe over the next few days," Roy continued. "And with that, let's turn to the morning's agenda."

An hour later Burt, whose mumbling had gotten even worse in the wake of his demotion, was presenting his "management is listening" posters to the executive team. Poor guy. Well, these dumb posters had been his idea, so maybe he actually believed in them.

"This is a great effort, Burt," Mark said with his tight smile, "but I slightly question how effective these posters can be, no matter how well they're designed and worded. Are we sure marketing is the right response to not listening? I wonder if it wouldn't be easier to just ... listen." He shrugged ironically.

"But I have an even bigger concern," he continued. "I think we need to make sure we distinguish Lumina Management from Big Brother. Does anybody share that feeling?"

"Absolutely," Andrea responded. "This could backfire big time with our engineers. I mean, there's listening when employees ask us to listen, and then there's just always listening. I'd hate to have a bunch of programmers staging a sit-in instead of finishing the 6.1."

Georgia suppressed a laugh and tried to catch Ken's eye. He was looking at his iPhone, his face flushed.

Georgia: *u r missing Grt Human Crcus.*

No response. When she glanced up at him he had set his iPhone down and was staring blankly at Burt.

∞

"So that's what you missed," Georgia concluded later in the privacy of Ken's office. "What was the distraction? Your family okay?"

"They're fine, Georgia, thanks." He paused. "This isn't very professional, but I'll show you what I was looking at." He scrolled down his iPhone for a moment, and then handed it to her across his conference table. "From Roy. It's about my bonus for the last six months."

Ken,

Your final score for your first half bonus payout is 40%. The key pluses were your settlement of the SAP lawsuit, and your drive to complete the side deal issue on time. The minuses, of course, are that you allowed our company to be pushed into the side deal audit and that you spent to great excess to complete it.

Best regards,

Roy

Georgia read it twice. "He took away part of your bonus because of the side deal audit?"

"I know this seems petty, and it's probably terrible leadership to show it to you, but I'm a little bit frustrated."

She returned the iPhone. "He doesn't have a clue."

"He really doesn't, does he? He seems to think we had a choice. He seems to think we had time and leisure to find a cheaper way."

"Well, or maybe he's just cheap. Does he realize Jean-Claude told you 'no budget limitations'?"

"Probably not. But here's the other thing that bothers me: If you were going to do this to somebody, would you do it in an email? It didn't warrant five minutes in person?" He studied his iPhone screen. "Look at the ending: 'Best regards.' Evidently he thought it was a cordial message."

"Okay. So I'd say the scorecard is 'comprehension: zero' and 'people skills: minus five.' Are you going to talk to him about it? That's what you'd tell me to do."

"I don't know, Georgia. You're exactly right that I *should* talk to him in order to preserve the relationship. But if you have to point this out to somebody, doesn't that mean he's incapable of understanding it? He'll probably just miss the point and tell me I'm greedy. Or repeat his ludicrous belief that we had a choice."

"Or offer you Andrea's job."

He snorted, staring vacantly at the table top. "Exactly. Not sure I could take it right now." Then he looked up. "You know, Georgia, it's not very satisfying to work for a person who can't understand anything you're doing. Eventually, you ask yourself what's the point?"

"Yeah. Pearls before swine," she acknowledged. She was torn between anxiety that Ken was so discouraged, and gratification that he felt free to share it with her.

"Sounds kind of arrogant, doesn't it?" he said sheepishly.

She shook her head ruefully. "No. And this was a big pearl. Poor old swine really tripped over it."

Ken laughed. "Georgia, you're a piece of work."

"Anyway, our team knows what you did. Jean-Claude knows."

"What we all did," he corrected. "Yeah. That's right, they do. And we go the extra distance because it's the right thing to do, not because somebody praises us for it." He sat for a moment. "Well, in any case, this isn't a good use of anybody's time. I'll talk it over with Laura. How's the options research coming? Need some help?"

"Nope. I'm on it. Can I ask you something else? How likely do you think it is that Glen really didn't know about the side deal in Home Depot?"

He didn't owe her an answer, of course. He looked into her eyes, considering. "Not very likely," he acknowledged finally, "but I hope it's true. When you don't know for sure, it's always best to give people the benefit of the doubt. I'm a pretty big believer in second chances."

"And what about all those bad disti deals?"

"Between you and me, Georgia, Charlie Reebuck doesn't strike me as the kind of independent thinker who would risk this on his own. I think Terkes probably knew about those, too, and if Horace had looked at a few more emails he'd have found that out." *Still Terkes instead of Glen.* "Why? What do you think?"

"Agree with everything," she responded, "except maybe the benefit of the doubt. Have to think about that part. So, why did this great independent law firm never question Terkes' self-serving denial? Why did they do such a window dressing job of investigating?"

"Because that was their job, Georgia. Window dressing, and I'm sure they perfectly understood that. We were on the brink of a corporate meltdown, and Horace's job as independent investigator was to make sure the investigation ended before we got there. Terkes—Glen—needed to be free of further suspicion so that the company could be free of further suspicion and file on time. Our team had a very different job. We were obligated to conduct a real investigation, and we took it wherever the evidence led us."

"Should we finish the job now?"

He looked slightly horrified. "You mean look at the rest of Glen's email? That would be very dangerous for the company. Suppose we find another whole line of side deals, and go through this again? Horace rightly or wrongly relieved us of the responsibility to look at anything else, and we just need to leave it there."

"What about the retaliation against the employee in Boston?"

"You mean Ben Larkin, the flippee? What about it?"

"Is Glen responsible for that?"

"Absolutely. He allowed Buck to retaliate against Ben Larkin, and then talked Roy out of firing Buck. Glen has a lot of influence with Roy, and he seems to pop up in a number of less-than-admirable moments for the company."

She decided to press her point. "But if he *did* know about the side deals and either encouraged it or else let it go on for years, isn't he still a huge risk to the company?"

Ken brushed his palm over the top of his hair. "Yes," he admitted, "but chances are he'll lie low for a while. This was a pretty big mess."

"Lie low until we forget. But not change his ethics about it."

"Well, now that's an interesting question." He smiled slightly as he searched her eyes. "Do you believe people ever change their ethics? I personally believe they can, but it's hard, so they have to be quite motivated. I've never seen anybody care enough to change their ethics because of work. It's always been something in their personal life. So I guess we step up our vigilance, and beyond that, Glen is just our cross to bear."

"We're getting a traffic jam in our cross-bearing lane."

"Beg pardon?"

"We keep concluding that people who don't do their jobs are just our cross to bear."

Ken snorted, but his smile was suddenly vacant, signaling the end of the conversation. "I guess we've had several of those, haven't we? Wish I knew a better answer."

It was alarming to see Ken this discouraged, she thought as she headed back to her cube. The stupid bonus insult was a big part of it. Nothing she could do about that. But whatever idiotic scheme Terkes was going to come up with next was already a storm, slowly building to hurricane strength somewhere out over the ocean. Probably. Maybe not. Would be great to be certain about Glen's involvement in those side deals, one way or the other. Too bad the company couldn't look at his restored emails.

Of course, Georgia wasn't the company, was she? She personally had no obligation to tell the public anything. She was nothing but a snoopy, low-level employee with a certain amount of spare time on her hands.

CHAPTER 20

Georgia and Quan were with Ken at his conference table when Maggie stuck her head in. "You have a letter from the SEC in the lobby. I'm going down for it."

"SEC." Ken lifted his head away from the palm that had been supporting it. "Thanks, Maggie, and would you ask Zack to join us?" He turned to Quan and Georgia. "Pardon my French, but qu'est-ce que hell?"

"Maybe there's just a formality with regard to the 10-Q," Quan suggested.

"I hope you're right. Must be something about the 10-Q."

A few minutes later Zack appeared with copies of a formal-looking document, ironically entitled Informal Request For Cooperation. Georgia scanned it quickly. Accusation of keeping dual sets of books. Forty-three categories of requested documents, mostly financial stuff. What did this have to do with the 10-Q?

"Oh no," Quan said quietly as he paged through the request. "They're investigating us."

"At least it's still informal," Zack noted. "We probably don't have to disclose it yet."

Georgia's eyes fell on a name near the end of the document. "You see who the complaining witness is?"

"Does it tell us?" Ken asked, looking up. "They don't usually reveal that."

"This guy might have wanted full credit." She reached across the table and pointed it out to him.

"Jesus, Mary and Joseph! 'Benjamin Larkin, sales executive.' That's your flippee, isn't it Zack? Page 13, halfway down."

"I take it you mean Buck Gibbon's flippee." Zack flicked to the correct page and scanned. "That would be he," he confirmed with bitter satisfaction. "I guess Ben wasn't quite the punching bag you were all hoping for." *'You?' He was blaming Ken along with the others.*

"Well," Quan said, "at least we don't have to worry about them putting him on a Performance Improvement Plan now. That would be suicide. A textbook case of retaliation."

"Does death by stupidity count as suicide?" Georgia asked innocently.

Ken stared at her for an instant, then said, "Zack, would you step out and call Buck Gibbons now? Tell him he can't put Ben Larkin on a PIP. Let's explain why Ben is their new lifetime employee. Assuming Glen hasn't fired him already."

"Would he do that without telling anybody?" Zack hurried out without waiting for an answer.

"Is there a chance we really do keep double books?" Quan asked, raking his black hair back from his face.

"Boy, I don't think so, but we obviously have to find out." Apparently this had nothing to do with the 10-Q.

"Can I just ask?" Georgia looked up from her copy of the document. "If we think we don't keep double books, why are we so afraid of an inquiry?"

"The last place any company *ever* wants to be is on the SEC's radar," Ken explained. "An SEC investigation is so toxic to a company's reputation that just disclosing it could tank the stock, regardless of the outcome."

"And once they start poking around," Quan added, "they might turn up something we did do."

"No reason to think that's going to happen here," Ken reassured them. "But the point is to get in, cooperate fully, and get out."

Zack reentered the room. "Well, they haven't fired him yet. Or if they have, they haven't bothered to tell HR. He's still on the payroll, and I've left messages for Burt and Glen to call us right away."

"Boy, Zack. I know how strongly you felt about Ben Larkin. You probably think I could have done more to protect Ben, and maybe you're right. This must make you quite upset."

"I don't think 'upset' quite covers it, Ken. Those jokers have brought the whole SEC down on our heads. Which serves them right, but I can't even get any satisfaction from that...!" He slammed his fist down so hard the binders jumped. "...because you and I are the ones who have to deal with it." *So loyalty trumped blame. It did for her, too.*

"Maybe now they'll fire Buck after all," Quan suggested.

Ken shook his head. "Don't think so, Quan. Probably just confirm their bad opinion of Ben. Friends, it seems the Big Circus is back in all three rings."

So it was, thought Georgia, and Glen Terkes was proving quite the ringmaster.

∞

At 9:30 that night, Georgia and Katie-Ann were sitting across from each other at the folding table in their living room. Katie-Ann was in her flannel pajamas and T-shirt, one heel up on the chair seat, absent-mindedly twirling a strand of shoulder-length blond hair as she bent over her homework. Georgia was in jeans and a wrinkled plaid shirt, searching through the restored Glen Terkes' email that was recent enough to be uploaded by thumb drive onto her ancient, cracked, cherry red gumdrop desktop.

"Nailed!" Katie-Ann pronounced, slamming her geometry book so decisively that it jiggled Georgia's monitor.

"Great. That makes one of us," Georgia muttered without looking up. She was on her fourth batch of Terkes' email, and it was going more slowly than she'd expected. Here at home she wasn't set up to sort by search term, so she was cruising thousands of subject lines, opening anything that looked promising. It was inefficient, but at least this time she didn't have to find every bad email. She only needed one.

Which she still hadn't found. Well, she'd sort of found it. From the first three batches, she knew that Terkes had been copied five times (at least) on email from sales reps that actually offered side deals. So unless he *never* read his email, he surely knew plenty. But he'd wiggled out of that once already. This time she wanted to catch him red-handed, either offering a side deal or telling one of his reps to offer one. So tonight she had switched from incoming to outgoing email.

Katie-Ann was at the kitchen sink, looking with distaste at the crusted lasagna pan, when Georgia said, "Whoa!"

"You found it?"

"Not exactly, no. I found something different."

"What?"

"Mr. Sales-Gorgeous has a thing for porn."

Katie-Ann shrugged, and resumed scrubbing the lasagna pan. "Like a lotta people. But how do you know?"

"I just opened an email called 'Project Carmen,' and it wasn't the kind of project I was looking for."

"In his email? Who's he sending it to?"

"Some guy called Brotkin. Maybe that's B. Rotkin? Outside the company."

"Sort on that email address, and see if he's done it more than once."

Georgia punched some buttons, and said "About ten times in this two-month batch. They all have project names. Hold on." She was silent a moment, and then she said, "Holy Shit."

"So much for not swearing in this house. You found more?"

"Just opened one called Project Alice." She hesitated. "It's a kid."

"Gross. Something that would suit Reverend Awknell?"

"Honestly, I think this is beneath Awknell. She looks like she's about ten."

"You serious? Maybe she just looks young." Katie-Ann headed over to the table.

"No! Don't come over here. Hold on." She punched a button and waited. "This one's a grown-up." She punched again. "I'd say ... young teenager." She continued opening email. "But here's another little kid. Grown-up. Another little kid. At least, I think these are different children. Where did he get these?" She folded her screen down onto her keyboard and held her hand over her mouth.

"Isn't he really stupid to be sending kiddie porn on company email?"

Georgia barely shook her head. "This guy isn't stupid."

"Any chance he didn't know what was actually in there?"

"How could that be? He's the one sending them."

"Then he must just believe he can do whatever he wants and nothing bad can happen to him."

Georgia was silent.

"Don't look at them any more, Georgia. They're freaking you out. Ken will know what to do."

Georgia continued staring at the lid of her computer for a moment, and then looked up. "I can't tell Ken. I'm not supposed to be looking at these emails at all, and I could sink the company right back into a crisis. I wasn't expecting this." She opened the monitor again and closed the photo image, the back of her hand pressed against her mouth. Her stomach was sort of bucking against the lasagna all of a sudden. "With those gold cuff links. What a dirtbag."

"Gives me a good idea for my debate topic."

"What's that?"

"I'm going to do 'Sex: Boon or Bane to Humanity?'"

"Katie-Ann, I don't think ..."

Katie-Ann threw her head back and laughed. "Can *not* believe you think I'm serious."

Georgia snorted in spite of herself as she punched more keys. "Don't jerk my chain right now, okay? I'm a little preoccupied."

"No worries, I'll be totally age-appropriate. How about 'World Peace: Achievable in Our Lifetime?'" She laughed again and began tilting the soapy lasagna pan back and forth under the hot water from the faucet. "You'll figure out how to handle it, Georgia. You always do." Katie-Ann could still joke because she hadn't seen the pictures. Anyway, this wasn't her issue, and Georgia was determined to keep it that way. She'd sleep with the gumdrop laptop right next to her pillow, just in case.

She continued her search, carefully avoiding B. Rotkin, while Katie-Ann wiped down the counters and disappeared into the bedroom. Just before midnight she found the email she'd been looking for. On March 17 at 3:32 a.m., Terkes wrote to the head of the Denver office:

... Your linearity for the quarter is alarming. Begin offering our special distributors the standard buyback provision.

Georgia propped her head on both fists and stared at the screen. "Standard." Side deals were so common there was a "standard"? She could never whisper a hint of this to Ken. As an officer, he'd be obligated to resume the investigation, and now it would be the whole company. But how likely was Terkes to stop this, even temporarily? Could he stop it? Wouldn't sales for the quarter plummet without side deals?

And now she knew about the kiddie porn. Georgia was no crusader, but how could somebody just hand those pictures of real children around like Pokemon cards? And she had those images stuck in her brain. This job had more hazards than a hog had spots.

Who was B. Rotkin, anyway? How did these perverts find each other? Had he returned the favor, sending stuff to Terkes? She went back to Terkes' incoming email and sorted for Rotkin. Four messages appeared in a list. One had a subject "Right here in Tulsa." She opened it:

Hey, look what I found in a chat room right here in Tulsa. Sent me this herself, though she thinks she sent it to 'Timmy' the high school track star. Ha! Time for another one of your field trips? This one wants it bad. ;-)

Attached was a photo of a blond girl, naked from the waist up and looking boldly into the camera. *Katie-Ann??* Georgia gasped, looked again, and saw that the girl was a complete stranger. She looked even younger than Katie-Ann, thirteen, maybe fourteen. Georgia checked the date. The email was already more than four months old. Too late, but then maybe it had just been pointless bravado, or maybe the girl had escaped on her own.

Georgia sat with her hands tented over her nose and open mouth, closed her eyes in a long blink, and exhaled. What was she going to do about this? Seemed like an FBI thing. But how could she go to the FBI without having a cast of thousands pawing through the side deal email? She fought off a memory of a filthy undershirt, the stench of tobacco-stained teeth. The terror that remained long after Gramma Griffin appeared in the barn and called her name in the nick of time … She bolted for the bathroom and heaved what was left of the lasagna into the toilet.

Well. If Georgia knew anything from her colorful past, she knew the value of recovering her wits promptly. Ten minutes later she was in her pajamas, teeth brushed, in the lotus position on her round cushion, visualizing the most beautiful mountain she could think of. Whenever a porno image floated into her head, she noted its presence, and then watched the beautiful mountain reappear. Gradually her breathing slowed, and her shoulders relaxed. Glen Terkes required some analysis. This problem required a right perspective. And Georgia required a good night's sleep.

∞

It was 6:30 p.m., and Georgia was in her cube, finishing up paperwork for the new subsidiary in Belize. Katie-Ann had promised to make ground beef with mushroom soup over rice for dinner, and Georgia wanted to be home in time to make a salad to go with it. As she worked, she tried to shut out worries about Glen Terkes, along with the pleasant murmur of Quan's voice drifting over the top of her cube from down the hall. Quan sounded like he was in Joe's doorway, and they were talking with Angela and Miles, two of the contracts admins.

"Hey, Georgia," Quan called over the tops of the cubes. "Want to go to lunch with us a week from Monday?"

"Sounds great," she called back. Not like Quan to be a social secretary. Was something up? The hell with it. Belize could happen tomorrow. She shut down her computer and strolled over to where they were gathered around Joe. "So what's the occasion?"

"The occasion is the annual sales kick-off," Joe responded. He was one of the lawyers who negotiated license agreements, so Georgia didn't work with him much. At the age of thirty, he was the sole support of a wife and four children, but instead of seeming burdened he radiated that wholesome, slightly lacquered optimism she was learning to recognize as Mormon. "All the salespeople are busy partying and doing things the legal department probably shouldn't know about," he explained, "so they don't have time to call us with their many demands. So our whole licensing team gets three days with no phones ringing, and that makes us so happy that we want to party, too. So we're gonna have lunch."

"Which just proves happiness is contagious," Quan laughed.

"Too bad it's only three days," Angela said, turning to Georgia. "The second it's over they start calling us like crazy again."

"And then there's actually extra work for the legal team," Quan added. "Especially Zack."

"How so?" Georgia asked.

"Well, the sales team's idea of good times sometimes gets them into trouble." Joe's tone was carefully nonjudgmental. "Or threatens to get the company in trouble. And then Zack or Ken have to step in to clean it up."

"Yeah," Angela said, "remember last year? It was the whores in the hot tub."

"Angela!" Miles said with mock disapproval. "Those weren't whores. They were exotic dancers. Very talented, I believe. One of them was

John Linden's fiancée."

"Yeah, for about three hours," Angela scoffed. "That's what he said to get her past security in the hotel. But then it turned out he'd met her at a strip club the night before. She and her friends took all their clothes off in the hot tub, and the other hotel guests got totally offended."

Joe the Mormon chuckled stiffly along with them. "Actually, those weren't just any old hotel guests who got upset, they were customers, and it was actually a user conference."

"You know what, that's right," Angela confirmed, wagging a finger near her temple. "So what happened at the kick-off?"

"Wasn't there a guy from Phoenix who complained that his boss made everybody chip in to pay for a stripper?" Miles asked.

"That is accurate," Quan confirmed. "I dealt with that one myself. I called the guy up and he said yes, he did ask for contributions for a stripper. And when I asked why, he said he thought it would be wrong to expense it." Loud laughter.

"That was Reebuck's guy, remember?" Joe added. The story was gathering steam. "And then it turned out Charlie and Glen were both there, and didn't stop it."

"Their defense was probably that they'd paid good money like everybody else," Miles said, and they laughed again.

"Well, in fairness," Quan clarified, "they didn't seem to know how she was being paid for."

"So what happened to the manager?" Georgia asked Quan.

"I told him he was halfway to paradise. I congratulated him for recognizing that it would have been wrong to expense it, and the next time he just needed to figure out it was also wrong to hire the stripper in the first place. Then I put a warning letter in his file."

Angela shrugged, unimpressed. "Big deal. The real punishment is this year he might have to pay for the stripper himself." They laughed again, but this time Georgia barely heard it. She was suddenly visualizing a map to buried treasure.

She realized Joe was calling her name, and reluctantly returned from her reverie. "What? Oh, sorry. What was that?"

"You okay?" Angela scrutinized Georgia's face. "We didn't gross you out with our raunchy stories, did we?"

"Oh." She held her palms up. "Not at all. Just visiting a distant planet. When is kick-off?"

"Starts a week from Monday," Joe said. "Can we count you in for lunch?"

"Absolutely. Lunch sounds great. I sort of have to go now."

A week from Monday. Wasn't much time. Was Charlie Reebuck even around this week? She was pretty sure there was a drug dealer at the church dinners she could use to score some coke. Incredibly expensive, unless she could get him to just lease it to her for a day or two, which seemed like a long shot. The whole scheme seemed like a long shot, but then so was landing a man on the moon. As Ken said, how would you know what's possible unless you tried?

∞

As luck would have it, Charlie Reebuck showed up for a visit from the San Francisco office two days later. Georgia slowed down as she neared the open visitor's office door, making sure she'd correctly identified that glib, staccato voice, then hurried back to her office to prepare a little midmorning playacting.

She was zooming past the visitor's office an hour later when a little brown medicine container shot from a manila envelope she was carrying and rolled to a stop at the toe of Charlie's glossy, chestnut-brown lace-up.

"Oh!" she said, and stopped just outside his open door, her gaze traveling from the medicine container up to his startled, hyper-alert face.

He bent over and picked it up. He held it up to the light and shook the loose powder thoughtfully. He opened it and sniffed. She used both hands to squeeze the manila envelope open, inviting him to drop it back in.

SUSAN WOLFE

"Good thing this wasn't glass," he commented as he walked to where she stood in the doorway and dropped it in. "Could've lost a whole party down in the carpet."

"Thanks!" She smiled at him. "Didn't mean to assault you in there."

"What's the rush? Free beer?"

"Nothing that fun, unfortunately. One of our executives needed a refill on his medicine, and now we want to get it to him before he heads out for a client dinner."

"His medicine," he said slowly, savoring the phrase. "Works for me. Whose 'medicine' is it?"

"Mr. Terkes'."

"No way. Glen? How would I not have known this?" He studied her face for a moment. *One con artist seeking to recognize another?* She made her face deliberately blank. "Tell you what, I'll be at the dinner with him tonight. Why don't I just take it to him?"

"That would be great." She held the envelope out to him. "Oh, you know what, though?" She pulled it back again. "I promised Mary I'd take it. Better stick to what I'm told."

He shrugged. "Suit yourself. Seems like a waste of time. Wait, aren't you the person from the legal department?"

"Oh yes, Mr. Reebuck, I'm Georgia. I was taking notes in that interview. Sorry it was sort of uncomfortable."

He searched her face again, considering, then waved his hand dismissively. "Hey, that was nothin'. You oughtta see some of my sales calls. Well, at least you're doing something important for a change, instead of getting all wound up about stuff nobody cares about."

"Yeah, I know what you mean. It's not like filing those 10-Qs is gonna pay our salaries, now, is it?"

He lifted his palms expansively. "I'm sure it's all very important. You're probably keeping us out of trouble in ways I wouldn't begin to understand."

Georgia shrugged. "Sometimes. I guess with sales, it's always pretty exciting.

"Exciting like going to your own hanging, but yeah, it's exciting."

"You always seem pretty upbeat about things."

"Well, we party now and then to blow off a little steam. We work hard, why not play hard when we get the chance?" He was waxing philosophical, half-sitting on the front of his desk, his shirtsleeves rolled up to reveal his skinny forearms and a gigantic gold watch.

"Absolutely," she said. "I've heard about your parties. Are you planning anything for sales kick-off?"

"Sunday night. Big tradition. Sort of an ice-breaker to kick off the kick-off."

She smiled a little wistfully. "Must be great, to just let go and be wild."

He appraised her body. "It is great. You should join us sometime. Bring Nikki."

"Could I really? Wouldn't want to interfere with the fun. What if I see something you wouldn't want me to see?"

"What's to see, assuming you don't object to a little 'medicine' or a couple of friendly girls?"

"Oh no, not at all. It's just that maybe if I'm from 'legal' "—she rolled her eyes and made air quotes—"I could sort of put a damper on things."

"Maybe you should join a department that doesn't interfere with your social life."

Georgia laughed. "You could definitely be right about that one. Speaking of which, I better get going now. Nice to see you again."

"Don't do anything I wouldn't do," he said with a wink. What could that even be, she wondered as she headed back to her cube.

∞

The board was fifteen minutes into their 8 a.m. meeting, and Georgia was actually bored for once, relying on the pungent steam spiraling up from her purple-stamped Peets cup to keep herself warm and awake.

She hoped Eddie would be at the backlog meeting again this afternoon. "Nice to see you again, Georgia," he'd say with the frank, slightly eager look she found so attractive. She was wearing her shirt that matched her dark blue eyes, just in case.

Roy didn't appear to be listening to Ken's presentation at all. He was focused on something across the room, and she followed his gaze to an apparently oblivious Sally, who was confidently sporting braided, purple epaulets on the shoulders of her brick red suit. Funny. You'd expect Roy's scowl to soften when he looked at his most ardent butt-smooch, but this was just the opposite. Roy's typical run-of-the-mill glare had hardened into one of downright hatred. Must be looking at her and thinking of something else, unless she'd finally managed to puncture his fashion oblivion.

"I'm certainly not surprised that there is no basis to this claim of dual books," Jean-Claude was saying. "I would have felt some shock if you had reached a different conclusion. But can you explain a bit about how this completely baseless claim got the attention of the SEC?" Now this was less boring. She sat up straighter and leaned forward to hear Ken's answer.

"Usually you have to speculate about these things," Ken responded, "but in this case we actually know. The accusation was filed by an employee in our Boston office who had complained of sexual harassment, and didn't like the way the company handled the investigation."

Jean-Claude raised his stiff, white eyebrows. "So she just said some lies to the SEC, as a kind of revenge for the way we treated her?"

"Him," Ken corrected. "Employee's a man. And we don't know whether he knew the allegation was false, or whether he believed it was true because he saw something that confused him. We do know that he didn't go to the SEC until after he saw the outcome of his harassment complaint."

"Can you say what this harassment claim was regarding?" Jean-Claude continued with a frown.

"Gentlemen," Roy interrupted, holding up the palm of his hand

and glaring a warning to Ken. "We're lost in the weeds here. Basically, we investigated this guy's claim and handled it responsibly. You can't control or predict what an individual will do sometimes. This particular employee evidently wanted an excuse for not doing his job, and became irate when we didn't give him one.

"The point is, this whole mess has no basis, and the SEC doesn't want to waste their time on it any more than we do. In fact, my only concern is that the SEC investigation will get out of control, exactly the way the side deal audit did. To prevent that, I've asked Sally to work closely with Ken and Cliff, to provide some much-needed perspective."

Ken and Cliff jerked in unison, exchanging glances to confirm each other's astonishment. How could Georgia possibly have thought any board meeting could be boring? Sooner or later, she always became an eyewitness to history.

"I share Roy's optimism that we can convince the SEC we don't keep dual books," Ken said. "I think we should be very careful, though, about trying to shortcut the SEC's inquiry. If they get the slightest idea we're trying to rush them, they have the ability to cost us a lot of time and money."

"I want to second that," Cliff added. "The SEC will become extremely disruptive if we give them the slightest motive for doing so. We want to convince them we're a respectful, transparent and honest company, and that could take patience. We can't allow an inexperienced person to get within a million miles of them."

"You and Ken will handle the relationship with the SEC, of course," Larry said. "In fact, I'm a bit surprised that we need to involve Sally at all, but if you guys are convinced it's useful …" Which "guys" were those, exactly? Ken and Cliff were practically pantomiming horror at the very thought.

"I will personally ensure that the team works smoothly," Roy said quickly. "I'm confident this is the right mix to get the job done thoroughly, and with a minimum of waste. I notice we're coming to the end of our hour. Any questions before we close?" he asked, shaking his head from side to side.

"I do have one question," Paul Holder called through the speaker-phone. "Where did we ever come out on the employee part of the side deal investigation?"

"We concluded that nine people should be terminated," Ken reported, "and that is being done this week."

"Anybody senior?"

"The most senior person is Wilt Devans, the head of the San Francisco office. The head of the Western Region, Charlie Reebuck, is being given a warning."

"But how can this be," Jean-Claude asked, "when his famous $1.2 million deal contained a side agreement? And didn't these disti deals come from his offices as well?"

"Let me comment on that," Roy interjected. "We looked at Charlie very closely, but decided that these lower-level characters were fully responsible for their own actions. We've warned Charlie about being more vigilant, and I'm confident he'll heed those warnings."

'Ugh!' Georgia wrote in a text to Ken, but then decided not to distract him and deleted it.

"But the $1.2 million deal?" Paul's voice persisted through the speakerphone. "Who was responsible for that?"

"That was just a misunderstanding," Roy reassured him. "Apparently Charlie thought the buyback was in the main agreement."

Text to Ken: 'Rbuck sd tht?' But Ken was focused on the board.

"Well," Jean-Claude said, "I am a bit surprised by that conclusion, but I guess it's a good one for the company. Anything else? Okay, then the meeting is adjourned."

"Did Reebuck really say he thought the buyback was in the main agreement?" Georgia whispered to Ken as they headed back to his office.

"Yeah, as soon as somebody out there coached him on it for a week. It's ludicrous, frankly, and I just hope it doesn't come back to bite us like this flipper thing did. My bigger concern is Sally. How did she manage to plant herself in the middle of this SEC problem?"

"By convincing Roy your spending was out of control. Why didn't the board speak up for you when Roy said the side deal investigation got out of hand?"

"They probably thought there wasn't much point. Unless he's convinced them it did get out of hand. Let's not worry about that right now. Let's figure out how to keep our momentum on this SEC thing, now that Sally wants to prove she's indispensable."

Well, Georgia thought modestly, she might be able to help distract Sally. If attrition couldn't hold her attention, Georgia was pretty sure she knew something that would. It would have to wait a few days, though, because for the moment Georgia was definitely overbooked with Glen. Well, maybe she had time for one more little confidence-booster. She glanced at the time on her iPhone. In fact, maybe she could take care of that now.

She knocked on Sally's invariably closed door (so much for 'management is listening') and stuck her head in. Sally was at her computer with her back to the door. "There's a reason my door is closed," she said to her computer monitor. Those purple epaulets looked even weirder from the back.

"Oh, sorry, Sally," Georgia said, ducking her head and starting to withdraw.

"Georgia!" Sally cried, swinging around to her desk as she motioned her in. "I can break for a moment. What's up?"

"Well, I just wanted to be sure you knew about the meeting on the second floor in half an hour to wrap up the warning letter for Charlie Reebuck."

Sally stiffened. "I certainly didn't know, and it's not convenient for me. I'll tell them to reschedule it." She reached for her phone.

"You know, Sally, I kind of wish you wouldn't do that. They don't know I'm running as a sort of go-between, and how would you explain how you found out about it?"

Sally considered, and put her phone back down. "All right. I'll rearrange my schedule so I can be there."

"Maybe you could just be sort of passing by, you know, and happen to see the meeting?"

"Of course, Georgia. That's exactly what I'll do. I won't forget this, you know. I won't forget this at all."

Georgia winced as she hurried back to her cube. Sorry Ken, she thought. Now you're stuck with the Nusty Beech in your meeting, and she's bound to be pissed. But all in the service of a greater good.

CHAPTER 21

Georgia found Zack standing at his office whiteboard, using a bright green marker to create a chart. Beyond him she could see morning light filtering through that luminous, pearl-gray cloud cover that was unique to California.

"What's that?" she asked, pointing at Zack's chart.

He turned around in that lethargic way that made people underestimate him. "Hi, Georgia. I just got the first draft of the earnings release, and the numbers look funny."

"You think they're wrong?"

"They all look higher than I remembered."

"Higher than the preannouncement?"

He entered a final number and stood back to consider the whole chart. "Yep."

"So our preannouncement was wrong? That's what Ken was afraid of."

"What was our original guidance?" He flipped efficiently through a seemingly random drift of paper on his credenza. "Here it is. Read them off to me, will you?" He started a new column on the whiteboard.

"So we basically hit our original guidance," he concluded a moment later.

"Then why did we preannounce?"

He picked up his phone. "Let's ask Ken."

After Ken arrived and studied Zack's whiteboard, he used the speakerphone to call Jill at Woodrow, Mantella.

"That's unfortunate," she said simply in response to Ken's description.

"Are we likely to get sued?"

She considered. "Probably not. Shareholder lawsuits usually start because companies inflate their numbers to get their stock price up. Deflating your numbers and depressing your stock price isn't self-serving, it's just … not very bright. I don't think a lawsuit would go anywhere."

"What about the SEC? How are they likely to react?"

"There's really no precedent that I'm aware of. Companies don't often shoot themselves in the foot like this." She was silent a moment. "What I'd worry about is bad publicity. You're a business intelligence company. The analysts could get pretty nasty about you not knowing your own numbers. It undermines the confidence of the street."

"Thanks, Jill. I'm heading into prep for the analyst call now. I'll call you if I need backup." He hung up and looked at Zack. "Thirty percent of our market cap. $1.3 billion dollars. Out of sheer incompetence."

"We lost more than we saved by filing on time," Zack agreed. "What was the point of killing ourselves if we just ended up in the same place?"

"You told them so," Georgia reminded him.

"Not very effectively, it seems. Well." He stared out Zack's window, where the clouds were darkening and picking up speed.

"We'd have lost something in the market, anyway," Zack reminded him, "because our license revenue was below the analysts' expectations."

"Yeah, but it wouldn't have been 30 percent, and we wouldn't be facing a firing squad on the analyst call this afternoon. Anybody got a blindfold?" He sighed and stood up. "I need to help them get ready. Funny, what I want to do is leave the building and never come back."

She hated that discouraged sound in his voice. "Maybe you should go to one of your church services."

He snorted softly. "I probably should, Georgia. But I've gotta get through this meeting first. Can you copy Zack's chart into your computer and join us? We'll have to generate the Q&A right there in the prep meeting."

When she entered the boardroom twenty minutes later, she found a dozen people with their computers open, and piles of paper in drifts. Monica, the head of investor relations, and finance and marketing people were peppering Roy with questions and then critiquing his response. The white board listed their key themes:

- License revenue strong recovery in Q4.
- Calypso strategic success, and boon for Lumina customers.
- Full Oracle compatibility in 6.1 release.

All just so gosh-darned positive. (Calypso was Roy's Plan B that replaced the Futuresoft acquisition.)

"Have we thought about how we're going to defend the erroneous preannouncement?" Ken asked when there was a pause in the questioning.

"What was erroneous?" Roy asked, glancing up.

Ken turned his astonished gaze on Cliff, who kept his face carefully neutral. "Well, pretty much everything. We not only came in higher than the ranges we gave them, but we also came within our original guidance."

"No, we didn't," Cliff objected. "We missed on revenue."

"By $300K on a $53 million number. That certainly wasn't enough to warrant a preannouncement."

"Actually, it was even less than that," a finance person pointed out. "We rounded down. If you look at the raw data, we only missed by $160K." The finance person flinched as Cliff turned to glare at her.

"So what?" Roy declared. "We were conservative. That was the best data we had at the time. And we did come in well below street expectations on license revenue." Which even Georgia knew by now was completely irrelevant.

"That's great, Roy," Ken said, " and I think it's more or less what we need to say. The problem is, the street doesn't want us to be conservative. They want us to be accurate. If it was the best data we had at the time, why didn't we wait until we had better data? In hindsight, there was no reason to preannounce anything."

"Of course there was," Roy snapped, crossing his arms combatively. "We were substantially below street expectations on license revenue."

Ken sighed. "I know I sound like a broken record here, but we didn't give guidance on license revenue, so we had no obligation to preannounce anything."

"Are we really going to rehash this now?" Cliff asked. "The analyst call is going to start in ... thirty-two minutes."

"My only point," Ken persisted, "is that we need to be ready when the analysts bring it up."

"They're not going to bring it up, Ken," Roy said. "I plan to keep them focused on our new Calypso acquisition and the release of 6.1. What else? Monica?"

An hour later there were 72 lines open on the call, which meant a minimum of 72 analysts. The dozen or so Lumina people who remained in the boardroom were, as always, utterly silent as the moderator commenced. Cliff gave five minutes on the numbers, and then Roy provided ten minutes of color and background.

"Our first question," the moderator intoned in her sing-song voice, "comes from Natalie Brickle at Deutsche Bank."

"Thank you." Natalie's voice came clearly through the speakerphone. "I'd like to extend my congratulations to the company for the Calypso acquisition. That sounds like a very good match."

"Thank you, Natalie," Roy responded warmly. "We think it will prove to be so." Well. Listen to Mr. Smooth.

"My question relates to the numbers you announced today and the preannouncement you released seventeen days ago," she continued. "Why are they inconsistent? Is this indicative of some weakness in your financial reporting systems?" *Very first question.*

Roy glared at the phone over the rims of his narrow glasses, but his voice remained completely pleasant. "Well, Natalie, no, we think our financial reporting systems are very sound. We're a pretty complicated company, and it takes a while to close and audit our books. We're pleased that the final numbers turned out to be a little better than we expected."

"Our next question," the moderator intoned, "comes from Tony Fried of First Boston."

"Thank you. I have two questions, if I may. First, I wonder if Mr. Tanco can comment on the product mix that made up the license revenue for the Americas, for Europe and for Asia."

"Unfortunately, we don't comment on that, Tony," Cliff said, "because we don't want that very granular information to get into the hands of our competitors."

"Understood. Thank you. And my second question is for Mr. Zisko. If you hadn't closed your books at the time of the preannouncement, can you say a little bit about why you timed the preannouncement as you did?"

"I'd be happy to, Tony." *Like he'd be happy to attend his own funeral.* "We knew our results on license revenue were going to be disappointing compared to street expectations. We are a conservative company, and felt it was prudent to disclose as quickly as possible. It was the best data we had at the time."

The next three questions went smoothly. Then the representative from Credit Suisse asked, "Mr. Zisko, you're a business intelligence company. Does it worry you that you didn't get accurate business intelligence from your own team on the quarterly numbers for the preannouncement?"

"My team and our software are only as good as the data," Roy responded, a dark edge of annoyance creeping into his voice. "And the early data gave us some misleading indicators."

"If that was a risk, why didn't you wait until the data was more reliable?"

"As a conservative company, we felt it was important to share what we knew with our investors right away."

"Even if what you quote 'knew' unquote turned out to be wrong?" *Whoa. This guy was a real bulldog.* She glanced at Ken, whose face remained politely neutral and attentive.

"It was fairly accurate on license revenue, and that's where we had the biggest concern. I wonder if we're ready for the next caller, please?"

Rod Bancott of Morgan Stanley asked about anticipated revenue from the 6.1. He then said, "I'd like to return to that issue of license revenue for a moment. Did you give guidance on license revenue for last quarter?"

"No." *Uh-oh.*

"I didn't think you did. Then why go out with a preannouncement on license revenue? Do you feel you had an obligation?"

"We didn't worry too much about whether we had a legal obligation, Rod. We felt it was the right thing to do."

"I see. So you felt you had a moral obligation?"

"Well, in a way, yes."

Ken sat bolt upright and gestured to get Cliff's attention, as the caller continued, "So we should expect to see more of these moral obligation type disclosures in the future?"

Cliff waved rapidly a couple of feet in front of Roy's face and shook his head emphatically.

Roy acknowledged Cliff with a slight nod and responded into the speakerphone, "Not necessarily. We will evaluate every situation as it arises."

"And one final question: Since you believe you have a moral obligation to help the street have realistic expectations for license revenue, will you now begin giving that guidance on a quarterly basis?"

Cliff dropped all pretense and made the exaggerated gestures of a man trying to flag down the tanker before it hits a cement wall and bursts into flames.

"No!" Roy barked, causing a ripple of discomfort in the room. "That is to say, we'll continue to evaluate that request." He waved at Monica and raked his thumbnail backward across the front of his neck.

"I note," Monica said brightly, "that we only have time for one more question."

"And that question," the moderator intoned, "comes from John Bignew of Morrow Hedge Fund. Mr. Bignew?"

Mercifully, Mr. Bignew had something other than the preannouncement on his mind. The call ended ten minutes earlier than scheduled. Roy disappeared immediately into his office and the group dispersed. Twenty minutes later Georgia heard Ken lock his door and head out. She glanced at her watch. Only 2:30. Maybe he was headed to that church service, after all.

By the next day the shareholders had lost another $500 million.

∞

Georgia was speeding past Mark Balog's office on her way to the kitchen when she noticed him at his conference table with his face in his hands, the comb tracks visible in his neat brown hair. She knocked on his open door.

"Hey, Mark," she said to the head of customer support. "Can I get you anything? Lunch? Advil? AK-47?"

Mark raised his startled, hyper-alert eyes and barked a laugh. "Georgia! Come in come in! Didn't realize my mood was so transparent."

"You don't have too many off moments, so they sort of stick out."

"They're becoming more frequent, I'm afraid. Have a seat." His dark mood hadn't tarnished his buttoned-up look one bit. His crisp aqua dress shirt matched the small aqua diamonds of his gold tie. A tiny black dot in the center of each aqua diamond picked up the black of his onyx cuff-links, and also, no doubt, his polished black shoes under the table. She'd be lucky to look that put together on her wedding day.

She accepted his invitation and sat down. "Don't suppose it's anything I can help with?"

"I was actually just thinking of looking for Ken, but I know he's in meetings all day."

"He'll find time for you. Let's ask Maggie." She started to rise.

"No. I shouldn't interrupt him. I'm just losing my mind again." He reached over and pushed his door closed. "I had a conversation with

Roy a few minutes ago."

"Ah. About?"

"Well, you know this whole change in reporting structure, which I knew would be a disaster from day one. I managed to extract a promise from Roy that I could go to him directly if I ever felt tech support was in real danger. Knowing, of course, he'd hate it to death if I ever really did.

"So I didn't. Even though I'm convinced the people on my team are going to start leaving in droves, Georgia. I have people who haven't had a day off in twenty-six days, and these are people whose whole job is dealing with unhappy customers. Can you imagine?" His wide-stretched smile was once again distractingly at odds with his words. "Glen and I butt heads on this every time I bring it up, so this morning I finally went directly to Roy for help. I laid out my concerns, and he said, 'Mark, I'm emotionally exhausted by the troubles with your tech support team.'"

She snorted. "Well, I hope you were able to comfort poor Roy in his moment of terrible exhaustion."

His appreciative laugh was tinged with hysteria. "Oh, Georgia, am I crazy? *He's* emotionally exhausted by tech support? *He's* never spent thirty minutes thinking about it. My whole team has been living it day and night ever since we put out that miserable 6.0."

"So he made this mess, and now he doesn't want to be bothered with it. The good news is, you're not losing your mind. You're pissed, which is sane and healthy."

Mark's tight smile collapsed into a look of naked fear. "We have a catastrophe on our hands, and nobody's listening."

"I think you really should talk to Ken. When was the last time you had a day off?"

He propped his forehead on the heel of his hand. "I honestly don't remember. It wasn't this month."

"So can you just leave for the rest of the day? I'll get Maggie to set you up with Ken tomorrow morning."

"How can I leave my team here, when they all need a day off more than I do?"

"What good are you here with your head in your hands? Your team needs you to take care of yourself. Your secretary can call you if there's an emergency."

He stared at her. "You know what? I feel like I *am* talking to Ken. That sounded exactly like him."

She laughed, slightly embarrassed. "Yeah, well, he's been busy lately, so we just channel him. Anyway, can you meet Ken early tomorrow? Maggie will confirm the exact time. Hang in there, Mark. The company needs you."

Wow. That really did sound like Ken.

She felt amused and flattered as she continued on to the kitchen. Sounding like Ken, indeed. Sounding like Ken and thinking like her father, what kind of hybrid did that produce? Cross between Mother Teresa with Bernie Madoff. But she wasn't a hybrid of anything. She was Georgia Louise Griffin, the only one there would ever be. Which meant she should be the finest one possible.

CHAPTER 22

Georgia followed the red dress of the sultry, olive-skinned reception-ist down the carpeted hallway and into Charlie Reebuck's corner office on the 17th floor of Embarcadero Center in San Francisco. He rose to greet her from behind a desk that seemed too big for him, tuck-ing in a creased, pale gray shirt and straightening his diagonal-striped tie. His professionally mussed hair had been flattened on one side, and he ran one hand over it as he used his other to grip hers. Sunset was streaking the wispy clouds with pink as she accepted a bottle of water and sat down at his round table.

"Wow," she said, gesturing with her Crystal Geyser bottle at the window. "I see why you prefer to work out of San Francisco."

"Yeah. So, is this a friendly visit from a gorgeous doll named Georgia, or is 'legal' on my tail again?" She could hear his knee jiggling under the table as it had in the interview with Zack, but his brown eyes remained on her face instead of darting around the room. He wasn't afraid exactly. He was cautious. Her job now was to help his lousy impulse control defeat that caution.

"I'm not really here as part of the legal department, Mr. Reebuck. That's one of the two things I wanted to talk to you about."

"Call me Charlie. What did you want to talk about?"

"Well, when I saw you in the San Jose office a few days ago, we talked a little bit about our two departments. I just wondered if the sales team would ever hire somebody out of the legal department to become a sales executive."

His shoulders relaxed a bit. "Salespeople can come from anywhere.

But why would you want to? Haven't you spent years on a fancy education?"

"Not really. I'm not a lawyer. I'm a paralegal, and that was only a year of training."

"Why sales?"

"Well, I'm thinking I could use something a little more ... social than what I'm doing now. Discovery and document retention can get pretty lonely sometimes." He waited. "And then, the other thing is that I have a little sister to support, and it's quite a challenge to do that on a paralegal salary. Wouldn't I make a lot more as a sales executive?"

At the mention of money he settled back in his chair and loosened his tie again. Her visit seemed suddenly to make perfect sense.

"Either a lot more or nothing," he counseled. "It's very, very tough for a sales executive in the first six months, even if they have experience. Ever sold anything?"

"No. But isn't it persuasion? I can persuade people to do things sometimes."

"Yeah, but this is subtle stuff. You don't want people to know they're being influenced."

Excellent advice. So she probably shouldn't bat her eyelashes. "That does sound sophisticated. Do you think I could learn?"

"Hard to say. The other thing is, sales might not always be quite as black and white as the law. I couldn't have anybody on my team bleeding stuff back to her legal buddies."

Well, maybe one tasteful little bat, to offset her solemn "Of course not."

He shrugged. "Possibly could work. I might be willing to try it, but I'd want you to shadow one of my sales guys for a few days, so you'd know what you were getting into. Can you do that?"

"At the right time I can. I have to do some things on this SEC investigation first."

"Yeah, I heard about that. Some troublemaker out of the Boston office. How's it going?"

"Well, it's a huge amount of work, but I think it's going okay. You know about the person who complained?"

Charlie snickered. "Yeah, Ben Larkin. Buck thinks the guy got a little freaked out by his management style."

"So it seems, and in fact that's the other thing I wanted to ask you about. You know Buck very well?"

Charlie shrugged. "Medium. Why?"

"Is he a good sales executive?"

"Okay, from what I hear. Not as good as I am. Why?"

"Well, I wonder if he's bothered by all the rumors since the harassment complaint."

"What rumors?"

"That he's, you know, homosexual."

Charlie's whole body jerked with astonishment. "Buck? A faggot?? I mean, a gaaayy person, right, legal?" He winked. "Nah, Buck's as straight as they come. Wife and kids, as a matter of fact."

"I'm sure you're right. I just wondered if the rumors were affecting his self-confidence, or making it harder for him to manage."

"No idea. I'm heading out to Las Vegas for the kick-off next week, I can check it out." He narrowed his eyes slightly, appraising her. "Don't take this wrong, but why do you give a shit?"

She shrugged. "I don't want our legal investigation to damage the business. If he is having trouble, it would be great to get the rumors to stop."

"Sure, be great to get world peace, too. How could Buck make the rumors stop?"

"Well, didn't you tell me you have 'friendly girls' at your parties sometimes?"

"As often and many as possible."

"Well, if Buck and a friendly girl, you know, with some other sales guys around, maybe he could start a counter-rumor."

He raised his eyebrows and then cocked his head to one side, his leg very busy under the table. "Surprising suggestion from a 'legal' person.

You wouldn't be trying to set us up, would you?"

Her alarm was genuine, if slightly exaggerated. "What would possibly be the purpose of that?" She hesitated, as if slightly flustered, and averted her gaze. "You know what, maybe I'm in over my head here." She looked back at him. "Sorry if I offended you. Honestly, I had the impression it was pretty routine."

"It is, sort of." He stared past her shoulder a minute, jiggling his leg and drumming his lips with two fingers. Then he grinned and flung his hands wide, embracing a vision. "What the hell, save a buddy in need! Genius, really! In fact, we're set to have a party in Glen's hotel suite on Sunday night, I'll just plan it for then. Pick somebody really hot for him, you know, and tell her to stay on him." He mimed by moving his torso from side to side like a downhill skier. The idea was picking up speed. "Be fun for all of us," he nodded, eyes sparkling. Then he pointed at her. "You know, maybe you'd be good in sales."

She feigned modest embarrassment. "And would other people from his office be there?"

"Sure. We'll get several girls, you know, so he won't feel self-conscious."

"Will Mr. Terkes allow that?"

"Don't see why not. Little bigger than we've done before, but that's the beauty of it. Something we'll all remember."

"And you're pretty sure Buck will react in a good way? Have you seen him at parties before?"

"Hm, well, I can't actually think of a time . . . There were the exotic dancers in the hot tub in Orlando, but I mostly remember Buck laughing so hard he just fell down on his knees in the grass. But all men react the same to pretty girls, don't they?"

"I suppose, but does everybody like to be public?"

"I see what you mean. Wouldn't want to do this and have it fall flat, so to speak." He considered. "We'll just do some bluey."

"Bluey?"

"Viagra. Why not?"

"It won't make him feel bad that you think he needs bluey?"

He threw his hands up. "How can I win here? I'm trying to do the guy a favor."

"Of course. I just wondered if cocaine would be a little less … medicinal."

He tilted his head from side to side, lips pursed. "Could be right. Though Glen seems to think it's 'medicine.'" She kept her face deliberately blank, refusing to share the joke. "Hell, it's a party. We'll do both. Anyway, I'm not gonna broadcast it. In fact, why tell him? I can drop it in the whiskey. We'll all have some before the girls show up, and nobody the wiser. We'll all just think we're amazing studs. Fabulous way to start the week. Huge favor to Buck, even if he's never heard the rumors."

"Well. That sounds great, then."

"Too bad you can't join us. Maybe by next year, you know?"

"Well," Georgia said, smiling, "I could hardly be part of this party, even if I was in sales."

"Don't sell yourself short. I think you could be one of the friendly girls." He shrugged. "They get paid, but they aren't really any better looking than you are." *He thought that was a compliment. Too bad Charlie didn't have a heart condition.*

She made her smile grateful, if slightly shy. "Thanks, Charlie. Appreciate the ego boost. Anyway, I'll think about what you said about moving into sales. Maybe I'll call you in a few weeks, after this SEC thing dies down. Have fun at the kick-off."

Done, she thought, as she waited for the elevator. Do your work, and then step back. The outcome was beyond her control, of course. Now it was up to Glen, and if it didn't work, there'd be time to figure out something else.

Why was she so uneasy?

∞

Katie-Ann stood in the open doorway and watched Georgia climb the stairs. She held a piece of paper in one hand and Wizard, their new black cat, in the other.

"Hey, Katie-Ann. What's up? Letter from Daddy? Traffic from San Francisco was nasty tonight."

"This is up," Katie-Ann said triumphantly, handing her the paper as she entered. It was a geometry exam, with red letters scrawled across the top that read, "90. A-. Extraordinary improvement!"

"Wow. Impressive."

"I even got an exclamation point from the old bullfrog. I'm gonna ask him tomorrow if I can retake the 'F' exam."

"That would be great. It's great already. Now you know you can do geometry."

Katie-Ann nuzzled the cat and set him down on the carpet, where he stretched languorously before sauntering away. "So this means donuts again, right?"

"Serious donuts. We'll head over as soon as I grab a sandwich. I need the fuel, anyway. I've got some thinking to do."

It was 11 by the time she'd cleaned up the kitchen and made it down to her car. She pulled her feet into a cross-legged position under the wool blanket. So what was bugging her? Something Ken had said about benefit of the doubt. He said they should give Terkes the benefit of the doubt. Instead she had eliminated the doubt by reviewing the email. Wasn't that a whole lot better?

But what if that wasn't what he meant? He'd also said something about second chances. Would he want Glen to have a second chance, kiddie porn and all? Why on earth would he want that?

And anyway, what if he did? That was Ken's whole weakness, letting toxic employees stay on when they needed to go. This was one tiny area where she saw things more clearly than he did.

Unless. What if she could offer Glen an alternative that was slightly less drastic, but would still get him out of the company? More trouble for her, of course. Could even be risky, if both plans fell through. Well, maybe not so risky. Retaliation would be a risk for him, too. After all, he knew what was in his email as well as she did.

What the heck. Be interesting to try something straightforward for once. If it worked, so much the better for both the company and Glen. And this second chance wouldn't depend on Glen being high-minded, exactly. He'd just need to see his own self-interest. If you were going to give Glen Terkes the benefit of the doubt about something, it should probably be about that.

∞

Georgia was rushing by Sally's office, clutching the draft earnings release, when Sally's new admin called out, "Georgia. Do you have a minute for Sally? We've been looking for you."

Well, no, as a matter of fact, she didn't have one single second for the Nusty Beech right now. Which of course was the wrong answer. She forced herself to slow down and turn dutifully into Sally's office with a friendly smile. Maybe now was as good a time as any. She just had to keep things separate.

"Oh, hi, Sally. How you doing today?" Sally was wearing an acid yellow, shiny blouse with speckled egg shapes on it.

"I'm fine, Georgia. Close the door. I wanted to thank you for alerting me to the meeting the other day about Charlie Reebuck's warning letter."

"Oh, no problem. Good meeting?"

"I think we got it under control. And while we were at it, I was able to set some parameters on the SEC inquiry. I can't believe what they intended to spend on document production. Good thing for the company I was there."

"I'm sure it was," Georgia agreed.

"So, what's new in the department now?"

Georgia pretended to consider. "Oh, well, nothing much. I mean, you know the latest on the options memo."

"I heard we didn't have any backdating issues."

"True. But it looks like we might have another issue that isn't so great."

"Which is …?" Sally acted like a dog who's just heard the word "walk."

"Well, we may have allowed departing employees to exercise their options after the options had technically expired."

"Really. And that's a problem because…?"

"Well, there's nothing to exercise. I mean, 'technically expired' is 'expired.' So some people might think they own stock that doesn't really exist."

"Well, of course." Sally waved her hand, dismissing the explanation as obvious and unnecessary. "How could we do something that stupid?"

"Evidently our policy was that a person had to submit their exercise notice within the thirty-day time limit, but they could get the check to us a few days later. Which cannot work because payment is required to complete an exercise, and by the time the check arrived the options had already ceased to exist."

"How utterly incompetent," Sally exclaimed with relish. "Why haven't they told me about it?"

Georgia shrugged. "I think they just wanted to get all their data, so they'd know exactly how big the problem is. I'm pretty sure you'd have found out about it sooner or later."

"That's not acceptable. I need to be involved now, while I can influence the process."

"Sure glad I mentioned it, then. Do you think you could do just a little camouflage, you know, like you did with the meeting? That way, he won't catch on that you got advance warning."

"Of course I will, Georgia. I always take care to protect my friends. You can count on it. Anything else?"

Georgia hesitated a little too long before delivering an uncertain "No."

Sally was instantly alert. "Nothing at all?"

"No, nothing else about our teams."

Sally cocked her head and smiled encouragingly, revealing those sparkly eyeteeth. "I'm interested in all aspects of the company."

"No, it's nothing. I'm sure he'll be able to right himself in no time."

"Who?"

Georgia's hand rose to cover her mouth. "Nothing, Sally, really. Didn't mean to worry you. I should get this press release over to investor relations."

And Georgia hurried from Sally's office.

That had probably gone well enough, she decided as she continued down the hall, but she really couldn't worry about it one way or the other. Very stressful to have two situations requiring special talents pile up like this. Right now she needed to forget that Sally even existed, and devote herself 100 percent to Glen.

∞

At 6:30 p.m. she cruised past Glen's office for the fifth time. The light was still visible under the door. The later she waited, the less likely they were to be interrupted, but he might leave for dinner soon. This was probably her best shot.

She knocked and cracked the door open. "Mr. Terkes?"

He hit a button on his cell phone and looked up. "Yeah. You need something?" He apparently hadn't been expecting anyone. His perfectly tailored suit coat was thrown over his table, and his deep purple silk tie was loosened.

"I'd like to talk to you for a minute." She stepped inside and closed the door.

"Whoa!" he said, holding up his palm. "No can do. Georgia, isn't that right? I'm in the middle of something now, Georgia."

"I'm here to talk about the side deal investigation." She sat down.

"Definitely no time to talk about yesterday's crisis. Got a crisis of my own right now. If you need something signed ..."

"I'm afraid this is still a crisis, too."

He frowned. "No it's not. Q's filed, problem solved."

"Not exactly, Mr. Terkes. I know there are still a lot of side deals that haven't been found yet, and that you told your salespeople to do them."

His mouth fell slightly open and he stared for several seconds, like he'd just spotted a rat in his office and regretted misplacing his baseball bat.

"You obviously have no idea what you're talking about." He stood up. "So by all means, stop talking about it before you get yourself in trouble. If you'll excuse me."

Georgia remained seated and scooted an email across his desk. "You might want to look at this."

He read for ten seconds, and tried to hand it back. "So what? The lawyers didn't think it was worth asking about."

Georgia kept her hands in her lap. "The lawyers didn't have it."

He dropped it on the desk between them. "Then why do you?"

"There are some others. I didn't think it was good to print them all."

"Good for what?" He remained standing, towering over her. "Help me out here. Are we talking about something? You are Georgia, the girl from our legal department? Does Ken know you're here?"

She snickered slightly in spite of herself. "Yes, I'm Georgia. I take notes in the executive team meetings. Ken doesn't know anything about this yet. That's why I'm here."

"Meaning?"

"Well, I just learned about these other side deals, and of course I will have to tell Ken. We both know what will happen then. If you're still doing these, it means we're lying to our shareholders. He'll have to reopen the investigation, just when we thought we'd managed to survive it. Our next 10-Q will be delayed, and our stock will tank."

"But, why do you ...?"

She spoke over him. "We'll spend time and money crawling through every single email you've sent or received in the last three years, and who knows what'll turn up? We're bound to find things that will be terrible for you and the company. Maybe even beyond the side deals."

A cloud passed across Glen's face and vanished.

"A lot of innocent shareholders and employees will get hurt," she continued. "You don't want that any more than I do."

He stared at her face while he decided on his next step. Then he sighed and sat wearily down. "Let me get this straight. You think this email is some kind of evidence of side deals?"

Nicely done. Sincere. Convincing.

"Oh, I really do," she said solemnly. "I've read thousands of emails in this side deal investigation, so I'm not exactly a novice. And it's not a matter of explaining away one. There are lots and lots of them." Which she was pretty sure would be true, if anybody continued looking.

"Well, my dear, you're 100 percent wrong. You're obviously in way over your head. But even if you were right, what's your point? You want something from me?"

"I want you to make it unnecessary for me to tell Ken anything. You can still make this a win-win for you and the company."

"Okay. And how's that, exactly?"

"Well, if you should decide to leave the company, you know, to spend more time with your family, then I won't have to go to Ken. The bad deals will stop, and everybody's reputation ..."

Glen Terkes' eyes widened to the size of golf balls. "You mean resign? You'd like me to resign? You thought you'd hand me a piece of paper, and then I'd resign?" He laughed, embarrassed for her. "Oh. Forgive me, Miss ...?"

"Griffin. It's Georgia Griffin."

"Right. You know, if I resign, Miss Griffin, it would be different from somebody like you resigning." He straightened his cuffs. "I really *am* this company. If I leave, the whole enterprise will tank within a week. Roy would never let that happen. By the way, I wonder how you could possibly think you're in a position to second-guess the lawyers on this."

"I'm not second-guessing anyone. When they see the email I've seen, they'll reach the same conclusion."

"They've seen everything they wanted to see. This is really quite ridiculous. I'm afraid you could be the one who needs to resign, if you try to kick up trouble. I'd hate to have you fired."

She shrugged. "How would firing me help? Once I tell a company officer, he has a duty to investigate, whether I'm still working here or not."

"Not if he realizes it's the confused rambling of some low-level admin who had no idea what she was looking at. Stuff she wasn't authorized to look at in the first place. What officer is going to listen to that?"

"It's the email he'll be listening to," she said evenly. "And anyway, the SEC listens to everything."

He cocked his head and raised an eyebrow. "The SEC. You're threatening me with the SEC? Let me get this straight. You want money."

"No. I want you to do the right thing for the company."

"And you believe you know what that is."

His astonishment was drifting toward full-blown indignation, judging by that flush in his cheeks. She couldn't blame him, really. Here he was, a Captain of Industry, and some germy, no-account rat was sniffing along his credenza as if it owned the place.

He studied her face for a moment and shrugged. "Well, Miss Griffin, you might not know how to spot a side deal, but you apparently do realize you're threatening to blow up the company. If your motive really is to help the company, then you won't go to Ken no matter what I say. You certainly won't go to the SEC. If you were going to, you'd have done it already. So forget this nonsense and go back to doing your job." He sighed. "Roy would be so disappointed to learn that our General Counsel can't keep control of his own employees."

"I'm sure you don't want to threaten Ken."

Glen barked a short laugh. "Was I born as young as you are?" He wadded up the email, and dropped it into his wastebasket. "If you care about this company, Miss Griffin, worry about some low-level nobody who makes irresponsible claims about the people who actually run the place."

"Sure you want to leave that for the cleaning people?"

He snatched the ball of paper out of the basket, then slowed down and tossed it toward her across the desk. "If it worries you, by all means shred it. You're quite right. We wouldn't want a cleaning lady to become as confused as you are, would we?" And with that he turned his back on her, and began hitting keys on his keyboard.

Well, that was quite a failure, she thought, as she headed down the stairwell to her car. She wasn't sure this second chances thing paid off, really.

Would her father have found a way to puncture such impenetrable self-confidence? He'd probably have known better than to waste his time in the first place, but then he didn't have Ken Madigan to think about. Which he would certainly disapprove of as a dangerous distraction, by the way.

Could she have done something to be taken more seriously? Threatening him with the kiddie porn would have been out-and-out blackmail. Way too risky, and almost certainly unnecessary. More side-deal email? Wouldn't have mattered. Why should Glen Terkes use a safety net under his high wire act when he was so confident he could simply never fall?

So where did that leave them? He seemed confident that she wouldn't go to Ken, and of course he was right. She felt confident he'd be afraid to have her fired, since he knew what was in his email even better than she did. Stalemate. Nothing for it now but to see what happened with the Charlie Reebuck gambit.

One thing was certain. Ken would have found this interchange as fascinating as she did. What a shame she could never share it with him.

CHAPTER 23

"Georgia, somebody's in trouble in this company, and I need to know who it is." Sally and Georgia were standing just inside the closed door of Sally's office, with a rather pronounced slam still vibrating the air, and Sally's hand guarding the handle. Georgia felt a slight panic that Sally was blocking her exit, which was of course irrational. This was what she'd been building toward. She was about to test her father's assertion that flattery is the lie most likely to be believed.

Looking uncomfortable was certainly easy enough. "Oh well, Sally, I'm not sure about that. If you haven't heard about it, then I probably misunderstood something. And if he is in trouble, I'm sure he can fix it himself."

"Who?"

"And if he can't, it probably won't have an impact on you."

"What??"

"I mean, you know, a negative one, anyway."

"Georgia, is this a joke of some kind? I should warn you, I have a very poor sense of humor."

"Oh, I'm sure that's not true."

Sally twitched with annoyance. For some reason she was sporting a perfectly tasteful cream-colored, silk blouse this morning. Forgot to do her laundry, maybe.

Georgia's pulse began to thud as she made herself hunch her shoulders and avert her eyes. "Well … Okay, I'll tell you. But I just overheard this, okay, so you won't blame me if it turns out I misinterpreted something?"

"Of course I won't blame you. Just tell me exactly what you heard, so I can judge for myself." She let go of the handle and brushed past Georgia to her desk, so that Georgia had to pivot on the thick carpet in order to face her. She noticed that the sickly rubber plant had finally been removed for decent burial, replaced by a healthy new plant with big green fronds. Poor thing.

"Well," Georgia began, "on Wednesday afternoon after the board meeting I started to go down to my car because I'd left my cell phone in it, and I like to keep it with me in case Katie-Ann calls."

"Yes." One urgent syllable.

"Well, and I decided to take the stairwell on the east side of the building, even though it's hot as blazes in there, because my car's right at the bottom and I wanted to be fast."

"Fine," Sally prompted, "and then you heard something?"

Georgia nodded. "As I was going down the stairwell from the third floor, I heard some male voices on the landing outside the door to the second floor. You know, nobody ever uses that stairwell in the summer, so I was surprised somebody was there."

"Yes!" Sally hissed through slightly clenched teeth.

"Well, I recognized Jean-Claude's voice and I just stopped."

"Jean-Claude. Go on."

"Jean-Claude was saying how disappointed he was by the latest stock drop. He's afraid we'll become a takeover target if we don't get the price back up. He said he was reaching a crisis in confidence that we had the right leader in place."

"Go on!"

"Well, then I heard Larry Stockton's voice, and realized there were several board members. Larry said if we'd reached the point of considering a change, we have to think about who's going to lead the company while we look for a replacement. Jared Winters asked Jean-Claude if he wanted to come back, and Jean-Claude did this little croaking sound that made everybody laugh.

"So then Jared said that on an interim basis he thought we should consider *you* in the role." *So implausible. Hard not to wince.* Georgia forced herself to breathe slowly.

"Really." Sally's impatience vanished, and she tilted her head to the side and smiled slightly, considering.

"But then Larry said that wouldn't work, because you're so loyal to Roy, you probably wouldn't even do it, and if you did, you'd just continue Roy's bad policies."

"This was Larry Stockton?"

"Yes, and Jean-Claude said it was unfortunate, but he agreed. So then Jared said maybe Andrea Hancock could do it, but Paul said we can't do anything that would slow down the 6.1 and Oracle compatibility. So then somebody said maybe Ken."

"Madigan?"

"They didn't say a last name. And then somebody else said maybe we'd have to get an interim leader from outside."

"And then what?"

"Well, then Larry complained he felt like he'd gone swimming in his suit, standing in that hot stairwell. They agreed that Jean-Claude would get all the non-employee directors on a call to discuss it further, because they might decide to move quickly."

Georgia shrugged. "And that's it. I was scared to death one of them would come up the stairs and find me there, but they all just went down and out. As soon as I heard the door slam, I ran back up to the third floor and waited in my cube until I was sure they were gone."

"Very interesting." Sally stared into the distance for a moment, then looked back at Georgia and asked lightly, "Have you told Ken about this?"

"I felt like maybe I shouldn't tell anybody, since I wasn't supposed to hear it myself. But do you think it's what I think it is? Is Roy in trouble?"

"Of course he's in trouble," Sally snapped. "What on earth else could it mean?"

Score!

"Then maybe I should tell Ken ..."

"No!" Sally barked and then smiled sweetly. "I mean, you have to do what you think is best, Georgia, but this is so serious that I think you'd be wise to keep it to yourself. If the board finds out you were eavesdropping, you might not have a job here much longer."

Georgia made her voice timid. "But you wouldn't tell ..."

Sally's reassuring smile was completely at odds with her glittering eyes. "Of course not, Georgia. I won't breathe a word of this to anybody. I'm surprised you even need to ask. It's good you told me, though, because I am in charge of Human Resources, and this is the most serious personnel problem there is. I need to think carefully how to handle it." She looked out her window and touched the scar above her eyebrow. "I just wonder what has upset them so?"

She needed to spoon feed this dimwit?

"Oh, you know what?" she said. "They were talking about that when I first opened the door. Something about releasing the 6.0 version of the software when it still had so many bugs in it."

"I see."

"And then refusing to acknowledge to our customers and employees how much trouble it caused. And they thought Roy should give Mark Balog the new staff he needs to prevent his current staff from quitting, instead of spending so much on a renovation employees don't even like or want.

"Yes."

"But it sounded like the biggest thing was that preannouncement, you know, that turned out to be wrong. And the way he keeps insisting it was the right thing to do, when the board seems confident it was actually sort of ill-advised."

"Well, of course," Sally sighed, shaking her head. "So misguided. Really, just the last straw." *So much for loyalty in Sally's butt-smooching little heart.*

"Well," Georgia continued, "I just hope we don't get stuck with somebody from outside who doesn't know a thing about our business.

It would be great if you could, you know, demonstrate you're ready to do the job if anything happens to Roy. That might put their minds at rest that they have the right person internally, which could make things easier all around."

"Very sensible, Georgia," Sally said, rewarding her with a soft smile. "You've evaluated this quite well."

"You might have to act pretty quickly, though. They could be working on an outside interim person already."

"Why do you say that?" Sally asked sharply.

"Oh, no information." Georgia held up her palms to prevent misleading her. "Just what I'm worried could be happening."

"Well, let me know right away if you do hear anything. And by the way, if I do get the job, I'll surely want a reliable right-hand person to help me out."

"You mean a really good admin?"

"Oh, Marla's going to be my admin. I think something more like an executive director position. Is that a job you'd like?"

Georgia widened her eyes. "Wow! You really think I'd be qualified?"

"I think you've shown real promise lately, Georgia. Keep your head down, say nothing about this to anyone, and we'll see where we end up."

"Thanks, Sally, that's exactly what I'll do. Bye now."

Yes! she thought as she heard Sally's door click shut behind her. She resisted the impulse to do a little dance right in the corridor, and began walking decorously back to her cube.

Of course, this was still very much a work in progress, she reminded herself. Sally was sniffing the bait but hadn't yet swallowed, and plenty could still go wrong. What if Sally decided to test the waters by taking one of the board members into her confidence? Could be messy. Well, Georgia couldn't control everything. Do your work and step back.

In the meantime, she was racking up some impressive job offers around here. Sales Team Friendly Girl. Sally's Henchperson. Executive Henchperson, no less. Who knew such brilliant careers were available, right here in Silicon Valley?

∞

On her way home, Georgia retrieved a fat envelope from her father's lawyer. Finally! This must be her father's literary effort. She'd read it after dinner, but she could at least take a peek before she drove off from the Mail Boxes Etc. She smiled up through her windshield at a blue jay bobbing on a poplar branch, then tore open the heavy envelope.

The contents were confusing. There were ten or more xeroxed pages of crabbed, slanting handwriting that didn't look like her father's at all. And from the copy, it looked like the pages of the original document were brittle and flaked around the edges. When she noted that the pages were set up with entry dates, her curiosity was replaced by stirrings of alarm. She found the first page, read the first several entries, and then slapped the pages onto her lap. Honestly. If her father wasn't careful, his boredom was going to get him in trouble after all. Literary effort indeed, Daddy. Outside her windshield, the blue jay gave a raucous squawk and flew away, leaving the poplar branch bouncing gently in his wake.

∞

The group lunch on Monday was at the Cocky Robin, planned to coincide with the first day of the sales kick-off. Afterward, Georgia rode back to the office with Zack, who looked cheerful and relaxed in his wraparound sunglasses as he maneuvered his black Lexus along Zanker Road. The sun felt hot on Georgia's forehead with the top down, and she kept reaching up to anchor her black hair, which was blowing in annoying little egg-beater circles around her face.

"Wish we could do that more often," Zack said, his left elbow resting on his door as he used his right hand to steer through traffic. His car phone rang, and he pressed the button on his steering wheel.

"Zack?"

"Hey, Ken. Georgia's here in the car with me."

"Hi Georgia. Zack, could you pull over for a minute?"

"Yeah, hold on." He and Georgia exchanged a quick glance of alarm as he maneuvered out of traffic and stopped on the shoulder. "Hope something hasn't blown up with the SEC," he said quietly, as the motor whirred and the top rose out of the trunk to enclose them. "Okay, Ken, we're here. What's up?"

"I just got a call from Sally. Guys... Glen Terkes is dead."

Zack yanked off his sunglasses and stared at Georgia. "Dead?!"

So they must have done the kick-off party as planned. Suddenly in the hot car her hands felt icy.

"He didn't show up for the keynote speech at the sales kick-off this morning," Ken continued, "and he was supposed to introduce Roy. People got worried, and it turned out the police had already found him ... passed away in his hotel room."

"Do they know what he died of?" Zack asked. *Terminal perversion,* Georgia thought.

"The paramedics think he had a massive heart attack around four or five this morning."

"Oh, God, that's terrible," Zack said. "I'm stunned."

"It's very bad," Ken agreed. "Rumors are spreading like crazy, and the whole kick-off's in chaos. I've been asked to talk to his wife, so I'm headed over there now."

"You have to tell his wife?" Zack asked with horror, staring at the phone. Georgia certainly hadn't meant to involve Ken in the family stuff. She wondered if Glen's wife knew about the kiddie porn. She rested three fingers against the pulse thudding in her neck.

"Well, I think the police have already told her, but I need to be there to help in any way I can."

"Of course. How can I help?" He glanced at Georgia, who was now grateful for the small privacy of her tangled hair obscuring part of her face. She had known this was possible, of course, although she hadn't really expected it. But now that it had happened she felt not only shock, but dread as well. If Ken knew she'd played any part in it, he'd be horrified. He would never think it was okay to wish for the death of another person. More than wish. Facilitate it, really, even though it depended upon Glen's choosing to behave abominably. She focused on her breath to steady herself for a moment before returning to the conversation in the car.

"…thinking about what we announce and when," Ken was saying. "We're going to need to say something both internally and externally fairly soon. I'd like to get a first draft ready by the end of the day."

"Let me handle that with the communications people," Zack offered. "How old was he?"

"Forty-seven."

Zack groaned. "Dying by yourself in a Las Vegas hotel room. How lonely is that?"

There was a brief silence. "Actually, Zack, that's why I want to get started on the internal communication. He apparently wasn't alone."

∞

Maggie let Georgia and Zack know that Ken was ready for them that evening just after six. Quan was already with him, and Ken's tie was undone, hanging in crooked, red ribbons against his creased yellow shirt.

"How'd it go?" Zack asked.

"As well as it could go, I guess." He closed his eyes in a long blink and brushed his hand across the top of his hair. "Anna Terkes seems to be a pretty strong woman. The sons are flying in tomorrow. The company learned for the first time today that Glen had a hereditary heart disease that killed both his parents—his father in his forties, his mother in her fifties. Glen and Anna have been managing his health together for their entire married life, and Glen's been taking powerful medication for years. He and Anna certainly knew this could happen. Which makes it even more surprising…" He glanced at Georgia and lowered his voice. "Apparently there'd been quite a party in his suite the night before, and he was engaged in activities that he knew were dangerous." Which was quite an understatement.

"Anna told me she and Glen haven't had all that close a marriage for a number of years now. I guess Glen always traveled a lot, and Anna went back to school while she was raising the boys and has a PhD in linguistics. They've been leading fairly separate lives for a long time.

"She has her suspicions, but I don't think she knows about the—what?—orgy? Sorry, Georgia, that's an awful word. Probably more of a party that really got out of hand. I just hope Anna never finds out. Can you imagine an executive of our company participating with his own team in some group sex and drug ...!" He covered his eyes and waved a hand in the air. "I guess I'm just going to be a naive choir boy all the way to my grave."

She hoped so. It was one of his finest qualities.

If Ken was that shocked by prostitutes, what on earth would he make of those crotch shots of children? She wondered with a twinge of despair what it meant about her that she was better able to take kiddie porn in stride than big, ex-military Ken Madigan. Well. No point in dwelling on that. Somebody had to take it in stride in order to deal with it.

"I don't think you're naive," Zack was saying. "I'm shocked by it, too, if only because of the sheer stupidity."

"I gave it 50-50," she murmured.

"Sorry?" Ken said, looking at her. "You gave what 50-50?"

Dumb. Get a grip. "Oh, you know, just the idea that he'd sleep with a prostitute at a party." She made herself shrug. "I mean, I would've said 50-50 if I'd ever thought about it."

"Boy, not me. Anyway, Anna's asked not to have an autopsy. She doesn't have a lot of illusions, but I think she feels the less focus on his last few hours the better. And the coroner has agreed because of Glen's heart condition.

"I tell you guys. We really need to cherish the people we're close to, because we could lose them in an instant. We know that, but it's always shocking when something like this happens."

He was silent a moment. "So. There's going to be a memorial service, but I think we need to get the internal message out tonight if we can. That a draft? Great, let's take a look." He took a copy from Zack and read through it. "Let's add the part about his heart condition, okay? And his parents' heart condition." He made some notations and handed it back. "Okay, read it out loud, Zack, will you? Let's try to focus on this so we can all get home to our families."

Dear Colleagues,

It is with great sadness that I inform you Glen Terkes has passed away. He died from the hereditary heart disease that claimed both of his parents at early ages. Glen was 47.

As most of you know, Glen was our VP of Worldwide Sales for just over two years. During his short tenure, annual sales grew from $1 billion to $1.2 billion. Glen consistently exhibited the highest standards of leadership and integrity, and we are very lucky to have had him for as long as we did. We'll miss him greatly.

Glen is survived by his wife, Anna, and their two adult sons. Our sympathies are with them, and I am pleased to report that the company will accelerate the vesting of Glen's options to assist the family with financial security. Plans for a memorial service will be announced when they have been finalized.

On an interim basis, I have asked Charlie Reebuck to step into Glen's role. Please give Charlie your full support as he serves the company in this critical temporary capacity. The search for a new VP of Worldwide Sales will begin immediately.

Roy

"Nice email," Ken said.

"And generous," Quan added. "*'Highest standards of leadership and integrity.'*"

"True," Georgia agreed. "Maybe when I die they'll say I was Mother Teresa."

"Come on, guys," Zack protested. "Shouldn't we be slightly respectful?"

"Glen was a good person," Ken said. "There aren't a lot of us who meet the highest standards as often as we should."

Seemed snarky to ask whether Stalin was a good person. After all, Ken didn't know what she knew: that Glen was definitely causing the side deals. That he enjoyed kiddie porn, and apparently kiddies themselves. (Had that thirteen-year-old Katie-Ann lookalike in Tulsa managed to escape?) She realized she had put her hand over her mouth and dropped it back onto the table.

"True," Quan agreed lightly. "Anyway, hypocrisy has its benefits, and I guess this is one of them. It wouldn't be good for the relatives if you said 'lowest standards of leadership and integrity.'" And he didn't even know about the porn. She sucked in her lips to suppress a smile, and allowed herself to shoot him a perhaps mystifying look of gratitude.

"Besides," Zack continued, "they weren't the lowest. Did you see who's replacing him?"

"Can you believe that?" Ken rolled his eyes to the ceiling and threw his hands in the air. "How could Roy possibly put Charlie Reebuck in charge? We're really gonna have to scrutinize the deals now."

"It should motivate everyone to move quickly on the right replacement," Quan said. "Ken, can you be part of the interview team?"

"I can try." He was silent a moment. "I think all of us should plan to go the memorial service."

No. No way.

"I don't think I should," she said.

"Why not?"

"I think everybody deserves to only have people at his funeral who really cared about him. I didn't respect Glen when he worked here, and I'd feel phony going to his funeral."

Ken looked puzzled. "I'm not sure it's ever phony to express respect and sadness for a person dying."

Georgia shrugged. "Dying doesn't turn a bad person into a good one."

Ken's look of alarm made it clear she had said something inappropriate. Must be a Catholic thing. Only imagine what he'd think if he knew she'd played a part in it. The feeling of dread returned with a vengeance, and to her astonishment she was suddenly blinking back tears.

"Sorry," she said in a constricted voice. "I didn't express that very well. Of course, it's always sad when a person dies. I just mean we should sincerely respect the person's death."

His look of alarm lingered an instant, then evaporated. "We should, Georgia. Absolutely. Then it sounds like you shouldn't go. I'll be there for the family, for Anna in particular. The rest of you should only go if you feel right about it. In the meantime, I'll see if I can get myself onto the hiring committee, like Quan suggested."

That night she left Katie-Ann bent over an essay and made her way downstairs and into the passenger seat of her car. The air sure was hazy tonight. Was there a wildfire somewhere? She had to search a while to find even the brightest star in Orion's belt.

It was certainly sad for Glen that he died, but was it sad for anybody else? It wasn't just the company that was better off without him, it was also his own wife, vulnerable teenagers, and basically the whole human race.

That was so callous. Did she really believe it?

Yes, she admitted a few moments later, she just really did. Ken was a nicer person than she was, but she'd seen some things she couldn't ever un-see, and that made her more realistic. Or maybe just more cynical. It was confusing. Terkes the pedophile had to be stopped, and he was stopped, impaled on his own vices without tanking the company. But her involvement was something she'd find it unbearable to have Ken know about. Was that her conscience, or just her need for Ken's good opinion? Were they different? She pressed her fingers against her closed eyelids and focused on her breath.

CHAPTER 24

Georgia sat in the boardroom, her pale forearm resting on the dark, polished conference table as she waited for Roy's voice to come through the speakerphone so the executive team meeting could begin. He was late, and she distracted herself by leaning over the table and checking different angles to see whether the highly polished surface could be made to reflect her pale, freckled face, or at least the outline of her black, blunt-cut hair. Perhaps in honor of Roy's physical absence, somebody had located the thermostat and savagely throttled back the air conditioning, so that the bright sunshine streaming in through the floor-to-ceiling window seemed consistent rather than taunting. Ken had draped his suit coat over the back of his chair, and was absent-mindedly rolling up his white shirtsleeves as he concentrated on a document on the table in front of him.

Lumina stock was being pelted daily by analyst reports that ranged from skeptical to scathing in their evaluation of the preannouncement. Although the stock price was now sticking around 17½, rumor had it that Roy's tour to meet with financial analysts had taken on the hunkered-down feeling of a siege.

So why wasn't there a feeling of crisis here in the room? Instead, the mood was one of lethargy as they waited for Roy to come onto the speakerphone. The only human sound came from Sally and Giuseppe, who were whispering calmly with their heads together. Andrea was draped over her chair sideways, thumb-typing on her iPhone. Charlie Reebuck, dynamic new head of worldwide sales, was slouched down until his chin nearly touched the table. At one point Georgia felt his eyes on her, but when she looked up his glance skittered away before she could make eye contact. Even having Sally and Andrea in the same room lacked the usual crackle of danger. Were these guys just giving up?

Only Mark Balog radiated his usual high energy. He sat firmly upright, his spotless yellow tie perfectly centered on his starched blue shirt, his fingers flying across his keyboard. She decided to check in with him.

"*Hw R U?*" she texted.

A minute later he responded. "*Horrbl. Thx 4 asking :-)*"

"*smthing hppnd?*"

"*15 resignatns this am.*"

She glanced up with raised eyebrows. He smiled brightly from across the room and tilted his head to indicate a stack of documents resting under his palm.

"*15 n 1 day?*"

"*15 n 1 hr. nvr seen anthng like ths.*"

"*!!! Xactly as u predicted.*"

Well. This should get the energy pumping.

The speakerphone crackled and Roy called a curt hello.

"Hey Roy," Ken called back. "How go the analyst interviews this morning?"

"Much better. We've turned the corner. I'm finally getting through to these people that the preannouncement was an appropriate and necessary response to what we were seeing in the numbers."

"Great," Sally muttered. "Maybe they can explain it to the rest of us."

Ho, and the big fish swallows the bait!

Andrea's thumbs froze over her iPhone, and she caught Ken's eye.

"What was that?" Roy called through the phone.

"That was me, Roy," Sally called back sweetly, batting her eyes theatrically for the benefit of those in the room. "I just said that's great. Maybe they'll retract those nasty analyst reports they've been putting out."

"That's behind us," Roy declared. "They just needed to be reassured by talking through the rationale with me."

"No doubt," Sally responded with an icy little smile.

Andrea swung her feet around onto the floor and rested her chin on the heel of her hand as she scrutinized Sally. Sally appeared not to notice.

Georgia text to Ken: *Whts ths?*

Ken text to Georgia: *No idea.*

"In any event," Roy continued, "we're getting momentum around the Calypso acquisition, so we're in good shape there. All under control. Cliff, take us through the agenda, and make it quick. I have another analyst meeting in half an hour."

"I realize time is of the essence, Roy," Mark interjected, "but I do have something I need to bring up."

"Sorry, there's no ..."

Mark shouted, "Fifteen people resigned this morning!"

After a moment of shocked silence, Ken said, "Jesus, Mary and Joseph!"

"Did you say fifteen?" Roy asked.

"One five," Mark confirmed brightly into the phone through his tight grin. "I guess that's the silver lining. At least it's not five oh—yet. They've all given two weeks' notice, so they'll be gone on the 28th."

"Sounds like organized insurrection." The words 'organized insurrection' evidently tasted like quinine. "And this mass exodus occurred because ...?"

"Nobody's told me that yet. The letters arrived on my desk just before this meeting. But you know, Roy, these are people who've been telling us for months that conditions were intolerable."

"Yes, your group has always enjoyed whining. You should've shut it down a long time ago, and now you'll have to show some actual leadership to turn it around."

"I'm certainly hoping to turn it around, Roy," Mark said brightly. "I'll need to speak to you about what we can do after I talk with them."

"Sally needs to become involved now. Sally?"

"I'll be on it right after this meeting," she confirmed.

"To be clear, I expect good news on this shortly."

Georgia text to Ken: *Dz he care if its accurat?*

∞

Dearest Daddy,

Thanks so much for letting me read the first installment of the lost diary of Robert E. Lee. General Lee's handwriting is excellent. I found samples on the Internet, and I do believe it would take some real scrutiny to detect any difference.

Your fascination with the Civil War shines through, and of course I see the appeal of such a challenge at a time when your other opportunities are temporarily unavailable. General Lee certainly has more dimension and personality than has formerly been supposed. His description of the whore with the hornet up her skirt is funnier than a hairpiece on a frog.

But Daddy, isn't that sort of a problem? I'm pretty sure there are some well-researched biographies of General Lee. Did he ever even make it to Arkansas? A newly unearthed diary could potentially alter more than a hundred years of scholarship, and might attract the kind of attention you'd prefer to avoid right now, especially when your address is so fixed.

I wonder if it would be safer to forge—She couldn't write that. Too dangerous.—*simulate*—no, still too dangerous—*research somebody slightly less famous while you're waiting for your parole hearing. I would love to read the diary of General Lee's favorite cook. You could keep a lot of the local color, and you wouldn't have to worry about the handwriting. I'll bet you could get good money for it.*

Anyway, those are my thoughts. Katie-Ann and I are doing fine and looking forward to the day we can show you first-hand how comfortable our little apartment has become. Katie-Ann named

*our new cat Wizard, in the hope that we can retrieve Blizzard
one day, and then we'll have black and white cats whose names
will rhyme.*
We think of you always.
Your loving daughter,
Georgia

∞

Georgia didn't know why she'd been called to a 7:30 a.m. emergency
meeting in Ken's office, and Ken wasn't there to tell them. She and
Zack were joking that it must be serious if they were being bribed with
scones as well as coffee, when Sally marched in through the open door
and seated herself at one end of the table. Zack shot Georgia a look that
meant "There goes the neighborhood," and they lapsed into awkward
silence while they waited. Through the window she could see raindrops
dotting the parking lot and pattering onto the tops of dusty cars. Her
first fall in California. Would Katie-Ann remember to take her windbreaker to school?

Ken and Quan hurried into the office together. "Okay, everybody,"
Ken said. "Thanks for showing up on short notice. We're here to consider
the SEC's somewhat surprising request for testimony under oath, which
came up in Quan's meeting with them yesterday. Quan, fill us in?"

Quan adjusted his rimless glasses. "I was there with Marcus Baker
from the finance department, because they had asked me to make him
available for what we thought was a wrap-up meeting. You recall they
have now reviewed thousands of documents we made available here
in our document room. Despite their irritation that we asked them to
come here instead of providing them with copies, they made it clear
last week that they viewed the dual books complaint as baseless.

"So we marched cheerfully into the wrap-up meeting, but unfortunately they didn't wrap up. Instead, they started asking Marcus a lot
of questions about backlog."

"Backlog?" Zack's hands dropped from the top of his head onto the table.

"Yes. Backlog."

"What's backlog got to do with anything?"

"Exactly," Ken nodded. "As you can imagine, we were quite disturbed."

Georgia raised her hand just above her head. "I'm probably the only one here who's never heard of backlog."

"As you know," Ken explained, "we have to ship our product to the customer before we can count the revenue. Backlog is when we have unshipped orders at the end of the quarter, meaning we don't count the sales revenue until the following quarter. This builds up a reservoir of guaranteed revenue at the start of each new quarter, which is what we call backlog. Completely unrelated to dual books." He nodded to Quan to continue.

"So Marcus answered their questions, and then I ran down to my car and called Jill. Apparently the SEC has been complaining for a while now that companies can arbitrarily build up backlog and then ship it all out in a bad quarter, to prevent investors from realizing that the business is in trouble. Jill thinks they're looking for a test case, and now we fear the test case will be us."

"Well, great." Sally let her crossed arms drop heavily against her neon orange midriff to emphasize her disgusted sigh. "I told Roy it was stupid to antagonize them by being cheap about the copies. I wonder how he'll like living with the consequences."

Ken raised his eyebrows. "I'm surprised to hear you say that, Sally. I thought saving money on copies was your idea."

"Don't be ridiculous," Sally snapped. "I was just the messenger carrying another witless message."

Roy was now witless. Excellent.

Zack texted Georgia: *bware. aliens hve abductd Sally nd snt us ths impostr.*

Georgia texted back: *mayb hr suckg muscles jst wore out.*

"And then," Quan was saying, "they made this alarming request to have Marcus testify under oath. Isn't that quite unusual for an informal investigation?"

"Unusual and dangerous," Ken confirmed. "Have they asked us for anything in the way of documents?"

"Not yet, but I feel confident the request is coming. I'm just wondering what we should do about it."

"The only thing we can do is recognize the danger and prepare," Ken replied. "Their request for documents will again be 'voluntary,' and we'll smile and cooperate. Same with Marcus's testimony. If we don't cooperate, they'll just serve a subpoena on us to make it formal, and then we'll have to comply and disclose it to boot."

"I don't seem to know what our backlog policy is," Zack confessed, glancing around the room. "Does anybody else?"

"All I know so far," Quan responded, "is that we use it, apparently like everybody else in Silicon Valley."

"Okay," Ken said. "Here's what I'd do. Get Cliff and Jill to give us a briefing on backlog tomorrow morning. Ask Jill to bring that young lawyer—Fallon?—to join us. Maybe he can start pulling together a list of documents, if not the documents themselves."

"Pull the documents now," Sally directed. "Let's try to cooperate promptly for once." She ignored the incredulous stares.

Fallon, Georgia thought. Eddie must have done something smart to show up on Ken's radar screen. What would it be like to run into him again? Probably forgotten all about her by now.

"Could I have prevented this problem from developing?" Quan asked, raking his black hair back from his face. "For example, should I have prevented Marcus from answering their questions?"

Ken shook his head. "Heck no. That would only have made them twice as suspicious. You did exactly the right thing, Quan, and now you're doing everything possible just by getting out in front of it."

"Maybe before we congratulate ourselves," Sally suggested, "we should try getting something right."

"Any news on attrition?" Zack inquired cheerfully.

∞

"Here you are," Nikki said, handing a folder across her desk to Georgia, who stood just inside her doorway. Nikki's dark hair was swept into a ponytail that revealed her little square earrings with tiny diamonds in the center. "He's still in a meeting with one of the finalists for the worldwide sales role, but everything he signed should be in here. I don't think there was anything..." She looked past Georgia into the doorway behind her. "Hi, Sally, did you need something?"

"I need to stop this nightmare renovation," Sally responded, sighing dramatically and passing her hand over her eyes as she pushed past Georgia into the little office. "But if you can't offer that, I'll settle for an appointment with the genius who started it."

Nikki frowned. "Sally, did you just imply that Roy is stupid?"

"I don't need to explain..."

"Because here's the deal." Nikki's ponytail bobbed emphatically. "Even if Roy were a moron, he also happens to be my boss, and I don't care to listen to his subordinates being disrespectful. What if a customer heard you?"

"All I said was..."

"I know what you said. Don't say it again in front of me. Now, you wanted an appointment with Mr. Zisko?"

She signaled for Georgia to shut the door the instant Sally was gone. "Did you hear that? What was that even about? She usually acts like this renovation is the greatest thing since the invention of sex."

Georgia shrugged. "Don't know, but she's been criticizing Roy about other stuff, too. Did they have a big argument or something?"

Nikki frowned, considering. "Boy, not that I'm aware of. She still just sails in and out of his office like she owns the place. Ugh! The only thing worse than a suck-up is a back-stabbing suck-up."

"You never know," Georgia said. "Maybe there's something even worse we haven't seen yet." Nikki glared silently at her desk, and Georgia decided to seize her opening. "You think you should, you know, warn Roy or something?"

"If this keeps up I'll have to. It's just so weird. Anyway, you got all your signatures? Let me know if you see her do that again, okay? It's just so fucking weird."

∞

Georgia was unlocking her car in the dark parking lot at midnight when a voice whispered "Georgia!"

She suppressed a scream.

"Georgia!" The voice was urgent. "In here!"

She whirled around to see Charlie Reebuck, bent over and looking up at her from the driver's seat of the car next to her. "God, Charlie. You scared me a little."

"Need to talk to you."

"Great. Why are you whispering?"

He reached across and popped open the passenger door. After the slightest hesitation, she got in and closed the door.

"What's up?" she asked cheerfully.

"I think we killed him." *Did Charlie Reebuck actually have a conscience? You couldn't count on anything in this world.*

"Sorry?"

"Okay. Okay. You could say it was me, mostly ..."

"Who are you talking about? Glen?"

"Somebody else dead? Listen. Can they, you know, put me in jail?"

Georgia cocked her head, frowning. "For what? I heard he had a heart condition."

"I know. I know. But you don't think the blue ..."

Georgia held up her hand. "Do not tell me *anything* you don't want me to testify to in court. Or anybody else, for that matter. You understand me?"

He nodded.

"Did you know Glen had a heart condition?"

"No! I swear! I'd never..."

"Well, that's just it. He's the one who knew. You didn't make him pair off with that stripper, if..." she held up her hand again "... he did happen to pair off with a stripper. Or a dozen strippers, for that matter. All you did—possibly—at most—is slip him a little recreational enhancement."

"I did it for Buck! He..."

She held up her hand again and emphasized each word. "Glen chose poorly."

"I warned him that girl was dangerous. Not because of the heart problem—who knew? But just because she was jail bait, you know?"

Jail bait.

She tilted her head and asked thoughtfully, "What exactly do you mean by jail bait, Charlie?"

"She looked like a kid playing dress-up, far as I could see. You know, wearing her mother's lipstick? Couldn't possibly have been more than fourteen. Not what she told him, apparently, so what could I do about it? But I bet that's why she ran away instead of telling us. Maybe if we'd found him sooner..." He was gripping his steering wheel with both hands and looking through the windshield into the dark lot.

So Glen Terkes really was a full-blown pedophile.

"She came with the other strippers?"

He shrugged. "I thought so, but then they couldn't find her after ..." He shook the steering wheel with both hands, still staring forward.

"Look," Georgia said, "It's very, very unfortunate, and you might consider other ways to liven up your parties from now on. But I don't think you need to worry about criminal liability here, especially if you keep your mouth shut. Now, if you did start talking..."

"I won't! Jesus, are you kidding?" He was quiet for a good five seconds, his hands still locked on the wheel. "You know what? I think you're right. He chose poorly. Yeah. I was just trying to help Buck, you know? You're definitely right." He let go of the wheel and sighed. "Good to talk about this. I was getting a little excited. You ever want a job in sales you've got it, no further discussion, okay?" He glanced away from the windshield just long enough to make eye contact and then back again. Still inviting her to join the fun sales team, but his heart definitely wasn't in it.

"That's great, Charlie. I really appreciate it. You know what you can do for me in the meantime?"

He looked at her warily. "What's that?"

"Stop with the phony deals."

"What phony deals?"

"Charlie."

"All right. All right. Sorry."

"Stop doing those phony deals with distributors, okay? The auditors are totally onto it now, and you're gonna take the whole company down. Tell your buddies, too. No more phony deals."

"Well, they aren't phony, actually, they're just . . ."

"Charlie."

"All right! I'll do it. I will. No more pull-forward deals. I'll tell 'em. And if we can't make the quarter, well . . ." His eyes sort of bulged as he imagined it.

"I'd be very disappointed if another one of those pull-forward deals comes through."

"I know. I got it covered." He paused. "Glen chose poorly. He chose poorly." He pulled his key out of his pocket and stuck it in the ignition. "Tell you what, let's have a drink sometime."

"Great. One of these days I'd love to have a drink." She opened her car door, and then surprised herself by turning back. "Look, can I say this once more before we never talk about it again? If you didn't know about his heart condition, then it was not your fault. It couldn't be your fault. You understand me?" She stood next to the car and lifted her palm in farewell as he started his engine and backed out.

Jail bait, indeed. Where had that kid come from? Could B. Rotkin be an alias for somebody inside Lumina?

She hoped Charlie wouldn't be upset for long. Waste of good conscience, really, and he didn't have much to spare. He should redirect his newfound scruples toward those phony deals. Which, sadly, he would never do.

Ah, well, she thought as she turned out of the parking lot. The auditors would find the next bad deal, and then, without Glen to protect him, Charlie would be gone for good. Stopping the side deals cold would have been pure gravy. She could accomplish quite a bit sometimes, but trying to persuade Charlie to think more than four seconds into the future was about as effective as a screen door on a submarine.

CHAPTER 25

Georgia was idly listening to Nikki's half of a phone conversation while she waited to get a signature from Roy. "Roy's finishing up with Jonathan Bascom now," Nikki reported into the phone, her plastic bracelets clacking as she used her other hand to flip through files in the bottom drawer of her desk. "If they're not done in another minute, I'll stick my head in."

Bascom, Georgia thought. Bascom. She'd heard that name before, and had some vague, negative feeling about it. She was about to question Nikki when Roy's office door opened and Jonathan Bascom emerged.

Surely not, Georgia thought. Large Romeo, the world's fattest sales guy from the yacht? She looked in horror at Nikki, who nodded once, almost imperceptibly, in solemn confirmation.

Roy slapped Mr. Bascom on the shoulder as they shook hands. They were both beaming. Roy waved good-bye, noticed Georgia and reached out for her document folder. "Make this quick. I'm about to announce our new VP of Worldwide Sales."

This was just downright discouraging.

∞

Jean-Claude called the board meeting to order in the slightly nasal accent that Georgia had begun to eagerly anticipate. Who knew nasal could sound so alluring? One of the few genuinely attractive men in this testosterone-drenched company, and old enough to be her grandfather. Too bad Katie-Ann had interrupted that invitation-in-the-making from gray-eyed Eddie Fallon. Now that had been a man with promise.

Larry was seated next to Jean-Claude, his jet-black hair firmly in place, his red tie pinioned against his silver shirt by a vicious-looking stick pin. Nobody was ever going to accuse Larry of being alluring.

"We have a quorum and should begin," Jean-Claude called with a smile. "Today we must start with the happy news that the 6.1 is nearly ready for release and will after all achieve compatibility with all thirteen configurations of SAP. Roy, you will please convey our big congratulations to Andrea, who once again has met a very important goal for our company.

"Now Ken will speak about the SEC inquiry, and then Sally will report to us on her efforts to reduce attrition." Look at that, Sally was wearing her favorite mustard yellow suit jacket with the red embroidered cherries. Something special doing in attrition?

Ken reported that the SEC investigation had now morphed completely into a backlog investigation.

"So why are they pursuing this with us, Ken?" Jared's navy blazer accentuated his elegant and very white hair. "Do we stand out somehow in our use of backlog, or were we just in the wrong place at the wrong time?"

"As far as I know," Ken responded, "our backlog practices are consistent with those of every other Silicon Valley company. I just think once they'd assigned somebody to investigate this complaint about dual books, they found it convenient to use the open channel to investigate their new pet project."

"And to punish us for being uncooperative," Sally added.

Larry swiveled a frowning gaze onto Sally, his forearms planted firmly on the table. "What was that?"

To Georgia it sounded like a warning to shut up, but Sally apparently heard an invitation.

"Ken and I were directed to cut costs in responding to the SEC, which forced their staff to come to our offices to review documents instead of getting their own copies as they requested. In retrospect, it does seem unfortunate." *Bold.*

If Roy was troubled by Sally's remark he didn't reveal it. "The SEC loves nothing better than to waste other people's money," he declared. "I don't know why we should make it easy for them."

Sally's smile was tinged with triumph.

"Well," Ken continued, "however we got here, we have now moved into an area of investigation that is more dangerous than the original one, simply because the rules about backlog are shifting under our feet. The SEC evidently wants to rewrite those rules in the guise of 'clarifying' them, and plans to use us as their poster child."

"Poster victim," Jared corrected. "Well, the first deposition should tell us more about their theory. Get back to Jean-Claude at that point, will you, Ken?"

Sally smiled ruefully as she stood for the attrition discussion. "I wish I were bringing you good news. Unfortunately, our bleak picture has only gotten bleaker. What I do hope to bring you is insight into the causes of this crisis and a new, more radical plan to meet the attrition goals the board has so wisely mandated.

"Let's start with the numbers." A slide with three columns of numbers appeared on the big screen. "We were at 40 percent attrition six weeks ago, and you mandated 28 percent within a year. This shows the quarterly milestones to get us there.

"We ran the numbers in preparation for this meeting. In fact, there has been a change, but it's been in the wrong direction. It seems we have now gone from 40 percent to 43 percent. This means at current course and speed, almost half of our employees will leave within one year." She looked directly into Jean-Claude's eyes for one beat, then Jared's, then her eyes came to rest on Larry's.

"That's a kind of progress, certainly," Jared responded dryly. "Is there an explanation?"

"Well, the unfortunate micro-trend seems to be occurring in two parts of the company. First, in the last month we have lost a number of fairly senior sales executives, and then we had a mass resignation of tech support people last week."

"Take those one at a time, if you please," Larry directed, adjusting a French cuff.

"Of course. To be specific, we have lost thirty sales executives in the last month, concentrated partly over in the UK, but really just an exodus of our best sales executives across the company." The board members murmured in alarm.

Roy asserted his control of the discussion. "The sales team was very shaken by the unexpected loss of Glen, Larry. That pretty much accounts for the numbers there."

"Actually," Sally contradicted, her eyes remaining on Larry, "that doesn't seem to be quite accurate. We've started doing exit interviews on these folk, and Glen's death is pretty far down the list. If you don't mind, I'll get to that data in a minute.

"On the tech support side, a week ago Friday Mark Balog received fifteen resignations in one day..."

"Really!" Paul remarked, the waxed dome of his head reflecting more light than the polished table.

"And this week there have been three more."

"We're turning all of those around," Roy declared.

"Great," Jared responded with a bright smile and elevated eyebrows. "And how are we doing that?"

Sally's smile was indulgent. "Well, Roy may be a little more hopeful about that than I am. But before we get to solutions, I'd like to talk about causes."

She tapped her keyboard and a new slide appeared on the screen.

"In the last two weeks we've had the dubious pleasure of interviewing thirty-seven employees who have announced they are leaving the company. The departing sales executives cited: poor product reputation due to the premature release of 6.0; inadequate tech support when issues with product installations arise; and lack of confidence that the management team can tackle the hard problems facing the company.

"Three people did cite the loss of Glen Terkes," she conceded.

"That's one reason I moved so quickly to get Jonathan Bascom," Roy inserted.

"What those three said," Sally continued, raising her voice slightly to drown out the interruption, "was that since they're going to have a new boss anyway, why not move to a company where the product's reputation actually helps the sale instead of hindering it?" *Had Sally decided to distance herself from Roy under his very nose? Could explain the favorite mustard-colored suit.*

"On the tech support side," Sally continued, "every single person says they are leaving because they do not have adequate resources to allow them to do their work. They feel they've been telling that to Mark Balog for weeks, but Mark couldn't get Roy..."

"Was there another reason for tech support, Sally?" Jean-Claude interrupted. *So he realized what was happening. Did Roy?*

"Yes, the second reason is once again lack of confidence in management. They don't think management listens, and they don't believe they're getting the straight story. Specifically, they think the multi-million dollar renovation is terribly ill-advised, especially when people don't have the tools and staff they need to do their jobs. They also don't understand why we were so good at 'Ship When Ready' for many years, and then shot ourselves in the foot by putting the 6.0 release out there prematurely. And finally, they were very discouraged by the erroneous preannouncement." *The exact list Georgia had given her. Well done.*

Text from Ken: *Roy approvd ths prsntation?*

Georgia text to Ken: *Unknwn. Nt n bord bk.*

"Well," Roy said, "that means we haven't done a good enough job of educating our employees about why we had to go out with the 6.0 when we did. The real failure was that R&D lagged so far behind in their development efforts. And I've explained that damned preannouncement until I'm blue in the face,"

"Actually," Sally said sweetly, "it seems to be the continuous justification that's caused the problem. Employees might have accepted that we just blew the numbers. What they can't accept is the continued insistence that the preannouncement made sense." *Pow! Right in the old kisser.*

"It made perfect sense," Roy snapped. *Good morning, Rip van Winkle. Glad you decided to join us.*

"Maybe," Jean-Claude suggested, "we could just quickly move to proposed solutions. Sally?"

"You know," Roy said. "Sally and I haven't been over ..."

"That's very true." Sally nodded, "I didn't have the chance to go over any of this with Roy before the meeting, so I take full responsibility. Or, did you want me not to offer my thoughts, Roy?"

Roy seemed utterly disoriented for a moment as he stared blankly at Sally. "Have at it," he muttered. *What?!*

"Well, wait," Jared objected. "Roy, if you feel the solutions haven't been thought out properly, maybe we should ..."

Roy held up his hand, his eyes still on Sally. "No, we'll proceed. Just keep in mind that I'll be hearing these ideas for the first time along with the rest of you." *Giving her rope to hang herself, maybe. Could be clever ...*

"Thank you, Roy." Sally's smile was courteous. "I recommend doing several things. The single most important thing is to acknowledge our mistakes and spell out changes being made in response. I see no other way to restore confidence." She brought up a new slide. "I've listed the key mistakes here. At least the key ones that can be addressed. There's really no way to go back and adequately staff the 6.0, now is there?" she asked with a wistful smile. The board did not react.

"First, we should acknowledge that the preannouncement was a flat-out mistake based on erroneous assumptions and inaccurate data. Then we outline the steps we'll take to get accurate data sooner."

Georgia text from Ken: *"????????"*

She caught his eye and carefully kept her face neutral. Any second now, Roy was going to swat Sally like a fly.

"Second, we acknowledge that releasing the product before it was ready has caused huge problems for our customers, our sales execs and tech support. We then outline the steps we're taking to minimize those problems. Which starts with authorizing Mark to hire twenty new tech support people immediately to help ease the burden."

"Good," Clarence called. Georgia glanced at the speakerphone. She'd almost forgotten he was there. "Is that in addition to rehiring the ones who resigned?"

"Yes," Roy affirmed, as if it had been his idea all along.

"The problem," Sally cautioned, "is that a number of these people who resigned have already accepted new jobs, and emotionally they've moved on. That's the risk when you decide to push people to the limit. Sometimes they're beyond the limit before you realize it. It would have been so much better if..."

"Thanks, Sally," Jared interrupted. "Sounds like you know what you have to do there. What else?"

"Well, you recall that one of the big issues is the belief that management isn't listening. A perfect example of which, by the way, was nobody listening to the tech support team. Another example is our insisting on pushing ahead with the renovation, when the sentiment against it is overwhelming."

Roy was now looking at Sally with frank astonishment. Why on earth didn't he shut her up?

"So the last thing," Sally continued, "is to stop the renovation now, and tell the employees we are stopping it because we hear and respect their views on the matter."

Text from Ken: *Tryng 2 sink rnovation rite undr Roy's nose!!!*

Georgia response: *I-witness 2 hstry. Tiger escapes frm Grt Hmn Circus and bites Sacrd Cow!*

"Can you explain why this renovation is quite unwelcome?" Jean-Claude requested.

Roy finally interrupted. "Gentleman, this is something that has been fully budgeted for many months, and we're not going to waste your time on it. The plan will improve communication among the rank-and-file and management."

"But the so-called rank-and-file don't agree with you, Roy," Sally pointed out. "That has now …"

"Sounds like Roy doesn't want to spend time on this, Sally," Paul said. "If there's nothing else …"

"Well, there is one more thing." Sally pushed ahead, undeterred by restless stirring among the board members. "We've talked about certain ways we haven't been listening. The other problem is what we're doing to convince them that we *are* listening."

With that, Sally turned the cover page of a flip chart near the back of the room to reveal a poster with the heads of two cartoon characters, each with a hand cupped behind a grotesquely enlarged ear. Across the top of the poster in big, red block letters were the words "Management is listening!!" Then around the two heads in wavy blue or yellow letters were the words "Free Friday donuts!" and "More wine at parties!" and "Suggestion boxes on every floor!"

"We seem to have gotten the idea," Sally said, "that posters saying we listen are just as good as listening." *Wow, she'd thought up something beyond Georgia's list. Sally was trying to take Roy out at one fell swoop.*

The board members stared at the poster for a moment in complete silence.

"That's great," Jared said lightly. "Who's, uh, responsible for this poster?"

"Sally's team is running the initiative," Roy responded.

"Exactly as Roy directed," Sally added sweetly. "This one garnered seventeen mustaches in three days."

Text from Ken: *Pt Sally on suicide watch.* She already had. Those bright red cherries were starting to look like bloodstains.

"You know," Jared said, "I think it's about time to wrap this up for today. I've got a call scheduled in about ten minutes."

"Absolutely," Jean-Claude confirmed, "I'd say we are finished. Thanks to everyone for coming."

"Roy," Larry said, with his wide, cold smile, "the board would like to meet with you separately for five minutes. Ken, can you remain with us as well?"

Georgia rushed down the hall and ducked into a conference room. Holding her breath, she dialed the conference number and put her phone on mute.

"Roy." Larry's voice came through the speakerphone. "I just have one question. What bad thing did you do to your Human Resources executive to make her want to end your life?" Laughter. "Did you forget her birthday? Did you kidnap her children?"

"She did seem rather critical of me today. I was surprised. She never voiced these concerns before that I know of."

"Those weren't concerns, Roy," Jared corrected. "Those were stabbing motions with a sharp knife." Laughter. "That was Kill Bill in the corporate setting." More laughter. There in the safety of her conference room, Georgia pumped both fists in the air. *Score!*

"So our question," Jean-Claude continued, "is whether you know a good explanation for this, or do you need a different vice president of Human Resources pretty much immediately? We fully support a change."

"I'd say we even encourage a change," Clarence called through the phone. "I know I do."

"And Ken is right here to handle the legal requirements," Larry added.

"Well, wait a minute," Roy objected. "If one of my executives disagrees with me, don't we want them to speak up? Isn't that what we pay them for?"

Georgia's fists froze in the air above her head, and she stared at the phone in confusion.

"In the privacy of your office, absolutely," Larry agreed. "Not as a public hanging in the town square." Murmured agreement.

"I guess what we're saying here, Roy," Jared said, "is that this looked deliberate. It really qualifies as lying in wait, and we think that's a capital offense."

But Roy objected again. "Guys, I think we're going way overboard here."

Georgia dropped her fists onto the table and stared at the phone in utter dismay.

"I don't have an explanation yet," Roy continued, "but I'm confident this is just a misunderstanding. Sally is my loyal and trusted advisor, and I wouldn't want to do this job without her. I think my reputation is solid enough to withstand a little criticism. I'll talk to her. Some coaching is called for, but otherwise we're fine as is."

Georgia clapped both hands over her mouth to suppress a groan, even though the mute button remained brightly lit.

"Your call," Jared said. "Several of us would take a different approach, but of course we defer to your judgment. Just know that if you change your mind, we're right there with you."

"Understood. Won't be necessary."

There was a moment of awkward silence. "Then if we have finished," Jean-Claude said, "I can still hope to make my plane. See you all the next time. And Roy?"

"Yes, Jean-Claude."

"I hope you will think a bit more about the renovation."

"And lose those posters immediately," Larry directed. "They're ridiculous."

Georgia rushed back to her cube before Ken returned to his office.

∞

Georgia could concentrate under almost any circumstances, but for the next two hours she could only concentrate on the agonizingly slow passage of time. She envisioned Sally appearing in the entrance to her cube, brandishing a scythe and sporting black shrunken heads on a mustard yellow Grim Reaper shroud. She half hoped Ken would call her in to talk about Sally, but she didn't seek him out because she sort of feared that as well. The fact was that either conversation would require a level of play-acting she wasn't quite up to at the moment. She needed to find her bearings, which definitely required one of those after-dinner trips to her car.

At ten to noon she gave up. This couldn't wait for nighttime. She snatched her peanut butter and jelly sandwich and her purse from her desk drawer, and almost ran down the stairwell to her car. To avoid being noticed she made herself drive at an orderly speed out the exit and around the corner to the back side of the eucalyptus trees that bordered the lot. The morning cloud cover had given way to bright sun, so she parked in the shade cast by the eucalyptus trees and just stared for a moment at two squirrels twitching their buoyant, dandelion tails as they chased each other through the dappled shadows on the sidewalk and skittered up the rough bark of a tree.

Roy wasn't going to fire Sally. Which meant big trouble for Georgia down the road, unless she could find a way to head it off. Sally was bound to figure out she'd made up the whole stairwell conversation. And what if Roy figured out who'd tutored Sally?

But *why* wasn't Roy going to fire her? Here was a guy who absolutely reeked contempt along with his Old Spice deodorant, directing his withering gaze at every person who crossed his path. Just itching to catch somebody doing something he could blame and insult them for. But then when Sally staged a coup against him right under his beaky little nose, he rose to her defense like a knight defending a damsel. Why??

Was he possibly so dense he didn't get it? Sally hadn't been subtle. The only thing less subtle would have been to shoot him with a cannonball. Nikki said he had the social awareness of a fireplug, but even a fireplug would have popped a valve and started spraying. Not to mention the board had spelled it out for him.

He got it.

So was he showing his merciful side, giving his loyal henchperson a second chance? From somewhere inside the swaying eucalyptus trees, a crow cawed its throaty derision.

Okay. Not merciful. Maybe he was just really good at ignoring things that didn't fit what he wanted to believe. A surprising number of people had that skill, as any practitioner of special talents could confirm. What if all Roy's hostility and aggression masked a lonely soul who couldn't face betrayal by his one true friend?

She half expected to hear the crow again.

Okay, unlikely but at least plausible. Though if this guy did have a soft side, he certainly hid it well. He never courted favor with anyone, including the members of his own board. Unless you counted those vulgar poop stories, which had the opposite effect of making them run for the door. He almost seemed to prefer keeping people at a distance. Didn't even banter with Sally much, or make eye contact with her for that matter, despite the fact that she beamed at him with that dreamy, emetic admiration.

Georgia glared out the windshield and sighed. It didn't matter how clearly she'd read Sally if she'd missed something critical about Roy. She needed to rethink Roy entirely. She needed to look at the actual Roy, instead of just recycling her own ideas about him, exactly as her father had taught her.

Transferring her untouched peanut butter and jelly sandwich to the driver's seat, she scooted over to the passenger side, pulled her legs into the simple lotus position, closed her eyes and began to breathe deeply. After a few minutes, she noticed she was visualizing the look of hatred Roy had leveled at Sally in the board meeting that day, while he was thinking about something else. Why revisit that now?

Two minutes later she opened her eyes and smiled faintly as she luxuriated in another deep inhalation. *Sally had something on Roy.*

Well, of course. Roy's glare really had been directed at Sally, after all. His fault lines now floated lightly on the surface of her consciousness, like a magic map to buried treasure. Suddenly ravenous, she dropped her feet onto the floor mat, pulled open the Ziploc bag and savored a big bite of her peanut butter and jelly sandwich. Sally had something on Roy.

So what was it?

CHAPTER 26

Katie-Ann forgot it was her turn to make dinner, so Georgia made grilled cheese and tomato sandwiches with a side of slightly limp raw carrots. Then Katie-Ann scrubbed away at the heavy skillet in penance while Georgia used a Lipton teabag to make tea for both of them. Rotating the chip in her dark blue mug to the far side of the rim, she settled herself at the rickety card table in the living room to discover the source of Sally's leverage over Roy.

Might as well start with her black folder of board member and executive CVs that she'd brought home. She flipped through the stack, extracted Roy's resume, and began.

Dull reading it was. His last company, Trilobyte Memories, had merged with Microsoft. The company before that was MegaMind Software of Massachusetts. Never heard of it. And so on, stretching with no gap in employment all the way back to a PhD in Economics from the University of Washington in 1987. B.A. from University of San Francisco, random public high school in Oregon. Lovely wife Linda, two swell children, other interests were sailing and history, blah blah blah. About as conventional as it got. All checked out and confirmed when he was hired, no doubt.

Still, she might as well spend an hour verifying dates of employment and degrees, just to get some momentum. She used her old Mac to go online, but couldn't find a good site for employment stuff. That meant confirming the employment dates by phone during business hours, which was probably more trouble than it was worth. But she did locate a promising site called Degree Clearing House. She used her personal email address to sign in as an HR person from Hewlett Packard, checked a box saying she had Roy's permission, and requested verification of all three degrees.

That was a start, but it only took half an hour. Katie-Ann was now bent over her homework a couple of feet away, so Georgia quietly drained the last of her tea and carried both cups to the sink. What next?

What else did they do before they hired someone? Criminal background check, but that report had to have come back cleaner than a gnawed bone, or they wouldn't have hired him. Maybe there was something else in his personnel file, if she could think of an excuse to get her hands on it. She made a note.

Too bad they hadn't restored Roy's or Sally's emails as part of the side-deal investigation.

Could Sally have something personal on him? Maybe he had a boyfriend. (Katie-Ann glanced up when Georgia snorted.) Second family somewhere? Either of those would give fine leverage, but how would Sally know? Life insurance beneficiaries. Georgia made another note.

Had they worked together before? She pulled Sally's CV out of the folder and set it next to Roy's. No prior employment together. So Sally should only have access to HR stuff, plus anything he'd told her. Unless Sally knew Roy's family. She made another note.

She tapped her forefinger against her lips, considering. No matter what she found, Sally wasn't going anywhere as long as Roy ran the company. And nothing she found would keep Sally from coming after her once she realized what Georgia had been up to. *If* she realized. Was there some way to camouflage it?

Sally would come looking for an explanation, that seemed sure. What if she told Roy about the "overheard" conversation? Seemed unlikely. What would it accomplish, except making Sally look dumb and treacherous? But she was bound to find a way to do something nasty. She winced, anticipating the wrath of Sally. And even if Sally did nothing, Georgia would still be watching over her shoulder for quite a while.

She'd sort of fucked this up, really. So focused on Sally that she allowed herself to make unexamined assumptions about Roy. What if she lost her job because of it? She glanced across the table at Katie-Ann, whose only concerns appeared to be geometry and a worrisome lock of blond hair that refused to stay wound around her finger. Was it possible she'd actually gone too far?

She shook her head with one decisive snap. Regret was like a pigsty, only good for wallowing. She had no intention of losing her job. She did intend to be smart about what happened next.

∞

"Georgia," Ken said a few days later, standing in the entrance to her cube, "come on down to my office for a few minutes, will you? I'd like to ask you about something." She set the phone back in its cradle and followed him down the corridor. She'd return Eddie Fallon's voicemail message later. Probably just wanted more backlog data, although she had looked up to see his pale gray eyes flick away from her in the meeting the day before.

Why hadn't Ken sent Maggie to get her, the way he always did? Was this about Sally? She thought he looked slightly grim, his lips set in a thin, straight line. Or was she imagining it? Great. How long was she going to torment herself like this, imagining that every communication was about Sally?

Not long, apparently. "Sally stopped by here today," he informed her as he closed his office door behind him and gestured for her to sit at his conference table. Now his face definitely looked grim, despite the cheerful, cherry-colored bow tie against his pale blue shirt.

"To what did you owe the pleasure?" she asked innocently, her mind racing in instant hyper-alert. She hoped she was ready for this.

"She wanted to warn me about you."

"I'm sorry?" As she feigned surprise, she could already hear the rhythmic thud of her pulse in her ears. Beyond him she saw that gray clouds had thickened over the parking lot, and the tops of the eucalyptus trees were flashing their silver undersides as they churned in the wind.

"She says you've been tipping her to confidential matters within the department to try to curry favor with her."

"Ah." She nodded calmly. So no mention of the "overheard" conversation in the stairwell. This she could handle. "Well, she's right in a way, although 'curry favor' shows how futile it all was."

"Can you help me understand what's going on here?" No, she thought, looking into those green eyes that rested frankly on hers, she could only deceive him. He was leaning slightly toward her, listening attentively, trusting her candor. She firmly suppressed the familiar impulse to tell him everything, along with a less familiar feeling that might be self-loathing. There'd be time for that later.

"Well," she began, "we all knew it was Sally's fault that Beatrice quit, and I was afraid we'd lose Suzanne, too. I offered to help with the options memo and everything, but honestly, I thought Suzanne's days were numbered."

She paused, hoping that Ken's reaction would help her gauge her performance. He just raised his eyebrows slightly, inviting her to continue. Sort of like that very first job interview.

"Sally lost another admin around that time, and I offered to help her, hoping I could get in her good graces and run interference for the whole legal team. But the only thing Sally really wanted from me was dirt on the legal department." She shrugged. "And I thought, what the heck, maybe I could tell her a few things she was going to find out anyway, to make her think I was on her side. I thought I could get her to let up on all of us."

"So you decided to manipulate her." He wasn't going to make this easy. And why on earth should he?

"Well, yes, I guess I did, although I didn't think of it that way at the time. But it obviously didn't work, and now Sally wants you to think I'm disloyal. I'd say that pretty much sums it up."

"Why would she want me to distrust you, Georgia?"

She shrugged. "Why did she go after Beatrice? Why did she convince Roy you wasted money on the side deal investigation? I think she just believes in divide and conquer. Unless ... do you think she's embarrassed that I saw her screw-up with the board?"

He frowned. "Seems like a pretty strong reaction to embarrassment. Assuming she even felt embarrassed."

"Then maybe she's mad I stopped telling her stuff."

"Why did you stop?"

"The board meeting where she turned on Roy sort of freaked me out. I thought if she'd do that to him, she'd do it in a heartbeat to the rest of us. I started worrying she might try to use the secrets I gave her to drive a wedge between me and the legal team. More or less what she's doing now, as a matter of fact."

She paused again, and again to no avail. His face remained polite but impassive. This really sounded like crap, didn't it? She wished she hadn't eaten that greasy donut for breakfast. Her stomach was roiling like the tops of those eucalyptus trees.

"I know this could make you distrust me, Ken, but if you think about what I told her, they were all fake secrets. Well, temporary secrets. The investigation about the credit card fraud. The Italy problem. The meeting about the SEC investigation that she was supposed ..."

He held up his hand. "I'm not too worried about the specifics, Georgia. I agree they were relatively harmless. I do have to tell you I'm surprised and disappointed by your judgment regarding confidential information. At the moment, though, I'm much more concerned about her other accusation." Ugh. So she had talked about the "overheard" conversation, after all. Well, she'd do her best.

"What other accusation?"

"About the offer to alter her Change of Control Agreement."

Her surprise was suddenly genuine. "What??"

"Sally says you believed she was about to be promoted, and you wanted a job with her. So you offered to help her with a lot of things. At first it was just information, but then you told her about variations in the Change of Control Agreements, and offered to switch her from a double trigger to a single trigger."

Ye gods and little fishes! Sally Kurtz was pulling a con.

"Sally's lying to you," she said evenly.

"She wasn't lying about the first part."

"No. She wasn't. But this is a big lie."

"Why would she make this up?"

"To finish me off," Georgia said in rueful admiration, gazing away for a moment at the child's stick-figure drawing on his wall. The gaps between those blocky teeth made it look like a few had been knocked out. She realized her mouth was slightly open, so she closed it and turned back to Ken. "Obviously, I have pissed off Sally Kurtz big-time."

"Could she just be mistaken? Do you think you might have said something that she misinterpreted?"

"Not about Change of Control Agreements, because I wouldn't know what to say. I know we give them to executives who might lose their jobs in a merger, but I never worked on one. I don't even know what a single trigger is."

"It's when an executive gets automatic severance if somebody buys the company, even if she still has her job in the new company," he explained. "Could easily mean a payout of well over a million dollars. You didn't know that?"

"No, I didn't know it. Ken, does this story make sense to you? Why would I think Sally was going to get promoted? Was she going to get promoted? Promoted to what? And why would I ever want a job with Sally Kurtz? I think she's the devil, and her admins last about three days.

"And how could I change her from a double trigger to a single trigger? Wouldn't the board have to do that? Could I just change some document? What about ..."

Ken raised his hand to interrupt. "Hold on, Georgia. I'm relieved to hear you say you didn't do this, and I believe you. The whole Change of Control thing sounds like a misunderstanding." His mouth remained a thin line. "But I'm very disappointed that you were the leak I've been worried about. You have access to the most sensitive information in this company, and I've trusted you more than was strictly necessary."

Those sorrowful eyes were unbearable, and he didn't know the half of it. Her face felt so hot it must be neon. "I'm so sorry to have disappointed you. I was wrong and stupid, and I jeopardized your trust in me." God, had her voice cracked? She sat up straighter and swallowed. "For what it's worth, I will never leak anything out of the department again, no matter what noble purpose I think it might serve." It was a promise she intended to keep. Good thing she wasn't the sort of wimp who cried.

He seemed to relent. "Or just come talk to me about it. We could have thought this one through together."

"Absolutely. Really stupid." They were silent for a moment. "But what about this thing Sally's doing? She's accusing me of out-and-out dishonesty, and she'll destroy me if she spreads it around."

"I don't think she'll do that, Georgia. I must admit, though, nothing Sally does lately makes any sense to me at all. I wonder if she's having personal problems."

"Could you, like, remind her not to spread the rumor, so the company doesn't get hurt?"

He seemed to be half listening, taking his own turn staring at the stick figure drawing on his wall. "I wish I could figure out what she's thinking." He turned back to her. "I think I should just tell her I discussed it with you, and I'm confident it was a misunderstanding."

"Is there anything I should do? Should I go to Sally and try to sort it out?" Which of course she could never actually do.

"I recommend that you carefully avoid any private audience with Sally for a while. You never know how she'd characterize it."

She almost sagged with relief. This horrible conversation was coming to an end. "Thanks, Ken. I'm very sorry to have disappointed you and caused you trouble. I will work hard never to do it again."

Yi! Georgia thought as she headed back to her cube. Sally had evidently decided to vaporize Georgia out of (frankly justifiable) revenge.

And she certainly wasn't going to stop because Ken dropped by for a chat. Scams were a lot more fun when they came off without a hitch.

And Ken might never trust her again. She reached her cube, and rested her hand against the cool metal of the entrance to steady herself. She might have just lost her only real ally and friend in Lumina—in California—maybe in the whole nonincarcerated world.

Dear Daddy,

I am experiencing a challenge.

There's a person named Sally in our company who prevents competent people from doing their jobs, and champions destructive ideas in order to advance her personal agenda. She causes good employees to leave our company by her spiteful manner, and then hires mediocre replacements who she believes will be political allies.

For some time now I have been arranging for her departure. She sucks up to our CEO like a leech on a skinny-dipper's backside, and this has afforded her great protection. I therefore undertook to persuade her that her political fortunes were best served by turning on him, and honestly, Daddy, I succeeded big-time. She has insulted him to the board and to the executive team. She has taunted him to his face. By all rights she should now be only an unpleasant memory.

But she is proving difficult to eradicate. Although I accurately gauged both her ambition and her treachery, she has a power over our CEO whose nature I suspect but can't yet verify. Whatever the reason, he is impervious to her insults and continues to treat her as his finest friend. It seems if Sally sets his clothes on fire, he will pay a dry cleaner to remove the smell of singe from her skirt.

Now I have learned that she realizes my intentions and has decided turnabout is fair play. And unfortunately, she is exhibiting a certain hitherto concealed intelligence.

Frankly, Daddy, I'm afraid. Have I allowed myself to be surrounded, just like General Lee at Appomattox? I can't outrun

her. Should I lie low and hope she gets distracted by bigger battles, or should I take the offensive while she thinks she has me cornered, and hope for the advantage of surprise? Because this next step is a serious one, I would value your opinion soonest.
Your loving daughter,
Georgia

Dear Georgia,
I must tell you, my dear, that your letter has caused me some alarm. Your pessimism strikes me as shockingly premature. Are you getting enough sleep?

Or even worse, has something made you hesitate to use your special talents?

Georgia looked out her passenger window at a young woman in brown suede boots exiting the Mail Boxes Etc. Lying to Ken. That look of disappointment on his face. Of course. Her father saw her more clearly on the basis of one inarticulate letter than she had seen her own self. Behold the one true King of Special Talents. She continued reading:

I do hope you're not letting your personal feelings about this Sally person cloud your judgment. I know of no faster path to serious error, and this horsefly is surely not worth it.

Or perhaps you suspect that you caused your own setback. Which, frankly, Georgia, you probably did. But so what? Everybody makes mistakes, and one setback rarely amounts to failure. This is no moment for the faint of heart, however. You have made a fool of this puffed up egotist in front of the board, and she will never rest while you remain in her vicinity. Seize the offensive promptly. I doubt that time is on your side.

Continue to think creatively, my dear. Such a dreadful character must have a plethora of weaknesses just waiting to be exploited! And don't forget the secondary benefit: Although your primary objective is now to protect your position in the company,

---

you will also experience exhilarating professional satisfaction when you finally hoist this adversary with her own petard.

I don't mean to minimize your difficulties here. I know your situation is more perilous than I can fully appreciate from this distance, and it cannot be easy having responsibility for Katie-Ann. But I also know you will use your own excellent skill and judgment to find the right solution. I love you, Georgia, and am very proud of you.

Let me know what you decide to do and, when possible, confirm the success of your endeavor. Send news of Katie-Ann. Daddy

P.S. You say your scam was cleverly conceived and well-executed, but its failure suggests otherwise. When leisure allows (and I do not mean now), examine each element of your con, and squarely face any error in order to learn from it. (Could you have predicted the CEO's behavior more accurately? Are you confident Sally was the correct target?) Your healthy ego does not need the protection of self-delusion. Leave that to our marks, if you please!
P.P.S. When you are able to visit me, please take out flight accident insurance and name me as the beneficiary. For Katie-Ann's sake, of course.

She laughed and shrugged at an oblivious UPS driver who was hoisting himself into the driver's seat of his parked truck. Thank God for Daddy. Had anyone ever been so reliably himself? He always had her back, and his confidence in her was unshakable.

And then in the same breath he was betting against her on flight insurance. Was he trying to demonstrate his conviction that she'd survive the Sally crisis and make it down to see him? Or was he just betting against her on flight insurance? Hey, nobody was perfect.

342

CHAPTER 27

The next morning, after a late night of meditation, star contemplation and email drafting, Georgia sent an email to Roy Zisko, copied to Ken, and then forwarded the email to Nikki with a request to bring it to Roy's attention promptly:

Dear Roy,

I request your help regarding a matter that is of grave importance to me and possibly to the company.

Ken informed me yesterday that Sally has accused me of proposing to falsify a very important document. She claims I offered to alter her Change of Control Agreement to make it a single trigger instead of a double trigger. If you haven't heard about this already, I'm pretty sure you shortly will.

I have given considerable thought to what could motivate Sally to make such a hurtful and completely false accusation. She's an executive of unquestionable integrity, and so must actually believe what she is saying. Ken asked me whether I might have said something that Sally could have misinterpreted, but I have never discussed Change of Control Agreements with her, ever. Is it possible that she's beset by personal or professional problems at the moment?

Sally is such a respected person here at Lumina that I'm afraid her accusation could make it hard for me to continue doing my job. That is what brings me to write to you. Do you think you could talk to Sally on my behalf, confirm that she has no evidence for what she says, and then ask her as kindly as possible not to spread this story further? Whatever her mental condition at the moment, I know she will always listen to you.

Thank you for taking the time to read this email. I know how very busy you are, and would never presume to ask for your help if I didn't believe it would afford you an opportunity to assess Sally's impact on other, more important parts of the company. I assure you that this misunderstanding will not alter the respect I feel for Sally, or my willingness to cooperate with her in any way. I will certainly continue to do my very best to make a positive difference to our shareholders and the company.
Yours very truly,
Georgia Griffin
Paralegal

Bold action didn't always succeed, of course, but it did help you feel like the hunter instead of the sitting duck.

∞

The first reaction came shortly after 9 a.m.

"Georgia?" She heard Nikki's muffled whisper. Maybe Roy was close by.

"Yes, Nikki, hi. You got my email?"

"Like a brick between the eyes. You serious about this?"

"Completely serious."

"She said this about you?"

"Oh, yeah. She came and complained to Ken about it."

"And there's no basis?"

She made her voice sound appropriately affronted. "Of course there's no basis."

"Sorry, I didn't mean you'd actually done it. But why would she make this up?"

"No idea. But if I wait to figure that out, Katie-Ann and I could be out on the street, lining up for breakfast at Sallie's."

"Breakfast . . . ?"

"Sorry. That's what they call the soup kitchen at Salvation Army." *Dumb. Why reveal she knew that?* "No connection to our Sally. I just mean I had to do something."

"You don't think Ken should handle this for you?"

"I'm the one who knows how urgent it is."

She heard Nikki's slow, restricted exhale through puckered lips. "Your call. I'll take it to him now."

∞

The second response came a few minutes later. "Georgia," Ken called from behind his monitor. "Come in. I see you sent an email to Roy." When he stood up to join her he looked slightly pale, accentuating the bright kelly green of his bow tie. Had she actually given him a shock?

She seated herself across from him at his oval conference table. "You think I shouldn't have sent it?"

"Well, it certainly was quite daring. Especially the part about her 'mental condition.' We've had some impressive evidence lately of just how inseparable those two are. Given that they're so close, he's probably going to show her your letter, and then she'll be furious. You should definitely expect some fireworks."

So he thought she'd made a serious blunder by being so provocative. But then, he also thought she was actually seeking Roy's support.

She said, "What exactly is the polite way to accuse somebody of lying about you? I had to say something to Roy. She was going to tell him about this, and I'd never have known or had a chance to defend myself."

He smiled skeptically, mingled with what looked to her like sad but genuine respect. "Bless you, Georgia, you're a braver soul than I am." Then he threw his hands in the air. "And for all I know, you could be right. I admit she wasn't very receptive to my suggestion last night that she might be mistaken. You're often quite intuitive about people, and this definitely brings it all out into the open."

"I hope you don't get dragged into the middle of it."

He waved a hand. "Don't worry about that. I just hope I don't have trouble keeping my best paralegal."

Yeesh. Did he have to remind her what a narrow ledge she was on? She willed herself not to look down. "Believe me, Ken, I intend to stay right here."

"Well, I hope it works out exactly as you intend. You certainly have the courage of your convictions."

She thought it a fine compliment, and grinned. "I suppose I do. Have you got a minute on the SEC production? I need to finalize our response today, and since it's still informal I'm not sure what the tone should be."

∞

Katie-Ann dropped the spaghetti in to boil the minute Georgia entered the apartment. When they sat down at the table Georgia asked, "How's school?"

"Okay. I retook the 'F' test, and now it's a 'B.'"

"Fabulous. I hope you feel proud of yourself." Good news on the home front, at least. A welcome distraction. "Maybe you'll stop getting crap from that Ginger person now."

"Actually, she already stopped."

"You're on a roll here. Guess she got tired of it and moved on."

"She really did move on. She's not there anymore."

"Stroke of luck. Did her family move?"

"Don't think so. I think they found some kind of bad stuff in her locker."

"Really. How do you know that?"

Katie-Ann shrugged. "Just, you know, what kids are saying."

"I see. That's pretty convenient for you, isn't it?"

"I guess," Katie-Ann muttered, very focused on the spaghetti she was winding around her fork.

Georgia set her own fork down and stared at Katie-Ann until she looked up.

"What?" she asked defensively.

"You tell me what."

Katie-Ann resisted a moment, and then gave up. "Come on, Georgia. She had a choice. She could have chosen to leave me alone."

"Katie-Ann Griffin, this really concerns me, and it would concern Daddy, too."

"Oh God …!"

"No, I'm not going to worry him with this. What I am saying is that scams are no substitute for developing social skills and figuring out how to deal with your own problems. You could have toughed this one out. Did you get her in trouble with the cops?"

She gave Georgia a hooded look. "Don't think so. She just can't come to Lynbrook anymore. Well, or any other school in San Jose."

"What did revenge ever get anybody, Katie-Ann? Total loser's game. Not to mention that teenage bullies are like dandelions. How do you know another one won't pop up any day now?"

Katie-Ann crossed her arms in defiance. "It wasn't just revenge. I needed her to stop. And I don't think the next dandelion is popping up from that crowd anytime soon. Since Ginger left they look like they've been flattened under a bush hog."

Georgia planted her palms firmly on the rickety card table and leaned forward. "I'm very disappointed in you. When did this happen?"

"Three days ago."

"So it could still blow up right in your face, just when you're doing so well with everything else. You took an unnecessary risk of getting attention we do not need right now."

Was she yelling at Katie-Ann, or herself? Good thing people couldn't die of irony.

"Besides," she continued, "you never know when you might really need a scam for something important, and now you've left a trail." She winced. That last sounded a little less principled than she'd have liked.

Fortunately, Katie-Ann seemed too busy defending herself to notice. "You should see how you'd like getting harassed all the time," she flung out tearfully. "Day in, day out, by people too dumb to pour piss out of a boot with instructions on the heel. What's more important than stopping that?" Her glare wavered. "Well, other than your job. Money and stuff."

Georgia acknowledged the concession by leaning back again. "How about you getting into UC?"

Katie-Ann's glare hardened again in defiance, and then disappeared. "Fine. I suppose you're right. It was too risky, and I shouldn't have done it. It isn't going to blow up, though. I totally nailed it." A look of triumph flickered and was quickly suppressed. "And if another dandelion pops up, I promise to go after it with some totally appropriate garden tool." They resumed eating in silence, their forks scraping their plates. "You know what, though, can I just tell you how I ..."

"No!" Georgia barked, and then coughed into her paper towel to suppress a grin. Actually, she'd have loved to hear the details. Her little sister was shaping up to be tough as nails and twice as sharp.

Katie-Ann shrugged. "Fine. But speaking of social solutions, my name is Kate now, okay? Hyphenated names are totally lame."

∞

She had a note on her chair from Ken at 7 a.m. the next morning.

"Have a seat," he said, closing his door. "I need to show you something." His mouth was set in that thin, determined line again as he handed her an email from Sally. The email was directed to Ken and Roy, and the subject line was "Does this look like a misunderstanding to you??"

The body of the email was a forwarded message from Georgia to

Sally, with the subject line "For Your Eyes Only." The attachment was a six-page document titled "Executive Change of Control Agreement."

Ha!

The trap had sprung. Sally had manufactured evidence. Georgia coughed into her hand to keep from chortling. She had a breathtaking vision of Sally-feathers, wafting gracefully up through sun-dappled air.

"Let me guess," she said solemnly, hoping her eyes didn't betray unseemly glee. "This is a single trigger Change of Control for Sally Kurtz."

"That's exactly what it is, sent by you to Sally. Roy has asked me to terminate your employment."

"That would be quite unfair, since I didn't send this email."

"Georgia." His earnest green eyes looked so disappointed.

"I didn't send this email to Sally or anybody else."

His raised eyebrows expressed profound skepticism. "Then who did?"

"Don't know. Maybe somebody else sent it from my computer, or maybe Sally altered some other email to make it look like I sent this to her."

Ken leaned back and tilted his head to the side. "Would she even know how to do that?"

Not very well, hopefully. She widened her eyes and shrugged. "She could've had help. There has to be some explanation, because I didn't send it." She stared at it and sighed dramatically. "Look at this. 'For Your Eyes Only.' Can you *think* of a better way to get unwanted attention? She's even insulting my intelligence."

He stared at her for a moment, and then his grim expression wavered. "Let me get this straight. Are you saying you don't know anything about this email?"

"I only know I had nothing to do with it."

"Jesus, Mary and Joseph!" he said softly. He frowned at the document for a minute. "I have no idea what's going on here. I'm not going to take any action now, Georgia, but you'll have to go home while I try to figure it out."

"Does it strike you as strange that she didn't give this to you when she made the accusation?"

"She said she was trying to downplay it."

Georgia scoffed. "Yeah, subtle understatement was always her way. Look, before you send me home, can we just investigate it together for a few minutes? I'd like to see if somebody sent it from my computer, though that would be pretty bold with my cube right out in the open. And I think we should run a side-by-side compare of the document in the legal database with this one."

He searched her face for a moment, considering, and then he stood up. "Have at it." He opened his door and gestured for her to exit. "You lead the way. Bring the email. Maggie, clear my calendar for the next hour, will you?"

Ten minutes later Ken confirmed that there was no record of the email in Georgia's sent mail or her electronic trash. "That doesn't really prove anything, though, because you could have emptied it out of your trash. I'll get our IT people to search for it."

"That won't prove anything either, unless you find it. If I send an email, delete it immediately and then empty the trash, I don't think it ever makes it into back-up."

"So where does that leave us?"

"With my head on the chopping block, if the email turns up. Nowhere, if it doesn't." She shrugged. "But of course you have to do it anyway. Now, can we compare the Change of Control template in our legal database to the one Sally sent? You can forward her email to me electronically."

"Let's ask Maggie to do the compare. What will it show?" he asked over his shoulder as she hurried after him down the hallway, extending her long legs to keep up with his springy stride.

"Not sure. I just don't think anybody in the legal department would've altered the document for her. If we look at the changes, maybe we can figure out whether the document came from somewhere else."

Five minutes later Maggie hurried into Ken's office with two copies of the redlined comparison, and they flipped through them.

"There are quite a few changes," Ken commented after a few minutes. "That's not surprising, though. It takes a lot to alter the template to make it a single trigger."

"Has it been changed properly?"

"I'll need to study it. On its face it looks accurate to me."

"Look at this." She pointed. "See this change on page two? What does that change have to do with single trigger?"

He brushed his palm across the top of his short, red hair as he read it. "Nothing." He handed it back.

"Then why is it different?" They continued reading.

"Here's another change on page five that has nothing to do with single trigger," he commented, tapping the page with his forefinger.

"Then I don't think she used the template from our legal database. She was working with a different document."

"It's certainly similar." He gazed at the child crayon drawings taped to his wall for a moment, tapping his middle finger on the polished table. "Maybe the metadata for this email would tell us what the original email was, and when this one was created. Maggie," he called, opening the door, "would you see if anybody from IT is in this early?"

He sat back down, and Georgia said, "She'll never forgive you for pursuing this."

He looked directly into her eyes. "I have to pursue it. The time to avoid making enemies is when diplomacy still has a chance. We're beyond that here."

"Probably right. You sure you want me to go home? If I stay, you can blame the whole search on me."

He shook his head with a slight smile. "Sorry, Georgia, I think you have to go. And we're going to need your computer. Can you do something at home without it?" *Thank God those unauthorized Terkes emails were all on her ancient gumdrop desktop at home.*

"I can definitely read through the new documents we're planning to produce, if Maggie can print them out for me."

"Good, you do that. I'll work on this for the rest of the day." He stared out his window for a moment. "Boy, if one of our executives is really capable of this ..." He stood up decisively, causing her to do the same. "Let's get some answers and we'll take it from there."

∞

"It's not so much that you're working at home," Katie-Ann specified later, "even though you never do. It's that you won't tell me *why* you're working at home." She was leaning against the kitchen sink with her arms crossed, one bare foot resting on the other, her eyes narrowed at Georgia in the living room.

"I did tell you. I just need to concentrate on this stuff because it's boring, and people kept interrupting me."

Katie-Ann shook her head decisively. "Nah. Most of what you do is boring. And how come you're as nervous as a cat in a roomful of rockers?"

Well, Georgia thought, staring at the document in her hand and widening her eyes until they bulged slightly, how about because she was playing high stakes poker, and waiting to find out whether she'd gambled away the shirt off Ms. Katie-Ann Nosey's back?

What she said was, "You know that thing I just said about people interrupting me? My mental state is fine, thanks. Can the same be said of your homework?"

And could this family kindly focus its excellent intuition on somebody else for a while? She'd had about all the penetrating insight she could take. Katie-Ann appeared to be momentarily vanquished as she began yanking tuna casserole ingredients from the cupboard and dropping them heavily onto the counter.

She finished reviewing the box of documents about 8:30, and there wasn't much else she could accomplish without her laptop. Katie-Ann was seated across from her, twirling the end of her blond ponytail as she bent over a battered copy of *Of Mice and Men*. Well, she wasn't going to sit around stewing. Anything she could research on her old Mac? She went online to check her email, and remembered the inquiry about Roy's degrees. Seemed like forty years ago, even though it had only been twenty-four hours. She wouldn't have anything back yet. Still, she logged out of her work email and into her personal account.

To her surprise, she did have a response. His B.A. from USF was confirmed, although the date was off by a couple of years. No record of his PhD in Economics from the University of Washington, though. Really? She must have entered the wrong data, which she couldn't check because she'd already taken the resume folder back to the office.

But no record of his high school diploma, either. She must have uttered some surprise, because Katie-Ann shot her a quizzical glance and then settled back to her reading.

Well, this was weird. No record of graduating from Klamath Union High School, Klamath Falls, Oregon, 1979? How was that possible? She hadn't gotten both the high school and the PhD data wrong, and nobody would ever make up a degree from some random public high school. So either the service was about as useful as headlights on a bathtub (which seemed likely), or else somebody had gotten sloppy and put bad data in Roy's resume, in which case they'd been reporting bad data to the SEC since the dawn of time (unfortunately, also likely). Great. Now she'd have to think up some excuse for questioning his resume data, and then figure out how to correct it with the SEC. Assuming she still had a job.

And suppose they didn't turn up evidence that Sally had fabricated the email from Georgia?

She resorted to playing online sudoku.

Her cell phone rang an hour later. She could feel Katie-Ann's stare boring into the top of her skull as she snatched it up.

"Georgia, it's Ken Madigan." As if she wouldn't know which Ken it was. Honestly. "The company owes you an apology, and we'd like you to return to work tomorrow morning."

So they'd found proof that Sally had faked the document. She began breathing deeply to counteract the blood rushing out of her head. Important to sound matter-of-fact in front of Katie-Ann.

"Great, though you don't owe me an apology. You figured out what happened?"

"I think we understand mechanically what happened, but we surely don't know why. You were right. She apparently doctored a document that came to her personal email from a lawyer at Woodrow, Mantella, though it wasn't one of the lawyers who works with us. Our lawyers knew nothing about it. Those minor differences you noted were updates to their general template because of recent changes in the law."

"And the email that supposedly came from me?" She ignored Katie-Ann's little gasp.

"They're looking at the metadata now."

"Honestly, this is quite a relief. It was all kind of creepy." She swore she could see Katie-Ann's ears growing. "I've made it through the documents, by the way. There are three I'd like you to look at before I produce them."

"Georgia Louise Griffin," Katie-Ann demanded the minute she hung up, "what was creepy? And what email was 'supposedly' from you? Are you in trouble?"

"Precisely the opposite, Katie-Ann."

"Kate," she corrected her.

Georgia rolled her eyes. "Kate. An executive was trying to deceive our CEO, and I helped Ken prove it. Done and dusted, as Gramma Griffin would say. And you know what? I'm pretty done and dusted myself right now." She shut down her old Mac, stacked the Lumina documents back in their box, and set the box by the front door. Then she went and stood under the hot shower for a long time, letting her tension gurgle down the drain along with the shampoo.

Jesus H Bull Guano Christ, that was scary! Yuck. She shuddered. Triple yuck. Fucking miracle it hadn't come out the other way. Overconfidence was a terrible trait, really. (Just look what it had gotten

Robbie.) Standing under the cascade of hot water, she renounced it firmly and forever.

And totally not worth it. Lumina Software could have limped along indefinitely with Sally Kurtz in full, eye-scorching regalia. Of course, it probably wouldn't have to, now. This probably qualified as a public crack-up, or at least an insurmountable moral failure. Hard to see how Roy could protect her from the board now, no matter what she had on him. Assuming she had anything on him. Probably overconfidence to be so cocksure about that, too. And she surely wasn't going to snoop around and find out. Even if it was pretty interesting. She began scooping the water over her head with both hands to rinse out the conditioner.

No. She was darned lucky, lesson learned with her job still intact and Katie-Ann—make that Kate—with a roof still over her head. She might even be back in Ken's good graces, where she intended to stay. She was well and truly done with using special talents for any purpose as long as Kate depended on her. Might even think about a social life, which reminded her she still hadn't returned that message from Eddie Fallon. She turned off the shower, and groped beyond the plastic curtain for her towel.

Her father had been right as usual. Saved her bacon for sure. Here she'd been tempted to shrink back, just when bold action was most called for. But what about that predicted "exhilarating professional satisfaction" at seeing Sally defeated at last? Did she feel any of that? She punched her pillow and slid her bare feet luxuriously down into her warm sleeping bag.

Well, yes really, she did feel pleased. Quite pleased. And surely there was no harm in that. Well, except it might be hard to get to sleep. In retrospect, it had all been quite satisfying. Had they told Sally yet? *Har!!*

There was just no substitute for the old adrenaline pump, when she got right down to it. And since she was prudently locking her special talents away in cold storage, why not acknowledge that this whole Sally thing had ended up being one big, glorious hoot?

She lay on her back in the warm, dark room, elbows spread wide on the clean pillowcase under her wet hair, her whole body bobbing on a sea of exhilarating satisfaction.

CHAPTER 28

The next couple of months were exciting for Lumina Software. Shortly after the abrupt (and widely celebrated) resignation of Executive Vice President Sally Kurtz, the much-awaited 6.1 was launched at the beginning of March with the finest fanfare that could be mustered by a marketing team newly released from the challenge of "Management Is Listening." It was a testament to Andrea and her team that it also launched to exceptional acclaim in the technical press.

Readers of *eWEEK* and *PC Magazine* and virtually every other geek publication of Silicon Valley could learn from cover stories that "despite its recent revenue losses to the competition, and therefore the tremendous pressure to release yet another premature product, Lumina's Chief Executive and Chief Technical Officers have shown the integrity and maturity of focus to Ship When Ready. And is this product ready! Long-suffering and skeptical customers are about to experience genuine delight in Lumina software of the kind that created so many ardent, wedded-for-life fans in its early days."

Armed with these glowing reports, the sales team bounded forth to customer sites like parched gazelles bounding to a fresh watering hole. The exhausted, dusty Lumina Software caravan was pulling into a lush oasis.

∞

Georgia wasn't trying to conceal from Eddie Fallon the fact that she lived with her little sister. How could she, when he'd been standing right beside her as she'd answered that terrifying 2 a.m. phone call a few weeks back?

Still, she saw no reason to emphasize her peculiar domestic situation the first time she met Eddie outside of work. So even though Kate went with her to Gap and helped her choose the black dress with the short swingy skirt; and even though Kate was the one who found the perfect earrings at the Now & Again shop to set off Georgia's blueberry colored eyes; and maybe *because* Kate wanted to "seriously inspect this dude," Georgia persuaded her sister well in advance to disappear into the bedroom as soon as the doorbell rang.

So when Eddie arrived to take her to dinner at Reposado and rang the doorbell, Georgia paused just long enough to hear the reassuring click of the bedroom door behind her. Then she opened her front door and saw that Eddie had been as careful about his appearance as she'd been about hers. Too careful. He'd forced his unruly brown hair into submission, and his ultra-neat checked shirt was almost worthy of Mark Balog. Uh-oh. This date might be as lively as a blown-out candle.

"Hi," she said stiffly, her voice a little strangled down in her throat, "You found it okay? Let me get my sweater."

He gestured with his head toward the space over her left shoulder. "Introduce me?"

Georgia whirled to see Kate standing about one foot behind her in complete violation of their explicit agreement.

"Oh! Of course. Eddie, this is my sister. Kate, this is Eddie Fallon."

"Hi," Kate said with a little wave. Turning to Georgia she added solemnly, "*I* don't think he has too many freckles."

"What?!" Georgia said with disbelief as Kate let her smile widen into a wicked grin. A flush began to spread across Eddie's freckled cheeks.

"Sorry," Kate said, "bad joke. That was mean." She turned to Eddie. "Georgia never said one word about your freckles. The only thing she did say was ..."

"Katie-Ann!" Was that a snicker she heard from Eddie, or was he choking on embarrassment?

Kate pressed her left hand to her mouth in mock horror and extended her other hand palm down, inviting him to take it. "My!" she said with a pronounced Arkansas twang. "What I mean to say is it's a right pleasure to meet you, Mr. Fallon. I do hope you have a lovely evening with my bi-yutiful sister." Georgia almost bumped against Eddie's retreating back in her haste to get out of the apartment. She threw a furious glare at Kate's mock-sweet smile and pulled the door closed between them.

Near the bottom of the stairs she said to Eddie's back, "Wow! What the hell *was* that?"

He turned, and she saw with relief that a strand of brown hair had popped up and his gorgeous, slightly asymmetric smile had appeared. "Well, you'd know better than I would, but I'd say it was your gutsy teenage sister seriously jerking your chain." He held the passenger door of his dark blue Mini Cooper while she climbed in, then went around and climbed in the driver's side. "And is she ever your sister!" he continued, laughing as his gray eyes considered her face. "Not just the daredevil personality, but even her looks. She's a blond version of you."

"What makes you think my personality is daredevil?" she inquired as he started the engine.

∞

Georgia was eating her peanut butter and jelly sandwich in her cube and researching requirements for sales tax collection in all fifty states, when a company-wide email from Roy appeared in her inbox:

Dear Colleagues,
As you know, it is essential to the vitality of the business that we …
Well, okay, not the whole email. She skipped down to see if there was any substance.
Giuseppe Coppola, who recently joined us as our Director of

Business Development, is hereby promoted, effective immediately, to Vice President of Business and Product Development. He retains all previous duties, and now adds the crucial role of understanding our evolving market and leading our product development in the direction that will maximize our competitive advantage in the marketplace.

This change in responsibilities will free Andrea Hancock to focus more fully on managing the R&D team in a manner that maximizes their effectiveness and brings our products to market in a timely way.

Please join me in providing full support to Giuseppe and Andrea in their new roles.

Roy

The second reading confirmed her impression from the first. Part of Andrea's job—the creative part—had just been given to Giuseppe Coppola. All that grumbling about "amateur hour" and "SallyMan" when Coppola took over biz dev with no biz dev experience seemed rather to have missed the point.

Ken said Andrea was the crown jewel of the company.

This probably wasn't as bad as it seemed. She printed a copy of the email and headed down the corridor to Ken's office. His door was closed.

"Maggie," she asked, "is Ken going to be free for a minute sometime this afternoon?"

Maggie glanced at her watch, then pulled up his schedule on her computer screen. "Hard to say. He's supposed to be free right now. This is an unscheduled conversation he's having. I might be able to get you in for five minutes before his one o'clock call."

"Great. Can I ask who he's talking to?"

"Andrea."

"Thanks, Maggie. I'll be in my cube."

"Georgia," Ken said a few minutes later. "What's goin' on?" He was seated at his conference table, his body strangely still as he raised his gaze from the empty, polished table top to meet hers. In fact, the only visible motion in this usually lively room was through his window and beyond the parking lot, where the tops of sun-dappled eucalyptus trees undulated in the gusting April wind.

"I just saw Roy's email," she said, "and was hoping you could tell me it wasn't as bad as I thought it was."

"I would love to do that, Georgia Griffin, but as a one-time Eagle Scout and Catholic I am not permitted to lie." His rueful smile above his cherry red bow tie told her he was proud of her for spotting disaster as quickly as he did. Sort of a two-edged skill for both of them.

"Is she going to quit?"

"I am not at liberty to tell you that, either, but I will say she was just in here asking me whether a written resignation requires public disclosure."

"Oh no. Does the board know?"

"I don't know whether they know about the demotion. They don't know about a resignation yet, because there hasn't been one. She's waiting until quarter end."

"Won't they stop it when they find out?"

"I'm sure they'll try. I just doubt they can succeed. Andrea has decided this is one insult too many for her to keep working with Roy."

"Will she leave right away?"

"She's thinking of giving a month's notice. In a way it doesn't matter. She's irreplaceable, no matter how much notice she gives."

"This is bad."

"It is bad, Georgia, but don't get too upset about it. The way of the world, really. Just be glad Roy Zisko is the CEO of a two-bit software company and not the leader of the Free World."

Two-bit software company.

"Ken, are *you* going to quit?"

"I don't really know, Georgia. I don't see how the company can survive without Andrea, much less flourish. I'm not usually a quitter, but I can't remember ever feeling quite like such a fool for just showing up every day and taking my job seriously."

"It'll be horrible if you leave. For the company," she added quickly.

"Nobody's indispensable around here. Well, except Andrea. How's that for laughs? Certainly not me. I don't know what I'm going to decide, but you shouldn't let it influence you one way or another. You're doing a great job here, and the job lets you support Katie-Ann. You certainly don't want to jeopardize that on my account."

"Thanks, Ken. I'll look out for myself. And I'm sure you'll make the right decision."

"Thanks, Georgia. It's great working with you. Would you mind closing the door on your way out?"

For the rest of the day Georgia kept reminding herself that he hadn't said 'It's *been* great working with you.'

∞

"You go ahead and start your homework," she told Kate after dinner. "I'll clean up, and then I'm going down to my car to think a while." She began spooning the leftover ground beef in mushroom soup into a plastic container.

Kate, who was bundled up in her favorite red hoodie, lifted a book from her backpack and let it drop with a satisfying thunk onto the rickety card table. "Did you return Eddie's phone call?" She shook her head disapprovingly. "Can't believe you're giving up SFJazz with the Eddie dude just to think. Must be serious." Eddie dude. Kate's assimilation was complete.

"It is, sort of." She'd told the Eddie dude she had to work late, and it was only their second time out.

"Okay, but why your car, Georgia? It's cold out there tonight. Think in the bedroom, and I'll stay out here."

She shook her head and pointed a finger skyward. "Need celestial consultation for this one. You know the car's my thinking place.

I sorted out some important things when I lived in it, and I no longer decide anything without my buddy Orion."

A few minutes later she left Kate hunched over her geometry book, descended the drafty cement steps and locked herself in the passenger side of the car. She wasn't going to see Orion tonight. The moon was a pale glow behind thick clouds, and rain began to patter on the windshield. She pulled the old wool blanket from the back seat, tucked it around the front of her body, then closed her eyes and focused on her breath. At least, tried to focus. After a few minutes she gave up, opened her eyes again and looked up at the light in their living room where Katie-Ann was hard at work.

Andrea was leaving the company, and when she went, Ken would go, too.

Ken thought there was one crown jewel of the company. Georgia knew there were two, and now they would both be gone. The company wouldn't survive this, especially when the stock was still recovering. It would become a takeover target for sure, and how secure would her job be then? Without Ken to look out for her. She expelled a sigh against the back of her hand. So much for those stock options and Katie-Ann's college money. So much for achieving escape velocity from her no-account life in Arkansas. She'd be lucky to avoid living jammed up against Katie-Ann in the backseat of the Subaru. Good thing she wasn't the sort of wimp who cried.

Not to mention that when Ken quit, she'd never see him again. That was the difference between a business friend and a real friend, wasn't it? You could lose them in a heartbeat, and weren't even supposed to care.

It was amazing how recently her dreams of a long-term job in a successful company had seemed not just possible but secure. She'd been the finest paralegal she knew how to be, and for what? She'd been delusional to think a paralegal could ever really make a difference.

Kind of laughable, when you thought about it. Not even Einstein the Paralegal could compensate for this idiot CEO.

Because that's what it all came down to, a terrible CEO. All those other morons and misfits were just manifestations of Roy's bad judgment. If you got rid of every one of them, Roy would just hire some more. Look at Large Romeo replacing Terkes, for example. Roy had more bad ideas than a stable had horseflies. Withholding Ken's bonus. Promoting Coppola. Probably negotiating with Voldemort right now to replace Sally as head of HR. Pitiful.

And she wasn't the only one who'd sacrificed a lot for Lumina Software. Look how hard Zack had worked, and Quan, and all the software engineers working around the clock to get the 6.1 out. Staying up night after night to finish the audit on time. Winning the patent case. And for what? Dead bang nothing. The company was finally caving in on itself. There hadn't been enough collective energy in that last executive meeting to power a light bulb.

This was what Ken meant about feeling like a fool.

What good did it do to use your special talents if you just ended up here, anyway?

Of course, she'd been using those talents in a shortsighted way. Her father had warned her that Sally might be the wrong target. The only solution that had ever made sense was getting rid of Roy himself. Maybe if she hadn't been distracted by all the horseflies …

Not that she'd ever had the slightest chance of taking out Roy. The guy was invincible. After all, Sally had more or less accurately listed his many colossal failings in the course of her unfortunate power grab, and the board's only response was to tell him to knock off the little, obvious ones and then leave him in charge to wreck everything else. Must be because Wall Street loved him for all that cost-cutting. Nobody, including Georgia, was ever going to puncture that.

Unless whatever Sally had on Roy made a good shiv.

Georgia remained convinced Sally did have something on Roy, but who knew if it was bad enough to get him fired? If it had been, wouldn't Sally have used it against him already, after the humiliating way he let the board just frog-march her out of the company? Georgia certainly couldn't judge, because she'd shut down her research as part of her wholesome resolve to stop taking wild chances and stick to the safe, respectable job she'd actually been given.

See, now that was the thing: Being cautious sometimes posed its own risks (not to mention that it got a little boring). She drummed her fingers on the seat a few times. Who could say for sure what she'd have found if she'd pursued it? She might have been locked and loaded by now for the present emergency.

She sighed so heavily that her cheeks ballooned.

What was she talking about? Roy Zisko was unassailable. Start messing with him and who knew where you'd end up?

Where was she ending up now? Her company was being reduced to rubble by a CEO out of *Saturday Night Live*.

The harm was already done, or shortly would be. If Ken Madigan was giving up, it really must be hopeless. He had worked so hard with such intelligence and no encouragement for a long time. He had given his all, his completely talented all, to that stupid company. How could so much effort be allowed to just gurgle down the drain?

Maybe it couldn't.

Ken was giving up because he had used all his talents to the best of his ability and could see it wasn't enough. But Georgia had different talents than Ken. Not as laudable, certainly, but valuable at the right moment. Peculiarly suited to the problem at hand, maybe.

But she could never pull something like this off in a week, when she didn't even have a plan yet. When she hadn't studied Roy with her quiet mind and found his fault lines. There was simply no time.

Which was exactly what everybody had said about the side deal audit. And how did Ken respond? *People are counting on us to do it*, he said. *If we don't do it, I want to know it's because it we couldn't do it. And how do we know what's possible unless we give it our very best?*

At that moment the clouds thinned and Orion flashed an appearance, his belt and sword winking at her from the cold, black sky.

Well, thought Georgia. Well. She had such confidence in Ken's judgment, but she knew one thing that Ken didn't. She knew about the Griffin family special talents.

She had sidelined those special talents prematurely. The point had been to keep things stable for Katie-Ann, but now she didn't have that choice. The current situation was about as stable as a heifer on a high wire, with equally predictable results.

She needed to know what Sally had on Roy. Probably useless, of course, but 'probably' was no reason to admit defeat. What if this was finally her chance to make the decisive difference? How would she know unless she tried? Tried it for Ken. For Katie-Ann and her college money.

At that instant the moon broke free of the clouds entirely, and bathed the wet sidewalk in brilliant, silvery light. Georgia tossed the blanket into the back seat, jumped across a puddle and ran up the steps to her front door.

Katie-Ann had already disappeared into the dark bedroom. Good. Georgia pulled her chair up to the coffee table and opened her notepad. The best approach was to get the Board to fire him. After all, they'd definitely come through on Burt Plowfield and Sally. But Roy's sterling reputation on Wall Street insulated him from his own incompetence, so the board members needed a real jolt, and how was she going to deliver that in nine—ouch!—make that eight days?

Better to freak Roy out and get him to resign. Self-deport, as Mitt Romney would say. But how? Roy was profoundly unfazed by Sally's treachery, even though the Board members were horrified by it. He evidently felt invulnerable, exactly like Glen Terkes. Roy probably believed he was the finest and most prized CEO in Silicon Valley, and maybe the most beloved to boot. Must be great to be so stuck on your-self. Whatever Sally had on him had better make a good solvent.

∞

She knocked on the metal rim of the entry to Lucy's cube. "Lucy, can

I ask you something? I'm looking at the resume of a key employee at a company we might buy, and something on there just strikes me as implausible. Should I assume their HR department checked it all out before they hired him?"

"No." Lucy shook her head emphatically. "It really depends. A lot of times they just spot check for low-level people.

"But always for an executive?"

"Well, not always even then. We're more conscientious about fact-checking our senior people, but then sometimes a senior guy is terrified of having his current employer find out he's looking before he's landed the new job. So then we make the offer contingent on everything checking out after the fact."

"But you do check it after he's hired?"

"Well ... that's the thing." Her shrug was apologetic. "Sometimes we pretty much forget about it. I mean, we know it's all *probably* going to check out, and if staffing is a little thin ... Anyway, what did you find that's implausible? I'll look into it now."

"Would you? Perfect. I won't bother you with it yet, though. Let's see where the acquisition's going first."

When she closed her eyes to sleep that night she saw an old-time black-and-white wall calendar, where the days tore themselves off and zoomed away until there was nothing but a square of blank cardboard hanging on a paint-chipped wall.

The next morning she called in sick with the stomach flu.

∞

The University of Washington kept her on hold forever, and then referred her back to Degree Clearing House. If she didn't like the answer she got there, the woman suggested, she could always have the employee obtain a set of transcripts himself. Georgia hung up and sat there, tapping on Roy's resume. She noticed that Degree Clearing House said Roy's B.A. was granted in 1987, the same year he'd listed for the PhD. Coincidence? If the undergrad date was accurate, and if his employment history was right, then he couldn't have spent any time at all getting a PhD.

Was that what Sally had on him? He'd made up his PhD? Boy, that would be irritating. After all, why limp along with a paralegal certificate from Heber Springs Correspondence School, when she could have given herself a B.A. from Harvard?

But did making up college degrees wreck people's careers? She went online and investigated, and the answer was an unequivocal maybe. Looked like they often were fired in disgrace, but not always:

1. David Edmondson, CEO of Radio Shack: Fired.

2. Ron Zarella, CEO of Bausch & Lomb: Not fired.

3. Terrence Lanni, CEO of MGM Grand: Resigned (which of course just meant that by timely consent he'd avoided rape.)

4. Scott Thompson, CEO of Yahoo: Resigned (ditto.)

So it might be enough, but you couldn't count on it.

What she found even stranger was the seemingly fake high school degree. She could see making up a PhD out of need for prestige or whatever, but a high school degree? Everybody graduated from high school, and nobody cared which one. Well, maybe they cared if it was some snooty prep school, but nobody cared about a public school one way or another.

She called the high school. The front office shunted her off to the school librarian, who grudgingly went into her stack of yearbooks and confirmed that no student named Roy Zisko was listed in 1977, '78 or '79. When Georgia asked her to expand her search back to 1975 and forward to 1983, the gracious lady balked.

"You know, I'm sorry, but I'm starting to neglect my other duties here. If you want to look at several years, you're welcome to come in and take all the time you need. I'm here every day between 8:30 and 5."

"Sort of far for me to come, is the problem."

"Mm-hm." No sympathy.

"Can I just ask, is there another high school with 'Klamath' in the name?"

"Hm-mm. Not around here anyplace."

"Well. Okay, if I decide to come, do you need to know in advance?"

"Hm-mm. I'm here every day the school's open."

"Okay. Thanks very much for being so patient with me."

"Mm-hm." Evidently not that patient. But then a grudging, "You're welcome."

Had Roy actually fabricated his high school, too? Seemed like he must have, but why? Did something happen at his real high school he didn't want people to know about? And if he'd never gotten his PhD, what took him so long to get his B.A.?

In the middle of the night she sat straight up: *What if Roy had gone to that high school and then changed his name?*

She slid quietly out of her sleeping bag and crept into the living room on bare feet to look up the distance to Klamath Falls, Oregon. Ugh! Six hours one way, and the gas would be hugely expensive. They'd be stuck eating pasta all week. Probably a wild goose chase she couldn't afford in dollars or time, with only seven days to work with.

But the specificity of that nondescript high school... She drummed her fingers on the card table for a long minute, then glanced at the time on her computer. Two-thirty. If she left by 4 she could get there and be finished by lunchtime. Which left her an hour now to go online and find the earliest photo of Roy she could get her hands on.

She'd have to set the alarm across the room for Kate. Good thing she had new tires on her car. Where was that Punch Brothers CD? She stood up, stretched, and went to make coffee.

∞

It seemed like forever since she'd exited I-5 at Weed and begun winding through high desert ranch country along Highway 90. She finally entered the sprawling no-neighborhood of Klamath Falls at 9 a.m., and stopped at Terry's Donut Center to tank up on coffee and sugar. She pulled into the school lot at 9:40, and stopped at the front office for directions to the library.

Mrs. Jones, the librarian, acknowledged they had spoken the day before, then led her through the aisles to the set of yearbooks. She pulled the books for each year from 1975 to 1983, plunking each new volume onto the stack in Georgia's arms.

"Here. Why don't we set you up here where it's quiet? Looks like you might be here a while."

Georgia lined up the yearbooks in sequential order, pulled her blurry printer copy of the younger (but not that young) Roy from her backpack, and set to work. First she flipped through every book to confirm that there was no Roy Zisko for any of the years. Then she returned to the book for 1979, the year that had been listed. She began by noting the name below each senior class photo, looking for any Roy. The student named Roy Coleman had big blue eyes. The student named Roy Gaddis had evidently missed photo day, since the square above his name was occupied by some cartoon pelican. No other Roys. She began flipping slowly through the activity/organization photos, searching for any other photo of Roy Gaddis. When she looked at the wrestling team she gave a start of recognition, and leaned in to take a closer look.

A kid was squatting in the front row of the photo, staring out at the camera with little, close-set black eyes and a beaky nose. She glanced at the list of names: It was Roy Gaddis.

With shaking hands she opened the '78 yearbook and scanned the junior year photos for Roy Gaddis. There he was, sporting a cheesy and obviously fake smile, minus the jowls, the glasses, the arrogance, and yet...

She jumped up with the '78 yearbook and carried it over to the librarian. "I think I found him," she said. "Any chance you'd remember him?"

Mrs. Jones closed the cover to look at the date and scoffed. "Lord, honey, do I really look that old?"

"Oh, of course not. Ridiculous. I wasn't thinking how long ago it was. Would there be anybody here who is old enough to remember?"

She considered. "Well, our English teacher's been here quite a while. Mr. Lardy. He's probably your best bet, though he wouldn't remember every student, of course." She glanced at the big, round clock on the wall above the circulation desk. "Might catch him on his lunch hour. Let's walk over there."

Mr. Lardy stood up from his half-eaten lunch with obvious reluctance and came to the door. "Yes. How can I help you?"

"George, this lady is looking for a student named Roy Zisko, who graduated from here in 1979. I figure you're the oldest fossil here in our museum." She chuckled. "Would you mind taking a look, see if you remember him?"

"Actually, it was Roy Gaddis," Georgia corrected, holding the book out to show him the picture. "I had the name wrong."

"Gaddis," he echoed. "Then I don't need to look. You with the police?"

Police? She was confused. "He was a friend of my mother's. I'm trying to find him for her surprise birthday party."

"Well, I'd say you're outta luck. If the cops haven't found him in thirty years, you probably won't find him now."

A little chill raced across Georgia's shoulders. *Could she be this lucky?*

She made her voice sound casual as her pulse began to thud in her ears. "Sorry?"

"Hold on a minute," Mrs. Jones said, reaching for the yearbook. "This that kid they wanted for check fraud?" She brought the yearbook photo close enough to scrutinize it with interest.

"That's the guy," Mr. Lardy confirmed. "But they didn't just want him for check fraud. They were pretty sure he and some older guy were using the money to buy heroin and then selling it to high school kids, including one kid who overdosed and died from it. They never proved the heroin part, but they did convict them both of check fraud, and then managed to let Gaddis slip through their fingers before sentencing.

371

You never heard such an uproar. Year after he graduated, I think. They put out a reward and everything, but never did find him. Destroyed his parents, really. Alice turned gray overnight, and Roger developed heart trouble and died a few years later."

Georgia concentrated on keeping her jaw from dropping open. "Well, this is a surprise!" she said brightly. "You remember what he looked like, Mr. Lardy?"

He squinted into the distance, bobbing his head slightly from side to side. "Well, sort of. Why? You think you've spotted him?" That little smile was downright condescending. Unattractive, really, especially with those old guy wattles.

She held up the fuzzy printer photo. "Does this look like him?"

He took it from her and glanced at it. "No, not that I can tell. He'd be a lot older by now, anyway." He handed it back. "Not likely anybody could recognize him after all this time, assuming he hasn't out-and-out disappeared from the face of the earth. Lotta people said they'd seen him, but none of it amounted to anything. Sort of like Elvis spotting, you know? Too bad to disappoint your mother, but let her know she's better off. He'd probably just steal her silverware." He snorted. "What's your mother's name, anyway? Maybe I remember her."

"Oh. Not likely. She went to a different school." *Okay, time to end this conversation.*

"I'm surprised she didn't know all this."

"You know, Mr. Lardy, she probably did. She never told me about it, though, and she has no idea I'm doing this surprise party. I've just been following up on people who signed her old yearbook. Anyway, thanks very much. Appreciate your help."

She sat in her driver's seat, blinking at the windshield, waiting for her heart rate to slow. If something seemed too good to be true, it usually was. Definitely worth another hour of research, though, to see if she could be sure one way or another. She reminded herself to drive carefully as she turned her key in the ignition.

She found the Klamath Falls public library, and asked for any newspapers from 1979 to 1981. She ended up in the basement with several rolls of brittle plastic film and an ancient microfilm reader that squeaked when she turned it on and the spindle began to rotate.

Sure enough, the story was there. Apparently they'd forged $38,000 in money orders the year he turned 16, and then another $52,000 after he turned 18, which meant he was tried as an adult. Same photo of Roy Gaddis as the one in his junior yearbook. And Gaddis was the only one who disappeared, evidently. The other guy, Jack Drummond, had spent a year in jail.

So Roy Gaddis had indeed been a fugitive from the law for thirty-five years. The $64,000—make that the $90,000—question was whether he was also the Grand High Doofus who was destroying Lumina Software. Hiding out for more than thirty years in plain sight, glaring at people in that superior way of his. Oh, delicious! Just unbelievable!

Which of course was the problem. It really was unbelievable. Mr. Lardy had spent less than five seconds looking at the photo before shaking his head and dismissing it as just another Elvis sighting. Nobody was going to take her seriously. By now, maybe nobody cared. The machine whirred to life as she started rewinding the tape. Almost 2 o'clock. Anything else to research while she was here?

She returned the tape to the desk and asked for the current phone book. That guy Lardy had said Roy Gaddis's father was dead, but what about his mother? No listing for a Gaddis. What about the other guy, Jack Drummond? No listing for him, either, but she did find a listing for Jessica Drummond. She wrote the number down, then went outside and called on her cell phone to see if anyone was home. She hung up when a woman answered, and headed over to meet her in person. Jack's wife? Maybe Jack would be there as well.

The Drummond house was overgrown with weeds and needed a new coat of its dark green paint. An old blue Chevy in the driveway was propped on cinder blocks with one of its wheels missing, and the once-white picket fence was listing dangerously. Georgia saw a chicken coop in the side yard, and several different kinds of chickens were ambling around in the yard, pecking at the dirt. A woman in jeans with long gray hair was throwing them grain.

"Ms. Drummond?" Georgia called as she approached the sagging fence near the chicken coop.

"Yes." The woman looked up, set down her plastic bucket and walked toward Georgia. She was in her fifties, with deep creases in her sun-weathered skin. "Here for eggs?"

"Oh, no. Actually, I'm trying to find Mr. Jack Drummond." The woman's eyes hardened, and Georgia added quickly, "I was hoping he could help me find a mutual friend."

She looked Georgia up and down before deciding to answer. "Not likely, unless you've got a ouija board. Jack's been dead for twenty years now."

"Oh! I'm so sorry. I'm obviously out of touch." Ms. Drummond snorted. "You were related to him?"

She nodded, her mouth set in a grim line. "Sister."

"Really. Then I wonder if..."

Jessica Drummond held her palm up and cut her off. "Look, if you knew Jack even a little bit, you know he was one scary loser. I never allowed him in my house, because he'd have stolen from me to support his drug habit, just like he did every fool who ever trusted him. I didn't want to have to testify against him, though, so that made two good reasons to keep as far away from him as possible. So I have no idea who he did or didn't hang around with. You here about that kid who disappeared?"

"Roy Gaddis," Georgia confirmed ruefully. "I sort of need to find him. Personal connection through my mother."

"After all this time? Well, good luck to you, but I can't help."

"Would you recognize his photo, do you think?" She pulled the photo out of her purse.

Ms. Drummond took the photo and glanced at it, then handed it back with a shrug. "Sorry. You have no idea how many times the police brought me photos, but I honestly don't remember ever laying eyes on the guy. The way he disappeared like that, wouldn't surprise me too much if Jack did away with him."

Georgia reared back in surprise. "Good Lord! Did he and your brother have a falling out?"

"How would I know? Just seems surprising he never showed up, 's all I'm saying."

"I see your point. Can I ask how your brother died?"

"Boating accident, the police said. Some luxury yacht supposedly, owned by this big East Coast executive, only you tell me what business my brother would have with some legitimate businessman on a yacht." She planted her fists on her hips in disgust. "Couldn't even swim, the damn fool, required too much concentration."

She poked the air with her forefinger. "I guarantee he was either stealing stuff or running drugs on that boat, so I asked as few questions as possible. They wanted to ship his body back here for burial, but I even said no to that. Who knows who he was mixed up with there at the end, that coulda come around here causing trouble? It's a shame, but I kept away from him when he was alive, and I wasn't about to get tangled up with him once he was dead."

"Sounds like a very good decision, Ms. Drummond. Thank you so much for talking to me. I'll let you get back to your chickens."

Wow. So the teenage Roy Gaddis was involved with a real crook, she thought as she unlocked her car. That could be a whole separate motivation to disappear. Interesting, but sort of a dead end for her, really. Didn't get her any closer to proving Roy Zisko was a fugitive.

Assuming he *was* Roy Gaddis, the fugitive. How confident was she of that? She sat with both hands on her steering wheel, staring up through her windshield at the lower branches of a pine tree. Beaky nose. Close-set little black eyes. He was a Roy who graduated in 1979, and Roy Zisko had been telling people for years that he graduated from this same public high school in 1979. And Sally surely had something on him that kept him firmly on her side. So was Georgia certain that

Roy Zisko and Roy Gaddis were one and the same?

No. How could she be? And even if she had been certain, she had no proof. How could she prove that Roy Gaddis was Roy Zisko in seven—she glanced at her watch—soon to be six days?

Already 4 o'clock. Katie-Ann would have to get her own dinner. Better to call from the car, once she was zipping past the cows and horses on her way back to I-5. She pulled away from the curb and headed for Highway 90.

If Jessica Drummond was right about Gaddis being dead, then she was on the wild goose chase of the century. *Don't go there. No percentage in it.*

Okay, how to get proof that Gaddis and Zisko were the same person?

Roy Zisko did get a degree from USF in 1987. If he and Roy Gaddis were one and the same, then he must have changed his name between 1980 (the year he disappeared) and 1987. How would he have done that? You could just start using a different name, probably, but then what did he use for transcripts when he applied to USF? No, he probably needed a court order, and would a 19-year-old fugitive show up in court to do that? Not likely. Had he stolen some actual Roy Zisko's identity, and then used his transcripts? Maybe. Some dead guy, probably, so nobody would show up and complain. She made a mental note.

If you were a woman, you could just change your name when you got married. No questions asked, probably. Could a guy do that? What if Linda Zisko had always been Linda Zisko, and it was Roy who changed his name? Probably couldn't figure that out in time, either, although her father's lawyer would have access to marriage records. Worth shooting off a note to the lawyer to see if he could check marriage records in 24 hours. Another mental note.

She pulled onto Highway 90 and came to a dead halt behind a gigantic yellow tractor that was taking its own sweet time to turn around in all four lanes of the road, probably so that it could use both lanes in her direction for a good long while. Great. Her car and her investigation, both stuck, going nowhere fast. She pulled out her cell phone to call Katie-Ann.

Of course, the one person who did know whether Roy Zisko and Roy Gaddis were the same guy was Roy Zisko himself. Could she get the proof from him?

CHAPTER 29

Georgia's knees ached, and her quads were burning. For forty long minutes now, she'd been crouched down on her haunches behind a big gray dumpster in the parking lot in back of the Overtime Fitness Gym. She wanted a clear and covert view of Roy as he rounded the corner of the pale gray stucco building and found the note clamped under the wiper blade of his red Ferrari, which read:

What ever happened to Roy Gaddis?

What was taking him so long? His personal training had ended half an hour ago, and if this was a guy who primped after a shower, then he seriously needed a primping coach. The longer she stayed here the more likely it was that somebody would throw open the "Employees only" door in the otherwise blank stucco wall and send her scuttering into the stiff, scratchy shrubs along the chain link fence. She set her iPhone down on the blacktop, put a hand on each knee, and stretched her legs straight, lifting her butt in the air, breathing through her mouth to block the smell of rancid grease and tomato sauce wafting out of the dumpster. Shouldn't fitness people be eating carrot sticks instead of this fast food crap?

She noticed a big, orange cat doing a stealth walk through the thick underbrush of the hedge behind her. Closing in on something? When she glanced back at the lot, Roy was hurrying toward his car, neck stuffed into his tight collar, wearing his charcoal gray suit and carrying his canvas gym bag. He tossed the bag from his right hand to his left as he walked, pulled out his key and pointed the remote door opener.

He had already opened the driver's side door when he noticed the note. Tossing the bag across to the passenger seat, he snatched the note free and then hesitated mid-crumple, apparently realizing that it was a hand-lettered note addressed specifically to him. He glanced at the note and his whole body jerked. He darted a hooded, frantic look both right and left, then caught himself and reasserted careful composure. He stuffed the note into his inside coat pocket as he climbed into the driver's seat and slammed the door. Then there was a full minute's silence, during which Georgia expected him to jump back out of the car and drag her by her hair from behind the dumpster. God, her feet were so exposed between those dumpster wheels! Then the engine roared to life and the red Ferrari fishtailed out of the lot.

Well, shut the front door! (as Gramma Griffin used to say.) He really *was* Roy Gaddis. After a moment she stood stiffly and made herself walk calmly through the lot and across the street where she'd left her car.

Thank you thank you thank you, Mr. Gaddis, for your inadvertent candor. Because his reaction to the note could only mean one thing. Ye gods and little fishes! Hiding in plain sight for almost thirty years, using that glowery contempt to keep everybody at a distance. Fine scam, she had to admit. Remarkable scam. Her father would positively chortle with admiration.

As she sat with her hand on the key in the ignition, the big orange cat rounded the corner with a little rodent dangling limply from its mouth. Yes, Roy Gaddis had run a stunningly good, daredevil scam for thirty years. She let her smile widen into her slightly loony grin. And now he'd met his match.

∞

Should she go to the police? Probably not. Even if they took her suspicions seriously, they'd never get anything done in the short amount of time before Andrea quit. And they probably wouldn't take her suspicions seriously. After all, they ignored Ted Bundy's wife, even though she'd shown up with the makings of his signature plaster cast from the back of his closet, practically proving he was the infamous serial killer. So why should they listen to her, when all she had—at most—was a lead on a thirty-year-old check fraud case in some other state?

The third reason not to go to the police was that if they did follow up and catch Roy, the whole thing would become notorious and tank the stock at a time when it seriously needed not to tank. And the fourth was that what self-respecting person with special talents would rely on the police for anything?

One thing that was clear from her misadventures with kiddie-porn-guzzling Glen Terkes was that she didn't have the stature to shake the confidence of a Captain of Industry, no matter what she had on him. No matter how vulnerable he *ought* to feel. If she was going to shake Roy's confidence, she needed to do it anonymously.

She would become the Wizard of Oz.

It took a couple of hours of computer time in an Internet cafe in Sunnyvale to settle on Chatzy for her anonymous chat room. (She didn't really know how somebody could trace her, but why take the chance?) She chose Chatzy because they just assumed she wanted an alias, and efficiently asked her to choose and enter it right when she signed up. She named the chat room "Klamath History Lessons," with a greeting of "Welcome to Roy Gaddis," and then sent an email invitation from "Jack Drummond" to Roy's work email. The invitation said simply,

Welcome to Klamath History Lessons.
To enter the room, please identify yourself below.

The Wizard assumed her position behind the curtain.

She bookmarked the Chatzy site so she could check back every few minutes to see whether he had responded. While she waited, she wrote a note to be delivered to her father's lawyer the next morning, and then began a fruitless search for any subsequent criminal history for Jack Drummond.

Roy entered the chat room an hour and a half later:

> **Blackbox:** You aren't Jack Drummond.

Look at that. He wasn't even bothering to pretend he didn't know what this was about. She smiled triumphantly at the screen. And calling himself "Blackbox." Already way better than the Terkes debacle, since Terkes had never admitted anything. Score one for the Wizard.

How did he know she wasn't Jack Drummond? Probably knew about the boating accident. Either that, or he was bluffing. She replied:

> **Jack:** Not the point. You are Roy Gaddis, and that's what matters.
> **Blackbox:** What do you want from me?
> **Jack:** I want you to resign from Lumina Software.

If he was surprised, he betrayed it only by a slight delay in response. This one answer had greatly narrowed his field of suspects, of course. His mind was probably racing through every person who could want him out of Lumina. Satisfying, really, that she'd never be on that list.

He replied:

> **Blackbox:** And then what?
> **Jack:** Then Lumina Software rises to greatness, and you never hear from me again.
> **Blackbox:** What about money?
> **Jack:** I don't want money.
> **Blackbox:** Sally?

So Sally did know. Why hadn't she ratted him out already? Was he paying her? In any case, she needed him to think he had bigger problems than Sally.

Jack: You aren't thinking clearly. Why would Sally want you to resign?

Blackbox: Why do you want me to resign?

He was trying to narrow the candidates further. She drafted:

Jack: I know this is called a chat room, Mr. Gaddis, but I'm not here to chat. You have 48 hours to resign and live in peace as Mr. Zisko. On Thursday at 4 p.m. I contact the Klamath police.

Rereading, she deleted 'Klamath police' and entered 'FBI.' Neither agency probably gave a shit, but Roy couldn't know that. Might as well make it scary. She hit send, and watched it appear in the chat room.

A full minute passed.

Blackbox: I will work with you, but I need to know who you are.

Jack: You don't need to know who I am to resign.

Silence for three minutes, which was way too long. She'd lost him.

Blackbox: You don't have proof.

Ha!

Jack: If you were dumb enough to believe that, Mr Gaddis, you wouldn't have eluded the FBI for thirty years.

Blackbox: How do I know you won't go to the FBI anyway?

Was he stalling? Trying to trace her?

Jack: You have until Thursday at four, Mr. Gaddis. Use your time wisely.

She made herself log out of the chat room before he could respond. If he had a good cyber-snoop tracing her, they would definitely identify this Internet cafe as the first dot on their map. But a cyber-snoop would see the contents of the chat room, wouldn't he, and how could Roy take that risk? Maybe he could trace her himself, but that was bound to take longer, and it was real work. He probably preferred just to con her into revealing her identity. Get her to say something online that gave herself away. She'd definitely have to avoid sounding like Arkansas.

With any luck, he'd just twist in the wind for the rest of the day. Twisting in the wind was excellent preparation for what she hoped would happen next.

∞

She needed to return to the office, which required recovering from her feigned stomach flu. There was a board meeting on Thursday morning, and she intended to be there.

On Wednesday morning she stood under an ice cold shower, left her hair wet, wore her black sweater to look as pale as possible, and drove to work with a Ziploc bag of ice inside the back of her pants against her lower back. By the time she entered Ken's office at 10 a.m., she really did feel sick.

"Georgia, come on in. Good to have you back." His yellow oxford shirt was rolled neatly to the elbows, and he brushed his bristle of red hair with one hand as he pushed back from his computer. His open, steady demeanor betrayed absolutely nothing of the disgust he'd expressed on the day Andrea was demoted. What if she'd blown the whole thing wildly out of proportion?

He joined her at the conference table, studied her face and winced. "Boy, you still don't look so good, if you'll pardon my saying so. You sure you should be here?"

She made her smile wan as she looked back into his green eyes. "I'm just a little weak. Maybe we can take care of things for the board meeting tomorrow, and then I'll head home early. I'll be fine by tomorrow."

"We could use your help, no doubt about that. Nikki isn't here this week, and her substitute doesn't inspire much confidence. Tell you what. Why don't we go over the board materials, then you can head home and finish them up from there."

She tried to make her voice sound casual. "Any news on Andrea?"

"Not a thing, I'm afraid." His voice was suddenly grim, and his face darkened. "You know, I come in every morning intending to talk to Roy about it, but I'm just afraid of how mad I'll get when he doesn't listen. She's going to submit her resignation when the quarter ends next Tuesday, and then I fully expect all hell to break loose. But don't you worry about that. We need to get you out of here today as fast as possible. Let's start with the presentation slides."

She stopped by the Mail Boxes Etc. on her way home, and found a response from her father's lawyer:

Confirm call on Thursday.

No record of marriage to Linda Zisko. Did, however, find a Bill Zisko who divorced an Alida Zisko in 1988. Followed that back to a marriage certificate for Bill Gaddis and Alida Zisko in 1985. Enclosed copies are informational only. Advise if you need certified copies for proof.

She must have gasped, because several startled Mail Boxes Etc. patrons turned in unison to look at her. She smiled apologetically as she clutched the letter protectively against her chest. She was holding actual evidence.

∾

She was the first to push through the swinging door of the boardroom the next morning, fifteen minutes before the meeting was scheduled to start. The little pots of yogurt were lined up over on the side table, and some diligent fellow underling had managed to find fragrant, glistening strawberries here in February. Looking out across the patio, she saw thin strands of cloud drifting peacefully from right to left through a sunny spring sky. As she turned on the lights and dialed in the speakerphone, the room gave off every indication of a peaceful, orderly board meeting. Unfortunately, the company's future required a certain hubbub.

She'd had to calibrate her physical appearance carefully this morning. She needed a believable relapse as soon as the meeting was over, but didn't want some health nut on the board noticing how sick she looked and ejecting her prematurely. She'd finally decided to skip the ice against her lower back (unbearable, really, and what if it leaked?), opting instead to wash herself out with a shiny polyester Salvation Army blouse the color of radioactive pea soup. Too bad Sally wasn't there to feel envious. And surely her hands were cold enough from the raging air conditioning and her raging anxiety to convince anybody that her health remained fragile. She resolved to shake hands as often as possible.

Jared Winters arrived first, his navy sport coat draping elegantly over a pale gray cashmere sweater. Larry Stockton entered next, pausing at the side table to get his cup of steaming Starbucks coffee. His coal-black eyes above his proud and prominent nose began their usual insolent gaze along her body, but stopped abruptly at her appalling blouse and skittered away entirely. She coughed weakly into her fist to disguise a little laugh.

Jean-Claude arrived, followed by Paul Holder, their storklike and very bald tech guru. Did Paul have one inkling of the mortal blow about to befall his beloved R&D group? No, she decided, he was way too relaxed and cheerful. Evidently Andrea was playing her cards close right up until she quit. Georgia and Ken seemed to be the only ones who knew disaster was looming.

Ken arrived, sporting neon yellow kidney shapes on his navy blue bow tie, accompanied by Large Romeo, looking wildly obese in a gigantic pink shirt. Keeping Omar the Tentmaker in business. Ken settled himself and sent her a message: *How you feeling?* As she responded she heard a crackle of life on the speakerphone as Clarence joined them remotely. Then Roy swept in through the door from his adjoining office, and Jean-Claude called the meeting to order at exactly 10:07. Nick of time, really. She sat on her hands to warm them up and keep them from shaking.

"And so this morning," Jean-Claude was saying, "we have the uncharacteristic but welcome good fortune to be expecting positive news about the..."

A quiet rap sounded on the door from Roy's office, and the timid little substitute for Nikki stuck her head in. "I'm terribly sorry, Mr. Zisko, but a Mr. Gaddis is on the line, and he insists you'll want to take his call."

Roy's look of panic flickered and vanished so quickly that others might have missed it completely if he hadn't knocked over his Starbuck's coffee cup in his haste to stand up. "Sorry," he muttered as Jared jerked his arm back from the hot liquid that splattered the table. "I need to take this." He rushed from the room.

The board members exchanged glances as Georgia hurried over to the credenza for big, white paper napkins to soak up the spill. "Well," Jean-Claude remarked with deliberate good humor, "it seems we can say this call is quite exciting." Nervous laughter. "We can hope it's from an angry husband, and not the SEC." Now the laughter was genuine.

"Leave it to our Frenchman to think of that," Jared said.

She mopped the shiny black surface of the conference table, and then ducked underneath to soak up coffee out of the carpet. She took her time pushing a dry napkin as far as possible into the deep, wet plush, savoring an extra moment of privacy, then resumed her seat as Larry turned his wide, humorless grin on Ken. "Do you know what this is regarding?" He sounded accusatory.

Ken held up flat palms in response. "Afraid I have no idea, Larry. Which at least means it's not the Justice Department."

"Thank God for small favors," Paul responded against a background of murmured agreement. Clarence called through the phone, "Jean-Claude, should we take a short break? I know I could use another cup of coffee about now."

Leave it to Clarence to want a break. Break from what, really, playing solitaire on his iPhone? She glanced at her Timex, hoping Jean-Claude would refuse. This wasn't going to be a long call. In fact, Mr. Gaddis would be long gone before Roy picked up the receiver.

Sure enough, Roy strode back through the door a couple of moments later, resumed his seat and adjusted the knot of his stately maroon tie. "Sorry for that interruption, gentlemen. Let's resume."

"But is it something quite serious?" Jean-Claude inquired.

"No. Not at all. Nikki would have known better than to let it through. Please continue."

Jean-Claude gave a slight shrug and resumed the meeting. As Ken reported on the SEC investigation, she lowered her head over her notes and rolled her eyes up just enough to study Roy from under her eyelashes. Hard to tell how rattled he was. His jaw seemed especially rigid, and his little black eyes glittered like two nail heads in a whitewashed fence. But maybe that was how he always looked. No point in telling herself fairy tales here.

The meeting continued. She tried to calm herself by looking out the window. That gentle spring zephyr must be picking up speed. The clouds were moving faster, and through the gap between buildings she saw a glittery confetti of swirling yellow leaves against the bright blue sky.

Ken reported that the SEC depositions related to backlog would begin the following week. Cliff reported on the status of closing the quarter-end books. Large Romeo was droning through a list of remaining deals that could still close in the final two days of the quarter, when he paused so long that all eyes flicked away from the overhead screen to notice dark sweat stains spreading beyond the armpits of that ample pink shirt. "Sorry," he said. "I seem to be drawing a blank on this one. Cliff, can you help me out with the Gaddis Industries deal?"

At which all eyes flicked back to the screen and read, "Gaddis Industries. $370K."

Cliff dutifully squinted at the slide for a moment before shaking his head. "Sorry, I'm not familiar with this one. Roy?"

But Roy was disappearing through the side door to his office.

"This meeting really is becoming a bit bizarre," Jean-Claude mused to nervous laughter after Roy had jerked the door closed behind him.

"Maybe turning a profit causes disturbances in the force field," Paul joked. "Maybe it's been so long we've just forgotten."

"Now I think we really must take a quick break." Jean-Claude was still half smiling as he stood, but his eyebrows were up by his hairline. "I will try to speak to Roy. I hope he is not ill?"

"Sure hope it isn't the flu," Ken remarked. "I know it's been goin' around our department." Georgia hoped nobody else would notice his sympathetic glance in her direction.

At that instant another rap sounded on the door from Roy's office, and Nikki's timid little substitute shortened her neck between her shoulders and winced as she shot out, "Mr. Zisko has left the building and sends his apologies!" She slammed the door closed as the room erupted in a cacophony of futile interrogation. That little receptionist wasn't as inexperienced as she looked, Georgia thought. Evidently she'd delivered unwelcome news to Captains of Industry before.

∞

She drove directly to a cybercafé in Burlingame, and started logging on and off every fifteen minutes to make it harder for him to trace her. When she logged on at 1 p.m. there was a message:

> **Blackbox:** Are you there?
> **Jack:** I've been expecting you.
> **Blackbox:** You are gaslighting me.
> **Jack:** On the contrary, Mr. Gaddis. Gaslighting is intended to

confuse someone about reality. I want you to see reality while you still have time to act on it.

He didn't respond. Trying to trace her? Or trying to keep her talking until she revealed her identity, letting him gauge whether the threat was real. Should she try to make him believe she was someone specific and terrifying? After a moment she carefully composed:

> **Jack:** Perhaps this sudden resurrection of your long-buried past has left you feeling a bit disoriented. That would be understand-able. I hear you behaved strangely in your board meeting today. Why not show this chat room to somebody you trust to help you make the right decision?

She guessed there was no such person. Was that what he was considering as the cursor pulsed on the screen? He remained silent for an entire minute.

> **Blackbox:** I will quit only if I have insurance that you won't turn me in.

Hm. Looked like progress, but what did 'insurance' mean?

> **Jack:** You will resign because you realize you have no alternative. I offer no insurance.
> **Blackbox:** I need to know you would implicate yourself by turning me in.
> **Jack:** Meaning?
> **Blackbox:** I need to pay you to go away.

Interesting. She cocked her head and frowned at the screen. Was he hoping to set her up on a blackmail charge, to prevent her from contacting the police? Of course, once she prevented herself from going to the police, he'd have no motive to resign. Could he believe she was that dumb?

Or maybe he wanted to determine whether she realized that a legal requirement for blackmail was that the blackmailer receive something of value. Probing to see if she was Ken? Whoa. Couldn't put a stake in the heart of that one fast enough.

Jack: Paying me won't help. I told you, I don't want money.

She could have sworn the cursor was pulsing his disappointment out through the silent screen.

Blackbox: Resigning will mean the end of my career. I prefer that you terminate me, citing irreconcilable differences with the board.

Fishing to see if she was a board member? There were a lot of board members, so that would slow him down a bit while he tried to figure out which one. Seemed like a misperception she wanted to nurture.

Jack: And bring the SEC crawling through every detail of our business to find out why? You will resign for undisclosed health reasons.
Blackbox: That will mean the end of my career.
Jack: I am confident your health will improve.
Blackbox: If you are going to turn me in, I must prepare my family.
Jack: Turning you in would damage Lumina's reputation. I have no motive to do that, as long as you resign.
Blackbox: I must hear that from you in person. I must know who I am dealing with, to judge whether my family is protected.

Funny, how a narcissist in trouble could suddenly become such a family man. Touching, really.
Jack: No.

Blackbox: You owe it to me to give me the opportunity to talk you out of this. I have mitigating information.

Now that sounded whiny. Trying to get her to underestimate him? How would that help? Was he just stalling for time? The sweat in her armpits was icy, and she was still debating her next move when new text appeared on the screen:

Blackbox:
To the board of directors of Lumina Software:
I deeply regret that life-threatening health issues require me to resign my positions as CEO and director of Lumina Software, effective immediately. Please respect my family's privacy by not asking me to say more.
I feel strongly that we should follow our long-standing succession plan and appoint Cliff Tanco to the role of Acting CEO immediately.
I am grateful to have had the opportunity to work with you, and wish the company every success going forward.
Very truly yours,
Roy Zisko, Chairman and CEO

That letter was so beautiful. And so unsigned. He continued:

Blackbox: I will deliver this signed letter today, if and only if you meet me at my office at 2 p.m. I will present my mitigating information, then deliver the signed letter to you and leave my fate in your hands. If you care about the well-being of Lumina Software, you have nothing to fear and will do as I ask.

He left the chat room.

Now what? The minute he saw she was the one who entered that meeting he would smirk with contempt, like Terkes had, and then call her bluff by refusing to quit. She'd be stuck getting him the slow way, which was as worthless as a two-legged mule. She'd be too late, her timing blown and Lumina Software wrecked forever. She shouldn't go to the meeting.

But what would he do when she didn't show up? He might be bluffing. Maybe his nerves would get the better of him and he'd resign before the deadline anyway.

Maybe chickens could play Scrabble. What would really happen is he'd stay right where he was and see what happened next.

Which left her where? Roy was going to stay put whether she went to the meeting or not, burrowing deeper into Lumina Software like a fat tick on a tormented dog. She was failing, and time was running out. She pushed back from the computer and dropped her forehead into her palms, her fingers pushing deep into her hair.

Unless. Could she use his arrogance against him? Maybe when he saw that the Wizard was nobody but The Girl Who Takes Notes, he'd feel so relieved and expansive that he'd say something stupid and give himself away. She lifted her face out of her palms and sat back up. Maybe she could even prepare a little script to lead him there. Use the marriage certificate between Roy Gaddis and Alida Zisko to deliver a helpful shock. Record everything he said with both her iPhone and her pocket microphone, and play it back to him right then and there.

And lose her job the instant it didn't work. Katie-Ann waiting tables and doing her homework in all-night cafes. Sleeping with cardboard wedged into the car windows again, to keep the creeps from looking in.

Get a grip. Now was not the time for her mind to jump around like a flea in a hot skillet. She pulled her legs into a cross-legged position right there on the roller chair, closed her eyes and began to follow her breath.

Ten minutes later she opened her eyes and let her feet drop to the floor, her mind refreshed and clear. She'd remembered a story her father had told them one afternoon as she and Katie-Ann helped him groom horses in the barn:

Hunters in South America use a special trap to catch monkeys. They build a box with a hole just barely big enough for a monkey to slide his skinny little hand in, and then they put a fine-smelling, bright banana inside the box. When a monkey reaches in and grabs the banana, the hole is too small for him to get his fist out again.

Oh, no! Katie-Ann said, her brush pausing against the bottom of the horse's flank. *So the monkey is stuck?*

Well, he doesn't have to be stuck. All he has to do is let go of the banana and pull his hand out, but the hunter knows the monkey won't do it. So the hunter comes back and catches the monkey every time.

Poor little monkey, Katie-Ann murmured sadly, her brush resuming a slow motion down the rich brown leg toward the knee.

Sad for the monkey, indeed. So what's the lesson for us, girls?

Be the hunter and not the monkey, Georgia stated firmly, and her father threw his head back and laughed.

Well yes, that's the superior solution. But suppose you don't have a choice? Suppose you're the monkey?

She and Katie-Ann had responded in unison: *Then let go of the banana.*

Georgia Griffin hadn't come all the way out of Piney, Arkansas, on bald tires to get caught in a monkey trap set by the likes of Roy Zisko. She was going to oust that guy all right, but she wouldn't go anywhere near that meeting, resignation letter or no. George Griffin's daughter was smart enough to let go of a banana.

∞

Since she couldn't actually meet with Roy, she remained the Wizard and could wander by shortly afterward to find out how he was reacting. When she got to Nikki's office at 2:20, she wasn't surprised that the frightened little receptionist had disappeared, but she was surprised that Nikki herself had returned to take her place. Nikki's blinds were drawn firmly against the light, and she was wearing big, high-fashion sunglasses in the unlit room. Her body seemed locked in a permanent wince. Roy was nowhere in sight, and his door was closed. With any luck, he was in there ripping out tufts of his hair.

"Oh, no," Georgia lamented. "I see they dragged you out of sick bay for the afternoon. Aren't you supposed to be in a clinic somewhere?"

"I am. Apparently the girl this morning didn't work out so well."

"Well, in fairness she had a pretty tough job. You heard what happened?"

"Oh, yeah. Paul Holder's called here three times looking for him, and he gave me a real blow-by-blow. Who was that on the phone, anyway? Somebody named G-A-D-I-S? That's what the girl wrote down."

Georgia shrugged. "Don't remember. Roy hasn't told you anything?"

"Haven't talked to him yet. Haven't seen him all day."

"Oh. Then he isn't here?" She made her voice sound casual as her pulse began to thud in her ears.

"Nope. Sent me a text message a while ago that he's spending today and maybe tomorrow on his boat."

He'd never intended to keep the appointment. What was he up to now?

"He says he's doing some maintenance thing for his boat," Nikki continued, "but honestly, at quarter end? I think he's dodging the board to keep from talking about the meeting this morning." Georgia squinted into the gloom and thought she discerned a frown below Nikki's oversized reflective lenses. "Was it really that strange?"

"Sort of, I guess, yeah. So, Roy hasn't been here at all today?"

"Not since the meeting," Nikki confirmed yet again, turning her big lenses toward Georgia and cocking her head. "Why, you need him for something?"

"Oh, documents that need signing." She held up a folder with documents she'd culled for camouflage, and then let it drop back into her lap.

"Well, if you need them today, you'll have to go there. He told me I could start sending people over at a quarter to two."

"He's redirecting people to his boat?"

394

She shrugged. "Has to. It's quarter end. I just have to let him know exactly who's coming and clear it with him before they head out the door. No board members, I'm pretty sure."

He'd intended to learn her identity without actually meeting.

Unless he intended to keep the appointment, on his boat.

His isolated boat, bobbing gently in that windy, deserted marina. Hadn't Jack Drummond died in a boating accident? She put a hand on Nikki's desk to steady herself.

She realized Nikki was waiting for an answer, her face blank and unreadable behind those big, reflective glasses. "Oh, sounds like he doesn't need to deal with this now," Georgia said with a little dismissive wave. "Honestly, don't even mention it to him. I'll just double check with Ken to make sure they can wait until Monday."

"Be a while before you can do that. Ken's headed over to the boat himself, and you know he promised Laura he wouldn't answer his cell phone in the car."

"Ken's headed to the boat?" she echoed stupidly. Good thing Nikki's head was pounding. Nikki nodded. "Yeah, just cleared it with Roy. Too bad the two of you didn't coordinate. He could have gotten the signatures for you."

"Yeah, bad luck. You know how long ago he left?" The sound of her pulse in her ears was deafening.

"I'd say ten minutes ago, so that was just after two. Should be there by a quarter to four. Leave a message on his cell phone, and he'll call you back then."

He'd shown up at Roy's office at two. *Roy thought the Wizard was Ken.*

"Thanks. I'll do that. Hope they let you out of here early." She kept her hand on Nikki's desk to steady herself as she stood up.

She reminded herself to keep breathing as she raced down stairs, unlocked her car, and flipped frantically through her Roy Gaddis folder for the phone number of Jessica Drummond. Jessica answered on the third ring.

"Ms. Drummond, this is Georgia Griffin. I talked to you about your brother a few days ago please don't hang up. I need to clarify something urgently."

The silence on the other end seemed endless. "Which would be what?"

"You told me your brother died in a boating accident. Do you remember where it happened?"

"Somewhere off the coast of New England. What's so urgent about that?"

"You remember who owned the boat?"

"Supposedly some company big shot, like I told you. Bet he was really a drug runner, though. Why are you asking me this now?"

"Because I'm afraid you might be right about the owner, and that could mean somebody's in danger right now." Her voice cracked, which was mortifying but might make her more convincing. "Please, can you remember the owner's name? Or the name of his company?"

"No way. Twenty years ago, and I wasn't really listening then. The owner had a funny name, though. I remember seeing it in the news clipping the cops sent me. Started with an X, or a Z, maybe. Zuni? Xerxes?"

"Could it have been Zisko?"

"Yeah, could be. I probably still have that article around here..."

"Oh. Don't worry about that, Ms. Drummond. Thank you for talking to me again. You've been a big help." And she very rudely hung up on Jessica Drummond's protest.

She had to get there in time to stop Ken from getting on that boat. Could he swim? Surely he could, but it better not come to that. She'd call Katie-Ann once she was on the freeway, have her call the cops if she wasn't back by—No. Bad plan. Katie-Ann had nothing to do with this. This was Georgia's project, and hers alone. She'd call Katie-Ann and tell her to get her own dinner. She'd resist telling her she loved her. With a kid like Katie-Ann, that would be a dead giveaway.

Well, she thought as she accelerated out of the parking lot, the good news was that her Wizard strategy had worked as intended. He'd obviously taken her very seriously. That's why he wanted to kill her.

CHAPTER 30

She spotted Ken's silver Camry the minute she careened into the nearly empty marina parking lot at 4:05. It was right next to one of the gates in the chain link fence. She screeched to a halt, and left her engine running while she jumped out into the chill, damp air to confirm that his car was locked and unoccupied. She was surprised it was so much colder here by the ocean, which probably explained the overcast sky and the stiff breeze bringing fog in across the water. Was that Ken, way down along the main dock, just turning onto the walkway next to Roy's boat? As she squinted through the chain link fence into the early twilight, the fog shifted and she couldn't see anyone. In any case, she'd obviously missed him. She had to get onto that boat.

And do what? Hopefully just listen undetected, while Roy realized his mistake in time to avoid blowing his cover with Ken. But of course she couldn't count on that. She'd gotten Ken into this mess, and if necessary, she'd be the one to get him out again, although she surely didn't know how. Roy was bigger than she was, and meaner than a polecat. Her only advantage was that he wouldn't know she was there.

Looked like she was following Ken Madigan into battle, after all.

She got back into her car, pulled in next to the Camry, and then hesitated. Her old, battered Subaru was just so conspicuous here, new tires notwithstanding, and stealth was her biggest asset. After glancing around the lot, she sped back out the entrance, cursing the delay, and parked at the first spot she could find on the side of Brommer Avenue.

She shrugged her nylon windbreaker on over her black pantsuit to buffer the cold breeze, kicked off her low heels and laced up her running shoes, yanked the can of Mace from her glove compartment, and clipped its black canvas holder to her waistband. She snatched her thin running gloves from the pockets of her windbreaker, dropped her cell phone into one pocket and her little recorder into the other, stuffed the gloves back on top of them, then reconsidered and pulled the gloves on. Good for warmth, and maybe they'd help avoid fingerprints. Then she raced back into the lot and up to the chain link gate, where she came to a dead stop.

She'd forgotten they locked the gate.

How had Ken gotten through? She shook the gate to confirm it wouldn't open, as gulls circled and squealed above her. She stepped back to evaluate climbing over the fence, and heard a voice say, "Need to get in here?"

She startled, and took an involuntary step back. A man in yellow shorts and a windbreaker had appeared out of the fog near the gate on the inside.

Manna from heaven?

She resisted her impulse to shrink back into the hood of her windbreaker, and instead beamed her most ingratiating smile. "Oh, can you let me in? That would be just wonderful! I'm already late for a meeting, and I forgot to bring my cell phone."

"No problem. The *Chaucer*, right? I let your buddy in a couple of minutes ago." He pulled the gate open and stood back to let her enter.

"Oh, that must be some other meeting," she lied as she stepped through. "I'm on a different boat. Thanks so much."

"You know," he advised, "if anybody else is coming, you should probably wait here and let 'em in yourself. I'm about to head out, and there aren't too many folks around here right now." As he gestured with his head toward the boat behind him, she heard the rapid staccato of his engine, and saw the light from his cabin windows staining the thick mist.

"I'll let the owner know," she called over her shoulder as she hurried away from him. "We really shouldn't be bothering you anyway. Thanks again." A moment later she glanced back to make sure he was gone, raced down the dock toward the *Chaucer*, then ducked and crept along the little walkway that separated the *Chaucer* from the next boat over. The *Chaucer's* lights were on, which must be why Roy had the engine running. Well, unless he planned to take Ken out to sea and throw him overboard. Could he do that? Ken was a whole lot taller than Roy, but he wouldn't see Roy coming until it was too late.

She heard voices coming from the cabin. Good. As long as they stayed put down there, the boat wasn't going anywhere and Ken wasn't going into the water. Now Roy just needed to realize he had the wrong guy, and she'd be gone in the fog without a trace.

She lifted her foot to step onto the deck, hesitated, then set it back down on the walkway. What if the boat rocked, what if they heard her foot land? But she had to hear what they were saying. Too bad cat burglary had never been one of her father's special talents. At that moment she heard the sound of an engine, crouched down next to the *Chaucer*, and saw the gate opener's boat churn slowly past and out toward the bay, setting the *Chaucer* bobbing in its wake. That guy was turning out to be downright useful. She jumped to her feet as soon as the boat was past, bobbed her upper body once or twice in rhythm with the *Chaucer*, then leaped and landed both feet on the deck, keeping her knees soft to absorb the impact.

The murmured conversation in the cabin continued without interruption. Perfect. She crouched low, tiptoed across the deck and pressed herself against the slick, wet exterior wall of the cabin so that she couldn't be seen through the horizontal window slits. Only one window was cracked open, and she crept around until she was right under it in order to hear.

"… drink?" Roy was saying. Good, they were still doing preliminaries. She started her little recorder with gloved hands, and propped it against the wall with her shoulder while she did the same with her iPhone. Then with a slight shudder she molded her whole front against the wet, cold, metal wall, and held up one device in each hand just below the window. She hoped for Ken's sake that Roy wouldn't say anything incriminating, but if he did, she just might need it later.

"…have ginger ale," Ken was saying.

"Awfully dull," Roy teased mildly. She heard the chink of ice, and then fizz, and then murmured thanks.

"…appreciate you agreeing to talk to me today," Ken said.

"Oh, I wouldn't have missed it." Did Ken hear the menace in that voice? "I thought it was you. I'm guessing this all must be about Andrea."

"That's exactly what it's about."

"I'm surprised you thought it was worth it."

"It is worth it, Roy, because Andrea's the lifeblood of this company. I was ready to give up, but then Laura and I talked it over this weekend, and agreed I should do everything possible to keep Andrea with the company."

"So Laura knows about it as well." *No. No way.*

"Laura's my partner, Roy. I talk to her about everything, but I promise you, it never goes beyond her."

"Very reassuring. And have you told anyone else?" *Say yes, Ken. Please say yes.*

"Nope. No reason to."

"And does Laura know you're here now?" Why was he asking that, exactly?

"No, I really don't bother her with the details. Just found out you were here myself, and since it was urgent I decided to drive on over."

"Glad you did. So you've been holding this in reserve for a while."

There was a slight pause. "What do you mean by 'this', exactly?" Uh-oh. Roy needed to realize they were talking about different things now.

"Well, that's a fair question," Roy acknowledged. "Exactly what do you know? Let's start with my being Roy Gaddis." *Thar she blows.* Georgia squeezed her eyes shut and suppressed a groan. And what did he mean, "start?" What else did he think Ken knew?

There was a pause. What was Ken making of that rather startling remark? Did he realize he was in danger? Had he made the connection with Gaddis Industries from the slide a few days ago? Wait, that board meeting had only happened this morning. She gave her head a slight shake to clear it.

"Sorry, Roy, I guess I'm not following you. Are you talking about what happened in the board meeting this morning?"

"You thought I was going to avoid it?"

"Not necessarily, and I know it's probably very important. I guess I just don't see what it has to do with Andrea. I hope we're not talking at cross purposes here."

"Oh, I don't think we are. You wanted me to feel cornered, and I'm letting you know that I do."

There was another pause. What made a simple gap in conversation sound so clearly like stunned silence? "Now I know I'm missing something. Happy to talk about anything that will help the company, Roy, but remember I'm an officer. If you tell me something I think the board should know, I'll have to tell them." So straightforward and upright. Hardly something the Wizard would say. Would Roy have the subtlety to realize that and pull back now, while he still could?

"Don't expect you to do anything, one way or the other," Roy responded. "Too late for that. And by all means, drop the Dudley Do-right imitation. Dudley Do-Right doesn't blackmail people with their past, even in the name of truth and justice."

He'd made up his mind. He intended to kill him.

Ken surely knew he was in trouble now, but he couldn't know how much. She lowered her left hand and touched her black canvas Mace holster, then lifted the iPhone back up under the window. She couldn't spray Roy in that little enclosed cabin, not with Ken in there. She'd have to wait until he came out.

"You know, Roy, you're obviously still quite angry and distracted about the board meeting this morning. Not sure this is a good time to talk about Andrea, after all." Good. He'd get himself out of there and off the boat. But why did his voice sound a little strange?

"Oh, come. You've traveled all this way. We're not going to send you home empty-handed." Roy's barely audible chuckle made the hair on the back of her neck stand up.

"Say, can we open more of those vents?" Ken asked. His voice really was a little slurred. "I seem to be getting quite a headache." *Had Roy put something in Ken's ginger ale?*

"Are you? Probably just don't have your sea legs yet. Let's sit here a few more minutes, and I'm sure you'll be fine. Now, where were we? Roy Gaddis. So you know about the mistakes I made as a teenager."

"Don't really believe I do, but they're probably pretty familiar. After all, I had two kids by the time I was twenty." Ken was sounding too chatty for a guy who knew he was at risk. *Was he really that trusting, or was something affecting his judgment?*

"If you know about Roy Gaddis," Roy continued, "then you know I got caught passing bad checks, and had to leave town." *Was he so confident of killing Ken that he was going to spell it all out for him? First chance in thirty-odd years, maybe.*

Long pause. "Ya gotta be kiddin' me."

"Oh, come. You surely knew that much. So I had to leave my identity behind, and I did. Laundered it, really, the way gangsters launder money. I married Alida Zisko in college, and she got boatloads of credit from the dyke feministas when I agreed to take her name. Voilà! as they say. Out with Roy Gaddis. In with Roy Zisko." It was terrifying that Roy felt comfortable saying all this. Ken would surely try to leave now.

"This wasn't Linda," Ken said. *So what, Ken? Stand up and get out of that cabin.*

"Of course not. Her name was Alida Zisko, a lovely young Czechoslovakian in search of a green card. Three years later, Alida Zisko got her citizenship, I had my new name, and we happily divorced and went our separate ways. Linda, being a traditional sort, was more than happy to become Linda Zisko a couple of years later.

"That was more than 30 years ago, and I congratulate you. In all that time, you're only the second person to figure out the connection."

"Who was the first?" *Good question. Slightly better question: What happened to the first?* She inhaled deeply, and let the air out slowly with puffed cheeks.

"My old partner in crime, Jack Drummond," Roy answered amiably, "and you know all about him, of course. Well, not all about him, since you evidently thought he was still alive. He probably would have been, if he hadn't had the misfortune to recognize my picture in the *Journal* when I became the CEO of MegaMind. Drummer was down on his luck at the time, and decided to participate in my good fortune. Only it didn't work out for him."

"Boy, I'm really not feeling well. Sure seems stuffy down here. You sure that was just ginger ale you gave me?" So now even Ken was suspicious. Roy must be knocking Ken out so he could throw him over the side. If so, was Ken better off staying in the cabin? Either way, she'd have to Mace Roy the minute he put his toe on deck. "You telling me you ... Jack Dormand?"

"Let's just say he wasn't able to take advantage the way he'd hoped. And nobody else has made the connection in thirty years.

"Oh, Sally figured out I didn't have the PhD I claimed on my resume, and I was always afraid she'd figure out the rest, but she never has. Is that how you figured it out? Did she tell you about my made-up PhD?"

"You don't have a PhD?" Okay, now that response was just stranger than pantyhose on a frog. Ken might be trusting, but he was never oblivious. She desperately wanted to look in there and see what was happening with her own eyes.

"Well," Roy continued, "in any case, now that I see who you are, I actually do believe you didn't want money. You really did just want me to resign." His chuckle was tinged with regret. "Too bad I didn't realize that sooner. Who knows, maybe I'd actually have done it. After all, I've made enough money killing the other companies, I probably could have spared this one."

"This one what?"

"Company, of course. Your beloved Lumina Software. You see, I learned a long time ago that making a business succeed is a lot more complicated than you might expect, and most executives just made it harder. Some of these people couldn't do more damage to their companies if they tried, and that's been my perfect camouflage. Making a business succeed is hard, but it's easy to get a good Change of Control Agreement and then help the self-dealers and dumb guys in the company drive it into the ground. Nobody suspects a thing, because all I do is exploit the plentiful stupidity of the average executive." He barked a laugh.

Ken didn't respond. She decided to chance it, peeked in the window and saw with horror that Ken's head was slumping forward. Then he lifted it. "You know, I'm not getting enough air down here. I just have to …" He stood up and then sank to his knees. Roy had his back to her.

"Whoa there, Ken, think you better wait till your head clears, don't you? Here, let me help you lie down." He helped Ken to his feet, and maneuvered him over to the bed. "You didn't ask me *why* Drummer never reaped the benefits of his knowledge. Turns out he had a boating accident. He was down in the cabin of my boat, sort of like you are now, while I was up on deck, steering. I was running my engine to charge up my second battery, and there was an undetected hole in the exhaust hose." As he spoke, Ken staggered to his feet again and over to the stairs, where he collapsed and stopped moving. "So carbon monoxide was filling the cabin without Drummer realizing it, and by the time I found him and dragged him up on deck it was too late. Or so the police concluded."

Georgia groaned. Why on earth had she assumed a 'boating accident' meant drowning? He had drugged Ken to keep him in the cabin until he suffocated, and she was just standing up here recording it. She dropped her iPhone and recorder into her windbreaker pockets, and slid the Mace quietly from its holster as she crept around toward the cabin entrance. She had to get Ken out of that cabin now.

"...don't like having the same accident twice, of course," Roy was saying, "but you came on me so suddenly I didn't have time to invent a new one. And anyway, the other one was back east, and quite a few years ago. I think we'll be all right. We do need to get you off these stairs, though, so I can get up. I'm getting a little drowsy down here myself, even without the ginger ale."

She heard a thump. Ken being dropped onto the cabin floor?

"I've been pretty clever all these years, don't you think? And now you're forcing me to be clever again. Rotten luck, really, that I have to waste my time being clever about this. And you told Laura, which means I also have to deal with her in very short order, and won't that be a helluva coincidence? I wonder why you couldn't leave well enough alone. Well. See you in an hour or so, though of course that won't be mutual."

She heard Roy start up the stairs as she retreated back out of sight around the corner of the cabin and brought the Mace canister up slightly above her head, her finger on the spray button. Would his glasses block the spray from getting in his eyes?

She heard him walk onto the deck, close the door and fumble the hasp. She could not let him lock Ken in that cabin. She stepped out, and he looked at her with startled incomprehension as she sprayed the Mace into his face, shifting the can to spray over and then under his glasses. He bellowed, clamped both hands to his face and staggered backward. She snatched up the padlock and hurled it overboard, then ran downstairs to where Ken lay splayed, face-up on the cabin floor, his head a few inches from the bottom step. She sat on the next-to-bottom step, slid her forearms under his armpits, and started dragging him up the steep steps, one thump at a time.

She might as well have been hauling a boulder. In less than a minute she was losing the battle to get enough oxygen, and she rested her butt briefly on each step before bracing her feet against the stairs and straining to pull him upward, afraid she would pass out and pitch forward on top of him. As she hoisted her butt up to the third step from the top, she saw a faint shadow fall across Ken's body, and heard rasping, uneven breathing above the sound of the engine. Roy was standing behind her in the doorway, waiting to shove them both back down the stairs and lock them in.

She'd never get Ken up those stairs again.

Keeping her back to Roy, she suddenly rose straight into a standing position and reached both arms back over her head to yank him off balance. He tumbled into her, knocking her legs out from under her so that her left ear landed hard against the step, and all three of them began sliding down the steps together in a tangled clump.

No. No way.

She found traction for her feet against a step, planted her palms flat on the step under her chest, then reared up and bucked with everything she had. She felt Roy's weight shift on top of her, and then slide sideways, as he tumbled over Ken and down the stairs onto the cabin floor.

Her ear was ringing from the blow against the stairs, and she felt dangerously light-headed as she dragged Ken's body out onto the deck. The wind hit her and she stood for a moment, sucking in big gulps of clean, salty air. She heard Roy's tortured wheezing as he staggered back up the steps, and realized Ken's legs were still dangling in the doorway. She bent and rolled them sideways and tried to slam the door, as Roy wedged his hand into the opening between the door and doorjamb and begin to push. She braced her feet and pushed her back forcefully against the door, feeling the door buck against her each time he lunged against it.

She noticed a screwdriver on the deck against the cabin wall. Scooting herself lower an inch at a time to maintain her pressure against the door, she touched the screwdriver with extended fingertips. Teasing it into her grasp, she picked it up and jammed it with both hands into the skin between Roy's knuckles. He screamed and tried to pull his hand back into the cabin. She used both hands to pull the screwdriver free, watched the bloody hand slither and disappear, then slammed the door and closed the hasp.

The padlock was gone. She'd thrown it overboard.

She stared for an instant at the bloody screwdriver in her hand, threaded it through the hasp, and then backed away, watching in fascination as he lunged against the door, twice. The screwdriver held.

Was she too late for Ken? Apparently not. He was not only breathing, but beginning to stir. No time to let relief slow her down. She had to get off that boat before he saw her.

The blows against the inside cabin door were getting feebler, and it occurred to her that Roy could be the one to die from carbon monoxide poisoning. She couldn't let him out. She couldn't just leave him in there. Could she figure out how to turn off the engine? Maybe, but there was probably too much carbon monoxide in the cabin already.

She slid her hand underneath Ken's body, found his cell phone in his back pocket, and punched in 911 with her thinly gloved forefinger. Using her windbreaker to cover the phone, she made gargly Donald Duck noises that she hoped sounded like a bad connection, interspersed with her lowest possible octave: "—*kwee-whech-whech* Ken Madigan. We've had an accident on *kwee-whech-whech Chaucer* in Santa Cruz marina. We need *kwee-whech-whe*…" and ended the call. Pathetic, but who cared as long as it got them to come? And wasn't recognizable as her, hopefully. She dropped the phone next to Ken on the deck. Would they come by boat? Or by ambulance maybe, and then run along the dock? She was afraid to jump off the stern of the boat with the engine still running. She'd have to cross the wooden walkway and jump into the water of the next guy's berth.

Ken muttered something as she lifted her foot onto the walkway, and as she looked back her glance fell on the screwdriver. She couldn't leave that bloody screwdriver stuck there in the hasp. It would look like Ken had locked Roy in. But what if she removed it, and then Roy rushed out and killed Ken? Ken muttered again as she ran back, and she fully expected his eyes to fly open and recognize her as she rolled and shoved him up against the door. She heard a siren wailing as she yanked the screwdriver out of the hasp, ran to the end of the walkway, and jumped with the screwdriver into the water.

She came to the surface gasping with shock from the cold, and thought she heard the siren turning into the parking lot. Good. At first she could only gulp in air, so it took a moment to orient herself by the sound of the siren and begin swimming in what she hoped was the direction of the parking lot entrance. The water was gritty, and her clinging, draggy clothes were maddeningly claustrophobic. She forced herself to focus on calming her breath as she pulled herself through the water with strong crawl strokes, holding her face out of the stinking black water. After a moment her head cleared. She thought she spotted the next gate over, swam into the adjacent berth behind a dark, bobbing boat, and managed to pull herself with a belly slap onto the little wooden walkway, where the wind rolled over her and immediately set her teeth chattering.

Stealing along the walkway to the gate, she could see the now-silent ambulance pulled up next to the gate closest to the *Chaucer*, its flashing red light illuminating both the gate and Ken's car just a few feet beyond. Paramedics were standing by the open back doors of the ambulance, apparently readying a stretcher. Good luck that she'd parked outside the range of that flashing red light. She desperately needed to get to her car and out of this cold wind. That scratchy blanket waiting in the back seat was going to be heaven.

But she couldn't let the paramedics see her, so she flattened herself on the wooden walkway to get out of the wind while she waited, shivering uncontrollably. What would happen now? She was pretty sure Ken had never seen her, but Roy certainly had. Would he give her away? Assuming he'd recognized her. In that instant before she'd sprayed him, she could have sworn he was thinking "Do I know her from somewhere?"

And maybe he hadn't even survived. Was it wrong to hope he hadn't survived?

She heard the ambulance door slam and pulled herself up into a crouch, waiting for the paramedics to disappear through their gate so that she could safely run out through hers. But just as she was about to stand and run, another siren rounded the bend and entered the lot. She threw herself flat and watched a police car pull up behind the ambulance. Too bad, those cops were bound to snoop. Two officers jumped out and disappeared around the driver side of the ambulance. Now she'd have to wait until they went through the gate as well.

By now she was shivering so violently she was afraid someone would hear her body knocking against the wood. If Roy did turn her in, she'd have no way to defend herself. No, wait, she had his confession. She fumbled underneath her, and pulled a drenched, sand-crusted iPhone from her windbreaker pocket. Her recorder seemed to have washed away entirely. She'd try to play the iPhone after it dried out, but she already knew it was hopeless.

She thought of her keys.

Her keys had probably washed away, too, and she'd have no way to get into her car. Watching the back of the ambulance for the cops to reappear, she dug stiff fingers into the pocket of her blazer, touched metal through her cold, wet gloves, and extracted her keys that were nestled in a bed of sand, coated with salt and decorated with a thin strand of seaweed.

The police officers reappeared around the back of the ambulance, turned off their engine and ran toward the gate. Good. She was free to get up now, but really, what was the urgency? Lying there, she wasn't even really that cold any more. Maybe it was because she was out of the wind that her shivering had pretty much stopped. She was just really tired now, and if she got up she'd feel that terrible wind again. Better lie here instead and get rested. Picture little Katie-Ann in the stables, with that warm late afternoon sunlight slanting in through the door of the barn...

She snaked a hand up next to her face and slapped it, hard. *Get a grip.* She had to stand up now, while she still could. Her father and

Katie-Ann were counting on her. She teetered upright, confused and uncoordinated, and began lurching toward her gate.

Then she heard another siren.

Was she hallucinating? She dropped onto the walkway again, and saw a fire engine round the curve from Brommer Avenue into the lot. To her horror, the fire engine pulled in behind the police car, not twenty feet from her escape gate.

Now what? She was pretty sure there was still one more exit gate between her and the end of the marina, but she'd have to go back into the water to reach it. She was so stiff, could she even still swim? She imagined that black, cold water closing over her head forever, with a dozen rescuers less than forty feet way.

With a last glance at the hulking, too-near fire engine, she half crawled and lurched back along her little dock, zipped the sandy car key firmly into the pocket of her windbreaker, checked the zipper twice, and dropped into the black water.

Surprisingly, it was warmer in the water out of the wind, and she began moving her arms and legs, swimming with stiff, jerky strokes until she reached the dock to the final gate. She hung onto the pier a moment, then managed to pull herself one more time out of the water and onto the wooden walkway. This time she staggered to her feet immediately, and began lurching toward the gate, wiping the sandy car key against her pants leg as she went. She had to get to her car and under that wool blanket.

She was already at the end of the lot, rounding the curve onto Brommer Avenue, when she heard another siren. Shrinking back into the shadows, she waited while another ambulance passed. Different siren, and by the flashing light she thought she could make out "Harbor Patrol" on the side. Well, she needn't have worried about whether her call would get a response. They were having a regular hootenanny in there. She forced herself to count to ten after the ambulance passed, then staggered back out and spotted her parked Subaru with a sob of relief.

She couldn't tell how much time had passed by the time she'd started her engine, turned the heater on high, peeled off her wet clothes and wrapped her gritty body in the blanket in the back seat. She pulled the windbreaker over her icy hair and tied the sleeves under her chin, pulled her whole head under the blanket, and lay as still as possible, completely out of sight.

After a few moments heat began to fill the car, and her hands and feet began to burn. She was pretty sure that burning was good. She didn't think the ambulance had come out again. Either ambulance, come to think of it. What was taking so long?

Would Ken remember Roy's confession? He seemed pretty knocked out by that drug and the carbon monoxide, so maybe he'd never even heard most of it. The wet wool next to her face stank wonderfully of hay and something else (her cat, Blizzard?) and she was shivering again. Was Ken still shivering, or had he warmed up now inside that ambulance? She wished she could reach out and touch his face.

Or Eddie's chest, with both hands. Or Eddie's whole body pressed against her, his gray eyes resting on her face. Whoa! That sort of got the blood pumping.

She remembered Roy's startled face as she stepped around the side of the cabin and Maced him. Again and again she replayed it in her mind, studying his expression, and it really did seem he was trying to place her. Fucking snob never could remember who she was. Ha! Her chattery smile widened into her slightly loony grin, and she heard herself chuckle. Uh-oh, was this the beginning of shock? She really didn't think so, but she'd have to lie very still and silent until her violent shaking subsided and she could trust her driving. And she wanted the ambulance to pass. The last thing she needed was some wailing ambulance crawling up the Subaru's backside once she did get on that road.

How much would she tell her father about this? Probably not much. No reason to scare him, really, and why take a chance on putting any of this in writing, ever? What would the cops make of the hole in Roy's hand? What would Katie-Ann think when Georgia showed up naked with seaweed in her hair?

Through the thick veil of the blanket, she saw pulsing red light, and heard one engine and then another grow louder and then pass. Beyond her, at the end of the street, sirens began to wail again. Sounded like both ambulances. Good. In another minute she'd force her bare arms into the clammy sleeves of her windbreaker, climb into the driver's seat and get going. She was still shivering, and sharp needles pierced her feet and hands. But hey, no whining. Shivering might be painful, but it meant she was going to be fine.

∞

Dearest Daddy,

I have had an unpleasant scare. It is all right now, and except for a pesky bout of pneumonia, I am no worse for the wear. I won't bore you with the details, but I will say that a certain mark turned out to be a more accomplished trickster than I could possibly have imagined, and he very nearly got the better of me. This has taught me not to underestimate my adversary in any enterprise. If and when I next employ my special talents, I intend to incorporate that learning fully.

For the foreseeable future, however, I have regretfully accepted that I cannot allow my special talents to jeopardize my ability to provide a stable home for Katie-Ann. Until she is safely in college, I intend to sacrifice all use of artful deception to the greater good of being here for her, and for some other people. Well, only one other so far, but maybe there could be others. This last may surprise you, Daddy. I have developed a kind of gratitude that extends beyond our own family, and have not quite gotten my mind around it yet.

My other news is also good. Kate (formerly our own Katie-Ann) has earned herself an A- in her geometry class, which is a miracle of focus and determination. She is studying regularly, and has made a friend who is a bit of an animal rights nut, but otherwise satisfactory. The three of us intended to go to a movie this weekend with my new friend, Eddie, but since this pneumonia is proving stubborn, I have decided to let Katie-Ann drive there herself to celebrate her new driver's license, which I am confident she will handle responsibly. I believe she is maturing nicely, Daddy.

I also have some surprising news regarding work. My "paragon," as you call him, whose actual name is Ken Madigan, is finally getting the recognition he deserves. Our former CEO perished in an unfortunate boating accident a couple of weeks ago, and after only a short period of deliberation, the board has decided to make Ken the CEO of the whole company. The person he considers indispensable here, Andrea Hancock, has become the President and Chief Technical Officer, and I am their Executive Director, or will be when I manage to get out of this sorry sleeping bag. The shareholders are luckier than they know, and with a little timely execution on my part (of the purely conventional kind) we will now get some things done and take this company where it is capable of going. I am most excited.

Finally, I am applying to law school. Ken has reinstated Lumina's tuition assistance program, and I think I have a good chance to get the maximum if I do well on my entrance exam and get into a decent school. It will take four years of going to night school, and I will stop immediately if it means I cannot be available to Kate as necessary. Assuming, of course, I can even get in.

I hope you are doing well under your difficult circumstances and keeping your spirits up. Just a few more weeks until you meet your parole board, and Kate and I are hoping daily for your early release. Whatever happens in this first hearing, you can be confident I will look after Kate for as long as necessary, and hope to make you proud of us both.

Please write back to me soonest, as I particularly welcome all diversion while I am temporarily laid up.
Your loving daughter,
Georgia

P.S. Speaking of diversion, did you happen to notice that Christie is about to auction the handwritten journal of a cook who rode with Robert E. Lee? Almost unbelievable it survived and turned up after all this time, don't you think? Recipes and everything, including one for "Varmint and Barley Stew." (They're saying the varmint was wild rabbit, but then they haven't lived in the Ozarks.) Honestly, Daddy, isn't that just a hoot?

CPSIA information can be obtained
at www.ICGtesting.com
Printed in the USA
LVOW08s2309201116

513848LV00001B/86/P